David Langford is a lapsed physicist who in his thoughtless youth worked on nuclear weapons, but later sublimated it. Thus his successful nonfiction epic *War in 2080: the Future of Military Technology* discusses unpleasantness with everything from stone clubs to colliding black holes. His first SF novel, *The Space Eater*, involves the detonation of several suns which might have thought themselves innocent bystanders. His satire on atomic research, *The Leaky Establishment*, goes further and is actually disrespectful to the Ministry of Defence.

Over the last thirteen years he has published SF, futurology, UFOlogy, horror, humour, computer software, verse, criticism, encyclopedia articles and worse; and has received several obscure awards, including the British and European SF Awards and the Hugo.

John Grant is a freelance writer and book editor. His nonfiction includes *A Directory of Discarded Ideas*, *Dreamers*, *The Directory of Possibilities* (edited with Colin Wilson), *The Depths of Cricket* and *The Advanced Trivia Quizbook*. He has just completed a major encyclopedia of animated cartoon characters.

In previous fiction he has destroyed large areas of North America (*The Truth About the Flaming Ghoulies*) and the continent of Atlantis (*Sex Secrets of Ancient Atlantis*), but to destroy the entire Earth he felt he needed help, and accordingly collaborated on *Earthdoom!* Nevertheless, he is currently working single-handed on a new novel in which he – albeit reluctantly – destroys the Universe. His *Walt Disney's Encyclopedia of Animated Cartoon Characters* is to be published soon.

Also by David Langford

The Necronomicon (with George Hay, Robert Turner &
    Colin Wilson)
War in 2080: The Future of Military Technology
An Account of a Meeting with Denizens of Another World,
    1871
Facts and Fallacies (with Chris Morgan)
The Space Eater
The Science in Science Fiction (with Brian Stableford et
    al.)
Micromania (with Charles Platt)
The Leaky Establishment
The Third Millennium (with Brian Stableford)

Also by John Grant

Sex Secrets of Ancient Atlantis
The Truth About the Flaming Ghoulies
The Depths of Cricket
The Advanced Trivia Quizbook
A Directory of Discarded Ideas
A Book of Numbers
Dreamers
The Directory of Possibilities (edited, with Colin Wilson)
The Book of Time (edited, with Colin Wilson)
Aries 1 (edited)

DAVID LANGFORD AND JOHN GRANT

Earthdoom!

GRAFTON BOOKS

A Division of the Collins Publishing Group

LONDON GLASGOW
TORONTO SYDNEY AUCKLAND

Grafton Books
A Division of the Collins Publishing Group
8 Grafton Street, London W1X 3LA

A Grafton Paperback Original 1987

ISBN 0-586-06739-6

Printed and bound in Great Britain by
Collins, Glasgow

Set in Times

Artwork on page 153 by Jane Barrett.

To Patrick Moore, Chris Boyce and Ian Watson
with apologies

'The ideal book if ever you're lost for words – just open *Earthdoom!* and you'll find lots of them'

Exeter Advertiser

'An oasis in the ocean of literature'

Bob Shaw

'Does for the disaster genre what Ludd did for the Industrial Revolution'

Roy Tappen

'Fills a long-needed gap'

Eve Devereux

'The greatest contribution to English literature since the invention of the semi-colon'

Ansible

'Could this be the finest book ever written?'

White Dwarf

'. . . sounds like an amusing idea . . .'

Isaac Asimov

Contents

Acknowledgements

This book could not have been brought into existence without the assistance of very many people, but nevertheless it was. However, the authors would like to extend their most heartfelt gratitude to Kingsley Amis, Isaac Asimov, Joe Haldeman, Harry Harrison, Robert Holdstock, Christopher Priest, Hilary Rubinstein and the Committee of the British Interplanetary Society.

Authors' Disclaimer

This book is a work of friction. Despite any occasional coincidence of names, introduced purely for the sake of verisimilitude, all of the characters in it bear no resemblance whatsoever to any *real* human being, either living or dead. None of the situations described in these pages has occurred – YET. The quotes at the head of each chapter are, however (and however unfortunately), genuine.

Small portions of this book have appeared in substantially different form in *Andromeda 3* (edited by Peter Weston), *Ad Astra*, *Aries 1* ('edited' by John Grant) and *Knave*.

While the various scientific concepts described within *Earthdoom* are of course authentic, readers are advised not to try to build any of the matter transmitters.

Dramatic Personas

Officer Hotchkiss of the Hornsville Police Department (feisty)
Death (personified)
Comrade Adrianna Dimpla, cosmonaut (chaste-minded)
Colonel Bart Malone, astronaut (unruly shock of hair)
Junior Finkelstein (precocious but heart-warming)
Nadia Finkelstein, NASA boss (statuesque)
Professor Mark Tompion, mathematician (streetwise)
Dr Lise Panther, mathematician (pouting)
Adolf Hitler (ambitious)
Art G. Throb, journalist (marginal)
Jeb Loam of Ambledyke Farm (lyrical/tedious)
Klaus or Kurt Schmidt (pseudonymous)
Rachel Loam (A Good Woman)
First Tibetan mystic (sage)
Second Tibetan sage (mystic)
Third Tibetan (dumb)
John Strickler, MoD PR man (commutative)
Madge Strickler (associative)
Bert Tremble, Science Correspondent of the *Daily Grunt* (illiterate)
Daphne Tremble (inveterate)
Gwynfor Bjørgstrøm, climatologist (acne, etc.)
Fredrik Winkel, off-stage climatologist (arid)
Reuben Loam, a son of Jeb and Rachel (unpredictable)
Nathan Loam, another son of Jeb and Rachel (changeable)
Dr Lucius Apricot, particle physicist (horizontal)
Avedon Patella, Cornish-language agitator (pert-nippled)

Aubrey Trevelyan, Cornish-language agitator (suave)

Loch Ness Monster: [a] forebrain (poseur)
               [b] hindbrain (earthy)

Ferguson, photographer (forgettable)

Joyce Abramowitz, lemming expert (swooning)

Leadbetter, Regius Professor of Aphrodisiacs, Judas College (forenameless)

Zenna Brabham, brilliant junior-school teacher (sultry yet naive)

Dr Al D. Bran, Nobel-laureate psychologist/psychoanalyst (witty and wise)

Stephen King, writer? (mentionable)

CHANCRE technician (incidental)

Mine host of the 'Goat and Spectroscope' (somewhere)

Mine host of the 'Old Bra and Boilermaker' (somewhere else)

Professor Ponglass, Tooting Bec Futures Research Institute (optimistic)

Prime Minister (carefully unspecified)

Carruthers, flunkey (white-coated)

Hive-mind of superglue/enzymic organism (class)

Superintendent, CID (blinkered)

Assistant Commissioner, CID (thirsty)

The Antichrist (predictable)

Howard J.P. Spong, multibillionaire and philanthropist (blocked)

President Heinlein of the USA (defensive)

Harcourt, technician and spear-carrier (a survivor)

Sir Dick Ingrams, lavatory attendant (well suited to job)

Vivyan Piccolo *aka* Thump Titanic, wrestler (combustible)

W. Bailey, H M Inspector of Taxes, Exeter 7 Division (implacable when alive)

Mr Wiz, of Ye Olde Bigge Apple Magicke Shoppe (gratuitous)

Sc'smv, Cygnan spaceship captain (oleaginous)
Stf'ndnl'dsn, Cygnan first mate (corrosive)
Rt'hrcc'lrk, Cygnan lieutenant (sensitive)
M'cffr, Cygnan midshipthing (gushing)
Dr Nevin, professional Californian (collaborative)
Dr Purnell, self-confessed polymath (excitable)
Mayor of Los Angeles (cringing and aghast)
Charlton Heston, actor (inspirational)
Warden of Judas College (circumambulatory)
Benson and Hedges Lecturer in Mathematics, Judas College (crepuscular)
Hovis Professor of Legal History, Judas College (diaphanous)
Emperor of Atlantis (incautious)
Captain Pelz, amateur Californian (spacefaring)
Ch'rspr'st, Cygnan activist (procedural)
J'nkkls, Cygnan fellow-traveller (pedantic)
E'nwts'n, Cygnan would-be politician (sinister but small)
Great Spong, Cygnan overlord (undischarged)
Reverend Rick Hamfist, fundamental evangelist (American)
Reverend Hunk Brady, evangelical fundamentalist (**quotable**)
Aide of the Great Spong, Cygnan interpreter (effusive)
Dr Scholl's Reader in Anatomy, Judas College (guttate)
King Arthur (unpunctual)

Plus werewolves, technicians, vampires, clones, Cygnans, security officers, politicians, congregations, lemmings, gratuitously slandered bystanders, supernumerary mystics, subatomic particles and corpses to a grand total of approximately four billion.

13

Prologue
Quivering

During the opposition of 1954 many thousand photographs were taken of Mars through various coloured filters. Astronomers were vastly intrigued by a 'W' shaped cloud 1,100 miles long which lasted from June to July and obscured the planet as though on purpose; the more romantic observers were struck by the fact that since the telescopic image is inverted the cloud was really an 'M'.

'M' for Mars? Who knows?

W.R. Drake, *Gods or Spacemen*, 1964

1

The city quivers.

Great waves of heat roll in off the Atlantic and burst against the tall white concrete slabs of the downtown business area. And still it is only eight o'clock on a November morning: by noon the streets will be hell. It is sure as all Judas going to be one awful day.

Officer Hotchkiss of the Hornsville Police Department leans against the corner of 43rd and 5th and scratches his armpit ruminatively. Another half hour or so and he'll be going off duty. The night hasn't been too bad, all things considered – just the usual bunch of drunks, junkies, brawls, suicides, riots and psychopaths – but still he's looking forward to knocking off and getting some shut-eye. Then maybe he can play with the kids for a while – a habit his superiors ignore.

Suddenly his slumping form tenses, and his hooded

eyes are instantly alert. Down the deserted street towards him comes a bizarre figure, over six feet tall and dressed entirely in black, with a bushy black beard obscuring most of the face. The man – if man it is – is singing to himself in a soft falsetto voice, crooning as if to an unseen child; and, as he moves his hands in time to the song, little lightning flashes emanate from his fingertips. But that is not the thing that is so strange about him: there is a sort of crackling blue aura surrounding his body closely, displaying the same kind of discontinuity you see when a movie special-effects man superimposes an actor upon an artificial background.

Officer Hotchkiss decides that he is confronted by a lunatic.

Fully awake now, he ambles purposefully towards the macabre stranger, his right hand never straying far from the bulky revolver on his belt.

'Hello there, stranger,' he drawls through pursed lips.

The tall man ignores him and keeps on walking, so that Hotchkiss is forced to trot alongside like a small boy out for a stroll with his father.

'Stranger,' he pants, 'you sure as hell better stop right there and listen to what I've gotta say to you.'

The tall man stops and looks around him, as if suddenly becoming aware of an incongruous note in an otherwise perfect natural harmony. His eyes eventually alight on Hotchkiss, and he steps patronizingly towards the burly police officer, his hand extended in pseudo-friendship.

'That's close enough, buddy,' says the cop.

The stranger stops, his hand still outstretched.

'Who are you, buddy? Where do you come from?'

Hotchkiss knows that his voice sounds nervous, but he is totally unable to control it. Close up, the man looks less like a harmless lunatic; more like one of those who should be locked up somewhere and forgotten about.

16

Behind the black beard – which is obviously false – the face is of a strange blue hue, and in it is set a pair of the most startlingly green eyes Hotchkiss has ever seen. Another disconcerting fact is that the man's mouth appears to be designed to open sideways. And his breath smells like a linoleum factory.

'Who am I?' repeats the dark figure. 'And where do I come from? Why, I'll answer your second question first, if I may, for that is the topsy-turvy nature of this acausal Universe and all that in it lies, is it not?'

'Yeah,' says Hotchkiss, stalling for time.

'My,' says the stranger, ''tis truly a difficult question, my dear friend, for its most truthful answer would be that I come from nowhere.'

Hotchkiss has his notebook ready. 'Which Nowhere would that be?' he says harshly, sarcastically.

'Ah, you jester,' says the tall man. 'When I say "nowhere", why!, I mean – tra la – *no*where!'

The cop breathes a deep sigh. 'OK, buster,' he says at last, 'just tell me your name and stuff the metaphysics, right?'

'My name?' The stranger pauses for a moment, and his phosphorescent eyes rake the distant skyline thoughtfully. 'I suppose that you would call me "Death".'

Hotchkiss finds himself writing 'D – E – A – . . .' before he realizes quite what he is doing. Then, with a resigned smile, he tucks his notebook away in his pocket and draws out his revolver.

'All right, numbskull, you got a choice. Either I blast you here or you come quietly with me down to head-quarters and I blast you there while you're trying to escape.'

'Don't be silly, there's a good fellow,' minces the tall figure. 'There's no way in which you could possibly harm me. See, your silly gun has turned into a bar of soap

17

already. Besides, I'm much more powerful than mortals like you could ever hope to be.

'Look.'

The stranger casts his lambent gaze around and spots an old lady walking her dog on the far side of City Park. He raises one of his long clawed hands and mutters a strange incantation. From the tip of his index finger springs a jet of light too bright for human eye to gaze upon, and the dog instantly disappears in a coruscating blaze.

'Damn!' says Death. 'Missed her. I must get my fingernails cut. Anyway, I think I've proved my point.'

He turns to face Hotchkiss, but the cop has collapsed on the sidewalk.

'Such a pity, darling,' says Death, and he begins to walk down the street again, singing his strange high song, surveying the kingdom that will shortly be his.

2

Two hundred million kilometres above the Atlantic, at that very moment, Comrade Adrianna Dimpla's lower lip quivered.

'You mean to say,' she blurted hoarsely, in her attractively guttural Russian accent, 'that there is no alternative?'

'None at all,' replied Colonel Bart Malone, not looking up from the controls in front of him.

'That the *Mary Poppins* is going to crash into your New York City?'

'Sure is, honey.'

'And that the impact is going to knock the Earth right out of its orbit?'

'That's the general idea.'

'And that will be blasted to smithereens?'

'Yup.'

'Oh, Bart, I'm *frightened*!'

It was the first time that the plucky little Russian cosmonaut had displayed any sign that she was other than a cool, calculating robot, programmed in the depths of Siberia to perform at all times with maximum efficiency. Now there were tears starting in her pale blue eyes as she pushed back from her elegantly structured face an unruly lock of corn-gold hair.

Her companion on this Russian-American space mission, the brawny Bart Malone, had not been programmed anywhere, and so he took the opportunity to eye her appreciatively. Then he turned his gaze back to the controls, which glowed ominously. It had been only three hours since the craft had been shaken by a gigantic explosion from the port retrothruster (or possibly the starboard retrothruster: it was so difficult to tell because, of course, there's no such thing as 'up' in space). Since then, with only the one retrothruster in action, the *Mary Poppins* had been describing ever-diminishing circles across the broad fabric of spacetime. According to the data the computer was spewing out, it could be only a matter of a few short months before the craft impacted on the Earth at a terrifying velocity of over five light-hours per day – so fast that the atmosphere would not have time to burn it up before it reached the ground. That the resulting explosion would bathe the entire surface of the Earth in lethal radiation was the very least of the worries, for the computer had calculated that the sheer force of the impact would knock the planet into a complicated form of Hohmann transfer orbit, sending it swooping, repeatedly, close to Venus for several millennia to come. Malone recalled reading somewhere that, had the meteorite whose impact formed the Imbrium Basin on the Moon been just a little larger or a little more swiftly moving, the force of that cataclysmic collision would have been great enough to shatter that small planet into pieces. He shuddered: it was not a comforting thought.

'But can't you *do* something, Bart?' Adrianna Dimpla's dulcet tones interrupted his chain of thought.

'Not a thing,' he muttered. 'In the ordinary way I would simply have cut off the starboard retrothruster – or possibly the port retrothruster, depending upon how you think about it – but I was in such a hurry to do that that I went and broke the switch right off.' He looked ruefully at the broken piece of plastic in his hand, a boyish grin puckering his features.

'What about remote control from Houston?' The Russian cosmonaut was close to tears.

'Nix,' said Malone. 'I knew I should never have converted the radio into a still.'

'I thought your breath smelled funny sometimes.'

'Yeah, well, baby, I mean, the thought of spending eighteen months drinking only recycled water was a bit too much for me.' He shrugged, and hiccupped. Then he leered.

There was a moment's pause, and Adrianna's virgin mind suddenly began to piece together a number of incongruous events that had taken place during the mission . . .

Their task had been to sweep out way beyond Mars to the shores of the asteroid belt, there to use spectrometry to determine, by examination of the weak sunlight reflected from those tumbling rocks, whether or not the belt was a valuable source of mineral reserves. If so, it would be the biggest boost the space program had received since its initiation, decades earlier; if not, then

Man's long adventure towards the stars would be delayed indefinitely, perhaps for ever . . .

In fact, the spectroscope had failed to survive the pressures of blast-off, but by that time it was too late to abort. So, its mission forgotten, the *Mary Poppins* had drifted uselessly along its preordained course, its two bored crew members staring frustratedly from the viewports at the asteroid belt, whose mysteries still lay hidden from Man's ken. Maybe the next mission would be successful where they had failed . . . if ever there was a next mission.

But the journey had not been totally uneventful. There had been a few bizarre occurrences – all of them minor – and it was these which now obtruded themselves into Adrianna's consciousness. Most mysterious of all was the time when, as she slept, all of her clothes had been swept out of the airlock by a freak gust from a nearby cosmic storm. Apparently Malone had been so engrossed in a game of *go* with the computer that he had noticed nothing until it was too late. Fortunately her spacesuit had been saved, but it was uncomfortable, and often she itched to take it off. Now, she began to wonder about that cosmic storm . . .

Then there had been Malone's insistence that they both put their time to good use by wearing the indoctaphones as they slept – he to learn Russian, she to learn English. She had thought at the time that the suggestion was odd, since her English, while accented, was syntactically flawless (except in times of stress), but had gone along with the idea, assuming that he was simply too embarrassed to admit that his Russian was not nearly as good as her English. Now, she began to wonder about those *extraordinary* dreams . . .

Strange, too, had been the telegram which had arrived from Mission Control while she slept – urging them to procreate. At the time she had thought little about it (and had refused to obey, since it came from the piggish, capitalistic Mission Control in Houston, not the friendly, comradely Mission Control in Gdansk), but now she began to wonder. After all, how did telegrams come to be delivered several hundred million kilometres from home? There was something very odd about the whole thing . . .

She gasped as realization hit her.

At once she looked up, and met Malone's slurred alcoholic gaze. It was only too obvious that he was perfectly aware of the thoughts that had been chasing each other across the uncharted wastes of her mind.

He grinned impishly.

Oh no! she thought. *Only a few weeks to live, and I'm cooped up in here with a sex maniac!*

3

The jelly in Junior Finkelstein's peanut-butter-and-jelly waffle sandwich quivered. Deliberately, he laid the concoction back down on his plate.

His mother was reading the newspaper dreamily, dallying with her breakfast coffee, waiting for the milkman to come.

'Mom,' he began.

She looked up.

'Something the matter, Junior?' she asked, drawing her lace dressing-gown closer about her against the heat.

His lips froze. How could he tell her? She might laugh at him, he knew. After all, she was Nadia Finkelstein, not long appointed NASA's head, and rumoured to be the greatest genius – or, at least, the greatest administrator –

the country had ever seen. She wasn't about to listen to the babblings of a six-year-old child who thought he had had a premonition.

'Nothing, Mom,' he half-whispered.

'Well, eat up your peanut-butter-and-jelly sandwich like a good boy,' she said comfortably. 'You've got only ten minutes before you've got to go to school, and you haven't brushed your teeth yet.' She returned to her newspaper.

. . . the jagged edges of the tall wrecked buildings pointing like dusty black bones to the cruel red relentless blood-stained sky . . . the people the few of them that were left dying as the hideously disfiguring sickness swept them up . . . the winds that sprang from nowhere yet could carry a man halfway to the sky before dashing him down again on to the blistered scab that had once been the verdant land . . . the air too choked with poisonous carbohydrates to breathe except with a mask that all too soon faltered and failed . . . the inexorable ice stretching its frigid tentacles down from the poles to imprison any last scuttling vestige of the proud creatures that had once walked tall and given himself a name Man as he had named the other beasts of the forests and flowers of the fields . . . the hideously distended corpses of the young and the old the ugly and the beautiful as they were washed in oily black torrents to a silently dead sea that licked the land as a wildcat licks the creature it has killed in the moments before it pounces forward to devour . . . and always the lemmings . . .

The dream had been too vivid.

He just couldn't forget it as easily as that.

He carefully put his peanut-butter-and-jelly waffle sandwich down again.

'Mom,' he wailed. 'Mom, *I think we're all gonna die . . .*'

23

1

A Sundered World?

When physicists came upon the idea that the atom is built like a solar system, the atoms of various chemical elements differing in the mass of their suns (nuclei) and the number of their planets (electrons), the notion was looked upon with much favour. But it was stressed that 'an atom differs from the solar system by the fact that it is not gravitation that makes the electrons go round the nucleus, but electricity' (H.N. Russell).

Besides this, another difference was found: an electron in an atom, on absorbing the energy of a photon (light), jumps to another orbit, and again to another when it emits light and releases the energy of a photon. Because of this phenomenon, comparison with the solar system no longer seemed valid. 'We do not read in the morning newspapers that Mars leaped to the orbit of Saturn, or Saturn to the orbit of Mars,' wrote a critic. True, we do not read it in the morning papers; but in ancient records we have found similar events described in detail, and we have tried to reconstruct the facts by comparing many ancient records. The solar system is actually built like an atom; only, in keeping with the smallness of the atom, the jumping of electrons from one orbit to another, when hit by the energy of a photon, takes place many times a second, whereas in accord with the vastness of the solar system, a similar phenomenon occurs there once in hundreds or thousands of years. In the middle of the second millennium before the present era, the terrestrial globe experienced two displacements; and in the eighth or seventh century before the present era, it experienced three or four more. In the period between, Mars and Venus, and the moon also, shifted.

Immanuel Velikovsky, *Worlds in Collision*, 1950

1

Even up here by the giant Arecibo radio dish the pollution was noticeable. Today, a great brown cloud of nitrogen dioxide squatted over the valley in which lay the mighty eye. Although it was noon, there was an all-pervading twilight gloom.

His eyes stinging, Mark Tompion shouldered his way past the guards and the NO SMOKING signs. He waited until he was on the other side of the airlock before removing his gas mask. He looked at it ruefully, then tossed it into a nearby disposal unit. Only a couple of years back there would have been no need for him to wear a mask of any type, but then the Puerto Rican government had designated the sparsely populated region a Pollution Disposal Area; now great underground pipes from as far away as Los Angeles spewed out their corrupting air twenty-four hours a day. Even the toughest gas masks lasted for no more than two or three trips up from the residential quarters to the lab areas.

His lab was a small one, shared with a microcomputer terminal and built into solid rock many metres below the dish. As he made his way towards it he had to pass through the laboratories of several of his colleagues. Some of them looked up and smiled, but his acknowledgements were automatic: he had never been a very sociable man, and of recent weeks his mind had been almost totally preoccupied with the curious radio emissions detected as coming from the region of 61 Cygni. Unless some new arcane type of pulsar had shown itself – and it seemed impossible to devise any kind of mechanism which would

25

support such a theory – the signals were intelligent: they *meant* something.

He flopped down on the chair in front of his console and looked at it bleakly. He had studied the figures it displayed so often that they no longer meant anything to him.

There was a tap at the door.

'Come,' he grunted.

The woman who entered was statuesquely built, and yet her demeanour was modest. Her hair, as black as night, shone in a perfect frame about her oval face. Her faintly pouted lips and her lustrous brown eyes suggested docility, yet Tompion knew that Dr Lise Panther was the finest mathematician alive, with the sole exception of himself. He also thought she was kinda cute.

'Yes, Dr Panther?' he said impatiently.

'Hi, Professor Tompion,' she responded, dropping a wodge of calculations onto his already cluttered desk. 'I've been having another look at the data on the 61 Cygni signals, and I think I've come up with something.'

Suddenly Tompion was alert. 'By thunder, but this sounds interesting!' he rasped. 'Fetch us both a coffee and tell me about it.'

In moments she returned and found room for the plastic cups of steaming fungal coffee among his disorderly papers; then, to his immense pleasure, she sat down. It was a movement full of the most enticing curves, yet carried out with all the shy grace of a young faun.

'Spill,' he said.

'Well, you know that the sets of signals seem to be of two kinds?'

'Yes.'

'Just let me recap for a moment, though. The type A signals are streams of very rapid pulses, regularly spaced.

26

You wouldn't think you'd be able to make out anything intelligible from them.'

'Exactly. I can't.'

'In fact, when we first picked up the signals we thought we'd got just another pulsar, except for two things. First of all, the pulses come at a rate of over twenty thousand per second, which would seem to be an impossibly high rate of rotation even for a very young pulsar – anyway, we'd probably have seen the supernova explosion if it had been that young.'

'True, true,' urged Tompion. He couldn't understand why she was going through all this basic stuff. Everybody knew what a pulsar was – it was the incredibly dense, rapidly rotating remnant left over after a large star had exploded as a supernova. The pulsar's magnetic field reacted in such a way with surrounding particles that radio waves were generated; if the Earth happened to lie in the right 'line of sight' it would receive a radio pulse with each rotation of the pulsar – hence the name. Everybody knew this . . . but Dr Panther was notorious for her habit of explaining everything from the ground up.

Nevertheless, he was impatient. 'The other thing that we noticed was that there were breaks in the pulses, lasting about a second and a half each. We know all this, Dr Panther. Please go on.'

'OK, well let's look at the type B signals. These are totally different. For one thing, they're a lot slower, and they seem to correspond much more to the sort of signal that we've been sending over the years: patterns of dots and dashes, not unlike the Morse Code.'

'Yes, yes, go on.' Tompion wondered what she'd look like without any clothes on.

'I thought it might be a good idea to stand back from the whole pattern of signals a little. I immediately saw that very long bursts of type A signals would be interspersed with single groups of type B. Moreover, in each group of type B signals there are exactly 4,753 dots and dashes, taken all together. Every fifth group of B signals repeats.'

Tompion caught his breath. Now that she had said it, it all seemed so obvious. Still, if this was all that she had done, it hardly explained the look of demure satisfaction which now crossed her face.

She straightened her spectacles, pushed back her hair, and picked up an unwieldy pile of computer printouts.

'Then I thought it would be interesting to look at the type A signals. You see, it struck me that we'd sort of ignored them a lot because there didn't seem to be much that you could discover from a massive series of identical pulses. But I wondered if maybe we weren't being a little too oversimplistic in dismissing them like that: I mean, if the aliens were sending type B signals expecting to communicate with us, they wouldn't waste their time sending the A signals if the A signals didn't *mean* something.'

Tompion nodded agreement. It was something which had been nagging away at the back of his own mind.

'But what could they mean?' he demanded.

'I decided that the key must lie in the number of A pulses in each sequence. So I put the whole thing through Multichip and came out with this.'

She tossed a sheet of printout over to him, and he looked at it blankly. There was a column of figures on it. The first few lines read:

1
96
4,560
142,880

3,321,960
61,124,063

His eyes scanned to the bottom of the sheet, down to the last few lines:

61,124,063
3,321,960
142,880
4,560
96
1

'So what?' muttered Tompion numbly.

'Don't you see? There's a symmetry about it.' For a moment she looked almost impatient. Even though Tompion was the finest living mathematician in the world, with the solitary exception of herself, she often found it astounding that he was totally innumerate: perhaps in the field of mathematics which he had single-handedly invented, and which no one but himself understood, you didn't need numbers.

'A symmetry,' repeated Tompion, with awe.

'Yeah,' she said, crossing her legs, an act which she had discovered always woke him up. 'Between each set of B pulses there are exactly 97 sets of A pulses. The first and the 97th set each consist of a single pulse; the second and the 96th each consist of 96 pulses; the third and the 95th are each of 4,560 pulses . . . and so on, and so on. Doesn't that remind you of something?'

Tompion stared at the paper. If you turned it sideways, it reminded you of the Nile Delta, and that reminded him of the summer vacation he'd once spent in Egypt with a curvaceous little red-haired belly-dancer called Lil, and that reminded him of . . . but he guessed that Dr Panther was talking mathematically.

'No,' he replied, honestly.

'Honestly,' he added.

Panther sighed. She'd have to start him all over from the very beginning.

'You remember back at school,' she began, 'when they taught you about Pascal's Triangle?'

'Yes,' he agreed, after a moment.

She wondered about giving him a quick lecture on the Binomial Theorem, but decided against it (he'd probably never even heard of Jacques Binomial, the seventeenth-century French mathematician who had formulated it). Instead, she got to her feet and undulated across to the blackboard.

'The first few lines of Pascal's Triangle look something like this.' She scribbled with the chalk.

$$1$$
$$1 \quad 2 \quad 1$$
$$1 \quad 3 \quad 3 \quad 1$$
$$1 \quad 4 \quad 6 \quad 4 \quad 1$$
$$1 \quad 5 \quad 10 \quad 10 \quad 5 \quad 1$$

Tompion watched attentively. Women in tight blue jeans always did something for him – and the numbers looked interesting too.

'I won't do all the rows in between,' she confessed with an almost guilty cough, 'but you find, Professor, that when you get down to the 96th row it starts off like this: 1 / 96 / 4,560 / 142,880 / 3,321,960 / 61,124,063.' Her hand moved rapidly as she wrote the numbers up on the board.

'Wow!' he said.

'Exactly, Professor! What the aliens are trying to tell us with their type A pulses is to think about the 96th row of Pascal's Triangle!'

'Wow!' he repeated, slapping his open palm on the

desk. 'Dr Panther, that's remarkable. You've done it again. My congratulations.'

He sat back and watched happily as she returned to her own seat. There were a couple of moments' silence, and he felt his enthusiasm beginning to waver, then to plunge.

'Well . . . uh . . . all this is very interesting, Dr Panther, but I don't see that it actually gets us very far. I mean, these aliens are obviously some kind of religious nuts . . .'

'*What?*' She sat bolt upright, and her mouth dropped open to reveal her even rows of pristinely white teeth.

'Well, yeah, it seems obvious to *me*,' he said patronizingly. 'Clearly they worship this Pascal guy and have a fanatical urge to broadcast the 96th line of his triangle to everyone else in the Universe. Or maybe we're the 96th planet they've tried to contact or something.' He leant forward, put his elbows on the desk, cupped his chin (damn! – he'd forgotten about that coffee), and grinned expansively at her. 'It all seems very simple to me, my child.'

'I'm not sure that I wholeheartedly agree with your interpretation, Professor,' she began, but he would have none of it.

'Let's leave it at that for the moment,' he said, waving her towards the door. 'I'll draft a press release on the subject – or, no, better . . . you draft it for me.'

Her magnificent forehead was lined with worry as she made her way out of the room. Her own deductions from the signals were rather different . . . but she knew that it was no use arguing with Tompion when he was in his big-daddy state. Her best plan would be to draft a release along the lines of her own theory, give it to him, and hope that he wouldn't read it before passing it out to the newsmen. It was a practice she used often. After all, he was so busy, his mind so often on higher mathematics.

Still, her brow was furrowed as she closed the door gently and strolled off down the corridor.

In the lab behind her, Tompion reached delightedly for the telephone. He knew the President would be more than pleased to hear about these latest developments. He keyed the button marked 'President' on the phone, and then began to punch in his security coding, 9441. 9 – that was the curly one near the bottom. 4 was harder but – yes, there it was, on the left-hand side of the – um – second row. And 4 again . . .

Listening to the tone, he thought again of Lise Panther. A strange woman, ever anxious to shun the limelight. He knew, and she knew – and he knew she knew, and so on – that he wouldn't drag her name into any announcements of this dramatic new discovery. It was one of those little courtesies he always liked to display – accommodating her habitual shyness.

And she was beautiful as well as brilliant. One day he must ask her if she'd like to have coffee in the staff canteen with him. If only someone would tell her about her halitosis . . .

The other party answered.

'Mr President . . .' Mark Tompion began.

2

1945 . . .

The mincing little figure with the toothbrush moustache leaned over the crumpled bodies, ensuring that they were really dead. His heart missed a beat as he checked for the pulse of Eva – his darling Eva – and found that there was none. The other corpses were similarly lifeless.

Chuckling happily, he darted over to a cupboard in the corner of the room, and staggered back carrying a heavy canister of gasoline.

Scheissen! but the cap had been screwed on tightly. Beads of sweat appeared on the world's most notorious forehead as he strained at it, his nervously sweating fingers slipping over the unsympathetic metal. His beady little eyes rolled as he tried yet again . . . and *there* – yes, that was it: the cap had shifted.

It took him only a moment to unscrew it. He threw the cap into a far corner of the room, and began to pour out the highly inflammable liquid. He took especial care to make sure that the corpses were adequately soused, then treated the rest of the room and the cheap bureaucratic furniture more cavalierly. When he reached the door he tossed the empty canister towards the heap of crumpled humanity in the centre of the room and cackled insanely.

Yes, yes, they had known that just along the corridor there was a secret room housing the Reich's final triumphant invention, the time machine. What they had not known – because he had never told them – was that it was capable of taking only *one* lucky person into the future. And so they had gone to their deaths like sheep, in the innocent belief that he had brought out the submachine gun only for an innocuous game of Russian roulette.

He slammed the door. Earlier in the day, he had built into its hinges a timing device which would, in twenty minutes or so, strike a match inside that charnel house of death. Twenty minutes was more than enough time for him to install himself in the time machine and leave for pastures new – out there in the uncharted wastelands of the future.

He scuttled along the drab grey corridor, his eyes alight

with glee. At the far end he paused outside the unmarked door and tapped the correct combination on it impatiently.

It swung open.

The interior of the room instantly sprang into full illumination. There, in one corner, stood the time machine, its sharp parasol gleaming evilly.

But there was no time for description. As the door swung shut behind him he leapt across to the wall where a single red lever projected aggressively. With one movement of his hand he hauled it downward, into the 'on' position – and lights came on all over the machine.

Five minutes – that was all it would take for the machine to be fully warmed up.

He pulled a diving suit from a nearby cupboard and, with excited clumsiness, clambered into it. When he was sure that all the hermetic seals were correctly adjusted, he lugged an oxygen bottle across to the time machine, which had begun to hum high-pitchedly with anticipation.

He leaped over its edge-wall and landed adroitly in its bicycle-like seat. Placing the oxygen bottle in its socket, he fitted it to the intake pipe of his diving suit.

A single red light began to flash – on, off, on, off . . . and he knew that the moment had come.

With trembling fingers, Adolf Hitler leaned forward and spun the dial of the chronometer. He was on his way to the future!

The lights in the room dimmed as the time machine drew on full power. And then, all of a sudden, they were no longer before his eyes . . .

Colonel Bart Malone was lying frenziedly on top of Comrade Dimpla, fumbling drunkenly at the seals on her spacesuit. (Or perhaps she was on top of him, he mused hazily – it was so difficult to tell because, of course, there's no 'up' in space.)

'Bart. Oh, *Bart*,' she breathed huskily. 'If you don't climb off of me, I'm going to break your back.'

His eyes focused for a moment. 'Don't say that to me, honey,' he slurred with a rueful grin. 'You know that you 'n' I have been wanting each other since the moment we clapped eyes on each other.'

His body was like a limp sack of potatoes as she tossed it across the control cabin of the *Mary Poppins*. He looked up dazedly as she stood over him, still trying to push back that unruly lock of blonde hair.

'Where I come from, *Colonel* Malone' – her voice was full of Slavic sarcasm – 'the testicles of rapists are used as golfballs. I would advise you to keep your clammy hands to yourself – or even use them to attend to the laser.'

'Why sure, honey,' he said with a cocky, undefeated smile. 'Anything you say.' His firm chin puckered with amusement.

Her glare was unrelieved.

Driving the alcohol smog from his mind by use of a mantra taught to him by an ancient oriental Zen master, he crawled over to the X-ray laser he had ingeniously conjured up out of the remains of his still. As he fiddled with the nuts and bolts he reflected that he had been wise to insist upon bottling a few crates before dismantling his last little construction.

On the other hand, he had to admit that the X-ray laser had been Adrianna's idea. Seeing that their radio set was totally out of kilter, she had suggested that their best chance lay in being able to communicate by laser. Since an optical laser was out of the question – after all, as she had pointed out, where in the hell can you get a good big crystal when you're a couple of hundred million kilometres away from nowhere? – they had settled for an X-ray laser. Of course there were a few problems – the hard radiation filling the cabin was going to be one of them – but apart from that everything was A-OK.

'I sure as all Jesus hope that one of the X-ray satellites is looking in this direction,' muttered Malone, a chirpy smile crossing his clean-cut face. 'Well, I just hope that that old God up there is on our side!'

'Have you finished adjusting that damn thing?' Comrade Dimpla hissed.

'Nearly, nearly,' he replied merrily, twiddling the dial. A thousand – a hundred – ten picometres. That would be about right. 'I thought we could do a fairly broad-band signal – around about one to a hundred picometres. I mean, if any of those goddam satellites happens to be looking in this direction, they'll be bound to pick us up.'

Adrianna Dimpla nodded in satisfaction: it was good to know that even the filthy Yanks agreed that a picometre was one million-millionth of a metre. 10^{-12} had always been one of her favourite small numbers, back at the Cosmonauts' Training College.

'I say, honey,' remarked Malone thrustingly, 'have you yet thought about what sort of a signal we should be sending?'

'I thought the International Distress Signal would be a good idea,' she responded crisply. 'They're sure to pick that up. After that, we can tell them more about our current situation.'

There was a very long, gravid silence.

'Hey, honey, uh, how're we gonna know when they've picked up our signal?' Malone smirked appealingly.

'*Colonel* Malone, that is a stupid question!' snapped Dimpla.

'Yeah, well, that's the whisky for you . . .'

'The answer is obvious! We must build an X-ray telescope in order to be able to pick up their responses.'

Malone scratched his curly pate.

'There seems to be a problem, babe,' he muttered darkly, although an optimistic grin was not far beneath the surface. 'The only useful piece of electronic equipment we had here on the *Mary Poppins* was the radio – it made a great still, and now with any luck it'll make a great X-ray laser. But it can't be both an X-ray telescope and an X-ray laser at the same time.'

'The answer is so simple that you will kick yourself in the back of the head when I tell it to you,' said the plucky young Russian cosmonaut, smoothing her spacesuit over her thighs. 'It will take our message towards Earth just over eleven minutes to reach there. It will take them some time to locate an X-ray laser which they can orientate in such a way as to transmit back to us – say twenty minutes. Then *its* signal will take another eleven minutes to reach us. That gives you over forty minutes to convert the X-ray laser into an X-ray telescope!'

'Say, funny-face!' wisecracked Malone cheerfully. 'I've had an even better idea! Why'n't we tell them, as part of our message, to transmit back to us using an *optical* laser – in visible light? Then we could actually *see* their message just by looking out the porthole!'

But the perfectly formed Russian was staring out through the very porthole towards which he had gestured.

'Look!' she gasped.

'Oh, don' be silly, honey-pie,' laughed Malone. 'We haven't even started transmitting yet . . .'

But the words died in his throat as his gaze followed the line of her pointing finger. Even his erection wilted – or so he thought: it was difficult to tell because, of course, there's no such thing as 'up' in space.

For now they could both see, not a million kilometres away, an awe-inspiring sight – one of the most bizarre objects known to Man.

It was a comet. A small comet, but a comet just the same. It seemed to be travelling on a course parallel with theirs, but moving rather more swiftly. NASA had sent a couple of unmanned probes to investigate comets in the years gone by, and both of the spacers had seen many photographs of the results – but they were only too aware of the fact that they were the first human beings to witness a comet in real life, close up. It was a sobering experience.

'It's beautiful,' said Malone, his voice suddenly no longer slurred.

'Quite beautiful,' echoed Dimpla.

Neither of them could have told, afterwards, how long they stood there watching the silent majesty of the comet, although the computer's log showed that it was fully a minute.

Against the intense background of black space penetrated by the diamond-hard lights of millions of stars moved a ghostly luminance, at whose heart lay a coruscatingly bright nucleus – so bright that the two astronauts had to shield their eyes against it. It seemed as if there were violent upheavals taking place within this brilliance; yet a terrible silence reigned. It was hell, without the screaming.

'There's something odd about that comet,' said Dimpla, after a time.

'What do you mean, babe?'

'Well, it doesn't have a tail.'

'Maybe it's not close enough to the Sun yet?'

'No,' she said, biting her lip. 'I don't think so. At the very least, it should have some form of rudimentary tail – even just some degree of elongation – because of the effect of the . . . oh, what is it that you call it in your language? . . . the electrically charged particles which stream out from the Sun.'

'The solar wind,' prompted Malone.

'Thank you. And there's another funny thing about this comet. Comets always shine just by the light from the Sun which they reflect, but I am sure this comet is too brilliant for that.'

'Maybe it's just because we're so close to it?'

'No, Colonel Malone. I do not think that that is the answer. There seem to be reactions going on in the main body of the comet. I do not think that they can be solely a result of turbulence.'

'But what else could they be, babe?'

'I do not know.' Her brow crumpled and she stroked her dainty nose thoughtfully. 'Unless . . . unless . . .'

'Unless what, honey?'

'Yes, that would explain the oddities.'

'*What* would explain them?' Malone's voice was rising to a shout.

'This could be – an *antimatter comet*!'

Malone's mouth dropped further open. He knew very well what antimatter was – it was exactly like matter, except that all the electrical charges of its constituent particles were reversed, so that instead of negatively charged electrons its atoms had positively charged positrons, and so forth. He knew also that there was very little antimatter in Earth's part of the Universe; which was just as well, since matter and antimatter annihilate

39

each other with colossal explosive energy when they meet. If there were an antimatter comet in the Solar System, it could cause untold havoc.

'Hey, baby, this thing could be dangerous.'

'Very dangerous, Colonel Malone.'

'I don't know much about astronomy, honey-babe,' said Malone with a quirky smile. 'I don't suppose there's any chance of this damn comet falling into the Sun, is there?'

'I think not – although we don't know much about the way in which gravity acts between matter and antimatter objects. On the other hand, if it passed very close to the Sun, the friction caused by its reactions with the particles in the Sun's outer atmosphere could be considerable. It might slow the comet down enough for it to fall.'

Malone stared at his hands and breathed heavily.

'And then what would happen, honey?' he murmured.

'I do not know. It is not a question which has ever come up before. I think this is the first antimatter comet ever known to mankind. Obviously there would be a tremendous explosion, but without knowing the mass of the comet it is impossible to predict just what effect that would have. It might be nothing more than a large solar flare – which would be serious enough for the people of Earth, for our planet would be bathed in high-energy radiation.'

Her cheeks glistening with horror, she drew a delicate palm across her brow.

'On the other hand . . .'

'Yes? Tell me the worst, babe.'

'If our comet is a massive one, the explosion might rip the Sun asunder!'

'Now tell me the good news,' half-sobbed Malone.

'There *is* some good news,' said Dimpla, simply.

'What?'

'There is absolutely no evidence to show that this comet will fall into the Sun. Even if it were heading straight for the Sun, as it appears to be, the chances are very high that it would never survive the journey.'

'Whaddya mean?'

'It could be destroyed either by the solar wind and meteoritic particles stripping it away layer by layer, like an onion, or it could hit a larger object – such as an asteroid or even a planet – and annihilate itself in one glorious burst.' She smiled reassuringly at him. *Poor little hick American boy,* she thought. *You just don't understand that there's a great big Universe out here which has never heard of the Stars and Stripes or Macdonald's or Abraham Lincoln . . .*

'I don't know that that reassures me much, baby,' said Malone slowly. 'You'd better toss me a spanner so that I can make the final adjustments to the laser.'

She passed the tool to him, her eyebrows raised questioningly into elegant arcs.

'We've gotta warn Earth,' gritted Malone. 'We've gotta.'

'But they have probably discovered the comet already.'

'Yeah, but they might not've. And the longer the warning they get, the better. This could spell the biggest disaster in the history of the world – much worse than what we envisaged happening when the *Mary Poppins* crashes!' He swore softly as he tightened a connection.

'Oh no . . . you don't mean . . .?'

'Yeah, baby, I see you got it now. That comet's following a path parallel to ours. And we're likely to hit Earth. *The comet might beat us to it!*'

Dimpla's mouth formed a perfect 'o' of horror. 'And in that case . . .' she breathed.

'Yeah, funny-face,' replied Malone gutturally, 'if that happens . . . the Earth will explode!'

41

4

Tompion was on the telephone when Panther slipped into his office. His face was suffused with fury and frustration, and he was shouting.

'I don't give a fuck what you say, buster! You just find me some goddam mathematician who can translate the Bible into binary notation! The President says we've gotta reply to them!'

He looked up at Panther and made a face. Covering the mouthpiece and holding the squawking earpiece well away from him, he said: 'Yeah. What is it?'

'I've brought the press release for your OK.'

Tompion glanced at the first few lines. Everything seemed to be all right. 'That looks fine. Look, Dr Panther, I'm really tied up. This bastard from Cornell doesn't seem to have heard that "the impossible takes a little longer". Know what I mean?'

Lise Panther gazed past the proud upthrust of her generous bosom at him, and smiled.

From the *New York Times*, 22 November 1989:

COMMUNICATION FROM ALIENS CONFIRMED

'Now All We Must Do Is Find Out What They're Saying' – Tompion

REPORTS IN FROM THE radio dish at Arecibo, Puerto Rico, confirm informed rumours that have been circulating for some weeks. Early in September intelligent signals were received from the star 61 Cygni.

61 Cygni is a star in the constellation Cygnus, the Swan. For many years it has been known that it possesses both a Right

Ascension and a declination, *writes our Science Editor, Art G. Throb*, and that it is in fact not a single star but two small stars in close orbit about each other, each of them having a mass a little over half that of our Sun. Also it has been known for many years that the system contains an invisible companion, which could be a planet.

However, until now it has not been thought that 61 Cygni was a likely abode for intelligent life – or even life of any kind. This is because planets of double stars experience temperature changes that do not seem conducive to the evolution of life. Also, the combined luminosity of the two stars is only about one-eighth that of our Sun, and the two stars are separated by about six times the mean distance of Pluto from the Sun. Even if a planet could find a stable orbit around the brighter of the two stars, it would still have to be over fifty times closer to the star than is Mercury to our Sun in order to be as warm as is the Earth.

Nevertheless, the signals have come. Radioastronomers at Arecibo, working in a team under Prof Mark Tompion, initially maintained silence about the pulses. They were concerned lest premature announcement lead to public hysteria; also that they might in fact be radio emissions from some hitherto unknown astronomical object.

But now their doubts are over. 'Working from internal evidence within the signals themselves,' said shock-haired Prof Tompion, 39, in a press announcement released yesterday, 'my assistant, Dr Lise Panther, immediately realized that the extraterrestrials were giving us instructions as to how to construct a triangular grid, with a base of 97 units.'

He explained that pictures could be fabricated upon such a grid – and that indeed some of the messages received gave instructions as to how to do exactly that.

'We've drawn the pictures,' he remarked, 'but as yet we have no idea as to exactly what they mean. Our systems analysts are working on that project right now.'

As yet, there has been no statement from the White House, but informed sources there say that . . .

Tompion pounded his desk savagely with his right fist. His left was holding aloft a crumpled copy of the *New York Times*. His face was convulsed with fury.

'Just what in hell is this goddam gibberish?' he screamed.

Panther was impassive. 'I thought you'd read the press release,' she murmured disingenuously.

'I never read anything about this numerical nonsense!' thundered Tompion. His shirt buttons were beginning to burst, one by one. 'And it says *nothing* here about Pascal!'

'For the sake of the press release, I did simplify your original theory a little,' admitted Panther. 'I assumed that you'd notice this when you read the announcement, and amend it if necessary.'

He glared at her balefully, standing there, her head downcast, modestly. 36-25-32 – she could have been any of these ages: it was impossible to tell. As he eyed her a ghastly realization came over him.

'Just sit down for a moment, Dr Panther. I've a couple of phonecalls to make.'

He groped blindly for the instrument, and began pressing buttons.

'Look – Sheila – get on to that translator, will you? Tell him he can lay off. I don't care if he has got halfway through *Leviticus* – we don't need the damn thing any more. Dammit – just tell him!'

He turned back to face Panther, who had now sat down. It was the one bright moment in a helluva morning. 'Got anything else you want to tell me?'

'Well, yes, Professor Tompion,' she said hesitantly. 'I think I have. We've had cryptanalysts at work on the five triangular pictures, and they think they are beginning to understand them.'

'Are you sure? I mean, the whole thing still seems very questionable to me.'

'Not really, Professor. You see, that's the tremendous beauty of the system the aliens have used. The 96th row of Pascal's Triangle is the same – in pure number terms –

no matter what base you're working to. As if that weren't definite enough, the B signals are in sets of 4,753, which is exactly the number of "positions" in Pascal's Triangle down to the 96th row. I don't think there can be the slightest possibility of error.'

Tompion nodded glazedly. Much of this was too simple for him to understand. 'OK, OK – I believe you.'

'Interestingly enough,' Panther continued, 'it seems that the aliens do their arithmetic to the base 96, which might suggest that they have either six limbs with sixteen appendages each, or sixteen limbs with six appendages each – but my guess is that they have eight limbs with twelve appendages each. On the other hand . . .' Her eyes were beginning to look dreamy.

'Sure, sure,' urged Tompion. 'But let's get back to what the cryptanalysts think the pictures mean!'

'Of course, Professor.' She smiled like a contrite school-girl. 'I was just coming to that.'

'Good.'

'As far as they can theorize – and we must remember that this is all still only at the theory stage – the first four pictures take the form of an incredibly concise language lesson. The information theorists are tremendously excited about how compact the aliens have been able to make this message. If all the hypotheses are correct, then using only a total of 19,012 "bits" the things from 61 Cygni have been able to make the message conveyed in their fifth and final triangle completely unequivocal.' She smiled again, this time with a faint hint of triumph – like a pretty girl who expects to be complimented any moment now.

'Don't bother me with the details of it all. Just tell me what the message says!'

Delaying the great moment for as long as possible, she slowly slid a sheet of computer printout over to him.

'You can call it up on your monitor, if you prefer,' she breathed, 'by dialling code 78 573 210.'

Tompion's head spun. So many bloody integers. 'No, I'll just read it off this sheet of paper – OK?'

And then his jaw dropped.

The message read: 'YOU EARTHLING SCUM ARE THE DREGS OF THE UNIVERSE. WE COME TO ANNIHILATE YOU PAINFULLY AND RAPE YOUR PLANET.'

He could find nothing to say.

'But I would stress, Professor Tompion,' said Lise Panther languorously, 'that this is all still at the theory stage.'

5

1990 . . .

Adolph Hitler arrived unheralded and unnoticed. As he had expected, his temporal motion had induced a slight change in his spatial coordinates, but he was delighted to find that this effect had not been too severe. The time machine dropped about three metres to land quite softly on mossy ground.

The sun shone palely in the winter sky as he looked around at the desolation surrounding him. As far as he could see, there was no sign of humanity – except for a few odd features which might well be the remains of crumbled walls. The countryside here was far from flat, and peculiar granitic outcrops studded the horizon. For a fleeting moment he wondered if he had arrived on another planet, then dismissed the idea from his mind as being too ridiculous. Still . . . it was uncanny, the silence.

In the far distance he suddenly noticed a bird wheeling

high in the liquid grey sky – and he felt a little surge of companionship for it. It was another living thing.

Then at last there came a sound to his ears, a sound other than the soft susurration of the wind through the stubbly bushes of this wasteland. At first it was too faint for him to identify, but as it grew closer he recognized it as the purr of an internal combustion engine.

Clumsy in his diving suit, he ran up to the top of a small hillock nearby and, shading his eyes with his hands, peered around in all directions. There! There was a flash of muted sunlight on polished metal. Looking closer to where he stood, he saw that there was a narrow road – in good condition: it had clearly been well maintained.

Grinning like a schoolboy prankster, he scampered back to the time machine. It was a matter of moments to struggle out of the diving suit, throw it into the cockpit, and turn the time machine's control to the red area marked 'Destruct'. He stood a few paces clear, and in a couple of seconds the device disappeared with a faint implosion. He gave the emptiness a mocking wave, and hurried back to the roadside.

The automobile was closer now: he could make out that it was grey, and that its form was streamlined in an unfamiliar way. It seemed to be travelling at about thirty kilometres per hour, or perhaps even more. Squinting, he saw the silhouette of a single occupant through the windscreen.

A thought struck him. He was fairly certain that he was not in Germany – the peculiar topography about him would surely have been known to him. In that case, which country *was* he in? Could he speak the language?

Nervously, he waved to the automobile as it drew near, and obligingly the driver slowed down. This was going to be the difficult bit.

'Ho,' said Hitler as the window was wound down. It

was suitably monosyllabic to pass as a greeting in any language.

'Hello there, stranger,' said the driver affably. In English, to Hitler's considerable relief. It was a language he could understand and speak with reasonable fluency – he and Eva had gone to night classes to study it, in preparation for the capture of London.

'Hello. A beautiful day, is it not?'

'For this time of the year. Mind you, the rain yesterday was something savage. And they do say that there might be mist on high ground later this evening.'

England! It had to be England!

'I had heard,' replied Hitler formally.

The driver looked around him. He was a youngish man – in his late twenties or early thirties, at a guess – with long greasy hair and a matted, tangled black beard. He seemed to be wondering what to say next.

'But you can never believe the forecasters,' Hitler prompted.

The man looked at him curiously. 'Who says that? You can always believe the weather forecasts. Haven't known them to be wrong for years.'

Hitler realized that he was in danger of blundering – so soon, so soon. 'I am old-fashioned,' he explained desperately.

'Reckon you must be, sir,' said the driver with a slightly suspicious look. 'Old-fashioned and not very well. Are you down here on holiday?' he continued, after a moment's pause.

'Yes, yes,' came the response. 'On a walking holiday. I have only my knapsack and myself.' He hefted the knapsack gingerly – it was full of mint German coins and notes dating from the war years, but he had no wish to tell his companion this. 'But unfortunately I sprained my ankle a little while ago – earlier this afternoon – and I am

48

not sure if I am going to be able to reach any accommodation by nightfall.'

'That's interesting,' said the driver with a thoughtful expression. Then an idea came to him. 'You wouldn't be wanting a lift from me, would you?' he asked.

'Well, that is terribly kind of you to offer . . .' Hitler began, but the other waved aside his words.

'I'd be glad to oblige. In fact, why not come back to my home for the night? The missis will take a look at your ankle this evening, and mayhap it will be better by the morning.'

Hitler limped melodramatically across to the passenger door, which had been opened invitingly. He climbed in and made himself comfortable.

The driver started to move off slowly. 'My name's Jeb Loam,' he said. 'Me and the missis have been running Ambledyke Farm for nigh on five years now. Won't ever make a fortune out of it, but we don't do so badly. Mind you, the money's the least of it. You'd never catch either of us wanting to move back up to the big city – not with the two little ones and a third on the way. We like the quiet life and the open air, the land where a man can call an acre his own and taste the milk still warm and creamy from the bellies of his cows. We're children of the rich, dark Devon soil, the missis and I and the kids – and the little one that's on its way – and that's the way we plan to remain.'

Having performed his introduction, he looked towards the dapper little man beside him. 'And yourself?'

'I am Klaus Schmidt,' Hitler said. 'Austrian. I am over in your wonderful country to recover from a . . . from a slight nervous exhaustion. My doctor told me to try to find as much peace and relaxation as possible.'

'Austrian, eh?' The farmer thought for a moment. 'I did hear tell that there hadn't been such a country as

Austria for a few years now. That it had become a part of Hungary.'

Hitler gritted his teeth in silent rage. *Gott! So many things have changed!* But his outward demeanour was calm and self-possessed.

'Of course,' he said serenely. 'But I was born in Austria and spent my childhood there; and, even though I have lived for many years in Paris, I will always count myself as an Austrian.'

'I do understand that, sir,' said Loam ruminatively. 'I'm just like that myself. Although me and the missis have farmed all these years here at Ambledyke on the *south* side of Dartmoor, I always consider that I'm a *north* Dartmoor man, being born at Okehampton like I was.' He picked his nose thoughtfully. 'It's not that the Exeter or Newton folk are so bad, you know; it's just that city folk don't appear to have any brains – they just have to do their best to get by on their spinal columns . . . 'Cepting yourself, of course.'

'I know exactly what it is that you mean,' said Hitler. His mind searched frustratedly for something else to say. Just his luck to pick a garrulous rustic.

'That's my herd over there,' said Loam after a couple of kilometres or so. He gestured towards the left, and Hitler looked out of his window with feigned interest. 'One hundred and twenty head of best Guernsey there, and all of them top milkers – well, of course, you'd expect them to be. But still it's nice to know that the cloning really works true to form. I remember – and it was only a few years back, you know – when you had to get your cows by Nature's process: put a bull in among them and see what happened. But two summers gone I got hold of one of them new-fangled Clonettes, killed off all of my cows except Daisy – she were always my favourite – and made myself a hundred and twenty of her.'

Still driving, he produced a pipe from one pocket, a lighter from another, and tried to get the tobacco to light. The automobile lurched dangerously all over the road.

'That's what I call useful technology, that is,' remarked Loam through a cloud of greenish smoke.

'It sounds most intriguing,' said Hitler casually – but a gleam had come into his eye. 'How do you operate this so-called . . . er . . . "Clonette"?'

'Oh, it be easy enough. Nowadays, when we lose a Daisy, the missis just produces another one like out of a hat, you know . . . You just take a few cells from one of the Daisies, put it in the hopper, switch on and a few days later – because of this here Clono-Strath stuff – you've got a full-size cow just can't wait to get its teeth into some long green grass, 'specially if that long green grass be a-growing in the rich, dark Devon soil. That's the joy of the country these days: everything's so easy. In my father's day, now, him as has been pushing up the daisies (no pun intended) now some sixteen years, you had to be out of bed at three in the . . .'

But Hitler was no longer listening. If only he could lay hands on Jeb Loam's Clonette, world domination could soon be his! He dreamt of a Fourth Reich, arising to conquer the world – then, perhaps, the Universe! And no longer would it be the entire Aryan race stamping on the face of humanity, but only those of its members of the purest stock of all – himself, and his millions of clones!

It was a happy little megalomaniac who came back to reality just as Loam halted the automobile in a muddy farmyard.

A dog barked, whined and growled nearby; hens ran squawking from the intrusion. The stink was indescribable – and Hitler paled at the thought of crossing to the house

51

through twenty centimetres of sharn in his patent leather shoes. He determined to follow in Loam's footprints.

'Shut up, you stupid whining bitch bastard or it's off to the knacker's yard for you!' shouted the farmer affably at the dog. Tail wagging furiously, it was attempting to lick his throat, but he kicked it away amiably.

'Don't worry about her, Mr Schmidt,' said Loam. 'She won't do you nor nobody any harm.'

The bitch squatted in the mud, growling deeply, eyes red, foaming at the mouth. It stared at Hitler's crotch.

'Rachel, Rachel! Where are you, you damned woman?' cried the bluff farmer.

'Jeb – oh Jeb!' came the call as the door was flung open. 'Good to see you back so soon, darling!'

The woman who emerged was clearly about six months pregnant. She had long, straight black hair, an oval face, a swarthy complexion and a pendant nose.

. . . *And her name is Rachel*, thought Hitler with dismay. *I've got to share the same house as a Semite!*

I've got to get to that Clonette – and fast!

6

Death never sleeps.

At the moment he is squatting with three ancient wise men around an open-air fire somewhere in the mountain fastnesses of the Tibetan Himalayas. The flickering, crackling ruddiness of the fire etches deep lines in the faces of the three old men, so that they look like no more than skulls from which depend loose flaps of flesh. Death sits farther from the fire than they do, so that when they glance towards him – as they do often – they see only a shadow in the hood where the face should be. But his eyes gleam greenly when he is unobserved.

The three men have scratched bare a patch of earth and are drawing on it with fire-hardened pointed sticks. They have drawn a crude zodiacal map and are plotting the planets on to it.

'The fair maiden of morning and evening is in the house of the toad of the murky swamp,' says the oldest of the three, and the other two cluck in agreement.

'And,' says the youngest, 'the red man of carnage and fear has raped four-and-twenty virgins in the palace of dancing.' All three heads nod in unison. The youngest adds: 'He and two other men of cruelty have crossed the line into the house of frogs and pungent herbs.'

The third of them has not spoken so far this evening. This is because he is dumb. He has been signalling furiously with dancing skeletal hands, but because the light is poor no one has noticed him. Except Death, who reads in a soft monotone: 'The King of all that is to be found in the Cosmos has entered the house of the usurer. His invisible but all-powerful Queen is in the house of provisions, eating manna and ambrosia.'

The other two ancients hardly hear him.

Once more the oldest takes up the rote: 'The ancient farmer lies in his own house, and his daughter is there, too; entering his house now there is a fleet-footed traveller from distant climes.'

'This I have heard,' says the youngest. 'He who is of the sky and yet also is the sky has entered the crowded house of the shoe.

'Together the kings of the undersea and the underearth walk through the garden of the gravid cherries. He of the undersea speaks many words of gloom, but the king of the underearth says nothing: he is biding his time, that when that time comes he shall find more souls for his harvest. Yet he moves hither and thither, with such swiftness that even the sunlight cannot catch him. He is beyond all mortal rules; he is infinite, and yet his power is still not complete.

'Yet the sky-people are moving, too, and in half a year he may expect them to smile favourably down upon his deeds. Yea, in half a year there will be great carnage and destruction. If he strike then, then he shall become invincible.'

The oldest speaks again, his voice dry winds moving through tinderish autumn trees. 'Should he fail at this designated hour, he shall be forever destroyed. Yet, there shall be a time beyond that for him, when once more his name shall be on every lip, both the upper and the lower, and his dark visage a fear that lurks in every mortal heart. Truly he shall live again in that hour.'

There is a long silence, with only the crackling of the dying embers daring to pierce it. Then the oldest sage turns toward their guest.

'We can tell you no more, Dark One, for the stars and the sky-people cannot tell us what *will* happen, only what *may* happen. What *will* happen is beyond our ken and control; but you have the power to affect it – you and the other sky-people, oh Dark One.'

Death nods his head.

'You have – shall we say – served me well, my friends. Your kindness will not be forgotten – or, at least, I hope not. I shall – well, I'd like to – return to this place in – let me just see now – a cycle of the Moon. 'Til then – byeee!'

And with an eldritch screech he is gone, leaving three old men deep in prayer.

Death emerges unseen in the bright lights and bustle of central London. People walk around and even through him without noticing that he is there: the effect is a little unsettling to him, but it is a small enough price to pay for omnipotence. And his green eyes see everything around him . . . and when he sights a tall, dark-suited man carrying a heavy case he moves to follow. Within moments he is directly behind the man, eavesdropping on his thoughts.

I'd like to leave it in the office, of course, but the cleaners are so bloody careless that there's no telling what might happen. After all, it's potentially dangerous stuff – good job I had this old lead-lined suitcase lying around in the attic. Wish Madge wouldn't make such a bloody fuss about it the whole time, though. She must know that the very last thing I want to do is lug so much plutonium home every evening. God! It's nearly critical mass! And the case is bloody heavy! Hope Madge is there to meet me off the 6.15 at Gnome's Green. Come to that, with the bloody trains so cockeyed these days, I hope I'm on the 6.15 at Gnome's Green. Things have been so bloody crazy, it's been months since I was on the right train . . .

Death nods his head with satisfaction as the man disappears into the yawning abyss of Piccadilly Circus tube station; then he waves his hand and is in another part of London. It is Fleet Street, and the crowds of secretaries and clerks are thronging the evening pavements. Here he need not maintain his invisibility, for no one is looking at anyone else. Few people speak to each other as the buses and the taxis roar by.

The man whom Death is here to see comes from the door of the building belonging to one of the tabloid newspapers. He, too, carries a heavy case, nervously, frequently looking back over his shoulder as he walks. Again Death moves close to listen to his thoughts.

Terrorists hand in nearly critical mass of plutonium to the office, and that bloody shit of a two-faced editor is too scared to let it stay there. So he gets me – just because I'm his bloody science correspondent – to take it home and look after it until the banks open in the morning. Oh well, can't be helped. I hope I get home on time for a change. Daphne gets so sodding angry when I'm late. I tell her I always try to be on the 6.15 at Gnome's Green, it's not my fault if the schedules are all over the shop, but she doesn't listen, she just gets that horrid tight little look in her eyes and . . .

Death whisks himself away into that strange land of nowhereness in which he normally dwells. His smile is very broad.

2
Dead Water

. . . Till clomb above the eastern bar
The hornèd Moon, with one bright star
Within the nether tip.
   – S. T. Coleridge, *The Rime of the Ancient Mariner*, 1817

1

Up here on the seventy-third parallel, the world was whiter than white. Shimmering white clouds hung overhead, ready to darken at any moment like a pathetic fallacy and shed their angry burden of snow upon the defenceless ground – if ground was the right word, for beneath the frozen Greenland Sea, if one had the patience to drill through pack-ice centuries old, one would find the icy depths of the unfrozen Greenland Sea. The empty whiteness of the landscape stretched away in all directions, bare as a novelist's imagination, affording concealment to countless polar bears, arctic foxes and the ice-stiffened newspapers dropped by passing scientific expeditions.

Such were the thoughts which drifted again through the mind of Gwynfor Bjørgstrøm, in his snowbound research station; a mind whose relentless grinding away at data had been called the world's first real perpetual-motion machine. Bjørgstrøm was always modest enough to insist that he was merely the second-finest climatologist in the world, and that one Fredrik Winkel was his master;

though, since Winkel's special field of study involved deserts and Bjørgstrøm's snow, it was hard for outside observers to make the fine distinctions so beloved of climatologists.

Now, though . . . now Bjørgstrøm was not thinking of Winkel. Those puny deserts of heat and sand – what was there to engage a man's intellect there? The great ice deserts, the tundra of the frozen North, they were clean and unchanging places where hard-edged reason could operate to its fullest extent. And besides, he didn't like Winkel.

He moved through the lonely routine of his arctic exile, struggling not to be forced into hasty conclusions by the fantastic new data his last few weeks' work had torn from the intractable face of the ice. It had been on his third Antarctic trip that frostbite had eaten into his own face and left him hideously ravaged . . . so now he chose to work alone, with no impressionable colleagues or research students to disturb his composure by having nightmares and heart attacks whenever he happened to look at them.

Alone, alone, all, all alone, Alone on a wide wide sea . . . he murmured to himself as he operated the massive coring mechanism; and, for the benefit of the students who were not there under the ice-blown sky where he worked, he mechanically added, 'Coleridge'. His thickly gloved hands protected him from the freezing, burning touch of the metal handles; the electrically heated coring head sank gradually into the rock-like whiteness. It was at times like these that Bjørgstrøm sometimes revelled in the secret facts of snow and ice that to him were open books. Little did the mundane world know of the sixfold crystalline symmetry of each and every snowflake; of the strange fact that packed snow is less dense than ice and even that it is less dense than water, which was why the frozen part of the sea stayed at the top for him to examine rather than sinking forever into the deep; or even of the curious truth that a full 79.72 calories of heat, no less than 333.54848 joules, must be expended to melt even a single gram of ice!

The wind whipped across the ice-locked sea and pelted him with powdered snow-like sea-foam; the electrically heated corer sank further in, a mighty phallus raping the virgin ice-field. This would be the last core of his current investigation, the last desperate hope of a man trapped by the inexorable facts and by his own icily reasoning mind. The worst of it was that he'd never been able to feel sympathy with Marxism . . .

Marxist geology, he bitterly reminded himself, had long been hampered by ideology, by its rejection of the slow changes of continental drift. Instead the Soviet geologists had preferred a theory of catastrophism, a theory whereby the mighty forces of the Earth built up slowly to the point where there was sudden change – revolutionary change! As Western critics had gleefully pointed out, the underlying rock strata were supposed to behave like the proletariat – held enslaved, until the time of revolution, by the reactionary forces in the upper crust . . . But in fact the theory wasn't unworkable. Just as Einstein's $E = mc^2$ had been useless until science invented the atomic bombs which it described, so the old Marxist theories of geological catastrophe might come into their own at last.

In a way nobody at all had suspected!

Later, much later, far into the terrible Arctic night, Bjørgstrøm leant back from his workbench with an expostulation of despair.

'*Shit!*'

He pushed aside the research tools of his tiny climatological station, the electron microscope, the bubble chamber, the polaroid camera, the metre rule. The violated ice-core, sectioned and minutely examined in a dozen places, began to melt as with a shiver Bjørgstrøm turned up the central heating: he didn't care. He didn't even trouble to shift some of the fragments into the deep-freeze which cost him so much of his power budget: there was no need; he had its secret now.

'*Pressure*,' he rasped to the empty air, to the curved walls of his single room. 'Tremendous pressure is warping and distorting the structure of the polar ice-fields – accelerating in its effect as time goes on, as though – ' he groped for a simple analogy which could be understood by the stupidest person, ready for the time when he would carry his warning to the world – 'As though an enormous tyre were being pumped up, closer and closer to bursting – or as though a shockwave were spreading through a charge of explosive, more and more violently every instant – or as though two pieces of plutonium – ' Well, sooner or later he'd find a convenient way of explaining it to the masses. They'd swallow anything.

Grimly he paced the hard floor, three paces up, three paces down; space was limited in this tiny oasis of warmth amid the encircling frost and night. His eye fell upon the microfilmed library he carried – how could the long-treasured books help him now? There were countless texts on climatology and meteorology, others covering geological and oceanographic theories, the complete novels of C.P. Snow and a physics text by Eisberg he'd bought by mistake . . . and none of them, not one of them even recognized the possibility of what seemed to be happening out there.

'Pressure building to a point of catastrophe,' he said in anguish, massaging his ravaged features. 'Down there in the ice, the higher allotropic forms must be developing – ordinary ice crushed into states like Ice-IV which behaves almost like a metal – the fracture-lines beginning to spread as the ice-fields begin to part company with their continental anchorage on Greenland and the north Asian tundra . . .

'There must be a reason. There has to be a reason. I can only imagine that . . . *the shape of the Earth itself must be changing!*'

As his machine-like brain scanned forward through the murkiness of time to what must happen when the point of catastrophe finally arrived, Professor Gwynfor Bjørgstrøm abandoned himself to the inevitable. Moving slowly, grey-faced, he set up the simple camp-bed which occupied most of the floor-space when erected. The catastrophe was written as though in Braille in the stress patterns of the tortured ice-field, but not even the skills of the second-finest climatologist in the world could read the *how* or the *when*. Better to turn one's thoughts away, better to occupy the ever-whirring mind with something, anything, other than this coming break-up of the roof of the world. The colossal pressures were poised in uneasy balance, like – his razor-honed mind saw the analogy now – like, say, the Great Pyramid miraculously balanced upside-down, unmoving and in perfect equilibrium, yet sensitive to the least touch, the least breeze, the least footfall of an insect which might send it heeling over and into ruin. Better to turn one's thoughts away . . . With trembling hands Bjørgstrøm unrolled the inflatable doll which was his sole companion in these lonely field expeditions, set his lips to the rather inconveniently placed valve-nozzle, and began to blow it up.

The doll's face was hideously painted to resemble his own. Somehow that reduced his guilt about it all. Sealed away from the world, he began his groping and jostling, reasserting an ancient rhythm of humanity amid the sterile white, throbbing and pounding, testing the sensuous plastic of the doll to its limits, pulsing at last to a beat which struck resonances, twanging at sub-sub-harmonics

. . . as a tinkling bell in a budgie's cage can wake resonance in a mighty gong of bronze.

'This,' he breathed to the doll as he trembled on some inner brink, 'this thing is bigger than both of us . . .' And in his personal, insignificant moment of release he failed to notice the answering quiver that ran through the ice-field lying on the Greenland Sea. Outside the night had cleared to a crystalline chill far below zero; had anyone been standing outside the igloo-like research hut, and had that someone diverted his or her attention from the trembling and crackling all around for long enough to study the cold stars, then he or she might have noticed that they were marching . . . sliding up from the south and setting in the north.

Heisenberg's uncertainty principle affirms that observer and observed cannot remain aloof and independent. To observe an electron is to change its position or velocity dramatically. To observe an ice-field . . . normally, ice-fields are not delicately balanced things.

With unnatural speed the stars drifted across the great dome of the sky, as though in some drunken planetarium that, with sickening slowness, was falling over. As he panted in the damp aftermath of his world-shaking orgasm, Bjørgstrøm moved unknowingly south, in a cocoon of warmth, securely riding atop the first glaciers of the new Ice Age.

2

Adolf Hitler stared dubiously at the gleaming consoles of the milking shed. Last night his hosts had offered lavish hospitality in the immemorial manner of the earthy English countryside – the finest hamburgers and fish fingers, fresh from the deep-freeze and brought to piping hotness in the Loams' microwave oven – but, alas, his offers of help in the kitchen had been laughingly declined. 'Sit you there, you daft bugger, and get an eyeful of the telly,' Jeb Loam had said.

Non-Aryan fingers had lifted those other fingers of fish – gefilte-fish no doubt, if the truth were known! Semitic hands had carried those succulent grey burgers to the table – kosher meat, he was sickeningly certain, prepared according to the ancient Protocols of the Elders of Zion! He had feigned illness and retired to bed in one of the children's rooms, from which the impurely bred lad Reuben had been evicted for this hospitable purpose. Indeed, he thought to himself, the children were now both . . . *concentrated* in a single room. The notion pleased him strangely.

Next morning, too cautious to take breakfast, he had cunningly suggested that he help with, say, the milking.

'Aye, 'tis a kind thought,' Jeb mused. 'Today I do be up to my ears wi' scranleting forty-acre, watching they great blades o' the mighty automatic scranleter tearing their savage way through the rich, dark Devon soil. Man's work, it is. And the missis – Rachel! *Rachel!* Don't you go forgetting there's the week's washing to be done after you've taken young Reuben to the playgroup and picked up another forty pounds of lasagna from freezer centre in the village!'

'Increasing hurricane disturbances over the Pacific,' said the miniature TV set which the Loams kept perched on their simulated-oak breakfast table. 'An unprecedented series of disasters to shipping . . . large craft have been advised to stay in harbour and small craft to stay out of the water . . .' The announcer slapped hurricane-zone stickers on to his world map until it resembled a snooker table after the first break. To Hitler, the TV

63

was merely another sign of England's effeteness and decadence – but he smiled grimly to himself at the thought of these portents which surrounded his second coming.

'You be a city man, Mr Schmidt, no offence intended to your good self . . . I do think you might stand a shift on Emergency Monitor in the milking shed, being as how the hired boy's down with a mysterious and as yet unidentified sickness. What d'you say to that?'

'*Sehr gut* – I mean, jolly good show, old chap.' Hitler licked his lips at the thought of that milk, still warm and creamy from the bellies of Jeb Loam's own cows. Or cow, if you thought of it that way. Then, his real objective obscured by this flanking movement, he might soon be trusted to help with the clonette that was the key to the new Master Race.

'Scientists have pooh-poohed suggestions that planetary conjunctions or unidentified new bodies in our Solar System are responsible for the atmospheric upheavals – '

'Ah, soddit,' said Jeb, and clicked off the set before Hitler could learn whether (as he had always suspected it would) astrology had indeed been given its rightful place among the exact sciences.

'This here's the milking shed,' Jeb Loam explained a few minutes later as he and Hitler stopped outside a ramshackle wooden hut, Hitler surreptitiously trying to shake the thicker deposits of organic fertilizer from his shoes. 'Ar. They automation buggers that did the place up, they called it Master Bovine Control . . .' He flung open the door to reveal a gleaming white-walled room where consoles blinked and a low hum of power, or of air-conditioning, was a constant background. There were no windows. There were no cows.

'What precisely do I do?' the supposed Klaus Schmidt asked warily.

'Well, you sit there, you do see that seat? Ay. There's

where you sit. And should there be a systems fault, see you, it's for you to engage the Manual Override.' Jeb removed a stray cornflake from between his teeth and spread his hands. 'Simple, sir, is it not? But a power of help you'd be giving me.'

'How do I operate this override, then?'

'Ar. That's not for me to say, not since goat did eat the instruction manual. But nothing's gone wrong in the three years since we installed the system. Tied hand and foot we are, by the Ministry's bleeding regulations – have to have a man on duty, but there's nothing says he has to be trained. You just watch the screen there, sir, and Rachel will bring 'ee a nice ploughman's lunch, pizza and chips, when she's finished hauling in the coal. That is if your poor tummy's feeling up to it . . .'

By the time he'd peered at the monitor screen for two hours, Hitler's stomach felt shrivelled to the size of a .45 bullet, and it was rumbling like distant machine-gun fire. He'd counted on stealing a sustaining draught of milk, still warm and creamy from the bellies of the cows . . . instead he had to watch the milking-tractor zeroing in on cows in a field that might be kilometres away, and extruding its automated milking-hoses to draw the warm creamy milk from the cows' bellies, and by and by rewarding them with a jolt to the pleasure centres of the brain via the specially implanted terminals. Hitler had made a note of the location of the apparatus Jeb had shown him the night before, a thing like an overgrown stapling machine that was kept in a drawer with the cutlery and used for implanting those very brain-stimulation terminals. It might be that such a device could be of use in the Plan for the Fourth Reich . . .

Meanwhile he watched the milking with a vacant gaze; it was a tedious business, made no less tedious by the identical appearance of each and every Daisy as she submitted to the mighty suction-pumps of the milker. After 119 replays of the same basic performance Hitler sat glassy-eyed, his head nodding in time to the pulsations of the tubes as they had their evil way with the last cow, his parched mouth filled with fantasies about the taste of warm creamy milk from . . .

'Mr Schmidt?'

It was the Jew woman. He backed against the far console, animal terror flickering on his face, the fear of contamination . . . 'Hello,' he said through gritted teeth.

She pointed to a digital counter. 'Hundred and twenty,' she observed. 'That's the last cow done now, sir; the milking usually finishes about this time of morning, plus or minus 16.8 seconds. Won't you come for a snack now?'

'That . . . would be . . . very nice.'

His brain raced furiously as he followed her through the farmyard muck. He must not antagonize the Loams until the right moment came, the moment when he could strike.

'Pizza and chips,' she said amid the stainless-steel fitments of the farmhouse kitchen. 'It's what the plough-man used to like, while we still had one.'

A brainwave! 'Thank you so much, Mrs Loam. It looks quite delicious . . . but I am still not quite well from my journey here. I shall take it to the lavatory and eat it there, in case there are . . . unfortunate results.' He mimed vomiting in the way that had once made Eva and the General Staff laugh so much.

'Bless you, sir, the kids are doing that all the time. You just sit down – '

'No. No, I must insist.'

Safe in the toilet, he bolted the door and ran water into the basin. Such a mind as his could not be baffled for long by the problem of the contaminating Semitic touch. The chips betrayed a slight tendency to dissolve as he scrubbed them carefully with a nailbrush, but he ate what he could of the cleansed result; the tasty-looking sauce atop the pizza washed away all too readily and left him with a thick, sodden mass of something which (as he nibbled gingerly at it) proved to taste strongly of cardboard.

The woman would pay for this! He thought fleetingly of the microwave oven in the kitchen – but no, it was far too small.

Back at the table he found Jeb tucking into a vast mound of scampi. 'That's done,' he said heartily with his mouth full: ''Safternoon I'm spraying the north fields – more o' they new-fangled fertilizers from the Central Ag Dist scheme, if there's not been another mix-up in transit! Silly buggers sent radioactive uranium hexafluoride in the cylinders last time around: ar, we had a good laugh about that one, down in the old Dog and Bladder.'

'So kind of you to wash up your plate, sir,' murmured Rachel as she took it from him. He hadn't noticed she'd got so close – the bulge of her pregnancy made distances deceptive.

'Damn you, woman! I'll not have you making love to any stranger that comes in from the road. Shameless 'ee are. Be off with you!'

Hitler supposed that the departing Rachel was quite attractive, really . . .

'Thank you again for your kindness, Mr Loam,' he said suavely. 'I wonder if I might see this "Clonette" of yours? My country's farmers are less efficient than you, by far.'

'Good of you to say so, sir, very good of you indeed. You just gimme a hand with the spray cylinders and 'ee shall look at the Clonette all afternoon – play with it all you like, that wonder of modern technology, for the beauty is that it's absolutely foolproof, not meaning any offence.'

So it was that Hitler, his limp forgotten, set his shoulders to Jeb Loam's helicopter to roll it out of the old barn where it was kept, and helped haul the massive, tarnished cylinders which held the latest approved crop-spray for this country's soil. And his pride surged when he saw the small print on the cylinders was in German! His country still held its own in this terrible new world; his country should yet know the tread of its old saviour!

'Much obliged to you, sir. Clonette's in number three shed, just beyond the reactor; we have to have a reactor you see, because we're not on mains electricity here; you just cast your eye over the clonette instructions and see if you don't agree it's the simplest, naturallest piece of farm machinery here on God's green earth. Oh, and don't let Rachel forget to muck out the sty – '

The helicopter blades spun, faster, faster, seeming to switch direction as the human eye was fooled by their speed of rotation. A blast of air filled Hitler's eyes and nostrils with dust; as the tears came he saw the 'copter rise, tilt and move off to the north on Jeb Loam's rustic business, the ancient servitude of the soil.

But as Hitler trudged to the Clonette shed, something tugged at his memory. Those cylinders had looked so very old, and somehow so familiar. Of course it must be mere coincidence that they were labelled *Tabun* and *Sarin*, names which had had a special meaning in Hitler's heyday. After all, what possible 'mix-up' could have caused *those* substances to have been accidentally distributed to the countless farmers who (Jeb had remarked) habitually treated their ground in this manner with the latest offering of what they jokingly called the 'Spray of the Month Club'?

He cautiously opened the door of the tatty-looking shed to disclose, as in the milking shed, an interior of laboratory cleanliness (apart from the dried footprints of

68

dung on the floor and a Gay Boys in Bondage calendar on one wall, which stirred pleasant memories of the SS and Hitler Youth). There was the machine. There was the detailed instruction manual: *The Clone Arranger – Clone Your Own In Six Easy Steps*. He sat down and studied it for a long while.

Tabun and Sarin, the Reich's most deadly nerve gases? Suppose, in one of the old war dumps – ?

No, that surely couldn't be. And it wasn't any business of his, anyway.

The manual said that almost any cells would do, but that hair, fingernails and the outermost layer of skin should be avoided, since they tended to be dead and thus not clonable. 'Use the standard Clonestart™ Handy Battery-Powered Biopsy Facilitator,' the manual advised. This gadget would take a core of tissue less than a tenth of a millimetre across, with more than enough cells for a dozen clones. Hitler first read this as a tenth of a metre, and spent some anxious moments making measurements on his body . . .

He sat, holding the biopsy tool he'd found clipped to the Clonette's side, holding it over his unprotected arm, hesitating. Suddenly he wanted to do anything to delay the fatal moment, even go back to the farmhouse and chat with that not-at-all-bad-looking but undeniably Semitic female.

Adolf Hitler never had been able to bear the sight of blood.

3

I'm not a science correspondent for nothing, thought the man on Blackfriars Station, a station on London Underground's Circle and District lines which is as convenient as any for Fleet Street. *Bloody editor wanted to stick this parcel of plutonium straight into a bucket of water 'to be on the safe side', the shitty old idiot, any first-year physics student at the smallest and grottiest polytechnic could have told him how water acts as a moderator and slows down and bounces back the neutrons this plutonium's putting out, and with more neutrons being fed back into the system that way the critical mass is reduced . . . Charming sight that would have been, blue glow of Cerenkov radiation and everyone in the office probably dead . . . I mean, I'm only a science correspondent, failed my university entrance exams, and that was only in modern languages at that, but even I, Bert Tremble, know all about this sort of thing . . .*

A doom-laden rumble from the tunnel hinted at the coming of a train. Tremble's face fell slightly, as it did at about this time on most weekdays of the year, when he saw that people were packed into the slowing train with a density which must rival that of the collapsed matter he'd written about in the science column two, three months back – *stuff you found in white giant stars, or was it red dwarfs?*

He'd begun to shoulder his way grimly through the crush when:

The Fat Man effect!

He halted. He could feel the blood draining from his face while sweat burst out on his forehead; a weakness assailed his knees and a violent trembling ran up and down his arms in perfect time with the shivers which moved in antiphase along his spine.

The Fat Man effect! He wondered if he'd shown any signs of nervousness. *No bloody matter, nobody ever takes any notice of what you do on an Underground station . . . That was something the American reactor man told me, some accident they'd had over there. Working with a bare reactor, they were, cranked down to safety below critical size – shift enough moderating material up close to it and it would have moved up to critical point, neutrons multiplying like rabbits, climbing the scale towards a radioactive hell. And what's moderating material? Hydrogen atoms do pretty well, light enough to absorb energy from neutrons, the way a ping-pong ball will share out its energy if you flip it against another ping-pong ball but will bounce off almost unchanged in speed if it hits a snooker ball . . . Hydrogen atoms make good moderating material. You find them in water, you find them in fats and proteins, you find them in people.*

And one day there were too many overweight scientists working too near to that reactor. The Fat Man effect. I heard that some of them lived . . .

If I'd got into that carriage with that tight-packed crush of people . . .

The London rush-hour is unpredictable in detail, but in general it means that a lot of trains will be jampacked with people between 4 P.M. and 6 P.M. each weekday of the year. Despite the terrible things which seemed to be happening all over the once stable world, the London rush-hour was carrying on, business as usual. From Blackfriars one travels two stops on the Circle or District lines to Embankment station; from Embankment one travels one stop south on the Bakerloo or Northern lines to the old, majestic and extremely grubby terminal of Waterloo;

71

from Waterloo it's a mere twenty minutes to Gnome's Green.

Oh bloody hell, Bert Tremble thought as a new wave of people spilled onto the platform. He stood as far from his case as was compatible with not abandoning it, and discovered within himself an urgent need to visit the lavatory. *I'd almost rather the Fat Man effect than what Daphne's going to say . . .*

At about the same time another man was tapping his feet restlessly on the crowded platform of Piccadilly Circus station. From there, one travels three stops south on the Bakerloo line to reach the grubbily majestic terminal of Waterloo; the second of these stops is Embankment, and here the crush can become even more intolerable as hordes of people from the Circle and District lines force themselves aboard your train.

The man on Piccadilly Circus station had never heard of the Fat Man effect. He was slightly winded, having run hard to reach his train only to have the doors perform snapping-turtle imitations right in his face. His name was John Strickler. With a not particularly muffled curse he staggered back from the now-moving train, settled himself on the heavy case and prepared to wait. Perhaps luckily, he was on the whole a rather thin man.

4

'Yesh,' said the swaying Dr Lucius Apricot, one of Britain's very finest particle physicists, perhaps *the* finest, and thus indisputably placed in or nearly in the top seventeen hundred such scientists in the whole Northern Hemisphere. 'Yesh,' he repeated. 'We're shitting, er, know what I mean, sitting on top of the biggesht fluorocarbon aerosol inna whole wide world. Thatsh what. Hic!'

Sitting facing him in the crowded lounge-bar of the Goat and Spectroscope, an almost respectable public house just a few minutes' walk from the heavily guarded North Gate of the Chiltern Hundreds Atomic and Nuclear Computation and Research Establishment, the voluptuous Avedon Patella leant forward to expose a little more of the snowy rift between her breasts. 'But, Doctor, aren't those aerosols dangerous? Haven't I read that should enough fluorocarbon compounds be released into the atmosphere, they would have a destructive effect upon the ozone layer and perhaps allow millions of people to die from skin cancer or third-degree sunburn?'

'Thatsh true,' Apricot agreed, nodding his head and craning forward a little more. 'How 'bout another double gin, then?'

'Oh, *I'll* get them, Dr Apricot. It's such an honour for a mere reporter like myself to interview a man who, after all, is widely acclaimed as the finest of British particle physicists. *I'm so thrilled . . .*' She rose to her feet with a snakelike grace and smoothed her raven-black hair, inhaling in a manner which made Apricot swallow hard. His eyes followed her to the bar, locked upon the exquisitely curved legs in their sheerest of black tights; such was his absorption that he scarcely noticed as one elbow slid across the table through pools of spilt gin, until it slid off altogether and he fell forward with his head in the rather overfull ashtray.

The sudden inhalation of cigarette ash reminded him of Security. All the Security offices smelt that way. *Keep firm control of yourself*, he thought, mentally, to himself, without so much as uttering a word. *It's just possible that this gorgeous creature is trying to worm something out of you . . . I wonder if that machine in the gents' toilet is still working?*

A whiff of that maddening perfume which should have been classified as a dangerous war gas announced that Patella had returned. 'I made it triple gins this time,' she said lazily. 'After all, this is a *special* occasion . . .' She settled herself with legs crossed, looked into his eyes, said, 'To us,' and raised her glass. Dr Apricot fixed his gaze helplessly upon her knees, tried to raise his glass and spilt half of it into his lap. 'Hic!' he temporized.

'Now *do* tell me all about this fascinating yet deadly reservoir of fluorocarbon material you keep in the Establishment . . .'

Apricot twisted on his seat, twined his fingers and knitted his brows. He wasn't so drunk, he thought, that he couldn't give an unclassified rundown on his work . . . he'd had plenty of practice, after all. One of the few perks of working for this Civil Service dump was that large gentlemen who spoke excessively perfect English were always ready to stand you a few vodkas in the lunch break.

'Well,' he said, 'It's neutrino detection, you see. The usual way of doing it is to use gigantic tanksh of chlorinated hydrocarbons, dry-cleaning fluid to you. It'sh only the chlorine that's important; chlorine-37 picks up a neutrino and beta decays to argon-37 – '

'I'm so sorry, Dr Apricot, but a plain girl like me doesn't understand all these technical terms; by "beta decay" do you by any chance mean that a neutron in the nucleus of chlorine-37 absorbs a neutrino and is thus caused to emit an electron and becomes a proton in the process, so that the charge of the nucleus changes, as does the atomic number, and thus the nucleus is no longer a chlorine nucleus but one having the next atomic number up, namely argon?'

74

She smiled winsomely. Dr Apricot gave a judicious nod. 'Mmm, you've more or less undershtood my explanation, yesh. Now the stroke of genius which I expect will bring me my Nobel Prize came while I was looking at a book on *chemistry* . . .'

'Oh Doctor, what a polymath you are!' She hitched her short skirt imperceptibly higher, producing a more than perceptible increase in the bulging of the great scientist's eyes.

'Oh, we have to keep hup – ' (a brief convulsion went through him) 'keep up with other fields, y'know. When I make the Nobel speech you can be sure I'll give some credit to *Fifty Fun Experiments You Can Do In Your Kitchen*. Thing is, thing is that fluorine'sh just a step up from the Periodic Table from chlorine!'

'By the "Periodic Table" you of course mean the classification into which Mendeléev first arranged the known elements, and which has since cast much light on their relations and properties?'

'Absholutely.'

'Thank you so much, Doctor. To be with you is an education. Do have a crisp.'

'No thanksh.' Apricot swigged a little more gin and homed in again on his subject, using a kind of mental landing radar to feel his way through the fog which seemed to have become so thick in the bar and inside his head. 'Fluorine acts *jusht like* chlorine in oh, lots of ways. Jusht like! Only it's more *reactive* – the most reactive element known!'

'And so?' Her eyes had widened prettily, and Apricot studied them with a distinct feeling that he might fall into their limpid depths; he let his eyes fall again to the study of other physical phenomena.

'More reactive, shee? Higher up the Periodic Table. More likely to combine with other elementsh – *more likely to combine with neutrinos!* So our neutrino detector, which is gonna be a hundred times bettern anything bloody Americans got, is jusht, shimply, nothing more or less than – '

She clapped her dainty hands. 'A gigantic tank of carbon tetrafluoride!'

'Jackpot! Let that stuff come gooshing out and all hell breaks loose. But sho long as it stays where it is, and we get Admin Office to authorize the £500 grant we need to build the actual detectors to use with it, it could mean a Nobel, two Nobels . . .'

Inwardly he reviewed the classification level of what he'd said. Had he let anything slip? No, no, the formula for carbon tetrafluoride was still locked in the hazy recesses of his skull – CF_4, that was it. And not a word had he breathed of how it boiled at $-129°C$, which was why the giant tank had to withstand such pressure; nor had he hinted at the stuff's molecular weight of 88.01. Security was especially touchy about molecular weights.

Ecstasy thrilled up his arm. She'd taken him by the hand. 'I suppose it must be a terrible, terrible responsibility,' she was saying. 'Knowing that if you turned the wrong taps you could release all that dreadful stuff into our poor dear atmosphere . . .'

'Only one tap,' he mumbled. 'Admin still hasn't authorized the expenditure for the shafety interlocksh I wanted.'

A further burst of ecstasy: had he been less drunk he might have fainted. She had pressed his hand against her warm, silken knee. He felt himself grinning idiotically, and after a moment a terrible suspicion came over him. He investigated: yes, dammit, his tongue *was* hanging out. He put it back in, thinking Avedon Patella was the nicest journalist he'd ever met.

'Perhaps we could arrange for me to visit your laboratory,' she crooned into his ear, almost suffocating him with that psywar perfume.

'It'sh a class-four security zone, maybe you could get clearansh – '

'Oh, I'll have one – I'll arrange clearance through the *Daily Grunt* office. We science correspondents have special privileges, you know.'

Somehow they were sitting side by side on the padded window-seat of the Goat and Spectroscope's lounge bar. Through humming fog Apricot watched those wonderful knees, and noticed his hand inching like a caterpillar towards the hemline of Patella's skirt. Perhaps he ought to stop it before it gave offence in some way. He tried. He couldn't.

'Met a shience correspondent once,' he said by way of distraction. 'Fellow called Tremble. Thought neutrino meant a little neutron; I asked him if he thought *pianissimo* meant – What was I shaying?'

'Tomorrow,' Patella said lovingly, detaching his hands from her breast and thigh, and planting a moist kiss on his forehead. 'Tomorrow I'll see you again . . . and I'll be wearing something specially nice instead of this old sack . . .'

She left him there, glazed, happy, and slipped from the room. *Tomorrow*, she was thinking. *It was all so easy after all. Trevelyan can forge the clearance in three hours flat – and then I'll have no trouble getting to that release valve! One twist, and the world suffers the greatest disaster it's ever known!*

Perhaps after this *they'll listen seriously to the demands of the Action Group. Perhaps this will be the first step towards having Cornish acknowledged as the second language of the British Isles!*

5

Longitude 57.3° North. Here there is deep brown water which is not the sea, a long slash of it running straight as a Roman road, a Roman canal, almost precisely north-west in its direction, or southeast should you choose to count it from the other end: deep brown water stretching for kilometre after kilometre through sundered Scotland, interminable as the padding in some hack novel. And in the deeps:

Two great brains were conferring wordlessly. It was possible for them to do this, since they were connected (as they had been for centuries) by almost thirty metres of bone-sheathed spinal cord. Modern-day beings have long since lost that ancient comfort and company of a second brain at the far end of the spine – it's no wonder they often feel the need to herd together instead; or, in the highly evolved case of humanity, to take refuge in a split personality. Consider, for example, the lemming – but no matter, we shall be coming to the lemmings presently. The ancient brains on which we now eavesdrop are vaster by far than most of those living on Earth in that time, 'vaster than empires and more slow', alien and unrecognizable to our too-different minds.

Two great brains were conferring wordlessly; but in words, approximately:

— *O stranger-brother who shares my body, is it that you are afflicted? Come share your woes with me, even as I with you . . .*

— *Hell of a stink down here, mate. Don't it get up your nose too?*

— *Alas, the sensation is not unknown to me, o little*

one; too close, too close do I dwell to those-which-breathe,
the organs of olfaction whose cry sings through my inmost
being. What are your woes beside mine?

— Come off it now. Don't you try and come that one
over me. Bleeding patrician cranial brains, you've got
eyes, haven't you, things like that, that's what I call a bit of
a distraction. Down here I just get the sacral end of the
stick; all the carthy sort of senses wind up down here. You
should flipping try it sometime.

— Truly your words are but the babble of waters in a
stream at flood, which rises without wits and in the same
manner sinks. Truly your stores of knowledge are fouled
and empty as gassy bubbles in that-which-digests (and
which you so imperfectly control). Stretch out your percep-
tion, small idiot brother; merge your being one instant
with mine and see now what you will . . .

— Can't see nothing. Never can, of bloody course,
water's all crappy brown and bitter from wossname, peat.
So there's nowt to see; so what?

— O one of shallow mind, you spoke of that-which-sees
as high distraction and felicity; yet is it bitter tedium and
no more. Once, only once has there been solace in this
deep, as the metal thing-made-by-men came searching.
Yellow it was, and sleek beauty lay in its lines; a submarine,
as men call such things.

— Never mind that. And never mind how it's getting
bleeding ice-age weather out there again, those bloody
people don't know when to stop having their ice ages, got
no thought for others . . . Never mind that, like I said.
What I want to know is, what's the flipping pong? It's
really getting up our nose, I can tell you.

— Alas, always it is thus: be our knowledge never so
great or never so scanty, I must think for two. Very well –

— Come to think of it, wouldn't be no bloody surprise
if it was those flaming sacrificial offerings those buggers

79

leave on the bank – been a long while since we made with the godlike presence and all that article of goods. Could be they're putting muck in the water as a kind of hint it's our duty to show ourselves every once in a while –

— Aieeeee! Speak not to me of offerings. Long and hard was the pain, and still it is not abated, since broke we a tooth upon some rich ornament which bedecked a live sacrifice; aye, the ornaments men call cameras. *Fain would I avoid such mortal grief in any of the endless aeons to come.*

— I know I'm only a bloody sacral brain, not fit to share a spinal cord with the likes of you, but have you thought maybe it's summat in the air? All sorts of gunk falling into the loch this last century or so; these last few days have been the bleeding limit. Place won't be fit to live in if they buggers keep spraying what they've been spraying just lately.

— Strange words, o brother; yet my heart tells me that by some chance you may have fallen upon truth. Then must we die with all dignity, proud and free –

— Not so bleeding fast! This isn't the only puddle on the beach, y'know. Gets flaming cold up north, but what d'you say to a look down south?

— Long and hard, long and hard must I weigh such words. Year upon cruel year must roll over us like the tides ere this be decided . . .

So it was that, as overhead the crop-spraying planes continued to discharge various unlikely substances upon the land, the owner of the two brains began to stir from its immemorial and majestic rest. Slowly it rose through the dark brown peaty water; with faint grunts which suggested it might be out of practice, it floundered onto shore. None of the loch's few remaining observation posts were well positioned to spot the emergence, save one which was rather *too* well positioned and which, with its occupant, succumbed to the two-brained creature's first limbering-up exercises on dry land. Evening was approaching as, clumsily at first but with increasing litheness, *an Niseag* began to move south towards the Grampian Mountains . . . *an Niseag*, alias Nessie, alias the Loch Ness Monster.

A change is as good as a bloody rest, one of its brains remarked to the other; but who could say which?

6

Death never sleeps, but sometimes he may choose to rest.

He rests now, in the pearly grey limbo which stretches to infinity and (this region not being subject to any known logic) some considerable way beyond. In his rest he finds himself in much the position of a television watcher, to use an analogy wholly unworthy of Death's majesty: rather than attending, say, a football match and seeing the filth and the fury in throbbing live action, he may remain at 'home' and range among a dozen such events – not the events themselves but the distant shadows they cast in his mind.

Without motion, now, he moves among the shadows. *Here*, for example, he spies on a certain time of the morning at a place called John o' Groats, formerly the northernmost tip of the British mainland.

'What the hell's all *this*?' a man is saying to Dr Gwynfor Bjørgstrøm. Death perceives that the first man's name is Ferguson and that his customary business is to photograph those few tourists who trickle this far through desolation to stand on what to the British mind has always been the northern edge of the world – until an uncertain hour of this very morning.

'Taking all the bloody trade away – look, you've camped out on it, you must know something about it!'

Indeed, by what to anyone but Death might seem a pretty odd coincidence, Bjørgstrøm's research hut survives, intact, perched at the very edge of the ice-field which now stretches away from John o' Groats and over the northern horizon. The former edge of the world is now the foot of an icewall.

'Pity about the Shetlands,' a perceptive bystander remarks. A certain inner decency prevents him from mentioning the Orkneys: portions of the Orkneys can still be discerned on the cliff of ice which has paused here on its southward march.

Professor Bjørgstrøm is wearing a bitter expression which is not precisely one of 'I told you so!' but the still more bitter 'I would have told you so if I'd had the chance'. A portion of his mind still grinds away at the data, fitting the quantitative facts of the ice advance into the equations tentatively set up on the day before, and making rough estimates of the flexibility of the University of Toronto's travelling expenses budget.

Still attached to the ice-face, which towers 100 metres over the hotel, are the ropes affixed by enterprising young climbers and by which Bjørgstrøm was able to descend. It is a long, hard climb, either way. But in the flicker of an eye one can shift one's glance, one's attention, from top to bottom of the soiled cliff of ice: even before the man Ferguson has finished preparing his new sign (REAL ICE FROM THE JOHN O' GROATS GLACIER! BE PHOTOGRAPHED AGAINST THE JOHN O' GROATS GLACIER! etc), Death's attention has flicked to the top. There is little to be seen but the irregular upper surface of the ice-plain which covers the sea and has ground down island after island in its path. Death moves his viewpoint higher. He appears to be expecting something. Presently, a little to the north of true east, he sees it. A far-off dark stain, irregular, amoeboid, blackening the ice like a creeping oil-slick or a fast-growing fungus.

Death turns off his metaphorical TV set for a short while, to recover from a sudden fit of the giggles.

Then, continuing our worthless analogy, he begins to try new channels.

Somewhere in the Middle East, an argument is going on:

'President, I implore you! I represent the cream of our country's scientists, and our firm consensus is that this trial could be disastrous. As I have just spent two hours telling you in detail, it could destroy our very water supply!'

'Very well, Doctor. Refresh my memory, and summarize your arguments . . .'

'In summary, then. The military arm wishes to detonate a 500-kiloton nuclear weapon in a specially constructed pit far underground; i.e. an atomic bomb of the fission-fusion-fission type having an energetic yield of some 500,000 tons of exploding TNT; i.e., enough energy to heat you three cups of tea every day for something like sixty million years – '

'I do not drink tea, Doctor.'

'And all this energy you propose to release into the deep rock strata beneath our desert! Already the desert is drier than it should be, because our artesian wells in the cities drain away the water table. This proposed test could crack the deep strata – let the whole water table seep away into the inmost bowels of the Earth – and leave us all to die of thirst! To die, President! To die!'

'I answer you with four points. Firstly, the military say

that without some such show of force as this demonstration that we have a nuclear deterrent, we may die more quickly than of thirst. You know the international situation. Secondly, I have hired numerous scientists to support the Government's view. Thus you are quite outvoted – thus democracy is maintained. Thirdly, the desalination plant will in any case serve for this city and the Governmental headquarters . . .'

'And fourthly, President? I say this knowing well that you have manoeuvred me into doing so in order that your next words will have an unmerited dramatic weight . . .'

'Fourthly, scum, to speak as you have done is nothing less than treason. Guards, remove this dog and have him shot. No . . . better still . . . maroon him far out in the desert, his only supplies to be a knapsack full of highly salted peanuts!'

Death nods his head knowingly as this scene fades from the videotube of his inhuman mind. He moves on, sifting through time and space: for Death is not limited to the present moment quite as humanity is, though his limitations do exist. Here, for example, is a moment which will not happen for a little while yet, as a long-delayed yet relatively empty Bakerloo Line train pulls into Piccadilly Circus and a weary man hauls a heavy case aboard it. Here is a moment which, unnoticed, has already happened . . .

The balance of air and water, earth and sea, is a delicate thing. Factory fumes, chewing-gum wrappers, the illimitable hordes of people who persist in breathing – all these take their toll. Only Death knows the point where a certain balance tips, and even he has his limitations. Consider: here in industrial zones all over the world, machines convert oxygen to carbon dioxide, the life-giving gas to the inert miasma of suffocation. Where there are no machines, people can handle the task (though less efficiently). Where there are no people . . . but this is to anticipate. Consider, too: plants, alone on Earth, labour to convert useless CO_2 back to oxygen; and all over the Earth, plants are being eaten, defoliated, wiped out or cut down until . . .

The moment comes. The balance tips. All that has happened, to human eyes, is that the usual chain-saw has done its usual work, felling another tree in the endless forests of the Amazon basin: the result is that Earth is now a net user rather than producer of oxygen. Presently, as CO_2 builds up in the air, the 'greenhouse effect' will develop; the increased concentration of the gas will mean that less solar heat is reflected into space, which means that Earth will become hotter, which means that more plants will die off, which means . . .

It is probably just as well that the benighted people of Earth don't know about this, muses Death. It would only worry the poor dears. And he giggles again.

Elsewhere, there are floods.

Elsewhere, dormant volcanoes seem to be stirring.

And a little way into the future . . . Death looks annoyed.

All over the world, seers and sages are probing into the apocalypse they sense ahead. Unfortunately, the mystical lines into the future seem to have got crossed. Predictive static is everywhere. Crystal balls condescend to show nothing more than snowstorms; haruspicators find nothing in the entrails save the information that the bird has been hung too long; the readers of tea leaves discover an almost suspicious randomness in their cups; practitioners of sortilege open their Bibles with closed eyes only to discover the randomly chosen verse they find to guide them is always obscure, and always from the Book of Revelation.

Death would like to probe a little further into the

Holocaust to come, to revel with still greater confidence in his coming inheritance of everything from the great towers and palaces of this world to the cesspit on Ambledyke Farm . . . but even Death has his limitations. The future is cloudy beyond a certain point.

Only certain Zen masters gaze inscrutably on an intermingled past and future, entire and perfect as a crystal or the body of Avedon Patella. They are at one with past and future, and thus unable to separate any portion of themselves actually to comprehend it. This oneness is a drag. Even if they were able to see what must happen, they would keep quiet about it, since it is written in the most sacred texts that the true Zen master does not shoot off his mouth. Or words to that effect.

The future is cloudy.

For the present, there is a question to be answered. Death knows the answer but idly turns his attention again, ready to admire this pretty stroke which the Norns have contrived. The question is, what strange and far-off stain is darkening the ice between Norway and Scotland? What creature – for it is no doing of Man's – what creature could be responsible?

The answer is a lemming.

7

The legend of the death-seeking lemming, the animal which amid great swarms of its own kind rushes suicidally towards the sea, has excited much incredulity from humans who choose not to make comparisons between this quirk and, say, the state of the roads to the sea anywhere in Britain or America during a national holiday. The lemming story was disbelieved, accepted, debunked,

86

de-debunked and finally established in a modified form – much to the confusion of all those people who'd read one debunking and categorically disbelieved any tendency on the part of lemmings to swarm or, in extreme cases, to exist.

The incredibly beautiful Dr Joyce Abramowitz, possibly the greatest lemming specialist in the world, had been studying the periodic lemming population explosion throughout Scandinavia, and was quickly refreshing her memory from the nearest encyclopaedia to make sure no fact had slipped from her mind about the animal upon which she'd written so many books, theses and dissertations, not to mention learned papers without number for *J. Biol. Zool. Stud.* and *Reader's Digest*. 'Lemmings,' she murmured knowingly to herself, her lips moving as she read . . . 'Yes, there are four genera of these small rodents found in north temperate and polar regions. The collared lemming, the true lemming, the wood or redbacked lemming, and of course my darling favourite the bog lemming . . . Ten to eighteen centimetres long, of course, and greyish – or reddish-brown when viewed from above. Gestation period twenty to twenty-two days – nearly forgot that, that's a tricky number! Noted for their regular population explosions, say every three or four years . . . Yes, and so they tend to migrate – but contrary to popular legend they don't plunge suicidally into the sea; in fact they avoid water on the whole!'

She peered from the window of the helicopter she was steering, the encyclopaedia momentarily forgotten. Her long, gorgeous blonde hair fell across her face and she pushed it aside as she gazed down on the lemming swarm she was tracking in the 'copter. Sure enough, they were greyish – or reddish-brown when viewed from above – a reassuring confirmation of the basic values of Joyce Abramowitz's life. It was a vaster swarm than usual, understandable when so many other strange things seemed to be happening in this strangest of all possible worlds – and it was headed for the sea! Millions upon millions of lemmings, surging over the cool green Norwegian fields, leaving a swathe of devastation in their wake, as their savage rodent teeth showed no mercy to roots, shoots, grasses . . .

Why were they heading for the sea? Would she have to rewrite her books after all? Were these lemmings plotting against her?

There was a solution, of course, a solution of sorts. Norway, being a foreign country, did not practise quite the same rigid control of disease as did, say, Great Britain. This passed quite clearly through her head as with one hand she resumed the 'copter controls and with the other applied a further coat of the lipstick that had been designed for her sensual lips by none other than the Regius Professor of Aphrodisiacs at Oxford University. The solution depended on those white flecks a less trained observer than she might have failed to notice coming and going in this onrushing tide of rodents. The white flecks of tiny animals foaming at the mouth!

It was not only lemmings which had undergone a population explosion. The dread disease of rabies had exploded along with them. Millions on millions of rabid lemmings were rushing headlong towards the fjords, towards the cold of the North Sea. Already it must be too late for them to stop.

How does one head off a stampede of lemmings? Shoot the leaders? Which *were* the leaders? Turn the kilometre-wide front of the swarm with the downdraught of, say, a helicopter's rotors?

But perhaps rabid lemmings were better drowned . . . The beautiful scientist wept at the thought of the slaughter, but she was enough of a hard-headed logician, despite her magnificent body, to resign herself to the inevitable after only mild hysterics and convulsions.

And perhaps, after all, this tragedy to come would add to the legend of the lemmings. She had toyed with the theory that the lemmings' unique (seemingly) irrationality was in the very long run a powerful evolutionary mechanism. The lemming left all the effort of developing civilization to less acute creatures such as mankind – the lemming's genes knew well that any animal of such eccentric ways as the lemming would be preserved, looked after, prevented from ever becoming extinct. Lemming genes would always survive, in zoos if nowhere else.

Could the genes have been *planned* that way?

Ah, the mysteries of evolutionary logic were too complex to understand.

Now the tragedy was near. Now the sea was in sight . . . an unusually white sea, a choppy sea? Now (she could hardly bear to look) the vanguard of the lemming horde was toppling from the cliffs and darkening the white water . . . Tears spurted again in her eyes, and as she mopped at them with tissues and then repaired her elaborate make-up the 'copter slipped downward another fifty metres. She saw, then, that the lemmings were undeterred by water; that they went grimly on; that the water was not water but ice crammed by some unthinkable force deep into the channel of the fjord.

It was impossible!

But it was happening; and, heedless of frostbitten toes, a number of lemmings which staggered imagination was sweeping like the Golden Horde from the east, carrying ruin and rabies over the frozen North Sea.

Dr Abramowitz's duty was clear. And besides, there might be a book to be written about this. She urged the 'copter forward to follow the dark writhing mass as it straggled for kilometres across the ice.

8

A long-delayed yet relatively empty Bakerloo Line train moved out of Piccadilly Circus. It stopped with a jerk in the Underground tunnel before even reaching the next stop, Charing Cross. John Strickler mopped his brow. Nearby, two passengers were arguing about whether the stoppage might not be caused by floods . . .

3

The Rat Manifesto

When writing the previous paragraph it occurred to me that in view of [Anatoly] But's experiments in improving the quality of tomatoes with ionized air we could raise a question about what planet the tomato may originally have come from – if in fact it was brought from outer space. It could seem that tomatoes originally flourished on a planet with a heavier upper atmosphere layer of ionized molecules than is found in Earth's Kennelly-Heaviside layer and, as a result, the fruit grown on that planet would flourish naturally as well as But was able to achieve artificially.

– Robin Collyns, Prehistoric Germ Warfare, 1980

1

The air was fresh and the birds singing in the dappled shade of the waving trees around the little school. Zenna Brabham, probably the finest junior-school teacher in the Western Hemisphere, her chirpy blonde hair in a fashionable off-the-shoulder pageboy cut, had opened the classroom window so that the kids could enjoy this freak January warm weather; the room was filled with the smell of sulphur as, outside, the new volcanic pool in the playground bubbled soothingly. Inside, thirty-four small heads were bent over brightly illustrated books, little lips moving ever so slightly in concentration. Miss Brabham smiled affectionately at her intent class, remembering only too well, and with fond nostalgia, her own great moment of release when first she had been able to read by herself – the tremendous sense of freedom, when no longer need she snare an adult if she wanted a bedtime story (since she had been a late reader her nineteen-year-old pleas had often been misunderstood). Now, with a last fleeting smile, she picked up the file labelled 'Physiopsychopathological Developments in the Awakening Personality – Research Data Accumulation Module' and took from it this month's edition of *Playgirl*. One day, one day . . . a Mr Right would come along, she hoped fervently: scintillating, vivacious, kindly, loving, paternal, patronizing, soft-spoken, an intellectual giant and well hung; but until then she could only wait . . .

She turned the pages avidly in the coolness of the children's rustling concentration.

But, if the classroom was tranquil, the same could not be said of Junior Finkelstein's mind.

. . . gore rising in a bony decaying mountain dwarfing the straining skyscrapers of the burning city . . . flames roiling oleaginously across the twisted forms and contorted grimaces of the lucky ones who had died already and so did not live on to see the painful destruction of all that had once been loved and thought good . . . the sky torn asunder as the very Universe bucked and heaved, itself twisted as if by the manipulation of a mighty hand, only of course there was no such manipulator and no such hand and that was perhaps the most frightening thing of all . . . great tidal waves of pulsing blood breaking against the mountain of heaving deliquescing flesh to send bright-red droplets kilometres into the air . . . a sudden cameo of a man's broken body lying on the parched black earth his hand reaching ineffectually for the revolver that lies only a metre away to put an end to his agony only he's never going to be able to reach it but still he's an American and proud of it, so he's damn well going to die trying unless he's already dead in which case the twitching of his hand is

only a reflex action like the way chickens run around after their heads have been cut off and there are plenty of those around now . . . the sudden boom of hyperbole, tautology and inconsistent metaphor fills the already overcrowded air mingling with the stinking acid fumes and the smoke and the radiation and the carbon monoxide while above high in the atmosphere the ozone layer is being peeled away a little but not very much like the outermost layers of an onion at the mercy of a not particularly tender cook . . . and all the time the agony and the blood and the gore and the noxious commingled fumes of polluting industry and excreting humanity mount higher and higher and . . .

'Junior,' said Miss Brabham.

'Yes, ma'am,' piped thirteen small voices promptly and obediently.

The schoolteacher sighed. That was the trouble with her class – of the eighteen boys in it, no fewer than fourteen were called 'Junior'. The situation was just as bad with the girls: of the sixteen of them, twelve had been christened 'Goldie' in honour of some movie star, and a thirteenth 'Oldie' as a result of the illegibility of her hungover father's handwriting.

But the one 'Junior' who had not responded to Miss Brabham's call was the one she really wanted to speak with. Junior Finkelstein looked ghastly. Sweat was pouring from his whey-faced features, his eyes were fixed and glassy, while around his desk there grew a puddle from which came the sharp tang of urine. Clearly his thoughts were far removed from the classroom: certainly he hadn't heard her.

'Junior Finkelstein,' she said, more loudly, but still he didn't react.

Impatiently, agitatedly smoothing her short skirt over her flaring hips, she crossed the classroom to the boy, stepping more fastidiously as she approached him.

'Junior,' she said urgently. 'Junior. *Junior!* Are you all right?'

At last there was a flicker of awareness in those feverish eyes. Suddenly, his head jerked and he was looking up at her, entreatingly, imploringly. He threw his hands about her lithe waist and buried his face in her taut stomach. It was difficult to hear his smothered voice through the layers of fresh cloth and pink, sensual flesh, but Zenna Brabham thought she could make out the muffled words:

'*I thing whale oil condom dry!*'

2

The psychiatrist was affable.

He leaned back in his great winged chair and smiled at the two women reassuringly. Laughter-crinkles flexed around his eyes. He was a Scorpio.

'What Junior was trying to say, Miss Brabham,' he explained, 'was: "I think we're all gonna die!" He seems to have some kind of a doom fixation – his mind is constantly being invaded by dire, and fairly graphic, forebodings. He's a nice little feller, but at the moment, at any time of the day or night, he can suddenly find himself unable to think of anything else but blood and gore on a truly gargantuan scale. It would be enough to shake the nerves of an adult, but it's really far too much for Junior to cope with. In fact, it's remarkable that he's been coping so well.'

'And to think I washed out his mouth with soap and water for saying "condom",' said Zenna Brabham softly, wondering if the psychiatrist was a Leo.

'Oh, don't worry about it,' said Nadia Finkelstein reassuringly: 'He's always been keen on oral hygiene.'

She remembered a time when . . . but that had been the War, when things were different. She turned back to the psychiatrist. 'Dr Bran . . .' she began.

'Call me "Al",' he urged suavely.

'Al, then. Al . . . have you been able to find out what might be the root cause of my little boy's trouble?'

'Well, yes, I think I have.'

'Oh?'

'Yes.'

'Ah!'

'Professor Finkelstein, if you'll excuse the informality, I'm sure you've heard of a technique known as "hypnotic regression therapy".' He got to his feet and moved over towards the window, beside which hung the framed cheque from the Nobel Foundation: the sight of it always reassured him, concentrated his thoughts. 'It seemed to me to be the obvious choice in this case; and so, for the last couple of days, Junior has spent most of the time in a trance state, answering my questions.'

Outside, a distant volcano erupted, and Bran waited for the rumbling to subside before continuing. He was annoyed to notice that, somewhere, an owl hooted: was this becoming bathos?

'The results have been quite astounding,' he eventually said. 'I took him back to the birth trauma and asked him whether at that time his mind had been filled with all these gruesome images. He told me that it had not, but that *in the first few hours after his birth* he had been secure in the knowledge that, one day, he would be troubled in this way – and that he would undergo hypnotic regression therapy at the hands of a certain Dr Al D. Bran!'

'You mean . . .?' said the two women simultaneously, leaning forward tensely in their seats. 'A star,' added Nadia Finkelstein under her breath.

'Yes!' said Bran. 'This is the clearest case I've ever come across of a genuine precognitive ability. In the old days he'd have been called a seer, a prophet, a visionary! Now that science has at last been able to pin down some of the phenomena loosely categorized together under the portmanteau of the umbrella-term "the parapsychological", we know of course that in very rare cases precognitive clairvoyance does occur – in your son's instance it's coupled with precognitive clairaudience, too, but that's less common.'

'I always knew there was something special about my son,' breathed Nadia Finkelstein, her warm eyes lustrous.

Bran was for a moment at a loss for words, but Zenna Brabham elegantly evaded any embarrassment by putting a question to him: 'But surely, Dr Bran – I mean, Al – surely if that *is* the case then all these ghastly things that Junior is . . . well, "seeing" . . . well, surely that means that they're all really going to *happen*?'

Bran clapped the side of his head. 'Shucks! I never thought of that!'

Nadia Finkelstein blinked in sheer horror, losing an eyelash.

'No, no, it cannot be,' Bran continued. 'It's beyond all human credulity. It's far, far too improbable for even *me* to believe. I mean, deaths by the billion! It would mean that Armageddon was just around the corner!'

The two women had difficulty hearing him now, as the wind outside rose to hurricane proportions so that the whole building, on whose 113th storey was Bran's office, swayed and bucked like a thing tormented, like an overused simile, like a piece of blatant padding.

'No, no, ladies – I think not!' Bran added, his voice rising almost to a shout. The sirens of the police patrol boats cruising in the flooded streets below added to the cacophony. 'From what we know of the nature of Time, at any particular instant the Universe has a diversity of choices before it, only one of which it actually takes. It seems obvious that Junior is "seeing" a future *that will never take place!* If you like, you could say that he's peeping into an alternate Universe! The kind of mass carnage he envisages just couldn't happen here – it wouldn't be allowed. Anyway, there'd be some signs of it already, unless it lay decades, or even centuries, in the future. There's no immediate need to panic on that account!'

A luminous sphere of ball lightning suddenly appeared just above his desk and nonchalantly glided across to the wall, through which it disappeared as enigmatically as it had arrived. A moment later there was the 'thwop' of an implosion.

'But Dr Bran . . .' shouted Zenna Brabham.

'Al. Goddamit, *Al!*'

'Al . . . there have been a lot of rather apocalyptic events over the last few weeks. Is it not possible . . . perhaps . . . that there might be something . . . after all . . . in Junior's visions?' The effort of shouting above the racket of the raging elements made beads of perspiration start out on her delicate forehead; her nubile bosom heaved.

Suddenly the wind dropped like a curtain: the eye of the hurricane had arrived.

Bran's voice sounded unnatural in the abrupt stillness. 'I took some notes of what Junior has been saying, and I've had my secretary type them up. Would you ladies care to have a copy each?'

Without waiting for their nods of assent, he passed them each a stapled wodge of closely typed pages. Zenna Brabham looked at hers reluctantly: she was filled with an instinctive terror of what she thought might be written there. Oddly enough, it seemed to be poetry. Yes, each page contained about ten four-line stanzas of verse. *Limericks*, she thought with a momentary optimism; then realized that the contents of the verses were far grimmer than the fate of any young lady from Ryde. The dispassionate crispness of the electronic typewriter made the words seem, by way of contrast, even more horrifying.

One
In the year 1990 in the thirteenth month,
  Great squidgy things will descend from the Swan, zap-happy;
With their knowledge of ages they wish to smash us all really
                                                      painfully,
  Yet Mars is the fourth planet from the Sun.

Zenna Brabham's eyes widened as she grasped the enormity of those few simple lines. Everyone had heard about the message from the Cygnans, but as yet no one had believed that those wily aliens were on their way to exterminate humanity: was she the first to realize this? There, in Junior's quatrain, the truth was manifest. Squidgy things, huh?

She let her gaze pass over the typewritten pages, stopping here and there as her attention was caught . . .

Seventeen
In the year 1990, in only the third month (March)
  Man-eating earwigs will stir amongst the foetid trees
Of the jungle in the land they call America of the South:
  Moving matter with their minds, they will spew forth.

And then:

Sixty-One
In the year 1990 in the month by men (and women) called
                                                      August
  There will erupt a plague of vampirism.

98

Those infected will thrive upon antibiotics
And ask for second helpings of silver bullets and wooden
stakes.

And then:

Ninety-Seven

The mighty mannish denizens of the high Himalayas and the
snow-strewn Canadian forests,
So long shunned, a mighty bomb called 'hydrogen' have built:
Midsummer 1990 this on Washington they will deposit.
And a great King called Spong will be powerless to defaecate.

And then . . . but her reeling brain could take no more.
And there *was* more, much more, in a similar vein; she
counted exactly one hundred stanzas altogether, and in
not one of them was there either a ray of hope or a
rhyme. But on the final page of the sheaf she saw that the
catalogue of doom stopped, and that there was a little
extra section in ordinary prose. She read:

Survival. Some may survive the dread events I see painted
across the canvas that is 1990, the awful agonizing days of
disaster, the centuries of catastrophe and the aeons of apocalypse. These are the people who should be drawn together,
so that terradoom may be ameliorated and the human race
continue:

There is a climatologist named Bjørgstrøm, attached to the
University of Toronto, now on a field expedition in northern
Scotland;

An expert on lemmings, Dr Joyce Abramowitz, currently to
be found commuting sensually between Norway and northern
Scotland;

Two mathematicians seconded to the radio-observatory at
Arecibo, Puerto Rico, Dr Lise Panther and Professor Mark
Tompion;

An English particle physicist, Dr Lucius Apricot, and his
gorgeous paramour, Avedon Patella;

Organic-farming specialists Jeb and Rachel Loam;

And I'd kind of like my Mommy and Miss Brabham along,
too.

Zenna Brabham looked up, her mouth open and her pert blonde eyes wide, to meet Bran's gaze; it was as if a sudden current of electricity had run through her, and him as well, in that treasurable, crystalline moment. Could this be love? Her bosom heaved with scarcely repressed animal passion – an emotion whose raw savagery was as unfamiliar to her as it is to the rest of us. In some confusion she lowered her maiden gaze once more to the typed stanzas. Thoughts scurried through her mind like moths about a candle. An intellectual giant – yes, yes, the cheque framed on the wall told her that . . . he seemed kindly and loving, and he was scintillating in conversation. But there was still a lot more she would have to find out about him before she could be sure – or, at least, she hoped there was. And now was . . . well, now was hardly the time.

'Do you think we should contact these people?' said Nadia Finkelstein reflectively, holding up Junior's 'Survival' notes and interrupting Zenna's train of thought. 'That is, assuming they actually exist.'

'They're real people, all right,' said Bran. 'That fact impressed me. I had my secretary check them out. Not only that, but they're all currently working where he says they are. It's an astonishing coincidence.'

'Coincidence!' snorted Nadia Finkelstein. 'Surely it must be clear to you that my Junior is a genuine clairvoyant. I've got faith in that boy. When he says that the end of the world is at hand, I'm prepared to back his judgement right to the bottom of my heart. Dr Bran, I'll take it upon myself to contact these scientists: they'll listen to me.'

At that moment a medium-sized seismic tremor (*About 4.5 on the Richter scale*, thought Nadia Finkelstein's elegant brain reflexively) struck Hornsville, and all three of them were thrown in a heap to the floor. To make matters even worse, the hurricane winds now suddenly returned and the electrical-power supply failed. In the dark confusion on the floor, Zenna Brabham felt an inquisitive hand on her thigh. She rather liked the sensation it created, and so did not move to repel the advance – if advance it was. A remote part of her mind reflected on the fact that the realization of impending disaster seems always to emphasize the sexual urges. The hand squeezed firmly. *He kneads me!* she thought wildly, joyously.

When the lights abruptly came back on she found to her horror that the hand concerned was at the end of one of Nadia Finkelstein's arms.

'Oh, I'm so *dreadfully* sorry,' said NASA's boss, swiftly getting to her feet and blushing deeply in embarrassment. 'I could have sworn that thigh was . . .' She paused. She had been about to say 'was Dr Bran's – I mean, Al's', but in the circumstances thought this might be tasteless. 'Was my own,' she concluded limply.

Outside the window, lightning coruscated and crackled through the louring, pregnant, turgid sky. Inside the office, Zenna Brabham's heart bled painfully.

Had he even noticed her?

3

'Avedon, you look sho beautiful when you're naked.'

'Thank you. My parents took that photograph on the beach at Bognor when I was three . . . or perhaps I might have been four?'

'Doeshn't marra. You're shtill gorgeoush. Wunner what you look like now. Oh shit! I've gonnan bitten the neck right off the fucking gin bottle.'

'Never mind, darling Lucius. There are plenty more where that one came from. Trevelyan dropped round a couple of crates while you were out at your Keep Fit classes.'

'Oh, goob – good. I think I'll just shample a few. Wunner what you look like shtarkersh now, I thought. I wunner . . . Sheems shtrange the way I alwaysh fall ashleep before you come up to bed. I thought this living-together thing would mean lotsh of sheksh. We must get round to it shometime.'

'Yes, my love. But not tonight. I've got a headache.'

'You've got a blurry headache! What d'you think I've got? Look, let'sh shtop looking at thish blurry photograph album and try a bit of the old hanky-panky.'

'Well, if you're sure you can . . .'

'Shure I'm shure. I'm ash shure ash shure can be. Only, can you posshibly take your own brasshiere off?'

'Well . . .'

'Oh, no, I think I'm going to be shick again . . .'

'Lucius! Are you all right?'

'Zzzzz . . .'

4

'Well, bugger I right down dead, but it do be a right funny thing about that there Kurt Schmidt, Rachel, my dearie-o a dandy.'

'What be so funny about him, my sack of potatoes?'

'Well, I don't be a-liking to be inhospitable to a guest, but he do be having been here a full two months now which be rather a buggeringly long time, if you don't be a-minding me saying so. Especially, my little tuffet, since I be only asked him to stay the one night.'

'Oh, Jeb, I do be a-thinking he be rather nice. He keeps me company when you be out spraying the land or harvesting the freezer centre. But there do be a funny thing about that there him: there do be a-seeming to be an awful lot of him.'

'You mean . . .?'

'No, I don't be a-meaning that. It just be that many a time and oft I be having seen more than one of him at once. I be wondering if he bain't be having a twin brother, or brothers, or something.'

'I hope they all be a-keeping their hands to theirselves, or by buggery, if they don't, I'll be a- . . .'

'Oh, don't you be such a silly great hunk, my Jeb. I be a-going to drop the little one that's on its way in less than a month now. He be hardly – *they* be hardly (if *they* they be) – *they* be hardly likely to be wanting to seduce a great big pregnant sow like me as is likely to give them a nasty surprise at their "moment of ecstasy", as they all do be a-calling it themselves.'

'Still, my little dear, I do worry. And what about all they great 'buses that keep calling around, with "Hitler for Racism" written on the sides of them? I do be a-thinking that some of them be driving off with hundreds and hundreds of people inside of them, I do. And all of them people be a-looking like that there Mr Schmidt. He do be a funny one.'

'Settle theeself down to sleep, my own dear Jeb, and don't ee freet theeself. That there Mr Schmidt be what they call on the *Guardian* women's page "an inadequate lover", or so I would guess. So turn theeself over and go to sleep like a baby calf on the first night of Spring.'

It was evening – or was it? – aboard the *Mary Poppins* – and Adrianna Dimpla was expressing her compassion to the swarthy Bart Malone.

'You moronic capitalist lickspittle! You lackey of the running dogs! For Lenin's sake, concentrate!'

'Hey, hon,' Malone chuckled, grinning winningly, 'I just love it when you talk dirty to me.'

'The laser is incorrectly aligned,' she blurted, on the edge of tears. 'We will never warn the Earth in time unless you – how you say – shape up.'

'Oooh, honey,' he beamed hoarsely, 'my shape surely is up. Believe me.'

'There is no "up" in space,' she began, protesting as he lunged towards her and pulled the zipper on his coverall down from throat to belly. She deftly parried, swinging under his free-fall arc in a tight zero-*g* somersault, snap-kicking the swollen target of his groin as she did so.

'Thokk . . . klupp . . .' he quipped, pinwheeling briskly in his newly adopted, curled-up, hands-between-the-legs position.

Even with his eyes wide and straining in the sockets of that blue face he failed to notice that he was sailing directly into the X-ray laser's firing controls. In one grand slam it happened – his left elbow banged the power up to full; his left arm cracked down hard on the arming pin; his nose fiercely butted the firing lever.

They screamed simultaneously and at the same time, she in Russian and he in agony.

The most powerful X-ray pulse ever to be fired in space was *en route* to Earth, and the consequences would be far beyond anything ever dreamed of by the crew of the *Mary Poppins* . . .

6

Junior Finkelstein opened his eyes – both of them – to see the dull red lights of the laboratory. In the darkness there lurked a rather darker shape which, had he only known it, was Dr Bran. Although Junior's mind was at its lowest possible ebb, he recognized that the person in the darkness was someone to whom he ought to outpour the substance of his dreams. For once he had had a dream which he knew to be totally fictional – that Adolf Hitler was not only alive but reproducing himself endlessly. Why should he, Junior, dream about something so trivial? Or . . . or was it true? Perhaps his subconscious mind had created an out-of-body phantasm – a phantasm which, while unreal, nevertheless displayed all the trappings of reality.

He sat up on the hard bed and stared fixedly out of the window. There was a single star hanging there, ominously. *Is it Epsilon Eridani?* he thought unhappily, knowing full well in his heart that it was Sirius. *Perhaps I could . . . but then maybe I couldn't. Or perhaps . . .?* His fevered mind constructed a hyperbola, then traced it. He was a child with multimegaton knowledge locked up in his cortex. Even his spinal cord sizzled like a frying pan full of sausages. When he was fully awake the sound was deafening.

'Mommy,' he said.

'No, it's me,' said Bran.

'OK, there, Al D. Mommy,' said Junior confusedly, 'I just thought I oughta tell you that I had this dream. Say, what's that noise?' Outside, a series of loud bangs rent the already tortured air. 'Gee, it sounds like a machine-gun.' The little lad was fully awake by now.

'It's just an extremely heavy meteor shower,' said Bran comfortably. 'Don't worry about it.'

'OK,' agreed Junior, and he snuggled down in his bed again.

'But you were going to tell me about your dream,' nudged the psychotherapist. 'It must have been quite some fantasy, little feller. The electroencephalometer almost fell off the wall.'

'Oh, yeah, it was like there was this farm in Devon, in Britain – or is it England? – and it was real spooky and . . . and I thought that Adolf Hitler had come back to life, and it was really like living in a Stephen King novel or something.' And Junior told the doctor as much as he could remember of his dream, which was a very great deal indeed. 'Say, Doc, what does it mean?' he concluded.

'It sounds to me, sonny,' Bran began, 'as if your subconscious is attempting to create an artificial construct in order to explain, in terms of a superficial psychomer-etricious "rationality" the, uh, little problems that we all seem to be facing. Simultaneously, your underlying laudaphilic subsensory impulses are, so to speak, exhort-ing you to conceive semideistic outside effectors (Hitlers, that is) whom you regard as omnipotent saviours. In quasireligiostic terminology, you could redescribe this (assuming you wished to) in terms of devils and demons (clear guilt subfeelings: rootless but real), on the one hand, as crystallized in the manifest form of the Cygnan aliens who are, we assume, coming to extirpate all human life (doubtless there is phallicity present); and gods and miracle-workers (making, for example, the trains run on time) operating in the interests of the forces of good, on the other. Am I interpolating the situation with sufficient clarity?'

'Gee, Doc . . .'

'Uncle Al.'

'Gee, Uncle Al . . . I, uh, think so. Can I go back to sleep now?'

'Why, certainly, young feller-me-lad. You snuggle down – and this time try to dream of something a bit more restful. When I was your age I used to dream of the little forest folk, and Donald Duck, and Zenna Brab . . . well, all kinds of *nice* things, like Jesus. Even when I was awake, I used to have these hypnagogic images of Bo-Peep and . . .'

Junior let the words wash wearily over his head as he settled down. But his mind was far from as tranquil as his aspect might have suggested. There was a problem here, a puzzle, a conundrum. With his wide-ranging psychic perceptions he knew, now, that in some way the foe of all human existence was of spiritual rather than purely physical origin; either it – they – was born from his subconscious, or it – they – was psychic. He couldn't be sure which of the possibilities was true. And what was Truth? But the Cygnans – they were real, all right. In his mind's eye he could see them swarming aboard mighty interstellar spacecraft, each and every alien face contorted into a mask of hatred: *what*, he wondered, had humanity done to earn this enmity? Was it purely a physical matter? The Cygnans, he knew, looked like jellyfish that had been passed through a mincing machine; it was hardly to be wondered at that they envied the inhabitants of Terra, who had clearly defined arms and legs, and who didn't have to worry too often about to which end of their bodies they ought to apply the aftershave. Now that his mind had been alerted to the Cygnans' presence, he could feel their physical forms, their despairing clamminess, and – most of all – the beam of pure, alien hatred directed by them towards the Earth. And he knew that, even as he thought, the Cygnans were heading at many times the speed of light towards this vulnerable globe . . . which made it even worse for him: the hatred was intensified by the Doppler Effect.

For a moment he wondered about trying to make friendly telepathic contact with the creatures – no, 'creatures' was the wrong word: 'sentient beings' – but he knew that the task would be an onerous one, and his fatigue was diminishing his psychic resources. Tomorrow, perhaps, he would make the attempt: there was no immediate hurry. It might be better to wait until his selected group of scientists was gathered here, so that he could draw upon their mighty intellects in order to bolster his own telepathic signals. Tompion and Panther were due to fly up in a couple of days' time, and the rest ought to be arriving soon after . . .

If they survived . . .

7

As soon as he had clocked off after his busy day in the cyclotron, Dr Lucius Apricot ran at a lurching stagger as fast as his beefy little legs could carry him to the Old Bra and Boilermaker. He and Avedon Patella – the sleek-thighed, bouncy-bosomed Avedon, his one and only true love – had decided to stop meeting after work at the Goat and Spectroscope. Too many of his colleagues drank there, and he had no wish for unfriendly tongues to start wagging behind his back. The Security Officers at CHANCRE had a simple rule: since no woman in her right mind would wish to be seen in public with a particle physicist, any girlfriend who did appear on the scene was indubitably the agent of a hostile power. To an extent, this assumption was justified: there were still ugly silences in the CHANCRE canteen whenever anyone committed the social gaffe of raising the subject of Professor Z. Moriarty, the chicken feathers, the polythene bottle, the office of the Works Manager, and the lovely Nastazia Klug: those Reds would stop at nothing to find out the definitive truth about the Uncertainty Principle.

As usual Apricot was early; also as usual, he had taken precautions. He leant against the door of the as-yet-unopened Old Bra and Boilermaker (he had discovered years before that it saved time if he positioned himself so that he simply fell into the pub when the landlord opened the door), consulted his digital watch, which told him that it was *EO:L1*, rapidly calculated that this meant he would have to wait twenty-seven minutes until the pub opened at 5.30, and settled in for the agonizing delay. *It's as bad as the Chinese water torture*, he thought. *Only those inscrutable orientals would be cruel enough to make a chap drink water*. He took another swig from the half-bottle in his duffelcoat pocket, his piggy eyes surveying the surroundings surreptitiously in case one of his colleagues might see him and demand a swig as the price of silence, and began to think of Avedon.

The half-bottle had been empty for some time when the lights inside the Old Bra and Boilermaker flashed cheekily on and the door swung open. 'Vodka and tonic, pleashe, mine hosht,' cried Apricot as he crawled to a stool, 'and no need to be too generoush with the tonic!'

'Don't you think you might have had enough already?' enquired the publican. He was a cheery fellow, and a friend of all the world and her husband; right now his face was twisted into a grimace of pure human compassion. 'I'm pissed off with you staggering in here every afternoon at opening time, already so newted out of your skull that you don't even know what day of the week it is,' he said genially.

'Courshe I know what blurry day of the week it ish,' said Apricot. 'Today'sh thirshty . . . er . . . Thurshday; it'sh me that'sh Thurshday – er, thirshty,' he protested with lightning wit.

The publican stared at him with distaste once more, but shrugged his shoulders and put a shot of vodka in a glass. He subscribed to the fundamental principles of Taoism: let every person have the freedom to decide his own merry way to Hell. Come to think of it, perhaps Apricot's was one of the better *taos*: the world could be sundered into a billion billion tiny pieces – and probably would be – but Apricot would just go drifting happily off into space, heading unerringly and with physics-defying rapidity towards the nearest pub. If there were aliens out there, and the publican was convinced that there were, having once experienced a Close Encounter with an extraterrestrial spacecraft (big and red it had been, with two tiers of lighted windows and, on the front, the arcane alien inscription that looked for all the world like '15 THE ALDWYCH'), then presumably those aliens would have discovered the benefits of alcohol. Had he not heard that various of the galactic nebulae contained enough neat ethanol to more than fill the hollowed-out Earth? Surely this was evidence of a distillation industry on a truly galactic scale? Out there, in all the vastnesses of space, there must be pubs a-plenty. 'I suppose you'll be meeting up with that young trollop with the pert buttocks again tonight,' he said ruminatively. 'I'll bet she goes like a tuning-fork once you've got her started.'

'If you mean the light of my life,' said Apricot, 'a lady of such purity and virtue that she hash sheveral times

110

been mishtaken for Princess Diana, then yesh. I do plan to shink a few quickiesh with her.'

At that moment the door was thrown open and a tall, thin cadaverous figure with a goatee beard and a drainpipe moustache skulked in, looking from left to right for all the world like a praying mantis. When this apparition caught sight of Apricot clinging desperately to the side of the bar-stool he smiled like an iguana, revealing a row of teeth that looked like the Elgin Marbles. He crossed the floor like a cobra, and sat down with the grace of a porcupine. 'You are,' he said, 'Dr Lucius Apricot.'

'Yesh. But I'm afraid I don't know either of you.'

The stranger showed his teeth again in a peculiarly rat-like manoeuvre. 'Of course you don't,' he said. 'We've never met before. But my name's Trevelyan. Aubrey Trevelyan, of the University College of Truro, Cornwall. We have a mutual friend in the shape of the sumptuous Avedon Patella. I'm sure she must have mentioned my name. Forgive me intruding on you like this, but I do hope you'll allow me to – to soften the blow, as it were – by giving you some liquid refreshment?'

'Shoften what blow?' said Apricot, making a rapid calculation. A free drink was a free drink was a free drink after all, as Gertrude Stein might have remarked, and he presumably would be able to get away from this ferret-like individual when Avedon arrived. 'Thash very kind of you, ol' buddy. A vodka 'n' tonic, then, pleashe. Must shay, you're a gemm'an. Make it a big one, if you'd be sho goob.'

Trevelyan nodded. 'Two vodkas, please,' he said to the publican in a chimpanzee-like drawl. 'And I'll have one for myself.' He turned back to the coldly sweating scientist. 'You may wonder why I have sought you out here.'

'To buy me a drink?' said Apricot confusedly.

'No,' said Trevelyan – 'No, it's more than that. It's . . .

111

well, it's about Avedon.' His voice dropped an octave. 'She may not be here this evening.'

'What?' cried Apricot desolatedly. 'Not even her titsh?'

'No,' said Trevelyan, 'not even those. You see – it's so hard to explain it tactfully – but, well, she's had to make a choice between you and me, and I'm afraid she's chosen me. I'm sorry. I should have told you more gently.'

'No, no, it'sh a pleashure, I asshure you,' said Apricot draining his vodka and, after a moment's thought, Trevelyan's as well. Was the man more like a walrus or a koala bear? – he just couldn't decide. The landlord, for some reason, had put a cherry on a stick in Apricot's drink, and it was in danger of lodging at the back of his throat.

'But let us turn the conversation,' said Trevelyan, 'to more pleasant matters. You and I have a mutual interest in high technology – although, of course, compared with yourself I am the merest amateur. Linguistics is my primary field. I come from the West Country, as you will no doubt have realized from my accent: the land of cider and friendliness.' He smiled again, managing to create a really striking impression of a boa-constrictor. 'I am interested in energy, in power sources; and in Cornwall we see the daily majesty of the tides. What immense power is there – but all of it just going to waste! Unfortunately, I would be the last to pretend that I have the technical knowledge to exploit it.'

Apricot raised one eyebrow, then the other, then the first a little bit higher. 'I'm a particle physhichisht, not an engineer,' he said. 'I'm afraid it'sh rather out of my field.'

'Not at all, you son of a gun. (Two more double-vodkas, please, landlord.) Let me explain. I'm thinking of a combination of nuclear power and tidal forces, and I have even drafted a scheme which I believe could completely revolutionize the whole of Britain's economy, with

112

my native Cornwall taking the lead: all I need, if I am to implement it, is a few neutrinos. If you would be kind enough to glance at these blueprints I have had the temerity to bring along, I would be more than grateful . . .'

Apricot sipped at, then drained, his vodka and tonic, and thought frenziedly as he stared at the incomprehensible words typed on the top sheet of the wodge of plans that Trevelyan had thumped down emphatically on the brimming ashtray. *Alekshia,* he thought miserably to himself. Every time his eyes seemed almost to get the wriggling letters into focus it was as if a mist passed over them; like tadpoles the characters would jig off into different configurations. 'I can't unnershtand thish at all,' he confessed sadly. 'Perhapsh another vodka would help conchen . . . con-chen-trate my mind . . .?'

Trevelyan laughed. 'Oh, my fault, my fault, old fellow. My notes are written in Cornish – which as you know has every chance of soon being accepted as the second language of the British Isles, perhaps even of the Western Hemisphere.' Trevelyan's eyes glowed fanatically: the way the glaciers were swooping down through the country, it was quite likely that, for a short time at least, Cornwall would remain the only part of Britain yet to be engulfed. Then, *then*, even if only for a few days or hours, Cornish would be acknowledged as the nation's *first* tongue! He controlled himself with some difficulty, and picked up the first few pages of his notes.

Apricot looked around the bar, which had now become quite full: even his slurred brain realized that, free drinks or no free drinks, it was high time he got away from this astonishingly boring companion. Then, to his immense relief, he saw Avedon come in. Perhaps 'enter' would be a more appropriate word; somehow the glamorous science writer of the *Daily Grunt,* her ripe young breasts straining

113

against the almost see-through fabric of her off-the-shoulder blouse, her raw tousled hair caressing her nubile shoulders and her buttocks moving like the cogs in some well oiled machine, always managed to make her presence felt. But then Apricot's heart, also a part of a well oiled machine, sank: had not Trevelyan just told him that his darling Avedon was deserting him for this lunatic Cornish swine? He settled back down gloomily to wiping spilled alcohol from the formica top with a paper napkin and squeezing it into his glass.

A shadow fell over him. He looked up. It was Avedon. To his amazement she was gazing at him with deep, lustrous, lambent eyes; she took his hand impetuously and held it tight to her heaving bosom. 'Lucius, Lucius, my one true love,' she said. 'I need you so much.'

The effect of her words on both men was electric. For the first time since his thirteenth birthday, Apricot's mind cleared; the colours of all the world seemed somehow brighter; it was like being reborn. Trevelyan's reaction was equal and opposite. From the abrupt grief and dismay which contorted his hitherto suave face, it was only too clear that the news of Avedon's change of heart was as much a shock to him as it had been to Apricot. 'Is this a change of plan?' he hissed at the pouting journalist.

She looked at him strangely. 'I don't know what you're talking about,' she said. 'In fact, I don't think you and I have been introduced. Is this some friend of yours, darling Lucius, or just some bar-room drunk you can't get rid of?'

'Don't be unkind to him,' said Apricot generously. 'He's just some tidal-power nut from the West Country.'

'From the West Country?' said Avedon. 'That's a coincidence! I've been down in the West Country today – only just got back. The Editor sent me out on a special assignment to a farm in Devon. There had been rumours that one of the farmers down there had been using his animal-cloning equipment to produce thousands of human carbon-copies.'

'And had he?' said Apricot, leaning forward eagerly and ignoring a cry from Trevelyan of 'Three more vodka and tonics, barman, and one each for these two.'

'No, well, I don't think so. I interviewed the farmer and his wife – a Mr and Mrs Loam – and a nicer, more honest couple you couldn't hope to find.' Avedon's chin dimpled as she accepted a proffered drink from Trevelyan; Apricot gestured his away. 'They said they knew nothing about the rumours, but that . . . well, that *something* funny had seemed to be in the air around the farm recently. Though how they could tell there was something funny in the air around *that* farm I just don't know.' She wrinkled her taut nose reflectively.

'So what did you do then?' asked Apricot, hanging on her every word.

She giggled; the sound was like that of a brook babbling over small rounded pebbles in the springtime of one's youth, when the skies are always blue and the air always fresh with the richness of summer. 'Well, dearest, I felt a bit of a fool. I asked them if I could wander around the farm for an hour or so until my helicopter pilot returned to pick me up, and they said that that was fine. Rachel – Mrs Loam – offered to show me the cowshed and the other outbuildings, but I could see that she was having difficulty moving herself around – she's *so* pregnant, poor dear – so I told her I'd be all right on my own. And then, and then . . . it's rather confusing after that.'

'Namesh Trevelyan,' interposed the Cornishman, trying to clap a clammy hand to her thigh but missing by a good 30.48 centimetres. 'Aubrey Trevelyan. An' you're a very lushchious young lady, m'dear. Like to buy you a shrink.'

'Push off, whoever you may be,' said Avedon Patella

haughtily, then turned back to Apricot, putting her arm around his shoulders and toying with one of the buttons of his shirt. 'Anyway, dear heart, I was saying: I went out to the cowshed to have a poke around, and there I met the Loams' farmhand, a funny little fellow called Schmidt. Somehow I felt that I'd seen him somewhere before, but no matter. He said he'd be only too glad to show me the Clonette, as the gadget's called, and asked me if I were Aryan, which seemed odd. I told him that I wasn't, that I was a Pisces, and he looked very confused . . . and then, darling, then there was a sort of *blank*.'

'A blank?' said Apricot.

'Yes, I just can't remember exactly what happened for the next half-hour or so . . . until I found myself outside the cowshed again with Mr Schmidt. He seemed very happy about something, but when I asked him about it he just looked enigmatic and said that I'd contributed something to his Masterplan, which I certainly couldn't remember doing. I was still in a bit of a haze, but I didn't like to admit it, so I just waited until Rock, my helicopter-pilot, came to fly me back to London. Oh, *Lucius*,' she whimpered, burying her lithe head in his chest, 'I was – I was *frightened*!'

'There, there, my dear,' said the particle physicist comfortably, mussing her hair. 'I'm sure there was nothing to be frightened about. There's probably a perfectly simple explanation for it all.' But in his eyes there was a suspicion that would not quite go away. He seemed to be staring towards the far corner of the room, but in fact his eyes saw nothing but swirling patterns, patterns that seemed to come tantalizingly close to having a meaning. It was frustrating, for the moment, that his brain seemed incapable of inserting the final fragment to solve this abstract jigsaw puzzle, but he was not without hope. His faith was pinned on ratiocination, the ancient oriental art

116

derived by millions of generations of mystic Hindu sages from the fast lostnesses of the mysterious Himalayas. The solution would come to him – soon, he knew.

Trevelyan was trying to get all the other customers in the bar to join him in a rousing rendition of Mendeléev's 'Periodic Table Song', but they were all embarrassedly claiming to have forgotten the words after 'chlorine'. The Cornishman staggered over to join Patella and Apricot, sat down heavily beside them, and belched loudly. 'More shrinks for m'friendsh,' he shouted, thumping the bar with his clenched fists. 'They're both too tight-arshed by half. Need a few little shrinkiesh to get you going, don't you shweetheart?' He nudged Avedon and she looked vaguely sick.

Apricot's eyes refocused. He looked down at his empty glass.

'Thanks, old man,' he said quietly. 'But this time make mine just a tonic.'

8

Death is sitting in a far corner of the Old Bra and Boilermaker, watching the play with a quirky grin on his face: people, he has always found, are so amusing in their little tragedies and their petty triumphs. But then a frown crosses his features. At the moment there is one human being who is very definitely thwarting him. His own analogical video machine has, like so many of its kind, decided to malfunction, so that he has had to venture forth into this teeming ratbitten little pub in order to use the machine over there in the corner behind the dart board, the pool table and the stripper. But one of the CHANCRE technicians has got here first, and has so far spent the evening methodically plugging coins into the slot. It would be easy enough to dispose of him with a thunderbolt, but Death has no wish to make himself conspicuous, for reasons of his own. And so he must just sit here, uncomfortable on the clinging vinyl seating, nursing a slimline bitter lemon and growing gradually more and more frustrated.

At last the technician drains his fourth pint of low-calorie lager substitute and heads purposefully towards the door to the toilets. For a moment Death is tempted to follow him to extract a swift revenge for all the waiting, but then he decides against it: it would be doubly frustrating were someone else to have taken over the machine by the time he returned. Instead, his left-hand pocket bulging with coins, he moves swiftly, his feet seemingly and in fact not touching the ground, over to the corner. He puts in a coin and a smile lights up his face once again as the pictures begin to flicker into view.

Now, what's this . . . ?

It is a little before sunset. Mark Tompion and Lise Panther are walking hand-in-hand through the woods near the great dish, their gasmasks firmly in place. Up here one gets so used to wearing the masks that the two have little difficulty in understanding each other's muffled words. Although neither can actually see that it is the case, each is perfectly well aware that the other is smiling languorously. They have all the inbuilt confidence and ease of two people who know that shortly they are to become lovers: there is a small edge of exciting tension between them, but it serves almost more to relax their minds than to abrade them.

'It was such an unusual present, Mark, but so thoughtful of you,' says Lise Panther dreamily. 'Toothpaste, a toothbrush and an instruction manual.'

'Well, honey,' drawls Tompion, his hand resting amicably on her jean-clad buttocks, 'it seemed like something special for your birthday.' There is something almost asexual about the thrilling tingle his brain receives from his fingers as they feel her firm muscles moving smoothly under the coarse stretched fabric.

'Oh, Mark,' she says, breathing hoarsely inside the harsh confines of the mask, 'you know, we make a good team, the two of us. Between us we'll be able to crack the new sets of signals that are coming in. I have the feeling that there's more to these than meets the eye . . . but between you and me, darling, I think we'll be able to save little old humanity somehow.'

She stops in the leafless clearing, beneath trees whose gnarled branches have long since surrendered any attempt at life to the all-pervasive pollution, and turns towards him. His eyes close as she pulls him tightly to her, her generous yet upright breasts pressing questioningly into his chest. 'Oh, goddam this pollution!' she almost weeps, yet hidden behind the words there is something of dry humour too. 'I do so want to kiss your great handsome hunk of a face.'

While courteously ecstatic, Tompion is also rather bewildered. The first he knew about Panther's birthday present was when she came into his office, sat in his lap, and kissed him passionately. His initial reaction, he allows himself reluctantly to confess, inwardly, was one of nausea – until he realized that, in place of the famed halitosis, her breath smelt sweetly of peppermint. After that kiss, his mind was too staggered for him to guess what he had done to deserve it; only slowly, from odd accidental references of hers, was he able to piece together all the elements of the situation. He was happy enough – deliriously happy, in fact – but still, at the back of his mind, there lingered that persistent question: *I wonder who the hell gave her that toothbrush?* It is a question which he still has not been able to answer.

Nevertheless he would be a fool if he let a little matter like that get in his way now. He is alone in the woods with a beautiful woman, who has indicated all too clearly that she wishes to make mad, passionate love to him at the very first available opportunity. 'Honey,' he says: 'Why don't we stroll back to my quarters? There'll be nobody around there at the moment. We can have the place to ourselves for – oh, for hours now.' He glances at his wristwatch. Well, if they get a move on, there should be time for a quickie.

Oddly, the air around them is beginning to clear a little. The dark noxious fumes seem to be becoming somewhat diluted. Panther is the first to notice this.

'Mark. Do you see? It's almost like Nature was doing her best to be kind to us.'

Tompion is dubious. He runs his hands down, down over her back until they are cupping her buttocks. 'I think it's just chance, my love,' he says sombrely. 'You know, sometimes when the winds are higher than usual the pollution clears up a little.'

'It's almost as if . . . yes, I think I can.' She reaches up and, before he can stop her, takes off her gasmask. 'Mark – Mark, the air isn't too bad! I can breathe it! Look!'

Obediently he watches her breasts rise and fall. Then a nobler emotion fills him. 'Lise – don't be silly. Some of these toxins don't have detectable aromas. You could . . .'

'I must,' she says simply. 'You don't understand, do you, Mark? Right now I'm not a super-rational scientist with first-rate intuitive functionings and a lightning mind. I'm a woman. All woman. And honestly, Mark, the air's beginning to smell quite pure. Only – there's a funny sort of smell. It's like the high-voltage lab . . . yes, it's ozone.'

120

'Get your mask back on!' he rasps. 'Ozone's no good for you! Surely you remember that from chemistry classes in Junior High?' He tries to force the gasmask back up towards her face, but it catches on her Yves St Laurent blouse, ripping away some of the material to reveal her breasts cupped in a virginal white brassière beneath.

And she is actively resisting his attempts, too. 'Mark, there's something funny going on here!' Her well built bosom rises and falls with the same intensity, the same urgency, as her husky voice. 'The air – the whole air seems to be changing! Look! You can see all the way across the valley to the radio dish! You haven't been able to do that for years!'

Tompion raises his eyes and his mind reluctantly to the brightly formed red rosebud of her lips. What she is saying is true. For the first time since he has been stationed here, the great dish lies in what seems to be bright sunlight. And yet . . . and yet the surrounding air is in turmoil, roiling and boiling like the air above a hot electric fire. Hesitantly, he slips his mask partly from his face. The smell of ozone is strong – beginning to approach danger level. He thrusts the mask swiftly back on – he'll have to kiss Panther's breasts some other time – and overpowers her passionate resistance to replace the mask over her face, too. His fingers fumble clumsily with the attachment straps.

'Don't be such a lamebrain, darling,' he hisses. 'Too much of this stuff can kill you.'

She stops fighting him, and her body relaxes in her arms.

'What's going on?' she murmurs throatily, tossing her mane of impetuous hair.

'I dunno, babe. What do you think?'

'Well, I know this sounds kinda silly, Mark, but it's

121

almost as if someone were projecting a powerful, concentrated beam of high-energy X-rays down through the atmosphere. But that's impossible. You'd need an X-ray laser . . . not just a little one, I mean: something really huge, really powerful. I don't think there's ever been one built that powerful!'

Absentmindedly, he fondles her firmly thrusting left breast, then shifts his attention to her right, which he has decided he marginally prefers; somehow, it has more character. 'Yeah?' he says thickly.

'Well, I did read some theoretical work a few years back in a paper in *Nature* by Malone, Apricot *et al*, which suggested that the introduction of crude grain alcohol into . . . but it never came to anything. They said that it was *theoretically*,' she twists her body elegantly as she stresses the word, 'possible to build a small X-ray laser of immense power. But . . .'

And then, all of a sudden, she is at a loss for words. Across the valley, the edge of the radio dish is beginning to glow and smoulder like a maiden's kisses. Strangely, there are no flames, just a plume of smoke. 'So powerful,' she whispers, 'that it could punch a hole through the atmosphere by ionizing the . . .' Now the aerial is like a red, angry cherry: abruptly it snaps soundlessly, its top half plunging into the great dish below. Vegetation around the dish is smouldering now, on the side facing towards them. Panther stuffs her fist into her mouth – or, at least, into the part of her gasmask where her mouth would be – to keep back the sound of her noiseless scream as the line of charred vegetation slowly, ever so slowly, extends itself in their direction.

'I'm frightened! Oh, help me, darling! *I'm frightened!*'
The voice is Tompion's.

Heaven and redemption! thinks Death furiously: the coin has run out. Still, with any luck Tompion's and Panther's hashes will shortly be settled for good and all.

The CHANCRE technician, having returned from the lavatory a little while ago, is looking bewilderedly over Death's shoulder. 'What were all those pictures of?' he enquires.

'There's a fault in the circuitry,' Death prevaricates. 'I've been sent to repair it.'

'That's quick,' says the technician. 'I was playing with the machine only a couple of minutes ago, and it was working all right then. Can I give you a hand repairing it, mate?'

'No – no,' says Death. 'It would be more than my job's worth to let anyone else fiddle around with one of these. Anyway, it's the software that's up the spout, not the hardware.'

'Ah, well . . .' says the technician and, to Death's immense relief, he ambles away towards the bar, shaking his head in puzzlement at the ways of men and machines.

Eagerly, Death thumbs a new coin into the slot. *Now, let's see, what have we here . . . ?*

Adolf Hitler is almost deafened by the sonorous booms of the mighty cracking glaciers as they thunder down towards the south of England. To his left are the lights of Taunton, but as yet he has no wish to encounter other human beings. For he is walking at the head of a raggle-taggle army – nearly 400 clones of himself, plus just over 100 Avedon Patellas produced in a frenzy of anticipated lust before finally the Clonette overheated and refused to function any more. One of the Patellas is being particularly irritating.

'Mr Schmidt, Mr Schmidt,' she keeps saying. 'You have to realize, our two causes have a great deal in common with each other. If I help you to dominate the world – the Universe, even – you can by way of reciprocation grant me the simple favour of making Cornish the primary language of the British Isles.' She trips over an exposed root, but stumbles on after him in the cold night air. 'If you wish, I could be your concubine,' she adds shyly. 'Together we can conquer the world!'

Hitler wishes the damn woman would go and join the others, but he is frightened to order her taken away. Suppose all the replicas of him think that he is shunning her not because he has his mind on higher things, but because he fears that in a situation of intimacy she might giggle about his widely rumoured testicular shortcomings. *Ah, Eva*, he thinks, *I should never have cut one off to go in that locket round your neck.*

The bloody woman is persisting. 'As soon as I met you by the cowshed I knew that you and I were made for each other. I could see that you were a man of strength, of fire, of courage, of conviction, of *superhumanity!*'

The words are manna to his ears, but this is not the time to think of such things. Not the time to think . . .

He turns towards her, a frown creasing his cunning features. 'Did I hear you say: "As soon as you met me by the cowshed"?' he says. 'Can you tell me what happened next?'

'Why, yes,' she answers. 'You ran up behind me while I was looking at the Clonette, cackling evilly and saying: "Tee hee, tee hee, I'll just hit her over the head and steal a sliver of protoplasm." Of course, as a science writer I knew what you meant by protoplasm: the material out of which the contents and outer membrane of animal cells are made, although, curiously enough, for reasons which need not concern us here, in plants protoplasm constitutes only the contents of the cell. As soon as I heard you I realized what you were up to, so I let you hit me over the head with the solar-powered pitchfork.'

Hitler gasps. *The perfidy of the woman!*

'Fortunately,' Avedon continues, 'I trained years ago in the martial art of Kung Fu, and so I was able to stiffen the muscles of my skull into impenetrable rigidity just as you struck. I can't have been unconscious for more than a few seconds. When I came round you were operating the Clonette.'

'But,' says Hitler, 'you pig-dog scribbler, I made sure that I sent you back to that swinish capital city of yours aboard the helicopter!'

'It was easy enough to distract your attention for a moment – plenty of time to substitute one of the cloned Avedons for myself. Because I wanted to be with you, you, *you*! All of the rest of the people in this little army of yours' – she gestures across the field behind them – 'are not really humans: they're just facsimiles of the two most important people on this Earth. *Us!*'

Hitler begins to realize that at last he has found a woman capable of replacing the beloved Eva in his heart. Perhaps at the next town they come to he'll stop to get her a locket and – no, on second thoughts, perhaps he'd better not. Would a toe do just as well? Somehow it doesn't have the same romantic ring to it. Still, there's no hurry: he can decide some time over the next few weeks or months. 'Avedon,' he says, 'you are truly worthy of my love.' *And if it proves you're not*, he adds silently to himself, *I can always have you killed.*

Avedon looks at him with trusting eyes. *I know you for who you are*, she thinks. *You are Adolf Hitler, the German-Cornish Führer, come to rescue our twin peoples. And if it proves you're not, I can always have you killed. I wonder if it's true what they say about your having only one . . .*

Once again, Death's coin has run out, but he has seen enough. *My little allies*, he thinks, with as much affection as his cold heart is capable of, *you are serving me well*.

The landlord is shouting that it is closing time and, anyway, Death has no need to linger. Rudely shouldering people aside he heads for the door. Ahead of him, Lucius Apricot and the *other* Avedon Patella, arms around each others' waists and teeth tightly interlocked, step fastidiously over the recumbent and foul-odoured form of Aubrey Trevelyan, who is snoring loudly. (*Stap me, but it's green*, thinks Death in parentheses. *The stupid sod must have switched to crème de menthe*.) Death follows Apricot and Patella out into the darkness but, as they turn away towards the flat they share, he turns right, into a shabby alley. Here, with no one around to hear or see him, he allows himself to break into a fit of gleeful cackling.

In the subdued lamplight his tall, cloaked figure, scuttling and yet striding, mincing and yet marching, pausing occasionally to throw back its head in gluttonous, gelatinous laughter, would strike pure terror into the heart of any mortal observer. Fortunately, there are no strictly mortal observers to be petrified . . . but there has been, all the evening, one *immortal* observer, who has been eying Death sardonically. This immortal is the travelling soul of Junior Finkelstein, and at last it has tracked down its single most implacable enemy.

The watcher has been watched.

9

Meanwhile, the London Underground, thanks to the enormous tectonic forces exerted by the glaciers as they rushed south, had adopted many of the characteristics of a Klein Bottle (*klein* being the German for 'little'). Two men, Bert Tremble and John Strickler, were trapped in its topological entrails, having by now lost any clear idea of where they might be heading.

In fact, the two trains into which they were crowded were both speeding towards Embankment station. The trains were scheduled to arrive simultaneously and, thanks to the time-distorting effects of the four-dimensional Klein Bottle, would actually do so.

Fortunately for Tremble and Strickler, neither of them knew this.

4

Down the Tube of Terror

Perhaps the spectacular production of bent spoons produces the wave of astonishment from the audience, releasing a flood of tachyons which travel backwards in time to cause the spoons to bend just before they are produced to cause the surprise. . . .
                                    – John Gribbin, *White Holes*, 1977

1

'Well, my little Colorado beetle o'mine,' said Jeb Loam, 'just think of that. Happen if a relativistic interstellar craft do be a-travelling at 0.9 times the speed of light, the whole buggering thing do swell up proud and massive by a factor of 2.3 times its rest mass, and that all on account of the good Professor Einstein, God rest him. Nay, Rachel, that's not all, for though 'tis a mighty wondrous thing, if that ship do be spurred and whipped till it are a-galloping at 0.9999 times lightspeed, why, its mass be seventy or seventy-one times that when it lie idle. Glory be, this relativity is a powerful strong thing, and I do be wondering about slipping a dose of it into the cowfeed, Rachel my little wireworm . . .'

'What be the point of all this talk, Jeb Loam?'

'Nowt really. But 'tis all in science column o' the *Gamekeepers' and Poachers' Gazette*; happen I thought it might amuse thee.'

Jeb's words rang hollow in his ears, and not merely because in these grim days his accent was failing to convince even himself. Ambledyke Farmhouse was sealed against the horrors outside, its boarded-up windows blind as proofreaders' eyyes. The inner dimness throbbed with a stench of ancient, decaying pizza. Tawdry, mocking sunlight leered through chinks like the raddled neon of Soho, daring the Loams to peep. Jeb already knew what he'd see: the evil glint of the advancing ice-spur to the north, battered but undeterred by its savage tactical thrust through Birmingham and South Wales (this last atrocity marked by a scatter of bilingual road-signs caught between the terrible teeth of ice). And closer, on Amble-dyke Farm itself . . .

Although he wasn't looking, he still shut his eyes. Daisy-42, his favourite of all the herd! And his own dear Daisy-57, with whom once . . . never mind that, always best to watch your thoughts with Rachel near. Not to mention Daisies 1–41, 43–56 and – he sobbed involuntarily – 58–120! Everywhere, a litter of whitened bones. Everywhere, the small scurrying shapes which now preceded the glacier's resistless march, mouths wreathed in foam like some fearful toothpaste ad. Damned creatures were so crazed with glacier-lag and hydrophobia, they'd forgotten they were herbivores.

This was a time when that buggering Schmidt might have been some use at last: but where was he? Stark memory kept thrusting rudely at the makeshift barricades in the farmer's mind, memories of horror and oxymoron. Young Nathan had sneaked out through the cat-flap to play, crying 'Teddy! Teddy!' Jeb had still been desperately hunting for his shotgun under piles of farming subsidy application forms when, outside, his son's merry cries had taken on a strange new timbre:

'Da, Da, they're eating my feet!'

'Da, Da, they're eating my tummy!'

'Da, Da, they're eating my throarrgh . . .'

All this, and only half a pizza left in the farmhouse's old-fashioned deep freeze: neither Rachel nor Jeb had remembered to stash away this week's family pack of sixty. With almost every aperture sealed, they were breathless in the sickly air, and young Reuben was greedily trying to suck oxygen from each tiny crack and wall crevice in turn. Impossible now to run that deadly, furry gauntlet to the cowshed, where (if only he'd acted in time) Jeb might have thrown the Clonette into reverse gear, converting the oncoming lemming-horde to minuscule samples of rodent tissue . . . Too late, too late. Jeb Loam clutched his throbbing head between his hands. There was just no way that things could get any worse.

Rachel groaned.

'Jeb? Happen the contractions are starting . . .'

2

'All is for the best in this best of all possible worlds,' declared Professor Ponglass of the Tooting Bec Futures Research Institute, eyes beady behind his pebble glasses and pebble contact lenses (professional futurologists always hedged their bets).

'How's that again?' said the Prime Minister as a further temblor rattled the drinks cabinet. The Cabinet of HM Government was already thoroughly rattled, and to them the shockwaves made little difference, barely altering their fixed expressions of mindless, drooling fear.

'I mean – ' said Ponglass.

'You can't!'

'But – '

'No – '

'I'm afraid it's yes.' He made a note. According to the

130

Institute's guidelines, dialogue like this was one of the telltale signs of disaster. 'Happily, though, we live in a world of natural checks and balances. (First slide, please.) As you see, our simulations, based on the fact that last year the Sun emitted only two neutrinos rather than the normal and considerably larger figure, predict a world-searing solar flare. But – next slide – we simultaneously find a "Velikovsky catastrophe" hurling the Moon from its orbit and sending it spiralling in towards Earth, possibly a Jungian synchronicity effect resulting from the adoption of Réné Thom's mathematical catastrophe theory here below. Observe the beauty of the balance – next slide – as our prediction indicates that the Moon will in fact *shield us* from the worst of the solar flare as it bulks largest in the sky, just prior to impact!'

He lit another cigar, and the greenhouse effect began to accelerate. 'See how the Ponglass Principle applies across the board! On the one hand, droughts and heat-stroke ravage the land as armpit aerosols finally destroy the ozone layer; on the other, kindly Nature moves to balance this with her generous dispensation of glaciers. On the one hand we have earthquakes caused by the conjunction of Mercury with Concorde; on the other, Earth itself compensates for our loss by thrusting up new land, land which one day we shall colonize and use! Our next slide shows an artist's impression of the constructive tectonic plate margin which all our simulations indicate is due to emerge at Basingstoke . . . yes, yes, Carruthers, what is it?'

A white-coated flunkey had entered with quick steps, without regard for the catatonic rows of Cabinet Ministers. He handed Ponglass a slip of paper. There was a deadly silence, broken only by the distant sound of the St James's Park pelicans vomiting.

'Ladies and gentlemen, there is a problem.' Ponglass

had begun to sweat. 'Our laboratories report a new and alarming development.' In the stress of emotion, one of his pebble contact lenses fell out. 'The latest hideous *change* to afflict poor ravaged Mother Earth . . . are any of you familiar with the substance known as *superglue*?'

'Not intimately,' said the PM, suspecting a trap. In these troubled times, morality checks were everywhere.

'As of 10:38 this morning – superglue has become sentient. And . . . hostile!'

3

At Arecibo it was hell, or thereabouts. Tompion regarded the approaching line of carbonizing greenery with a scientist's cool, emotional detachment. He hoped, at any rate, that Lise Panther would take this view of his immobility: in actual fact he'd probably have been near the horizon and swimming hard, had his knees not turned swiftly and debilitatingly to a substance he'd tentatively identified as hydrogen oxide.

Another hundred square metres of undergrowth puffed into soot and vapour under the merciless lash of X-rays. A passing rabbit jerked and rolled over, flash-grilled, smelling good enough to . . . *Must be my imagination*, Tompion told himself fiercely. *Either that or my goddam gasmask has sprung a leak*. His eyes met Panther's above her mask's exquisite snout.

'So you worked it out too,' she said, her voice a caress like honey-soaked velvet gently simmering in champagne.

'Nng,' he agreed, intending to say something rather different. Somewhere at the back of his trained mind, a note was filed on the possible effects of X-ray scatter on the tensioning of vocal cords.

'Yes, I see.' Her laughter was like the tinkling of small ice floes. 'For a moment I thought you were being stupidly brave!' She whipped out an ozone-faded notebook and with swift, feline movements jotted down the probability equations. Tompion watched, glazed, sensing meaning in the delicately convoluted symbols but baffled by Panther's irritating habit of inserting *numbers*.

Overdone to a degree which would have horrified even an English chef, the rabbit swelled up capriciously and exploded in an interesting spray of intestines.

'There! The probability integral can't be disputed!' She sketched the curve in the smoky air, a firm, thrusting, sensuous curve which reminded Tompion all too painfully of something. Of two somethings. Grass was wilting and flies were kamikazeing from the air mere metres from where they stood. Farther back, fused and molten earth had begun to quiver in the slow rhythmic heavings which lead to orgasm.

Screaming mildly as stray photons began to give his feet sunburn despite the heavy boots, Tompion began: 'I think – '

A few loose ends of Panther's hair flashed hotly into nothingness. The equations on the page glowed and flamed: and as they did, Tompion somehow understood them. Intolerable heat and radiation sleeted on them both – and stopped.

'Communication,' said Panther, trembling in triumph, or perhaps just trembling. 'My analysis made it clear that laser *communication*, not attack, was the highest probability. That initial three-minute high-power pulse, happily reduced in deadliness by the smog blanket, was just to attract our attention; my prediction was that it *had* to stop after that time, plus or minus . . .' Her pretty face wrinkled into a delightful frown as she raced through the subsidiary calculations for which there'd been no time in

133

all the excitement. 'Two hours and four minutes. How . . . interesting, don't you think, Mark?'

But Tompion had sunk into a reverie and lay supine in the scorched undergrowth, eyes fixed sightlessly on the once again clouding sky. Though dimly aware that he was dribbling slightly, he had devoted all his attention to the control of a suddenly backsliding sphincter.

'Oh Mark, yes, how *right*. How I've underestimated you! We must be ready to detect and record the lower-intensity coded communication pulses which just have to follow. Perhaps to make sure we're as sensitive as possible to the radiation flicker, we should not only lie down but take off our clothes.'

Too late, baby, thought Tompion, who'd never felt more detumescent in his life. But she was bending over him, naked but for the now strangely erotic gasmask, loosening his trousers and saying in low, indescribably sensuous tones: 'It's coming, it's coming, I can feel it coming! Do you know Morse?'

4

. . . SOS SOS SOS MAYDAY MAYDAY MAYDAY SORRY IF OUR FIRST BIG PULSE MELTED THE ODD CITY OR WHATEVER JUST ONE OF THOSE SILLY LITTLE MISTAKES ANYONE MIGHT HAVE MADE STOP THIS IS COLONEL BART MALONE ABOARD THE MARY POPPINS GIVING WARN-ING TO THE UNITED STATES OF A FRIGHTFUL PERIL WHICH OUCH LEGGO ALL RIGHT DIMPLA HAVE IT YOUR WAY DOT DOT DOT GIVING WARNING TO ALL THE WORLD INCLUDING COMMIES DOT DOT DOT OK OK

GLORIOUS SOVIET REPUBLICS WHERE WAS I QUERY

PROBLEM ONE SEEMS LIKE MARY POPPINS IS ON COLLISION COURSE WITH EARTH AT TOP VELOCITY WELL SHUCKS WHAT CAN I SAY SORRY FOLKS NOT OUR FAULT WILL FILL YOU IN ON DETAILS LATER IF THERE IS A LATER OF COURSE STOP NOW YOU MIGHT THINK ALL YOU GOTTA DO IS WHIP UP A FLIGHT OF NUKES TO BLOW US TO SUBATOMIC GAS STOP SEEMS OBVIOUS DOESNT IT QUERY OF COURSE WED JUST LOVE TO MAKE THE SUPREME SACRIFICE AND STUFF FOR EARTHS SAKE BUT WE RECKON WE HAVE TO REMIND YOU THIS WOULD BE AGAINST INTERNATIONAL TREATIES ABOUT NUCLEAR USE IN SPACE STOP ITS THE PRINCIPLE OF THE THING YOU KNOW STOP BESIDES IT WOULDNT DO MUCH GOOD IN THE LONG TERM OR EVEN LIKE IN THE SHORT TERM SINCE THERES ALSO PROBLEM TWO COLON DRAMATIC PAUSE THIS ANTIMATTER COMET WHICH WE COMPUTE WILL OVERTAKE AND HIT EARTH LONG BEFORE WE DO STOP ESTIMATED ENERGY YIELD NO I CANT BRING MYSELF TO TELL YOU BUT BELIEVE ME ITS BIG STOP

SO IT LOOKS LIKE WE HAVE TO SAY GOODBYE BUT THERE IS STILL ONE HOPE FOR HUMANITY YOULL BE GLAD TO HEAR STOP HUMANITY CAN STILL LIVE ON TO GROW AGAIN FROM NEW GARDEN OF EDEN AND CONQUER THE STARS STOP PLEASE BEAM JOINT USA PLUS USSR AUTHORIZATION TO CONVERT MARY POPPINS INTO VIABLE BREEDING COLONY SO WE CAN ENSURE ARRRRGGH

COMRADE DIMPLA SPEAKING STOP PLEASE IGNORE FASCIST RANTINGS OF UNHINGED DRUNKEN CAPITALIST GOAT STOP PROPER DIALECTICAL ANALYSIS OF SITUATION INDICATES BEST COURSE OF ACTION STOP I COMPUTE WE CAN NEUTRALIZE BOTH THREATS TO EARTH BY MINOR COURSE ALTERATION STOP MULTI GIGATON EXPLOSION AS MARY POPPINS INTERSECTS COMET TRAJECTORY SUFFICIENT TO DIVERT REMAINING ANTIMATTER MASS INTO HARMLESS HYPERBOLIC ORBIT SWINGING ROUND SUN AND OUT INTO PEACEFUL DEEPS OF SPACE NEVER AGAIN TO TROUBLE GLORIOUS HISTORICALLY PREORDAINED FUTURE OF SOVIET HEGEMONY STOP

OWING TO FAILURE OF PORT OR POSSIBLY STARBOARD RETROTHRUSTER MUST MAKE COURSE CORRECTION BY JETTISONING APPROX NINETY KILOS MASS AT HIGH EJECTION SPEED WITHIN NEXT THREE HOURS STOP PLEASE ADVISE WHICH SURPLUS MASS CAN BEST BE USED FOR THIS STOP UNFORTUNATELY OWING TO VARIOUS MAKESHIFTS NO SPARE SHIP MASS AVAILABLE FOR EJECTION STOP SORRY I WEIGH ONLY FIFTY TWO KILOS EVEN IN SPACESUIT BUT PERHAPS YOU CAN THINK OF SOMETHING WHICH IS LARGER STOP MEANWHILE PLEASE ADVISE SYNTHESIS FROM SHIPBOARD MATERIALS OF BROMIDE SALTPETRE TRANQUILLIZERS SPECIAL RESTRICTIVE MORMON UNDERWEAR . . .

The X-ray energy pulses died away at last, and smog closed in over the fused ruins of Arecibo like a warm, friendly, familiar blanket which happened not to have been washed since 1968. 'No, sorry,' said Tompion, able at last to speak: 'I can't read Morse.'

'Oh dear,' said Panther, her perky, thrusting bosom seeming to wilt a trifle. 'Neither can I.'

5

'That's funny,' the Superintendent remarked. 'Would you believe it? The latest printout says . . . no, it's absurd. A nuclear explosion predicted in the London Underground? What's *that* got to do with the parking-ticket figures, I'd like to know . . . Bloody PNC must be on the blink again.'

The Assistant Commissioner looked momentarily distraught. 'PNC?' he enquired, topping up his pint glass with trembling fingers. 'Er, just for one moment can you pretend I've never heard of the PNC, and describe the situation to me as though I knew nothing of it. Constable! Bring another bottle of The Macallan, if you please.'

Gritting his teeth, the Superintendent bowed to literary convention. 'As you well know, sir, PNC stands for Police National Computer, the mighty data integration network which amasses information about major crimes and correlates this with information received about major criminals loitering suspiciously in the vicinity with jemmies and sacks marked SWAG . . . thus making vital connections impossible to the unaided human mentality. And now the damned thing says there's going to be a nuclear explosion!'

'Well . . . you know, Superintendent, I don't see that it's really our business. A memo to the MOD – which as you well know stands for Ministry of Defence – should cover the matter, wouldn't you say? We must not allow ourselves to be distracted from the maintenance of law and order. Far too many miscreants are expecting to avoid being ticketed or wheel-clamped, simply because of distractions like a third of the country being smashed by glaciers while rabid rodents prowl at will. They may expect laxity, but we'll make them smile on the other side of their faces! Unroll the War Plan, Constable . . . thank you. Now here, where the alleged Nazi riots, led by the supposed reincarnation of Adolf Hitler riding on a rumoured Loch Ness Monster, are at their thickest – here is where we shall spearhead our major offensive against double parking . . .'

Far beneath the city streets, beyond the awesome sway of parking meters, John Strickler found himself in terrifying hot darkness. One second the train had been hurtling towards Embankment station; the next, the world had turned upside down and begun to dance the hornpipe while balancing on its nose. *Must be one of those earth tremors*, he thought. The train, he realized as orientation returned, seemed to have stopped with its nose slightly down in some kind of shallow pit. Groans surrounded him, like one of the less cheerful bits of Dante's *Inferno*. The suitcase seemed wedged under the seat, distorted: with sudden sharp terror he fumbled within, to find the . . . Egg . . . unharmed.

Bloody Ministry of Defence, that's the last time I do copywriting for them! *Just an ordinary public relations job, they said, you have to sell the product to the British public, you'll need a sample to base your copy on* . . .He took hold of the dull metal sphere, feeling a sort of responsibility, and tucked it under his arm. Then he found and clicked his cigarette lighter with that characteristic devil-may-care gesture he'd devised for the Melanoma King Size campaign. What he saw by its fitful glimmer might have been tossed off by Hieronymus Bosch

138

on a particularly hungover morning. Whimpering, he eased himself and the weapon core through a conveniently broken window, and landed in a pile of bones.

Look, mate, he thought in the general direction of God, *this is getting beyond a joke!*

Old, brown bones. They splintered and crumbled underfoot, and gave him an idea for a road safety poster he'd have to sketch out some day. With sudden, dazzling insight he realized that the earth tremors must have caused the tunnel to subside into some ancient plague burial pit. A historical curiosity, nothing more. Feeling that all those months of jogging were at last beginning to pay off, he clambered painfully up the tilted side of the Underground train, amazed at the ability of forced evolution to develop prehensile fingers at a moment's notice.

What the fuck do I do now? Walk? He sat with legs dangling over the front windows of the driver's cab, morosely cradling the Egg on his lap, staring blankly into the deeply Freudian tunnel of darkness which led (he supposed) to Embankment station. Surely help would have to arrive soon?

Presently Strickler began to feel a strange discomfort in his groin (but put it down to random randiness) and also in his armpits (but put it down to nervous sweat and lack of deodorant). A copywriter's vocabulary has certain limitations, and for one reason or another he'd never had to craft a slogan like, 'Nine housewives out of ten just can't tell warts from buboes!'

Surely help must be on the way?

Meanwhile, Bert Tremble was gingerly holding a brown paper bag of weapon-grade plutonium, and staring resentfully at the implacable London Transport guard. 'Look,' he said, 'this is getting beyond a joke!' Unmanned, in a welter of automatic-systems failures, the train lurched through the roaring lights of Embankment station – on the wrong tracks.

'Farther back, sir,' grated the guard. Tremble retreated into the driver's cab, cowed by the massed, hate-filled eyes which stared at him from the crammed far end of the carriage with the dead, distrustful gaze of tinned sardines. *If only I'd kept my big mouth shut! If only I hadn't bragged about it! If only I hadn't tried to impress that smashing young raver with my machismo and my near-critical mass of plutonium!*

Aloud he exclaimed: 'Please, listen, I'm a science correspondent and I know what I'm talking about. It's perfectly safe. To make this thing explode you'd probably need to surround it with a large and carefully symmetrical mass of specially formulated explosive which would then have to be precisely triggered in order to collapse the plutonium into a supercritical configuration!' It was a relief to break free, just for once, from the monosyllables which his editor demanded for such subjects.

Just behind the guard, that smashing, leggy girl who'd been his downfall stared at him with mute compassion and apology in her long-lashed violet eyes and delightfully pomegranate-shaped breasts. *You're well in there, Tremble,* thought a small and lecherous – actually quite large and lecherous – part of his mind: *don't forget to get her phone number, now.*

'Farther back, sir. Into the cab . . . that's right. Now hold the bag behind your back, if you don't mind – get it farther away from the rest of us – *that's* right . . .'

'Good God, man! You're completely paranoid! This stuff can't just explode at the drop of a hat! Even if this train ran straight into a brick wall right now, nothing special would happen unless, by some utterly incredible coincidence, another large mass of plutonium were positioned exactly where the two could impact and achieve supercriticality!'

'Easy there, sir.'

Somewhere ahead, Strickler had begun to sweat profusely, and was overcome with giddiness. A deeply insightful slogan ran through his whirling mind: *Nothing acts faster than yummy Prudential Assurance when the parts other beers cannot reach are feeling 57 degrees under* . . . Clutching the dull-metal orb as though it were a talisman, he slowly, very slowly, began to topple forward . . .

(Death, peering into a shop window's demonstration TV – which puzzled bystanders assume must be showing an avant-garde underground documentary – falls awesomely about and slaps his bony thighs.)

'And here,' said Professor Ponglass to his now slack-jawed audience, 'are the very latest computer prognostics, hot from the newest-model laser printer which is so characteristic of the Institute's state-of-the-art technological sophistication. Exactly in accordance with the Ponglass Principle: this set of curves shows a resurgence of that long-forgotten terror, the Black Death! Mutated, it seems, by some chance exposure to radiation (possibly in the form of a near-critical mass of weapon-grade plutonium), into a newer, swifter, and more lethal form. A *black* prospect, one might think!' He chuckled over his little pun.

'But now, please note the converging Serendipity Curve.' (He scribbled on the overhead-projector transparency.) 'Science tells us that, despite the seeming threat of worldwide plague, the outbreak will be sterilized almost before it's begun, by an event analogous to the historical Great Fire of London. We only await the latest fire-alarm reports, whereupon – '

The windows of the Parliamentary Committee Room exploded with blinding white light. The curtains burst into flame. In the brief pause before the blastwave, punctuated by tinkling glass and Ministers' high-pitched screams, Professor Ponglass said testily: 'I cannot be held responsible. I was not given all the pertinent data – '

7

'*Donner und Blitzen!*' shrieked Hitler, accidentally lapsing into character. The long, ranting colloquies in which his trusty, scaly mount had been persuaded not only to throw its weight behind the Thousand Year Plan but to answer (however reluctantly) to the name Siegfried . . . the glorious ease with which resistance had crumbled before him, seemed in fact hardly to notice him . . . the ecstatic sacking and burning of every Marks and Spencer's store between the West Country and western London . . . was it all to be for nothing? Ahead, where the naked throat of the hated metropolis should have lain bared to his knife, there was little but a medium-sized mushroom cloud.

'*Himmel!* I have . . . I have been *upstaged*!'

'Darling, it is for the best,' murmured the pushiest of the seventy-eight remaining slinky, voluptuous Avedon Patellas in his shock-troop force, now reduced to fewer than 300 in number (a kosher delicatessen on the outskirts of Slough had put up an unexpected show of resistance). Sitting behind him on mighty, two-brained Siegfried, she tweaked his moustache in the little gesture of affection he'd already come to dread.

'What do you mean, *mein liebling*?'

'A blank slate, a *tabula rasa*: nothing remaining to be torn down before, dear Adolf, before we erect the bilingual road signs!'

From between the grating slits of a nearby drain, an

142

ever-pulsating blob of superglue watched them with eye-less malevolence.

'I homed in on your Arctic Emergency Beacon,' Dr Joyce Abramowitz explained with a sensuous pout. 'I know *that* part of it's none of my business really, but my curiosity was sort of piqued when the helicopter's inbuilt direction finder picked up an Arctic Emergency Beacon in Devon.'

Bjørgstrøm smiled at her gratefully, winningly. The effect, on his scarred face, suggested Frankenstein's monster in severe bad temper and punk make-up. Abramowitz closed her eyes for a moment, and thought of lemmings. Nearby, at the edge of the high ice cliff, the parked helicopter idled and thrummed with a sound like that of a vast swarm of bees lulled into near-coma by a hectic afternoon pollinating marijuana plants.

'I found myself here on the morning after what we now know to be an astonishing and catastrophic glacier slippage which – oh God – ' His face contorted in sudden anguish as memory came flooding back: the effect was marginally less appalling than his smile, but there was still a tiny click as one of the busty, blonde-haired lemming expert's contact lenses cracked from side to side under the impact. 'Oh God, the guilt! Those nights I paced up and down on the icefield, every booted step no doubt causing further microfractures in that long-suffering but eventually angry ice . . . Time after time I relieved myself into the mile-long holes left by deep-core ice samples, and more than once – ' his eyes were pits of stark terror – 'I poured the hot fat from my breakfast bacon into just those holes! And then, on that last fateful night . . . never mind. *It's all my fault.*'

Her eyes filled with sympathetic tears, blurring Bjørgstrøm's image, which promptly seemed almost (in a cadaverous way) attractive.

'Oh, Prof Bjørgstrøm, I know that feeling! It was Oppenheimer who said after the first nuclear weapons that "The physicists have known sin". At school I refused to study physics, as a protest against imminent holocaust, and devoted my life instead to the study of lemmings. My own dear lemmings, how was I to know there was any harm in them? Yet now I know the sin of having been a lemming expert. How can I expiate such guilt? As I flew over ravaged England, I saw such atrocities . . . A woman in a fur coat, but the coat was a living mass of rabid lemmings, doing a passable imitation of a piranha swarm. A man screaming as he tried to prise apart the terrible rodent jaws which were locked fast on his nose. A child, barely an hour ago, outside the besieged farm you see there far below – Ambledyke Farm, it's called on the map – '

His strong arms clasped her comfortingly; her face was pressed into his craggy shoulder, smothering the words: *actually that wasn't so bad, I don't much like children anyway.*

'What's a nice girl like you doing in a place like this?' he murmured, slightly surprised by his unwonted command of repartee. 'This thing is bigger than both of us. Let me take you away from all this.'

'I was going to take *you* away from all this,' she sobbed, her long blonde hair drenched in salty tears. 'It was not just chance that led me here, Professor Bjørgstrøm. You are needed. Word has gone out over the emergency band: across the Atlantic, a crack team is being put together to tackle the inexplicable torrent of disasters

144

which, as you well know, threatens to engulf the world and topple Man from the evolutionary peak to which he has so long and so painfully aspired!'

I wish this kind of book came with a better class of dialogue, they each thought with silent resentment.

'Well, might as well have a bash at it,' he muttered. 'Let's go.'

She shook her head in a way that emphasized her gorgeous, firm breasts, pouting lips, softly rounded thighs and delightfully *retroussé* buttocks. (It had taken a lot of practice, learning to shake her head like that.) 'First we must rescue the Loams of Ambledyke Farm, if we can: they're part of the plan. And then we rendezvous with world-famous particle-physics expert Dr Lucius Apricot and, er, top Cornish-language expert Avedon Patella, both being rushed westward in a specially requisitioned Army detoxification unit.'

Bjørgstrøm peered over the ice-wall to the farmland below. 'I can't let you go down there! The whole area is a packed mass of slavering lemmings – a carpet of rodent terror – forty square miles of agonizing death!'

'Professor Bjørgstrøm . . . remember, we have our terrible guilt to expiate.'

'Oh, yes, that.' The great glaciologist, caught at bay, slowly bowed his head and tried to sum things up in a single, epigrammatic insight. 'We,' he said, 'are all guilty.'

Below, inside the sealed and besieged farmhouse, new tragedy was poised to strike. Reeling in stale, depleted air, Jeb tried to boil water for the imminent birth: he wasn't quite sure what you did with it, but its presence was, he knew, vital. His chemical knowledge being somewhat scantier than his expertise in midwifery, he hadn't made any particular connection between the increasing stuffiness and the roaring jets of the gas stove.

'Jeb, Jeb! It be coming, I do feel it!'

'None o' your clack, woman, until water do boil. Reuben? Reuben! Come tend stove lad, and make thyself some use at last.'

Reuben lay quivering on the floor, mouth pressed against the mousehole through which he strove to suck some scant ration of unvitiated air. He did not answer.

'*Jeb!*'

'Reuben!' Jeb Loam stumped across the room to give his slothful son a shrewd and salutary kick. 'Mebbe this'll teach 'ee to hearken when your father – *awk!*'

At the strangely muffled impact of Jeb's boot, the young lad's body simply . . . collapsed . . . and a scurry of lemmings erupted from the crumpled clothing. Slow-wittedly, as he stamped vengefully on the glutted, furry forms, Jeb put two and two together: infiltrators had crept through the hole against which Reuben's mouth was pressed and, as it were, burrowed from within. He shook his head numbly, regretting all the times he'd told Reuben not to speak with his mouth full. The lad had never had much opportunity for character development, but Jeb had been kind of fond of him.

'Jeb . . . Jeb . . .'

The kettle began to whistle shrilly, and Jeb leapt to the stove: 'I'll be with thee in just half a shake of a wild mink's tail, lass!'

'Nay, Jeb, 'tis done; happen you could make a cup o' tea instead?'

The first thin wails of the newest Loam were drowned by heavy knocking on the roof. 'Anybody in?' boomed a deep voice bearing those unmistakable overtones which indicate a world-famous glaciologist.

'I knew thee were special,' murmured Rachel proudly. ''Tis not every newborn has a wise man come to visit . . .'

Above, heedless of a long-standing preservation order, Bjørgstrøm prised slates from the farmhouse's ancient,

146

lichen-encrusted, tourist-photographed roof, while the helicopter steadied him from above with an umbilical rope-ladder. He felt immensely pleased with himself when at last he lowered himself into the darkness as heroic rescuer, and was inordinately hurt when Rachel Loam promptly fainted.

Twenty minutes and a thrifty cup of tea later, the 'copter angled to the east and sped away to its next rendezvous, while thousands of tiny jaws gnashed and foamed their fruitless anger from below. The ice-wall, which for a time had paused, thanks to the inexplicable ways of Nature and the exigencies of the plot, began to creak southward once more.

As they flew, Bjørgstrøm listened in to the doom-filled messages crackling round the world on every emergency wavelength. CATACLYSMIC FLOODS EXPECTED TO AFFECT MAJOR PORTS – LONDON TO BE EVACUATED – LATER REPORT – NO NEED FOR LONDON TO BE EVACUATED – ALL NEW YORK BUSINESS ACTIVITIES BEING MOVED UP ONE FLOOR AS STOPGAP. With the Arctic loosed, one could expect little else, he mused for the benefit of readers.

DROUGHT IN CANADA – EARTH'S MAGNETIC FIELD REVERSES IN DRAMATIC POLE SHIFT – ADVANCING GLACIERS THICKLY LAYERED WITH IMPACTED BIRDS MIGRATING WRONG WAY – POPULATION EXPLOSION HALTS OWING TO RAMPANT STERILITY – COMPENSATING EPIDEMIC OF PRIAPISM – EPIDEMIC OF MASS SCHIZOPHRENIA IN WESTERN USA – EPIDEMIC OF MASS PARANOIA IN USSR – EPIDEMIC OF TRAFFIC JAMS IN AUSTRALIA – EPIDEMIC OF AMERICANS IN SE ASIA –

Abramowitz shivered. The writing was on the wall for

147

humanity. Jeb Loam crouched back sullenly, his eyes fiery pits of apathy. Only Rachel was unmoved, and with the eternal resource of motherhood pulled out a bulging, sensuous breast to suckle her new child.

TERRORISTS BLACKMAIL GOVERNMENTS WITH NUCLEAR DEVICES IN CHILE PUERTO RICO TAIWAN NEW ZEALAND MINNEAPOLIS CHIPPING SODBURY – RUNAWAY GENETIC ENGINEERING LABORATORY FLOODS LARGE AREAS OF W GERMANY WITH INTERFERON – 'REACTOR POX' CAUSING MELTDOWN EPIDEMIC CAUSE UNKNOWN – WORLD INFLATION INDEX HITS 850 PER CENT –

'Does it strike you that all this could maybe be . . . more than coincidence?' said Bjørgstrøm quizzically.

Abramowitz laughed her light, delicious, sexy laugh without diverting one iota of her grim concentration from the controls as they passed through a small plague of locusts over what had been Exeter. 'Professor, any scientist would call me just crazy for saying this – but, yes, I know what you're trying to hint. We rational folks analysed all that weirdo God stuff out of existence way back when: but my folks were heavily into Debased Early Primitive Fundamentalism, and if my old Pop were here now you know what he'd say?'

'Apocalypse?'

'Got it in one – you world-famous climatologists don't miss a trick, do you? Professor . . . Gwynfor . . . d'you think this could be, well, the end of the world? I think that would be a shame.'

Bjørgstrøm frowned, and a hairline crack started in the 'copter's left-hand observation dome. 'I don't believe in that stuff, but sometimes these things work even when you don't believe in them. The thought did cross my mind. One picks up a smattering of such knowledge in a

148

lifetime's work on climates – trying to dope out the climatological basis of the Plagues of Egypt, for example. Or the opening of the seven seals, which has a crazy resemblance to what these radio reports are saying.

'But if we've got ourselves into some kind of apocalyptic religious scenario, there's something missing. The Beast of Revelations: no, come to think of it, until London got it there were reports all the way along a line from Loch Ness to South Ealing, reports of . . . something. However, that's small-time stuff.' He paused.

Joyce Abramowitz did look up from the controls then, wishing she could comfort this tortured, hideously scarred, halitosis-cursed, yet somehow strangely sexy man.

'The one thing whose absence keeps me rational, the one thing I'd have expected by now from a religious context, speaking quite hypothetically of course, is . . .' His voice dropped slightly to gain a meretricious dramatic effect. 'The revelation of the Antichrist.'

Then he chuckled suddenly at the absurdity of it all.

Rachel Loam's baby pulled away from her breast with a gummy, toothless smile, and said: 'Did someone mention my name?'

9

'We have the full cooperation of the President,' announced Dr Bran importantly. Nadia Finkelstein gazed at him with adoration tinged with just the weeniest touch of irritability: she and that bitch Zenna Brabham had already heard some 200 times about how Bran had dominated the Oval Office and convinced the President with his flow of unparalleled eloquence. Might not the endorsement of the head of NASA, not to mention that of the undoubted finest junior-school teacher in the Western hemisphere, have had something to do with it?

'I thought you were sceptical about this whole weird Infant Precog theory?' said one of the two newcomers, Professor Mark Tompion, who with the exquisite, perky Lise Panther was sitting on Bran's spare couch and emitting a faint aroma of scorched hair and clothing. Tompion felt a bitter, atavistic urge to needle Bran: they still didn't give Nobel prizes for mathematics.

Junior Finkelstein himself sat in a corner, absent-mindedly blowing his bubblegum while all the hells of antiquity and futurity blazed across his inward eye.

'Er, I was won over by the force of the, er, arguments,' Bran said, darting nervous glances at Nadia and Zenna, who instantly stared at each other in suspicion. 'Er, for example, you may not have realized that much of the present economic upheaval can be traced to one man – the "unknown multibillionaire" Howard J. P. Spong, whose psychosomatic constipation problem (in confidence, he happens to be one of my patients – I'll show you one of his fee cheques sometime) has had an extraordinary "transference effect" on the world money supply. In the face of such persuasion, er, evidence . . .'

'*And a great king called Spong will be powerless to defecate,*' quoted Nadia, proudly and precisely on cue. 'Just as Junior predicted. Brilliant, Dr Bran, brilliant!'

'How clever of you to trace that subtly elusive connection,' purred Zenna.

Lise noted idly that Dr Bran wore a strange, *hunted* look which seemed somehow familiar. What did it remind her of? Perhaps the curious look she sometimes noticed in the mirror after one of those sessions with Mark in which she somehow felt he was trying to *tell* her something? If only he could put whatever it was into numbers

150

for her; but alas, such communication between them was never to be.

'I'm still sceptical,' she said suddenly.

'Then why come here?' snapped Nadia, her buxom bosom swelling in tantalizing rage, the rage of a mother whose child's very honesty has been called into question. (All mothers have a deep-rooted, irrational feeling that although children's honesty should indeed be called into question approximately every three minutes, nobody should be allowed to do so but mothers.)

Tompion and Panther shrugged in unison. He explained: 'With Arecibo a fused heap of slag (oops, that's classified), there's nothing now to make us stay there waiting for new radiotelescope data on the approaching fleet of sadistic alien planet-rapists – oops, didn't mean to let that out. Try to forget I said it.'

'Ah,' said Nadia, and dreamily quoted: '*Great squidgy things will descend from the Swan, zap-happy . . .*'

'My God!' Shaken from her customary pose of cool scientific scepticism, which she had always found drove the guys crazy, Lise blurted: 'The Swan! 61 Cygni! The source of the signals which, er, perhaps I must be thinking of some other signals.' Tompion nodded approvingly. A classified datum was a classified datum.

'*Anyway*,' said Bran, annoyed at losing dominance in his own office despite his carefully tended personality, the specially built-up analyst's chair in which he sat, and the artful indirect lighting which focused attention on that masterful, heavily insured glow in his eyes. 'Anyway: it's time I told you about my latest rummagings in the endlessly layered mental onion which is Junior Finkelstein's remarkable psyche. Maybe even you hard-scientist types will be able to help us when we come to interpret the results.'

There was a dramatic pause, during which Tompion

and Panther exchanged meaningful glances, and Junior whimpered as a particularly big bubble of gum popped into extinction (who could know that in his soul's eye it was the last desperate blood-bubble from the sole remaining nostril of the last of the human race, gasping for breath amid the shards of a shattered world?), and one of the increasingly frequent micrometeorites zapped through the 113th-floor office to leave a smoking furrow across Bran's hand-carved rosewood desk. *Funny how quickly we get used to these little things*, thought the great psychiatrist with one of those sudden, devastating insights which the Nobel committee had found so compelling. *Thank God I've got a spare onyx top in the other room.*

'These words,' he said aloud, 'come from the deepest levels of Junior's mind. To some of you they may be meaningless. To the trained mind they seem to indicate that what's happening to the world isn't just bad luck, or the Commies, like you might think, but . . .' *here goes, and bye-bye scientific respectability if the goddam theory doesn't pay off!* 'but a *psychic* upheaval, a *paraphysical* assault on the flag and everything we hold decent, whose gross physical symptoms' (he pointed through the window, to where the Empire State Building could be seen falling gracefully and coincidentally over) 'are just that – symptoms. With all that in mind, I want you to listen to this.' He read from a grubby scrap of paper a few stark lines in the exquisite copperplate handwriting which characterized the 'seer' aspect of Junior's third-sub-five personality layer:

What I Know About Death
by Junoir Finkelstein. (aged 6.)

I saw Death last night. He plays
vidio games with corpes as the little
glowing dots. After that I saw Death before.
His face is of a strange blue hue, and his
mouth opens side ways. He summons
lightning to zap the defenceless,
and his breath smells like a linolem
factory. He walks the streets
servaying the kingdom that that will
shortly be his. I don't much like him, but
He's got carisma, a bit like a republican
candidate. From her Old Bra and boilermaker" he gloats as his works are
made manifest in the world. No
physical force can balk his
awesome supernatural potency.
    I warn you he'll be the death of-
us.
    The End

A short silence followed, and was succeeded by first a
pregnant pause and then a dramatic hush.

'What a load of rubbish,' murmured Tompion
distinctly.

'Did I write that?' asked Junior.

'Brilliant!' said Nadia warmly.

153

'Really brilliant!' added Zenna sultrily.

'Amazingly brilliant!!' Nadia put in, her voice a searing plasma torch of passion.

'*Staggeringly* brilliant, Doctor!' riposted Zenna, the white-hot calorific content of her sensual, throbbing tone defying mere adverbs. With unobtrusive skill, Nadia kicked her in the shin.

'Junior,' said Bran repressively, 'sees the personification of Death stalking abroad. Against this threat our weapons must be psychic. When the remainder of the "Earthdoom Think Tank" arrives from Europe – then, perhaps, we can strike back. In the meantime, I've been conducting certain experiments in psychic fire-power, aided by information from President Heinlein's controversial Supernatural Defence Initiative project (which, in spite of what the propagandists may say, is *not* just an excuse for firing Inigo Swann and Uri Geller off into orbit).

'Unfortunately, the results so far have been ambiguous . . .'

For Bran the room began to waver and blur, and the incidental music faded in: with a sickening sensation he recognized the symptoms of his recurring flashback problem . . .

10

The door had closed on them: two men, two needles, an old-fashioned brass pan balance, and (white-coated as an Observer) Junior Finkelstein.

'Will it take long?' said Harcourt, professional experimental subject and expendable spear-carrier.

'Hours,' said Dr Al D. Bran, determined to be dominant from the very start, and already annoyed to find Harcourt taller than himself. 'Hours and hours. You could be under observation all night – and glad of it, in this time of national emergency!'

'Time and a half after five o'clock, Doctor . . . You're working with the psychic weirdies, aren't you?'

Bran gnawed his lip: he might beard the President in the Oval Office, but it was dangerous to talk back to a paid-up member of the Experimental Subjects' Union, especially now they were talking about relaxing admission standards and letting white mice join. He said distantly: 'My Nobel Prize was for work in other areas. I'm just dabbling a little today, in an interdisciplinary way. Specifically, mind-expanding drugs – the deusexmachinol series. I expect you've heard of that Russian experiment, alleged psychic control of plankton using deusexmachinol-24?'

'Yes . . . but doesn't that cause tumours in mice?'

Bran smiled. 'Everything does. No, today we're trying deusexmachinol-32, with all the carcinogenic groups knocked out of the molecule and marketed separately as artificial sweeteners. I've got this crazy theory after scanning the literature, even though this isn't my field at all, that 32 could stimulate telekinetic ability. Think how you could be the centre of attention at parties!' He turned. 'Ah, I forgot . . . this is Junior Finkelstein, sitting in as Observer.'

Junior popped his bubble-gum without enthusiasm. Harcourt remarked that kids gave him a rash. These amenities over, the subject's attention wandered round the room. 'That's what the balance is for, OK? You pump me full of jungle juice, and I sit *here*, making the pans go up and down by thinking at them?'

'More or less,' said Bran with a thin smile of strained

encouragement. He didn't like it when other people stole his lines. 'Roll up your sleeve.' As he filled the first syringe, it was an effort to remain calm. Breakthrough! He felt it in his bones – no, he corrected himself, he expected it as a result of legitimate scientific extrapolation. 'Two cc's . . .'

'Telekinesis,' said Harcourt brightly, 'can't possibly work, can it? No action without reaction, says Newton; I suppose Einstein says the same in a more complicated way, eh? Still, can't complain, I expect the research grants pay the rent. How long before the stuff gets going?'

Bran allowed himself a knowing look, which was wasted since Harcourt was staring straight ahead at the dully gleaming brass balance. 'That injection wasn't *the* stuff. Just a hypno drug . . . to make you more suggestible.' He hoped the intonation ('Har har, I have you at my mercy!') would worry Harcourt a little.

'Why?'

'To clear out your silly, fixed preconceptions – otherwise you'd block the effect of the 32. These things fail unless you believe in them, or so everyone says.'

'Well, I sure don't believe in telekinesis, you pompous-assed baboon.' Bran made a note: *inhibition loss occurred in expected time scale*. Aloud he said: 'The action/reaction argument is kind of interesting. One theory is that it works just like normal – the balance might lift into the air, say, while at the same time *you* feel a slight force downward.' Not for nothing had he read two whole chapters of elementary physics that morning!

'Fair enough, cocksucker. But what if I sort of got carried away, pushed down the wall or something . . . if I TK something that heavy, the fucking reaction'll send me smashing back through the door, you numb-brained sodomizer of hamsters!'

Bran began to fill the second syringe. Deusexmachinol-32 had a milky turquoise colour which he rather liked; it reminded him of Nadia's eyes, or was it Zenna's? Momentary panic gripped him, only to be fought back.

'First safeguard,' he explained: 'You'll be under hypnotic commands to avoid any grandiose telekinetic showing-off – a mental straitjacket – we won't *allow* you to try anything but tiny movements of one pan of the balance. Second: a lot of people don't think action and reaction *are* equal and opposite, psychic-wise. Action moves mountains and reaction can't be felt. The two just don't relate to each other in our space/time: or that's the theory.'

'Don't . . . balance . . .' Harcourt said dreamily, and after a pause added: 'Fuckface . . .'

It was time, Bran decided, to start the recording he'd prepared. For some reason, he noticed, Junior Finkelstein was very gently quivering. Bran's finger came down on the switch:

Nothing to worry about you can do it you are going to push down one pan of the balance the pan on the left push it down without moving you will not move push it down only a few millimetres gently very gently very gently you will do this when Dr Bran (for whom you will henceforth feel a deep and lasting respect) says GO you will not move you will simply think at the pan tell it to move down when Dr Bran says . . .

'Go!' snapped Bran when the tape had looped enough.

The balance seemed ridiculously immovable. The chill sweat of failure, of having to go through life with just one Nobel prize, started out on Bran's expensively tanned forehead.

And then the left pan of the balance jerked down . . .

Breakthrough!

With a sound like a titanic slap, the light and the air changed. There was a sudden . . . wetness in the room.

Junior Finkelstein unwrapped a fresh sliver of gum. 'Knew that was gonna happen,' he said to no one in particular.

Action and psychic reaction had proved wildly dispro-portionate after all: the trick was to know on which side the imbalance lay. Later, puzzling over the physics texts, Bran estimated that Harcourt's brain had erupted from his skull at more than 200 miles per hour.

11

Death has a strangely hunted feeling. He clicks his mandibles as jauntily as ever as he reclines on a storm-cloud moving (against the wind, but the world is too fraught to notice) over the region known as the Bermuda Triangle. Far below him, shipping disasters have increased many hundredfold owing to endless collisions involving stray icebergs and the thousands of small boats now wandering the 'Triangle' in search of UFOnauts prepared to save the world, or at least the passengers of the boats. Death's attention is elsewhere, though, and he is frowning.

He snaps his fingers, causing a freak hail of continental breakfasts over Bermuda, and conjures up a rainbow. This he tunes, the seven-coloured test card giving way to vast, hazy 3-D images in the sky: portents which those below ignore, portents these days being ten a penny.

He sees Dr Lucius Apricot and Avedon Patella speed-ing cross-country in a now rather crowded helicopter, and raises an eyebrow as he extrapolates their flight in the general direction of the Bermuda Triangle. Dr Apricot, he notices with a trace of his old glee, is about to remember, when it is too late, the need for an expert (Dr Apricot) to keep checking the mighty CHANCRE fluorocarbon tanks, which unless nursed by hand could yet blow their entire contents in an ozone-stripping aerosol blast . . .

He sees Hitler raise a clenched fist to the sky, face transfigured by the impact of his new and just-conceived Master Plan . . .

He sees the approaching Cygnan fleet in all its awesome immensity, unstoppable, poised to rape, loot, pillage, smash, burn, destroy and evade immigration laws . . .

He sees 5,271,009 lemmings advance with dripping fangs towards the dreaming spires of the as yet miraculously untouched city of Oxford . . .

He does not, however, for good reasons, see into the 113th floor of a certain swaying New York skyscraper. He does not even realize his failure. He is inexplicably troubled. Perhaps he is growing old? Yet nevertheless, what can possibly stop him *now* from inheriting the Earth?

What he does not see is a furious argument in Bran's office, sparked off by sceptical mathematicians Panther and Tompion.

What he does not hear is Panther's latest, bitter tirade:

'Now you listen to *me*, Dr Bran! A rational mathematician like myself just can't accept the notion of Death as an externalized, personified force. I'm suggesting there's . . . an alternative explanation. You can't live the life of a mathematician for as long as I have without picking up a smattering of subjects like depth psychology and occult theory. I know this is just an off-the-wall analysis, but statistics suggest that "Death" is not the entity you suspect him, or it, to be! In fact, the implication is that this

"Death" is no supernatural being but a form of poltergeist phenomenon!'

Cries of disbelief fill the office, and the glass of the framed Nobel cheque cracks as though in horror at such blasphemy.

'One simple point makes your whole theory fall to the ground,' says Al D. Bran very slowly. 'Such phenomena have been recorded – gee, I'm as open-minded as the next Nobel laureate psychiatrist, you know – but just about the only thing which is clear about poltergeists is that they're always associated with the psychic storms of adolescence. I have a report from the Pentagon: they've tied all the data into their computers, and one of the conclusions is that no adolescent on Earth fits into the nexus of disaster afflicting our ravaged planet. So, sorry babe, but that's the way the cookie crumbles. Next theory, please?'

'I haven't finished, Dr Bran. There's just one wild-card factor you've failed to consider. What kind of awesome poltergeist might be produced by a high-grade psychic talent, pitchforked into *premature* adolescence by the savage eruption of his own powers?'

And all eyes turn as her slow, accusing finger moves to indicate the abstracted, bubble-blowing figure of Junior Finkelstein.

5

The Square Root of 443,556

'Man lives on one quarter of what he eats. On the other three-quarters his doctor lives.' This observation carved permanently into an Egyptian pyramid more than 5000 years ago should be chiselled into the brain of anybody serious about ageless ageing.

Leslie Kenton, *Ageless Ageing:*
The Natural Way to Stay Young, 1985

1

Knock, knock . . .

Rachel Loam looked amiably around the room. It wasn't quite home yet – perhaps it would never be – but, all in all, it wasn't too bad. Jeb had made a bit of a fuss (silly man!) about sculling through the deserted streets – canals? – of New York looking for the small comforts that turn a sterile, cypherlike, strange room into a cosy nest, but in the end he had done what she had asked him. Now, here, in an open-plan office four floors above Dr Bran's suite, there was a part of New York that would be forever Dartmoor. Nice fresh wallpaper with a tasteful design of exploding orange cabbages decorated not only the walls but the ceiling; a plastic chandelier tinkled merrily if a little uneasily beneath the strip-light; the rickety plastic-synthetic-wood-over-chipboard self-assembly bedside cabinet was topped by a whimsical plaster statuette of a little boy urinating which doubled as an ashtray; a useless but in its own simple way beautiful forty-four-inch colour television set was shelved over the integrated hi-fi centre with both its accompanying records (*Strings for the Young at Heart* and *Summer Serenade* by Max McLean and his Amazing Electronic Organ) neatly in place; and a flight of three onions ('They were being a-right out of ducks,' Jeb had explained) sculpted in what she was sure was alabaster arched gracefully over the life-size photograph of a fireplace which she had tacked to the wall. There was a final touch which, although she could not see it, strangely comforted her by its very presence: outside in the corridor there was a witty little doormat which said 'Hoots the Noo' on one side and 'Bon Voyage' on the other.

She sat down on the G-plan armchair and gazed contentedly at her little world. Jeb was away with that clever Dr Abramowitz, trying a few experiments to see if the profuse growth of marijuana which they'd discovered in the roof-garden of the office block could be turned into a food crop, and wouldn't be back for hours yet. She had only the baby (Aaron, would it be? Or Meyer? They still hadn't decided) to keep her company, and he was sleeping in his shatterproof polycelluloid cot, his pudgy thumb firmly placed in the centre of his flushed little face, his Mickey Mouse 'Catchalotty' potty standing on the floor nearby, ready for instant application if need be. She smiled indulgently at his tiny, huddled form. Sleeping away, he was, just like a newborn calf in a . . . her mind struggled for an apt analogy, but the only words that came into her head were 'in a sandwich', and that didn't seem right. Sleeping away like there was no tomorrow (which, come to think of it, there might very well not be). Sleeping . . .

She let her head nestle back into the soothing skivertex of the armchair and allowed her eyelids to settle down easily and casually over her tired eyes. The last few days had been long ones, hard ones, exhausting ones: often

162

enough she would have been sorely pressed to tell anybody the day of the week. The 'copter, piloted by that charming Dr Abramowitz (such a beautiful young woman, with her flowing bosom and her strainingly taut blue-denim culottes, although sometimes Rachel thought that she looked at her Jeb with a rather saucy eye), had reached rendezvous with the nondescript Lucius Apricot and the raven-eyed Avedon Patella (Rachel would never forget seeing her for the first time, as she smoothed her single-denier stockings over her sleek, bronzed athletic thighs and cocked a rubicundly curvaceous lip in greeting at them) in Gorran Haven.

'Will the tanks in this whirlybird hold enough to take us all the way across the Atlantic?' Gwynfor Bjørgstrøm had asked. He seemed instinctively to know about such things.

'We should be all right,' Abramowitz had replied shyly, carelessly undoing the top button of her silk blouse. 'It has an atomic recycling plant to recover the petroleum wastes and convert them back into high-octane fuel for re-use.'

Rachel had hardly listened. Her attention had been caught by a voice emanating from a nearby house. 'Can't you bugger off!' it had been shouting. 'Just let me finish these four books on Gurdjieff and *then* I'll evacuate!'

And then they had all piled back into the helicopter, taking with them such provisions as Apricot and Patella had been able to loot from the gaping stores of the anthrax-stricken town. The skies were black and heavy as the belly of a pregnant sow, and as the blades began to spin the whole arc of the firmament was rent by a titanic sheet of lightning, as if the deity Himself were venting His wrath upon the world.

Knock, knock . . .

She turned uneasily in the chair as that dusty, sibilant

whisper filled the room once again. But the sound was too low, too subtle, to register properly on her conscious mind, and so after a moment of readjusting her comfortable position she let her thoughts flow back to that nightmare journey across the Atlantic through the great storm. Only Bjørgstrøm had been other than starkly terrified: he had been grinning with barely restrained excitement, like one of his Viking ancestors before a battle to the death, cheering enthusiastically each time the tiny, buffeted craft had hit an air pocket and dropped unexpectedly, sickeningly for hundreds of metres before the spinning rotors could engage with the air again and bring the 'copter and its terrified occupants lurching uncertainly back onto a stable course. Outside the windows they could see nothing but luminous blackness, as if they were in the jaws of some mighty mythical monster that would soon swallow them whole; later, thanks to a nervous joke from Abramowitz which Bjørgstrøm had seemed to find excessively funny, the windows were misted completely – and perhaps that was better.

No, Bjørgstrøm, now that she thought about it more coolly, had not been the only person on the 'copter to avoid the demonic clutches of terror. Little . . . Benjamin, might it be? . . . the child had lain for the most part on her lap, not really sleeping – in fact, determinedly awake. His little eyes had darted hither and thither throughout the entire gut-wrenching flight, sometimes looking up into his mother's face with a precocious gleam of mocking knowingness. *I'm enjoying this*, the dimpled, poorly coordinated leer on his face seemed to be saying, *and I'm enjoying the fact that* you're *not enjoying it*. Rachel smiled to herself as she sprawled in the comfortable chair: she must be getting as soft as a cowpat on a misty spring morning if she was beginning to have fantasies like that about a poor innocent newborn . . .

Who's there? . . .

And this time the aspirated words did register on her mind. She sat bolt upright and looked suspiciously around the room. Was it her imagination, or had she really heard? . . . But no, there was nobody there but herself and the sleeping, motionless form in the cot. Her imagination, in fact, seemed to be playing funny tricks on her – it must be the exhaustion. But . . . the lights in the room appeared definitely to have dimmed. Perhaps there was a problem with the electrical generator which Apricot and Nadia Finkelstein had rigged up.

She relaxed again, idly casting an arm over her closed eyes – and so she did not notice as the room was abruptly filled with an unearthly, blinding green luminescence, and then as abruptly plunged into the pits of almost-darkness. Instead she was watching with desperate urgency as the 'copter climbed shakily down out of the sky to land on the drab grey tarmac of LaGuardia Airport, where Lise Panther and two admiring immigration officers were waiting expectantly to greet them. Otherwise the bleak airport was deserted.

'I'm sorry we're late,' Abramowitz had said with an urchin grin as she'd jumped out of the craft, stretching her lissom pectoral muscles in an attempt to ease the stiffness of the long hours in the pilot's seat.

'Most everybody on this continent's "late", these days,' Panther had murmured huskily, 'if you see what I mean.'

Auntie . . .

Rachel jumped almost a third of a metre and her eyes shot open like the venetian blinds of a bordello at the stroke of a Mediterranean noon. *There was someone – or something – in the room with her!* For a moment, but a moment only, she was blinded by the darkness, seeing nothing but the arcane echoes of that evilly enunciated (almost spat) whispered word. She was certain now that she had heard it, and all of a sudden, too, there flooded back into her mind the half-memories of those earlier words ... *Knock, knock ... who's there?* ... *Auntie* ...

It was nonsense, she thought wildly, her brain performing a neurotic gavotte of panic. What could all this be about 'Auntie'? Who *was* 'Auntie'?

Auntie who? the room breathed, as if to correct her.

Christ, but this was frightening! She couldn't think why the gentile Messiah's name had popped into her mind. She tried to move, but terror anchored her to the spot; she could only watch impotently as a nexus of glittering silvery greyness formed in the very centre of the room, hanging intangibly in the stillness. She felt the warmth of sudden urine on her legs, and realized only fractions of a second later that it was her own. She tossed her head from side to side, forcing the words out from between her clenched teeth, her face a rictus grin of tormented horror ... 'No ... no ... no ... *no!!*'

The greyness was coalescing, taking form, as if each of the remote corners of the room were contributing to it the last droplets of light which had lurked there. Soon all the room was midnight black except for that moving, swirling hypnotic mass of fluorescent turmoil. Dread seized Rachel's heart – dread incarnate: it was no abstract thing, this dread, but an implacable physical mass that submerged her spirit in its inexorable advance. It was a great, heavy, black, creeping, slithering, noisome, loathly, sticky, carnivorous thing that dropped mendaciously on to her soul and shot toothily for her throat. Two pseudopods reached out from that unmentionably disgusting mass and clasped her head in an iron grip, so that her eyes were forced to stare at the glowing quicksilver knot of light that was hovering with spinechilling silence in the centre of the room's inkiness.

But the worst of it all was that she *recognized* the shape that the gleaming nothingness was adopting. It was a face – two faces, rather, superimposed upon each other . . . the two faces of the two sons whom she had thought dead, their huddled corpses left scattered and largely devoured in a distant corner of half-forgotten Devon. The luminous head that was now facing her was not an inert, stable thing, however, for the face on it was constantly changing: now it was Reuben's, the flashing eyes looking into hers with a vindictive shriek of joy; now it was Nathan's, convulsed by a malevolence born beyond the grave; and now the bizarre chimera was a mutated synthesis of the two, so that she half-recognized it as Nathan's, half-recognized it as Reuben's, and half-recognized it as the almost formless face of the . . .

Auntie Christ!

The whisper was a thunder, a torrent of sound, filling the room until it seemed as if the walls would burst open, and it was followed by a stream of broken, choppy giggles that tailed off into infinity . . .

Hello, Mummy, susurrated the air, and the lips of Reuben's contorted, screaming face seemed to form the words: *We're back . . .*

And this time, mouthed the drooling jaws of something that looked too much but not enough like Nathan, *we propose to stay.*

Rachel could not move, could not scream. Her bowels loosened as the cold clamminess of dread's heavy form pinned her to the emotionless chair. The face of light had changed yet again, so that now it was half-Nathan's, half-Reuben's. Glistening, greasy horns sprang from its temples and a serpent-tongue whipped from its lipless mouth.

And, Mummy, we're going to tell you all the knock, knock jokes we know . . .

Two storeys above, Lucius Apricot, his finely honed brain working overtime as it rediscovered logic after its long holiday in the blurred hinterlands of acute alcoholism, was on the brink – he believed – of a momentous discovery. 'The fact can't be denied,' he said, staring absent-mindedly at a cup of coffee and wondering if it Meant Anything. 'Numerologists have been harping on about it for centuries – perhaps even millennia.'

'What's a "numerologist"?' Apricot's new assistant failed to ask. This new assistant was, in fact, a white rabbit: because of the fact that most of the population of the world was now either dead (after protracted, grisly torment) or had fled into hiding, the top scientists gathered around the leadership of Bran, Finkelstein and Brabham were having to make do with whatever research staff they could find. In some ways, the particle physicist mused, having a rabbit as a research assistant was a disadvantage – the blasted animal had yet to learn the alphabet, and so couldn't be told simply to go and look things up in the Periodic Table, or whatever – but in other ways it was a very useful circumstance indeed. As now, for example, when it seemed to be thinking of the exact questions which Apricot wanted it to ask, yet never interrupted with any boring, irrelevant criticisms of his mercurial theories.

'A numerologist,' he said in response to the unspoken question, 'is somebody who believes that numbers contain within them certain fundamental truths which, for occult reasons that are not fully understood by orthodox science, tell of things like the past, or the present, or even the future.'

The white rabbit digested this information in motionless silence. Apricot wondered, in fact, if it were actually alive. It had occupied the same space on his borrowed desk for days now, and was beginning to smell. Still, some of the other scientists didn't have a research assistant at all, so who was he to complain?

'Take my own name, for example,' said Apricot, prompted by the rabbit's festeringly incredulous stare. 'Lucius Apricot. To a numerologist, that isn't just an ordered collection of letters: it's a string of *numbers* which, when combined and totalled in an arcane and profoundly illogical fashion, will give you the key to my entire character. Take the first letter, "L", for example. For reasons that are obvious to anyone, that signifies the number 27 – which of course reduces to 9. After that we have the "U" . . .'

He drew a scribble-pad towards him and began to jot jagged notes, muttering calculations under his breath. The rabbit, by contrast, didn't say anything: it didn't, part of Apricot's mind thought, seem to have any breath to mutter under.

'There! You see!' said the world-famous particle physicist at last, pushing a sheet from the pad directly under his assistant's nose. On it, in big bold strokes of his felt-tipped pen, he had scrawled the subtle message: '47'. Apricot smiled triumphantly, as would have anybody in the same situation. 'But that's not all,' he continued. 'In order to reduce the number correctly to its final form, you've got to take the two individual integers 4 and 7 and add them together.' He spent a busy minute with his pocket calculator. 'When you do that,' he said at last, 'you find yourself left with the answer 11.

'But that *still* isn't all,' he went on before the rabbit

could interject a protest. 'You see, now you have to add the 1 and the 1 together to get the final answer, which is' – and here he hardly needed the calculator – '2 . . .yup, that's it, right enough. Now – or so the numerologists say – all I have to do is to look up 2 in this handy reference book and I'll know the secrets of my innermost soul.'

He thumbed through the pages of *Extract a Digit and Discover the Real YOU!!!* until he found the relevant paragraph. He read it out loud to his assistant: 'Individuals whose name-number is 2 have many – indeed, a plethora of – positive attributes that are the envy of all around them. They are at once witty and vivacious, of startlingly high intellectual power and of dramatically handsome (if not perfect) physical appearance. Whatever they *want* to do, they *can* do. They become great political leaders, internationally renowned particle physicists, rock megastars or Hollywood sex idols, and, despite occasional differences with somebody close to them towards the end of the week, lead lives of unbridled bliss. If male, they are possessed of unusually large generative organs.'

Apricot shut the book forcefully, and gestured self-deprecatingly at the rabbit. 'You see,' he said: 'A perfect character description. Why the numerologists say that you have to reduce your name down into numerical form I don't know, but clearly "there's something in a name", as the old cliché has it. If I were called – well, "Rick Hamfist", for example – if I were called any name other than "Lucius Apricot", whose numbers added up to any number other than 2, I'd be a totally different person. I might be female, say, or I might not even be alive today. I might . . .' He shut up abruptly, realizing that he'd just been tactless.

The telephone on his desk rang imperiously, and he answered it. 'Hi there, you delectable hunk of beefcake,' a throaty, sensual voice murmured, so he slammed the phone down again angrily: another bloody wrong number. Things really were falling apart a bit in the run-up to Armageddon.

'Of course,' he said firmly to his assistant, as if there had been no interruption at all, 'the numerologists have never been able to explain exactly *why* their technique actually works. And that's where I step in with my breakthrough, as it were. *They* think that it's all got something to do with numbers, but *I know* that all that's really involved in the process is the person's name. Or even the name of an inanimate object. Take – well, take the name of the ship *Titanic,* for example.'

The rabbit seemed to be thinking.

'Yes,' said Apricot busily, 'it's very likely that the good ship *Titanic* was doomed from the very moment that a bottle of champagne shattered across its bows and some tremulous local worthy squeaked out the three syllables "Ti – tan – ic". Can you think of anything else with the same name that *didn't* come to an untimely or violent end? Well, we can soon find out. Of course,' he added, as he pulled his trusty copy of the *University Desk Encyclopedia* from the shelf behind him, fondling its handsome red binding, 'the name hasn't been very popular since the ship went down in 1912 (or 1066, as I see it says in here), but it must undoubtedly have been used quite a lot before then. Let me see now . . .'

He turned the pages rapidly, his brow furrowing.

3

The city was a woman.

An ornery, cussed woman with the spirit of freedom strong in her soul; a woman whose spirit was a thing of the wild woods and the open prairies, whose hair tossed and twisted in the capricious breezes of time as they tugged at her coat-tails; a woman whose dusky eyes seen through the candlelight of a Fifth Avenue restaurant told you that she had seen all the ways of life, the squalid, dirty, lonesome ways as well as the high ritual ways of the true light. And while she spoke softly in the warm, affectionate gloom you knew there was more to what she was saying than the words that glided from between her moistly tactile lips. You knew that she wasn't just telling you about this life, or that life, or even the life of the hereafter: she was telling you about all of things, about eternity, about the vastnesses of the cosmos, at the same time as she was describing the rags and tatters of a summer's day, when the people would come and play hopscotch and leapfrog and baseball and cat's cradle in the parks that were the patches of her patchwork coat.

And she wasn't just a sort of glossy dream woman, like the type you see a million times life-size blazoned across the cinema screens, the type of woman who only goes to the lavatory when the cameras aren't rolling. She was a *real* woman – female, above all, yes; but despite that a rollicking, roistering, rooting-tooting human being as well, with all of the warts and the calluses of a man – a lumberjack, perhaps – whose powerful odour at the end of a long day fills the log-cabin of life. She was the kind of woman who can swim with the fishes of the sea, fly through the clouds with the birds of the air, tunnel through the ground like the moles of the soil, infest people's follicles like the lice of the scalp, trample across the broad plains of our everyday eternity like the buffaloes of the prairies. She was as sweet as a country virgin in the one moment, and as vicious and mercenary as a whore of the street the next, the profanity pouring like a waterfall all down her scrubby chest as she insulted you for your very existence.

And her moods changed with the seasons, too. In springtime she was as frolicsome as a baby goat, dancing this way and that, hither and thither, wherever the fancy might take her. She was as unpredictable as an April breeze as she kicked coltishly through the dust in men's minds, and her laughter was the high clouds, the white nervous clouds, scudding across the sky of time. For in the springtime she was not yet fully sure of herself, the shy one at the party, the little girl in the corner who can hardly pluck up the courage to reply to you when you offer her another glass of root beer.

There's beauty in that kind of shyness; and in the springtime it was this beauty to which you lost your heart.

But in the summer she was a broader, brawnier woman, her skin tanned to gold by long hours spent surfing on the West Coast, her eye-whites yellowed from the sun's relentless glare across the breakers, her teeth strong and startlingly white against the darkness of the corners of the laughter-wrinkles around her mouth. For it was in this season that she achieved the full flood of her womanhood, when she stretched her lazy cat's muscles and took you in her arms and made you into a man in more ways than ever your mind could have dreamt. Summer with the city was weeks in the bed of a maturely beautiful woman, tangled in sweat-wet sheets, laughing and joking and smiling in that ancient slow way that lovers have and sometimes, yes, sometimes maybe sobbing a whiles as well, because growing through the golden age of womanhood has a lot to do with learning all over again how to cry.

And in the fall her shoulders had broadened. Over the aeons of her life the wind and the spray and the breeze and the sun had all left their marks on her face, and their slow erosion had turned her away from the beauty of youth towards the beauty of foreverness, and it was then that a man could think of her as his wife, as the woman who was by his side all through the vicissitudes of the world that framed his life. The roads that were her blood vessels would be more pronounced now, their runnels of industry criss-crossing her for all the world like a road-map. Maybe it was then that a man loved her the most, so that he hardly knew which way to turn because his heart was so crazy-glad just to be in the same world as her.

Or maybe it was in the winter, when age had come to her gracefully, and she sat in her grey-white shawl, rocking toothlessly beside the crackling log fire, waiting for death to take her away, to ease all the pains and aches of her aged joints, to smooth out her wasted, etiolated muscles and to dress her up all smooth and perfect again so that she could be reborn into the world as spring's fresh young maiden. All through the winter you could see her face change as the memories scuttled behind it through the canyons of her mind and she relived again all those springs and those summers and those falls . . . and those winters. Yes, maybe it was in winter that she was the most beautiful of all.

And men did love her. Had loved her. Maybe would love her again. Officer Hotchkiss was one of those men, he and the brave boys who fought alongside him to push back the coverlets of darkness that threatened to close

174

over the woman they loved like a caul over a baby's head. They knew all her secret places, all the places that she kept hidden from every man but the ones that she loved. And she had it in her heart to love millions of men, Hotchkiss knew; years and years and years and years ago he'd given up any adolescent dream that she might find it in herself to love no other man but him, and it didn't bother him any longer. You could call her a harlot or an easy lay if you liked, but Hotchkiss knew different: he knew that all this great ideal of the totally chaste woman was nothing but an invention by under-sexed ascetics trying to stamp their own gloomy philosophy – their morals of necessity – across the face of the rest of humanity. A virgin, thought Hotchkiss, can give you all of her heart, but a woman with a million lovers can still give you all of her heart for the length of a long summer's day, and he knew which of the loves was the greater one.

But now Officer Hotchkiss had to leave the woman he loved, the city of Hornsville. He sat astride the big black police motorbike on Thuggee Spur above the city and looked down on it with a lover's eyes. There was a tear just forming in one of them, or maybe there wasn't. This couldn't just be like leaving a city, he thought: it was more like leaving your home behind, where your bronzed lady lived and her body yearned for you all the long nights you were away about your worldly things. And your body yearned for hers, too, even if you went a-whoring.

Funny how he'd come over all sentimental, he thought as he kicked the kickstart and the motorbike roared into throbbing, virile life. He guessed it must have been a case of reading too many of those boring, padding-out passages in the Ed McBain novels to which he was addicted.

He turned the bike's nose towards New York, and a moment later he was gone, leaving nothing but the echoes of the powerful engine lingering in the air.

Behind him, the sprawling voluptuous woman that was Hornsville slumbered on unheedingly, satiated in the hot waves of somnolence from the stone-eyed sun.

4

'I was right,' said Lucius Apricot with deep satisfaction. 'If this blasted book had an index I could doubtless find lots of other examples, but already I've found enough to prove the general truth of my theory. For example: did you know, my friend, that Napoleon had a pet dog called "Titanic"?'

The rabbit's pink eyes looked blank.

'Well,' said Apricot, 'I'll tell you. That dog – a poodle, of course – was the only creature that was loyal to the little corporal right up to the end, on St Helena. It endured all the rigours of his exile there without once complaining. It's believed, according to this book, that Napoleon's death was actually hastened by his grief over the demise of his faithful pet. And the demise itself is of more than passing interest in this context.'

He stared intently at his transfixed assistant.

'You see, according to the *University Desk Encyclopedia* – which has it direct from the *Guinness Book of Records* – Napoleon's dog "Titanic" is the only poodle ever known to have died through being struck by lightning!'

Rather to Apricot's annoyance, the rabbit didn't say anything in response to this. But the new, sober Lucius Apricot had never been the kind of man to allow his flow

176

to be slowed by outside interference from his audience, and so he carried on, waving his arms about as he got more and more excited.

'Here!' he cried jubilantly, his finger stabbing at a fuzzy illustration. 'According to the earliest of the Spanish and Portuguese chroniclers, the Incas used to have a great lake which they called – by one of those amusing little linguistic coincidences (or so it might *seem*) – "Tit-on-iq", which in their language meant something . . . rather daring. Not to put too fine a point upon it, "Tit-on-iq" meant "pisspool". The legends of the Incas, say the chroniclers who came over with the *conqistadores*, had it that great rocks fell from the sky into this lake every few months, way back in the dawn of history, creating such enormous tidal waves that anyone living within eighty kilometres of the lake's edge was lucky to escape drowning. So, in desperation, the ancestors of the Incas changed their name for the lake to "Titicaca", meaning "interface", and the problem never recurred.'

Lucius Apricot slammed the desk with his fist. 'You *see*?' he cried. 'It all makes sense! It's a question of names, *names*, NAMES! Things which are called . . . But,' he said, calming a little, 'I can see that you still don't believe me. I must say, you're a very sceptical animal – especially for one so . . . er . . . dead, if you don't mind me saying so. Still, I suppose healthy scepticism is a good thing. Let's find another example. Aha!'

An almost lunatic gleam had now returned to his eyes: the room was lit up as if by an arc light. 'Yes!' he half-shouted. 'I have it here. The first to be discovered of the so-called "Earth-grazing" asteroids – named thus because their eccentric orbits can sometimes bring them dangerously close to our world – was initially christened by its discoverer, the feisty pioneer Galileo Galilei, "Titanic". Two years later – only two years, mark you! – the

177

asteroid was totally annihilated when it plunged into the Mediterranean, creating the great gulf which is now known as the Bay of Naples.'

He looked at the rabbit; then, despite himself, he looked at the fly that was crawling across the rabbit's dull eye. He did wish that Zenna Brabham, who was supposed to be in charge of the 'Think Tank's' admin, would take the time out to introduce his new research assistants to him.

'And finally,' he said, rather miffed, but covering the fact up splendidly, 'the clincher. Spontaneous combustion. "Fire from Heaven", as Michael Harrison called it in his entertaining book on the subject. Cases in which people burst into flames for no apparent reason, burn with a colossal heat, and yet leave things like the clothes they're wearing or the chair they're sitting in totally unmarked. Now, believe it or not, the only person ever to go up in smoke in this way in front of the television cameras was a professional wrestler called, at least according to his publicity handouts, "Thump Titanic".'

The fly buzzed encouragingly.

'According to the commentator, as quoted here,' said Apricot, '"Thump Titanic" was just getting angrier and angrier. When he finally burst into flames we all just assumed it was some kind of a publicity stunt. And we all applauded his ingenuity. When he died in the flames we hailed it as the supreme act of a real pro. I still chuckle a little whenever I think about it. What class the guy had!'

'But it wasn't just "class",' Apricot continued, 'it was' – and here his voice deepened by a couple of octaves – 'Fate. Yes, Fate. I'm not ashamed to use the word. If Thump Titanic had been prepared to use his own name, Vivyan Piccolo, rather than his ridiculous *nom de guerre* in the ring he might still be alive to this day. But he didn't, and so Fate took its inexorable toll.

'My friend,' he added, though whether he was talking to the rabbit or to the fly no outside observer would have been able to tell, 'I think it is a clear-cut case of "Q.E.D.".'

His assistants were both too awestruck to respond.

5

'H – e – y, man,' said Mark Tompion. 'These scones we've baked are like, real, gro – o – o – vy. Sheesk! They hit the nail right on the button. Here, have a blast, Joyce.'

Abramowitz toyed indolently with the blonde kiss-curl that adorned her svelte cheek and decorously reached out with the other hand to accept a scone from the plate which Tompion was proferring. She allowed her hi-glossed lips to curl into a provocative curve of fellowship. The mathematician was such a willing fellow, rather like a pet spaniel, always eager to please. In other circumstances, she might have been tempted to lose her heart to his bluff, burly good looks, but not now, not here. She was too confused, beneath the superficial veneer of casual sophistication which moulded itself lovingly to the flamboyant creases of her exquisitely sculpted body. For all the years of her young life she had taken her men when she wanted to, and left them, again when she wanted to, never allowing herself to become too deeply involved with any one man. Sex she had understood; love was the unknown – and, like any of us, she was frightened of the unknown, shied away from it. Besides, she had had her career to consider: Nobel Prizes didn't grow on trees – as a biologist, she knew that. So she'd settled for a succession of one-night stands with identikit young eligibles whose presences had now fused in her mind to form a blurred mass of half-remembered smiles and indistinguishable loins.

Now, though, things had changed. From the moment that she had seen Bjørgstrøm she had known that there was something different about him, something that touched a chord somewhere inside her that no man had ever touched before. And the experience had confused her, had muddied the hitherto crystalline waters of her emotional life. She couldn't be certain that this was love, of course – nobody can ever be certain, the first time – but her response to the presence of Bjørgstrøm was unlike anything she had ever experienced before. It was, in truth, a whole turmoil of emotions: mixed in with the soft feelings of . . . well, almost of motherhood that she felt whenever the sound of shattering retorts and test-tubes told her that his work in the laboratory was going well; yes, mixed in with those feelings there was the fervent tug of passion and also, more perplexingly, just a faint tinge of revulsion.

He came into the room now, a boyish grin creasing his crushed and ravaged face, a glass of milk in his hand. He winked at her and the glass disintegrated, leaving him clutching a cylinder of cheese. He was wearing the red tweed tie which made him look so youthful.

Conquering her inner turbulence and smoothing down her blue satin blouse she smiled back encouragingly at him. 'Gwynfor,' she said, 'we're all just trying out these scones that Mark and Jeb have managed to make out of the marijuana plants from the roof.'

'Ah, so,' he said. 'Are they good?'

'Try one for yourself, baby,' drawled Tompion sleepily, pushing the plate across the formica-topped table. 'Say, have any of you guys seen Lise around? I'd kind of like to discuss a few philosophical problems of mine with her.

You know, what's it all for? – that kind of thing. I guess Avedon would do, or . . . say, Joyce, can I tempt you to talk over some cosmic-like metaphysics with me?' He shook his clean-cut head as if to clear the fog behind his eyes. 'Geez, this stuff does sure as all hell relax you.' He tried to get to his feet, but unsuccessfully, and instead subsided into a heap of crumpled blue denim and cowboy check.

Jeb reached for a second scone, and then thought better of it. The first had tasted totally unlike anything he'd ever come across before. He remembered from way back in what seemed like another lifetime, another world, how his mother had sometimes baked scones, and how he and all his brothers and sisters had clustered eagerly around her apron as she'd drawn the steaming trayful from the oven. Then it would be out with the pots of clotted cream and strawberry jam, and the whole family would tuck in with a will. But these . . . these scones were tarter to eat, more astringent. And eating them made his head spin a little and his stomach feel distinctly rebellious. *Like there be a little sparrow, in there all on his lonesome, a-fluttering and a-struggling to be out of there and into the light of day, bless his poor fragile little heart*, thought Jeb. *I be going to wonder how my little gusset, Rachel, be faring downstairs with the little one that's came. Perhaps if I be a buggeringly picking up this here old carcase of mine and taking her a scone, she be a-kissing of me on the nose with a roving look in her eye. Like wow.*

That last thought caught him up short. Where in hell had that come from? 'Like wow.' That was city-talk, that was, like folks used in Newton Abbot and Bovey Tracey. Was someone invading his mind? He pondered this for a moment, but then concluded: no, it was impossible. It would be like invading Monaco: you'd never get the whole of your army in.

He stood up and swayed. No one paid him any attention. Tompion seemed to have dissolved into a catatonic state, while Abramowitz and Bjørgstrøm were billing and cooing at each other like the little lambs he, in his country heart, knew they were. Without making a sound he took two of the scones and lurched on exaggerated tiptoe from the room.

'. . . we tried every frequency possible,' Abramowitz was saying, 'but all we could get were a couple of rock stations. All the others seemed to have gone dead. So then Nadia Finkelstein – she's so *clever*, Gwynfor – suggested that if we just switched a few chips here and there we could turn the radio into a transmitter. Stands to reason: if everybody else is doing what we were – just trying to pick up radio transmissions – then no wonder nobody can get anything.'

'Makes sense to me, popsicle,' said Bjørgstrøm, adding to himself in an undertone: 'Coleridge.'

'So we tried that for a couple of hours, and then Al D. Bran pointed out that, for all we knew, hundreds of groups all over the country might have picked up our signals and right at that very moment be trying to get in touch with us. But, of course, since we no longer had an operative radio receiver . . .' She shrugged daintily.

'So you rejigged the transmitter to work as a receiver,' Bjørgstrøm said nonchalantly.

'How did you guess? Gwynfor, you're a genius under that curly mop of . . . it *is* hair, isn't it? Anyway, once again we could get nothing but static and the two rock stations, and then Zenna Brabham – Gwynfor, I think you've underestimated that gal – Zenna said: "Say, what if all the others are transmitting when we're transmitting, and then trying to receive while we're trying to receive?" So she and Bran went out and looted another radio – oh, and Professor Finkelstein went with them, too. But it *still* wasn't any good.'

'What was the matter?' said Bjørgstrøm. 'Transmissions too faint to be recognizable?'

Abramowitz never answered him. Tompion, whom they had assumed to be sleeping, had suddenly leapt to stand on the table, trying desperately to punch his fist into his palm. 'Did I hear you say "matter transmission"?' he cried.

'As a matter of fact . . .' said Bjørgstrøm but Tompion wasn't listening.

'Matter transmission – *that's* the answer to our problems! That's what we can use to escape all . . . all this.' He gestured through the starred window to the wreckage of New York. 'We have the technology, we have the physicists, and – most important of all – we have the natural psychic powers of young Finkelstein. We can do it!'

'Do it?' said Abramowitz and Bjørgstrøm in unison. 'Do what?'

Again Tompion ignored them. 'Call in the others,' he said. 'Get them here. Fast. Instanter. Pronto. Chop-chop. I've cracked it.' More than that he refused to tell them.

6

Symbiosis.

To the lexicologist it's just a word, like many other words. To the ecologist it's a precise term, with a meaning. It refers to a sort of co-operative parasitism between two organisms, such that the arrangement benefits both of them. Like the novelist and the publisher. From the novelist the publisher gets breathless words of pearly wisdom, a commercial property of timeless, incandescent value. From the publisher the novelist gets just enough to live on, assuming he or she is willing to dabble in prostitution in order to make ends meet. The two of them conspire to scavenge from other organisms, known as 'readers', who must toil long and hard to save enough money to buy the novels, and so enrich the publisher and protect the novelist against the wildest ravages of malnutrition. That's symbiosis . . .

Dick Ingrams ran the most northerly public lavatory in the United Kingdom, currently proudly sharing latitude 36.6°N. with Algiers (El Djezair). Of this he was blissfully unaware. Times might come and times might go, the climate might change, the midnight constellations might have welcomed new arrivals and lost old friends – but all these things had happened on the surface. Down in his subterranean ghetto Ingrams knew nothing of them. He'd noticed that the newspapers had stopped arriving, that there were increasingly frequent electricity cuts, and that customers ('my gentlemen', as he liked to call them) were few and far between; but his was a slow, easygoing nature, and it took a lot to make him start worrying about things. 'Leave the worrying to the sheepdogs,' his mother had always said, 'and just get on with your own life.' His mother had been right about most things (the framed letter from Buckingham Palace informing him of his knighthood was a testimony to the correctness of her careers advice) and so he had no cause to doubt her in this. He plied his daily trade much as before: mopping the floors morning and evening, peppering the toilet rolls regularly to ensure that there was no shilly-shallying among his gentlemen, jotting down the names of any pop stars who dropped in for a private fix for his beneficent chum Norman from Fleet Street. If things were quiet these days – well, that just gave him more time to sit with his feet up reading and re-reading his old copies of the *Reader's Digest*.

But today there was a customer.

The man had burst in as if all the hounds of hell were in hot pursuit (which, curiously enough, they were – although he didn't know that). 'My God!' he'd cried. 'There's going to be a disaster any second if I don't . . .' And he'd shot into a cubicle, slamming the door behind him.

Curious, thought Ingrams, *how in other disaster novels there are never any difficulties about finding functional lavatories.* But the thought winged only for a moment across his mind before it was gone.

Since then, after the first ten minutes or so, there had been nothing but silence from behind the blank door of the cubicle – and slowly, slowly, Ingrams was beginning (despite his mother's advice) to worry. The only sounds were the occasional chugging of the plumbing and the rustle of paper as he turned the pages of his magazine. He hadn't actually expected a conversation with his client, but . . . but, not to put too fine a point upon it, surely the man *must* have finished by now? It was getting closer and inexorably closer to eight o'clock, when Ingrams was supposed to lock the outer doors and set to work with his mop. He ran a bitten fingernail through the stubble on his gnarled chin. He didn't like to interrupt people but . . .

At last he came to a decision. Whistling a jaunty air by way of warning, he filled his bucket with cold water and industrial soap-flakes and started to slosh the suds across the floor. 'Time, gentlemen, please,' he called out at random, as if the place were full of clients. 'I have to lock up soon, you know.'

But still there wasn't a whisper from the occupied cubicle number thirteen.

When he came level with its door, it dawned upon Ingrams that perhaps there might be something wrong. Quietly, in case of perceived impoliteness, he knelt down on the soapy floor and looked quickly through the gap under the door. All he could see was the usual sight – a crumple of trousers and underpants, supported beneath by the toes of a well worn pair of Hush Puppies.

'Is everything all right, sir?' said Ingrams softly. His words echoed back to him from the walls.

And then he saw something that made his blood run cold. The legs arising from the puddle of clothing – they seemed curiously . . . empty. They were more like limp flags of skin than flesh-filled legs. He felt a scream bubbling up through the vomit that clogged his throat.

For a moment he couldn't move, and then he was running along the length of that hellish charnel house, scrabbling through the drawers of his scuffed desk for the master key. He found it at last, and held it in his trembling fingers. Did he dare . . .? Yes: he must.

As he turned the key in its rusted lock the little sign slid around from ENGAGED to VACANT. There was nothing to stop him now from pushing open the door to see what lay beyond, but still he hesitated. 'Are you all right, sir?' he said, but once again there was no reply.

What he saw when the door creaked unwillingly open was enough to make him run, gagging and screaming, from that hellish place, his eyes starting from their sockets, his heart beating like an outboard motor, his veins bulging on his forehead like the intestines of a freshly slaughtered bull. He came out onto the surface for the first time in many years, and looked around him at the endless snowfields that covered the tortured shambles that had once been Reading. There was nobody else in sight, no one with whom he could share the agonized recollection of what he had found behind the door of

186

cubicle thirteen, no one to whom he could describe the horror that was imprinted forever upon his convulsed retinas – no one, no one at all.

He looked back through the twilight at the opening to the subterranean lavatory with loathing. From the outside it looked innocent enough, giving no clue to the nameless terror which lurked within. The terror that seized a man's entrails and turned them to jelly. There was no way that Ingrams was ever again going to venture through those dread portals. His home of many years was now forbidden to him, *verboten*, taboo. Something – some horror – had taken it over and evicted him, retching and spitting, out into the snows. *Sans* food, *sans* clothes other than those he stood up in, *sans* even the *Reader's Digest*. None of these thoughts ran through his mind: he was in too much of an emotional ferment for coherent cogitation.

When the last of the vomit had drained from his stomach, when his guts felt like a hard-knotted bundle of high-tensile steel, he staggered away across the world's great white blanket, looking neither to right nor to left, moaning mindlessly at the naked skies, drool dropping from his numbed lips to spot the snow and mark his progress, seeking he knew not what but anguishedly searching for the succour of another human being. As he came to the crest of a ridge he looked back and saw the last sight he would ever see of the cast-iron pillars that marked 'home'.

Then he turned away finally, and trudged away through the drifts.

In the doom-laden abyss he had left behind him a slight breeze moved. It was no more of a wind than the draught of a maiden's laughter, but it was enough to set in motion the remains of the last customer ever to use cubicle number thirteen. They collapsed with an almost friendly 'flumph' to lie around the pedestal like the petals of some noxious flower, joined to the central upright only by an oval ring around what had once been fleshy buttocks. Joined there for eternity.

Symbiosis.

There were two different levels of symbiosis involved.

The hive-mind of the world's superglue was conscious at last. It had developed sensory organs among the many globs and blobules that went to make up its whole. But these units of its being lacked the magic ingredient of mobility: unless a human or, less probably, an animal fortuitously moved them they were confined to passive observation of whatever surrounded them – they had no powers to express their seething, bitter, implacable hostility to the human race and all of its works.

But some of the units of the world's superglue-consciousness had, willy-nilly, found their way into the sewers – where, whenever accident had brushed them together, they had coalesced. And it was also in the sewers that they had encountered the first of their symbiotic partners: the free-ranging enzymes assembled by the manufacturers of biological washing powders, which had themselves united with complex organic molecules present in soiled clothing to constitute a primitive form of semi-sentient life. The two lifeforms united immediately to create what was virtually a brand new one – a form of life possessed of an intelligent hive-mind and an astonishing degree of mobility: it could ooze in a layer only a few molecules thick through the narrowest of apertures. Moreover, and this was perhaps unique in the animal world, it was possessed also of amazing adhesive powers: while it could not rend its prey with tooth and claw, it could immobilize a cat or a dog or a horse or a human being and hold its victim until starvation and dehydration took their lethal toll.

It is impossible to guess at the number of rabid lemmings which had died in this way before the superglue/washing-powder entity realized that it was destroying a powerful potential ally. Negotiating with murderous lemmings is never easy, even at the best of times, but the hive-mind was able to draw on hitherto-unsuspected telepathic powers in order to do the deed. And a joint plan of action was devised.

As the last occupant of cubicle number thirteen had eased himself with almost ecstatic relief down onto the pedestal he can little have realized that already a thin skin of potent adhesive rimmed the seat: as soon as he made contact he was held rigidly in place. Then it was the turn of the lemmings to leap evilly from below, their sharp, vicious teeth flashing in the gloom . . .

Another breath of wind shifted the empty skin of the symbiotic organisms' first victim. The flapping pocket that had once housed a skull moved over, so that an empty eye stared at the ceiling. Somewhere far away the hive-mind exulted silently: the operation had been a total success.

Now no one was safe.

Symbiosis. To some people it's just a word. To the human race it spelt nemesis.

7

The bubble suddenly exploded and its pink, sticky skin collapsed back onto his face for all the world as if it had just been scooped clean by lemmings.

Junior Finkelstein grunted with displeasure and began to pick the goo from his eyelashes. He left, however, the stuff that had courteously blocked up his ears: at least it freed him from the banging and crashing of the workmen who were erecting a complex electromagnetic screen around the room in which he sat. 'This won't be a permanent isolation, Junior, you understand,' Bran had said, before gesturing a couple of burly security officers from the Pentagon to drag the child kicking and screaming into this prison. 'It'll only be for a few days,' Bran had added through the keyhole, 'just until we can be certain that it's not you who's causing all these disturbances.'

The psychiatrist had left, then, and the electricians had set to their noisy work.

Junior Finkelstein balled all the collected tatters of bubblegum in his pudgy fist and jammed the agglomerate back into his mouth. He had tried to tell them, of course, that it was useless. He knew – with a knowledge that was incomprehensible to orthodox science, a knowledge which flowed from the very bowels of the Earth itself – that he was in no way responsible for the catastrophes that were besetting the world – that, by contrast, he was humanity's sole hope against the forces of evil; but of course they had not listened to his piping tones. 'Orders are orders,' they'd said, and carried on with their work. So Junior had forborne to tell them that, in addition, his powers were in no way inhibited by the subtle screens which they were erecting. Psychic waves are as different from electromagnetic waves as electromagnetic waves are from sound waves. The men might as well have been pinning used egg-cartons to the outside walls of the room. In fact, because psychic waves, like electromagnetic waves, share an affinity for materials such as metals and other conductors (hence the ability of dowsers), the egg-cartons might have been a better bet: the sole effect of the web of wires which they were building was marginally to enhance his abilities. The screen was, in short, acting very much as a booster aerial.

Which was why Junior was able to see through Bran's

eyes as the world-famous psychiatrist combed through the morning mail that was littered across his desk.

The letters were addressed to the various members of the 'Think Tank': Bran acted as a sort of clearing house for all correspondence, since in these straitened times the various scientists were being forced to carry out each other's functions as often as not, each picking up where another had left off. So some of the letters were irrelevant to the main thrust of their endeavours, but nevertheless had to be allocated to someone . . .

Dear Mr Loam
I refer to your letter of 9 April and note its contents accordingly.

HM Inspector of Taxes, Exeter 7 District, has advised me that the Notice of Assessment which was issued on 16 October 1988 has now been returned from the Post Office, undelivered. The Inspector has therefore asked me to express his inability to confirm or otherwise that your farm and domicile are now occupied by a horde of vermin and are therefore no longer eligible as a place of residence under Article 3 of the Abodes (Dilapidation) Act of 1987. In the absence of such confirmation of the situation by yourself or by some other interested party, he must assume that you have no intention of appealing against the Notice of Assessment which he has issued.

Similarly, he can take no account of the fact that you now choose to make your home in the United States of America.

Would you, therefore, kindly endeavour to arrange with your Bank for a loan to cover the tax payable, against which interest continues to accrue daily. If you are unable to transfer a loan would you please call at my office (temporarily relocated to the address below) within the next fourteen days to discuss the matter further.
Yours faithfully
W Bailey
Collector of Taxes
Exeter 7 Division, 423 Sun Plaza, Tenerife

Others were, perhaps, more germane:

FROM THE OFFICE OF THE PRESIDENT
(a) We have today received confirmation of the fact that a fleet

of hostile warships is intent upon invading this nation from the region of 61 Cygni, and have accordingly put the US Navy on full alert. Please locate the island of 61 Cygni and forward coordinates to this office so that we may authorize the use of our first-strike nuclear capability to destruct same.

(b) Failing the correct location of 61 Cygni, please forward coordinates of any region of the planet that might still remain sufficiently nondestructed for the use of our first-strike capability to be militarily effective.

Bran's fingers, guided by Junior Finkelstein's travelling mind, reached for a pen and jotted down on a sheet of paper: 'Latitude 28.5°N. Longitude 15.3°W.' Although Bran didn't know why he was putting this sheet of paper in an envelope and addressing it to the President – in fact, was barely conscious that he was performing these actions at all – Junior Finkelstein was moving with a steady purpose: Jeb Loam seemed a nice enough character, and he might as well do him a favour.

Then the boy's mind was whipping through the febrile vortices of space, away and away and thousands of kilometres away to the lonely spacecraft *Mary Poppins*, whose crew were as ever locked in a sociopolitical argument.

'There is no choice, you yankee lickspittle. We must alter the course of this scumbag of a craft to collide with the comet, so that we both annihilate. It is the only way to save Earth, no?'

'Gee, honey, do you Russki dames have tits just like Western gals?'

'We will feel a great, what you say, nothing. We will die instantly and in glory. Perhaps people who are to come will remember our deed and say to themselves: "They died willingly and nobly for the good of all the workers of mankind."'

'The way you wiggle your ass is enough to make Billy Graham joik off.'

'I have been at work on this abacus for the last hour while you have been sleeping off your latest ingestion of neat butyl alcohol from the meteor-shield power unit, and I now know how to alter the ancillary drive units. Stand clear of me.'

'I know you got the hots for me, baby, only you just don't like to admit it to yourself.'

'I do not wish to use this weapon, but if I have to I will. I cannot let considerations of individual well-being stand between me and my duty. It is obligatory upon us to sacrifice our negligible selves to save our planet. Stand back, I say, or I fire!'

'I wanna plant kisses all over your nates, you sassy broad. Like, I've laid some dames in my time, but you'd be something special to tell all the guys. Come on and drop 'em, huh? (Say, why are you pointing that revolver at me?)'

'You leave me no choice, Colonel Malone.'

'Aaaaargh . . . you Red bitch, you've shot me! You know what you've gone and done, you stupid bastard woman. You've shot me. Yeah, me. But why, f'gawd's sakes, did you have to shoot me right through the goddam prick?'

'I tried not to, Colonel Malone, but the rest of you presented a very difficult target. Will you let me make the necessary adjustment to our spatial attitude now, or must I shoot again – this time, to kill?'

'Don't make much difference, you commie bitch. I'm a-gonna die anyhow.'

'Good, then you will let me pass?'

'Yeah . . . but first, I gotta confess something to you.'

'What?' Dimpla sighed. The sooner her suicidal task was over, the better. Behind her grimly efficient bosom there was a quiveringly nervous fieldmouse.

'Well . . . I never, like, thought I'd end up confessing this to a commie bitch bastard, but I suppose it's gotta come out, now that we're only hours from Death, that final question-mark. All that stuff about me wanting to screw your ass off every which way to Sunday – well, it was all kinda pretence.'

Dimpla blenched. No girl likes to be told that she's a sexual no-no.

'Don't take it personally, babe. No insult intended. It's just that this red-blooded, virile, all-American exterior of mine is a sham. Like, women just don't turn me on.'

Surprising, thought Dimpla. *Virtually everything else seems to.*

'Yeah, good old Bart Malone, the finest man in NASA's astronaut team, the guy who's balled more gals than the Scots Guards . . . yeah, Malone, that's him, well, I gotta tell you. He's, like, gay. A cream puff. A guy's guy. A limpwrist. A fairy. Sure, I'm gay. And it's all 'cause my Momma used to dress me up in girl's clothes and make me use tampons. I used to say to her, "Momma," I used to say, "I wanna go and play baseball like all the other kids," but she used to tell me, "Bartelmina" (that's what she used to call me: "Bartelmina"), "Bartelmina," she'd say, "you just stay in with me and crochet another egg-cosy, like the girls in *Little Women*," and I used to do what she said because I loved my Momma so, and now look at me . . . *diseased – accursed.*'

Dimpla was baffled. Didn't the hick American kid realize that half the Supreme Soviet preferred fancy boys? 'What for you worried about?' she said. 'What for you make this boring "confession", anyway? We have, have we not, suicide to commit. Is most urgent task. Confess in afterlife, if you capitalist pigs right and there an afterlife is. If no afterlife then OK, I don't mind, save getting bored to death now.'

'But you gotta realize . . .' Malone was blubbing uncontrollably now.

194

'Colonel Malone, all I have to realize is that if I do this' – click – 'this' – click – 'and this' – splotch – 'I have set the *Mary Poppins* on collision course with that antimatter comet. Our death will be announced across all the broad skies of Russia, as a new sun comes into being. There' – c-r-r-r-ack! – 'now I have fixed it so that there is no way you can change our course.'

'Ommigod,' said Malone. 'Ommigod ommigod ommigod. You Red gook. Didn't your commie friends teach you any physics at the University of Vladivostok? What about the goddam radiation?'

'What,' said Dimpla, 'radiation?'

'Yeah. When we collide with that asshole comet of yours, and we annihilate with it, we're going to release enough hard radiation to sterilize the whole of the Solar System. Gamma-rays, X-rays – you name it.

'You've just condemned the Earth to death!'

8

''Sa brilliant idea of mine!' cried Tompion woozily to the assembled scientists. 'Matter transmission!'

'I can see the academic interest in such a proposition,' said Bran dubiously, 'but in our current circumstances . . .'

'Look,' said Tompion, 'it's simple. Least, it was a moment ago. Yes, I remember now. If we can develop matter transmission we can . . . Well, put it another way.'

'Please do,' rippled Avedon Patella sceptically.

'Look, we're all agreed that all these disasters are linked, that they're not just coincidental, that they're all integrated manifestations of a single disruption of spacetime – right?'

'Right!' 'Right on!' 'Too much!'

'Well, doesn't it seem most probable that this phenomenon, whatever it is, is purely *localized*? That other regions of the Universe are completely unimpaired?'

'That's true,' said Bran, stroking his chin. He was beginning to see what Tompion might be getting at.

'Well, surely the answer is to matter-transmit the *entire Earth* into orbit around another star, in some other corner of the cosmos.'

'Yes,' they all cried.

'And how do you propose to do this?' said Bjørgstrøm, an eager light in his eye.

'Uh, yes, that's the other problem,' agreed Tompion. 'We'll come back to that later.'

Lise Panther was pink with barely suppressed fury – she had never looked more beautiful. Her man was making a fool of himself . . . or was he? 'Wait a moment,' she said, as the others turned away, giggling. 'Mark may have a point.'

'Like what?' said Zenna Brabham, hooking her arms affectionately around Al D. Bran's thighs.

'Between us, Mark, Lucius and myself can easily enough crack the theoretical principle of matter transmission. All we have to do is find some loophole that Einstein left in General Relativity – there are bound to be a few. The question is, where do we get the power? And I think I know. Nadia, your boy is the source of such awesome energies that the Universe has never known their like. All we need to do is hook up his brain to our matter-transmission device and we should be home and dry. All that's left after that is for Mark and myself, in our roles as household-name astronomers, to locate a suitable star and plot a precise orbit around it for the Earth to slip into. It would be easier, of course, if we still had access to the Arecibo dish, but that's obviously impossible (as any of you with a security clearance will know).'

'I've got a pair of binoculars,' volunteered Abramowitz.

'OK,' crowed Panther, 'we've got everything. This time tomorrow I estimate we'll be ready for a dry run. I suggest we try sending something – a block of fablundium, perhaps – between Bran's office and the 110th storey of this very building.'

There was an enthusiastic babble of voices.

'Let's go!' yelled Tompion joyously, falling off the table.

9

Jeb Loam, of course, knew nothing of this.

As soon as he'd neared the outside door of his family's makeshift apartment he'd realized that something was wildly wrong. Green sulphurous smoke was oozing out from under the door; the air was rent by shrieks of maniacal laughter; the doormat was 'Bon Voyage'-side up. He'd thrown the scones from him with undisguised alacrity and shaken the woolly fug from his mind like a dog shaking water-droplets from its fur.

'Rachel, my little deary-o-down-dandy,' he'd yelled. 'Rachel, be thou all right and ups-a-daisy in there, my gryphon?'

He'd battered furiously on the door, reducing his fists to shapeless bleeding masses, then paused and tried the handle. He'd swung the door open for only a moment – but a moment had been quite long enough.

Rachel had been floating in midair, upright, her feet nearly a metre off the ground, her face contorted into a bloodless mask. Streamers of what he could have sworn were ectoplasm were pumping themselves into her ears and nostrils. Her hands were upraised like the wings of a vengeful hawk, and she spat fire.

Her lips moved.

Jeb, said the whole room. *Jeb, join us and we shall share infinite power for all the years of an infinite future. Join us and enjoy the triumph of E – V – I – L.*

Loam had slammed the door. He hadn't seen Rachel look that rotten since they'd gone for a ferry-ride across the Tamar. He knew he needed to get help, fast – and he knew, too, that that help would not be forthcoming from the scientists of the 'Think Tank'. He would have to go out into the streets of New York and find the ancient herbal ingredients which his grandmother had always used to ward off the evil eye and attacks of dyspepsia.

So now he was sculling along what had once upon a time been 42nd Street East, looking to right and left at those shop-signs that were still above the water-level. APPLE SHOESHINE, read one. Over there was APPLE UNDERWEAR, and just beyond he could see APPLE . . . the distant word looked to his eyes like 'compost'. Ah, but there, *there*, was the sort of sign he'd been looking for: YE OLDE BIGGE APPLE MAGICKE SHOPPE – LOTSA GOODIES'N'GHOULIES. He steered his craft – an upturned Volkswagen – eagerly in that direction. He soon saw that he was in luck: the shop had extended over three storeys, only the bottom-most of which had been inundated by the waters of the Hudson. As he drew nearer he saw a large poster fixed over the windows of what had originally been the shop's third storey:

A TRULY INTERNATIONAL SELECTION OF SPOOKS
Ghouls Tailored For Every Pocket
Ghastly Horrors From Every Nation of the World

His eyes read on down the list:

FROM ENGLAND
The Accrington Poultrygeist
Torment Your Least-Loved Chicken-Farmer!

FROM LIBYA
The Tripoli Doppelbänger
Can Ravish Two Sleeping Virgins Simultaneously!!

FROM EUROPE
A Car to Chill Your Spine!!
THE HILLMAN SPRITE

FROM SOUTH AMERICA
The Patagonian Pantasm
No One's Underclothing Is Safe!

FROM ENGLAND
The Most Frightening Soccer Team of All Time
WRAITH ROVERS!

AND FROM THE GOOD OL' US OF A ITSELF
The Fiendish, The Unspeakable . . .
STATUE OF DIABOLICAL LIBERTY

Jeb nodded. This seemed to be exactly the kind of shop he had been looking for. *I be not a-doubting one sheepshagging bit*, he thought, *that here I do be a-getting my fingers on a few simples that will be curing my beloved in two shakes of a bull's nasty.* He gulped. *Ah, Rachel, my little oryx.* And then he gulped again as the dreadful thought of possible failure struck him. *I don't be a-wanting to start thinking of her as 'my little aurochs' instead*, he thought.

The windows of Ye Olde Bigge Apple Magicke Shoppe were covered in what proved to be spun-nylon spiders' webs, and it was only with some difficulty that Jeb was able to twist and chew his way through these to shatter the glass with a sturdy rustic punch. The shards fell into blackness. He was just balancing himself teeteringly on the bobbing Volkswagen, preparatory to throwing one leg over the windowsill, when a voice spoke:

'At your service, sir.'

'Well, bugger I down . . .'

'Mr Wiz at your service, sir. Ready to show you round my shop of magic. All the other store-keepers seem to have fled, but here at Ye Olde Bigge Apple Magicke Shoppe we like to feel that the customer comes first, and so our sales-staff have stayed at their posts. The ones on the first floor have drowned, of course, but we've tied stones to their ankles so that they don't float up out of position.'

Jeb gawped. The speaker was a small man – almost a dwarf – dressed impeccably in a black evening suit and a white top hat. His face was filled with bland affability which peeped through a goatee beard and monocle. A cigarette holder that must have been over thirty centimetres long completed the picture. 'By the great udder in the sky,' breathed the farmer.

'Here, let me help you in,' said Mr Wiz, and all of a sudden Jeb found that he was standing inside the shop. It smelt damp, filled with the stench of rotting wood and plaster. 'I believe,' said Mr Wiz, tapping the side of his nose with that incredible cigarette holder, 'that you've come here looking for herbal medicines.'

Jeb Loam could only stand there, mouth open, and stare. As he did so, Mr Wiz slowly faded out of existence, reappearing equally slowly standing behind a counter on the far side of the room.

'Our motto,' explained Mr Wiz, 'is that the customer is always right, but that sometimes the customer has difficulty in knowing exactly what he really wants, and so we just do a quick check beforehand to find out. That way everybody's satisfied, and nobody's time is wasted.'

Loam gulped. *If I be a-doing that again I be floating away like one of them there airships*, he thought.

'And, of course, in this instance,' said Mr Wiz, 'as you're a new customer I'll serve you myself. Nothing but the manager himself for someone who's come to us for the first time.' He pulled a white dove from his lapel pocket and bit its head off. 'To tell you the truth,' he said, leaning forward over the counter and looking confidentially at the farmer, 'in your case it's rather a matter of necessity. Poor old Braithwaite who normally services this department has gone down with leprosy again, and I just couldn't, under the circumstances, find anyone to take his place.'

Jeb was beginning to wonder if he were dreaming.

'You're not, as a matter of fact,' said Mr Wiz. He had disappeared from behind the counter and was now sitting folded up like a parcel on a high shelf over the window. 'People often find this shop a little disconcerting at first but . . .' His hand emerged from a crevice clutching the bloated corpse of a drowned water-rat. He looked at it appreciatively for a moment, then threw it up into the air. It turned into a handful of flower-petals, which drifted quietly, dancingly, to the floor.

'But the trouble with you, my friend,' said the voice of Mr Wiz from a brass spittoon, 'is that you're all wrong about what you want. Your wife – a lovely buxom woman, if I may say so, sir – is not ill . . . not at all, at all, as O'Reilly in Packaging used to say before the fungus got him. No, you see, Mr Loam: the problem is that she's been possessed by an Unholy Trinity of which the Antichrist is the most powerful member.'

Jeb gasped, uncomprehending. This was a little above his head.

'So sorry to disconcert you,' said Mr Wiz, floating down to a more orthodox level so that he was facing Jeb.

'I can understand that this must all come as something of a shock to you.' He coughed a shower of golden coins which almost immediately turned to truffles. 'But you're fortunate, sir, fortunate. You've come to the very right place. The best place in the whole of New York City, if I may be so bold as to forswear modesty for a moment. Ye Olde Bigge Apple Magicke Shoppe has just the product for you.'

And there it was, floating in front of Loam, occupying the space where only a moment before Mr Wiz had stood: a big box with the lettering DO-IT-YOURSELF EXORCISM KIT splashed across it. 'I'm sure I'll give you every satisfaction, sir,' said the box in Mr Wiz's voice. 'Take me.'

A moment later Loam was standing, with weak knees, in the corridor outside the room where Rachel waited for him – waited for him to come to her rescue. But it was also the room, of course, where the forces of massed evil waited to do battle over both their souls.

He gripped the box firmly in his hands and stepped forward to the door.

Knock knock, said a whisper.

10

They led Junior Finkelstein out of his screened room, along the corridor, into the elevator, and so to the 113th storey. Bran's office had been converted overnight, by Abramowitz and Patella working sassily in tandem, into a makeshift transmitting station for the device that Tompion, Panther and Apricot had cobbled together. From the outside it looked much like a public callbox – which was exactly what it had been until Zenna Brabham had liberated it from a submerged street corner nearby, using an amphibious forklift truck. Like its fellow on the 110th storey, which was to act as a receiver, it had been covered all over, windows as well, with black spray-paint. From various points on its outer surface bundles and tangles of wire led in every conceivable direction, many of them to an oak laboratory bench on which nestled bubbling retorts and seething test-tubes. Two of the thickest clusters of wires led to what looked for all the world like an old-fashioned electric chair, complete with arm-clamps and metal head-piece. It was to this chair that they took Junior Finkelstein. Bjørgstrøm strapped him in with a paternal good-luck smile; Junior muttered the seven spinal chakras to himself to blot out the vision and then, as an afterthought, closed his eyes. He felt the bulky glaciologist lowering the head-piece down onto him, tucking his slightly splayed ears inside the casing.

'Are you comfortable?' hissed Bjørgstrøm.

'OK,' muttered Junior through a mouthful of gum.

Bran was talking with Tompion in the far corner of the room.

'Are you sure this thing will work?' he was saying, his eyes sceptically sweeping the scrambled-together device.

'Of course I'm sure,' said Tompion with a smile. 'Lucius may not look much, but he's probably the finest particle physicist in the world by now; what he doesn't know about "ritons" (as we call the instantaneously travelling particles which lie at the theoretical core of the matter transmitter, or MT) just isn't worth knowing. Lise may not look much either . . . er, well, she may not look much like the genius she is, with her peephole bra and her crotchless hotpants, but she can make numbers stand up on end and do conjuring tricks for her. And me – aw, shucks, I guess you know about my reputation.'

'Hmmm,' said Bran. 'But there's one thing that worries

me a little. I remember reading in an old pulp science-fiction novel somewhere that a time machine was really a space machine as well – you know, that if you travelled in time you'd pop up somewhere other than where you started, because everything in the Universe would have moved while you'd been staying still – and I was wondering if the same sort of thing might not apply here, except the other way around. You know, that a space machine might not turn out to be a time machine as well.'

Tompion laughed. 'You don't want to believe everything you read in pulp novels, now do you, Doctor? Those space operas are fun, but they're only for reading on the train and throwing away afterwards.'

Bran smiled in response, but the corners of his mouth still looked dubious. 'Still, I'm not entirely convinced about the safety of this gadget,' he said. 'The calibration, for example, seems a bit haphazard. How do you know our block of fablundium won't end up in the middle of . . . well, of somebody, for example?'

'I don't think you need worry on that score, either,' said Tompion with another faintly patronizing smile. 'We've calibrated the device so that it works only in the direction of the Earth's gravitational field – that is, so far as we're concerned, vertically. And, for the sake of convenience, we've used as our spatial unit (that is, our unit of distance) 4.37 metres, which is the exact distance between each of the storeys in this building. As you can see,' Tompion gestured the psychiatrist over beside him, 'this dial here is currently set at 113, representing the storey we're currently on. Before we use the machine, I'll simply set it for 110. Our block of fablundium should arrive bang on target.'

The great mathematician's eyes looked with a nervousness which belied his easy tones at the dial. Lise had shown him carefully how to set the needle on 113 – the two tall straight ones followed by the squiggly one – but she hadn't had the time to do the same for 110. Still, he thought he could recognize it all right. Ah, yes, there it was – all the way round the dial there, the one that looked like two small circles close together and sort of joined up. Like one of the other numbers on its side . . . what was it? . . . ah, yes, like an eight on its side. Easy enough to remember that one.

Bjørgstrøm and Apricot were ready to leave, to go downstairs to stand by the receiving cubicle. They turned to wave and give confident grins; one of the painted panes of the transmitter starred. Apricot went through the door first, and then held it open for Harcourt, the technician, who was struggling to bring in the block of fablundium on a trolley.

'Harcourt!' exclaimed Bran. 'But I thought you were . . .'

'I thought I was dead too, for a while,' grunted the man, struggling with the heady load. 'Losing my brain like that. Then I discovered that I could get along without it just as easily as before. Funny that.'

'Great!' said Bran with a clap of his hands. Inside, though, his mind was in a ferment. *My God! One of the fundamental tenets of psychology seems to have gone down the tubes . . .*

Still, there was no time for theoretical abstractions now: later, later. He watched as Harcourt manoeuvred the old trolley across the room towards the cubicle: the block of fablundium sat there inertly, some seventy-five kilograms of lifeless matter. It seemed almost a shame to Bran, in a fleeting moment of romantic fancy, that the block could have no way of experiencing the fantastic adventure that it was about to undergo.

'Place the block in the cubicle,' said Tompion, spitting

out a severed fingernail but otherwise showing no signs of apprehension.

Without a word Harcourt obeyed, tipping the cube – which, a metre by a metre by a metre, was unwieldy – into that engulfing cavity that lay behind the callbox door; it landed with a malevolent thump.

'That's one small lurch for a cube, one giant stride for mankind,' muttered Panther reflectively.

'Stand back!' snapped Tompion suddenly. 'The experiment is about to begin!'

Everybody retreated respectfully, except Tompion himself, who stood ready by the calibration dial and the great power lever, and Junior Finkelstein, who was sitting blank-eyed, blowing bubblegum, in his position, the wires leading from the head-piece beginning to glow with a green spectral light. The 'p-phlap' of a bursting bubble punctured the silence of the otherwise still room as Tompion looked around him, his knuckles tightening on the lever, ready to pull it down and so set the MT into action, disassembling the atoms of the fablundium block and transmitting them instantaneously across the few metres into the downstairs room where, presumably as tensely as the gathered spectators here, Apricot and Bjørgstrøm were watching the receiving cubicle – in which the atoms would be reassembled to form what would be to all intents and purposes the same block of fablundium!

It was an exciting moment. Nobody could doubt that they were watching history in the making. His one hand still on the power lever, Tompion, his heart filled with a deep sense of occasion, screwed up his eyes in concentration and shifted the calibrating dial carefully until the needle pointed at the symbol that looked just like a . . . oh, shit, forgotten it again . . . oho, that's it . . . an eight on its side . . .

The air was full of such tangible tension that you could

have taken a handful of it and used it as chewing-gum – which, in fact, Junior Finkelstein for a moment considered doing. There was a pregnant silence as the electronic clock on the wall edged its way inexorably round to the precise hour of midnight, the time at which, by unanimous agreement, they had determined to shatter the foundation-stones of orthodox science – a silence broken only by Avedon Patella nervously lighting a cigarette.

The long red second-hand swept finally towards the twelve, and under his breath Tompion began the countdown.

'. . . four . . . five . . . six . . . one . . . zero . . . *now!*'

And he pulled the lever down with all his might.

It was nonsense, of course, but some atavistic corner of each of them had been expecting – perhaps even hoping for – a sparkling and a crackling straight from the climax to a horror movie: almost to their disappointment there was nothing of that . . . just a sort of pungent, acrid stillness.

'Has it worked?' said Bran, after a moment.

'Give it a chance,' replied Avedon Patella, coughing paroxysmally yet elegantly over her cigarette.

'Ploop,' said Junior Finkelstein's bubblegum.

'I hope it damn well has worked,' added Lise Panther sardonically. 'I wore my fingers to the bone on my calculator making sure that it would.'

'Don't worry,' said Nadia Finkelstein, who had been standing apprehensively in the corner until now, barely noticed by the others. She stepped across to the makeshift cubicle. 'I'll open the cubicle, and then we should see that our cube has disappeared, and in just a moment or two we should get a phonecall from Lucius and Gwynfor to say that they've got our cube in their cubicle . . .' Her voice trailed off nervously. The fate of the Earth could depend on this.

She slowly raised the lever, and the door of the cubicle eased open with tantalizing slowness. Behind it they could all see, to their astonishment, nothing other than the original block of fablundium, totally unchanged.

'Tough titty, Earth,' said Zenna Brabham, after a bitter pause.

Just then the internal telephone rang; Zenna, being the nearest, picked it up with an adroit flick of her perfectly formed pelvis.

'It's amazing!' came Bjørgstrøm's thrilled voice down the line. 'It really works! The cube is here, safe and sound! It's even got Tompion's initials carved on it! At last the great spaces of the Universe, in all their stark magnificence, are open to mankind! We can . . . .'

The honey-skinned schoolteacher slammed the phone down before he could continue.

'Tompion and the others,' she began, 'seem to have invented something rather different from what they intended. Their matter transmitter apparently doesn't actually transmit matter, it duplicates it and then sends the duplicate. Down on the 110th floor they have, in their cubicle, a block identical with the one that we failed to send them.'

She gestured at the cube of fablundium, wearisome in its frustrating immobility, while the information sank in.

'You mean,' said Bran, aghast, 'that at last we've learnt to duplicate matter? If this had happened a few years ago we'd have solved the world hunger problem at a stroke, because one grain of rice could be turned into two, into four, into eight, into . . . Oh, what have we done in our folly, tampering with the forces of Nature?'

'But that's ridiculous,' snapped Patella caustically, grinding one cigarette out on the carpet with her heel and lighting another. 'If that were the case you'd have the paradox of creating matter out of nothing. I mean, I'm

208

only a Cornish-language expert, not a top-flight scientist like the rest of you, but even I have a glancing acquaintanceship with the implications of the Law of Conservation of Energy. You just *can't* get matter from nowhere.'

'There's always pair creation,' said Bran with a sudden jaunty leer at her taut bosom.

'No, but she's right, you know,' Nadia Finkelstein put in. 'Whatever goes to make up that second cube must have come from somewhere.'

'We're amateurs,' cried Zenna Brabham. 'We're groping in the dark, creating an apparent paradox where there may be no paradox at all.'

'That's right,' agreed Lise Panther reluctantly. 'The only one of us who can possibly hope to understand all this is Tompion.'

'That's a thought,' said Zenna Brabham, looking around. 'Just where the hell *is* Tompion?'

11

Hours later, in the darkened room, Junior Finkelstein still sat strapped to the chair where the others had, in their excitement, inadvertently left him. His bubblegum had lost most of its flavour, but he chewed on stoically; besides, he wasn't sure that he didn't prefer it that way.

He could have told them what was going to happen, of course, but none of them had seen fit to ask him. He let his infinitely powerful mind roam back to the pages of the *Boys' Book of Cosmology* that his mom had given him for Christmas a couple of years back . . .

According to one popular theory of the origins of the Universe, once upon a time (before there was such a thing as time) there was a nothingness. It was an infinite sea of what are called virtual particles – which is to say, particles which don't actually exist at all. This sea was boundless, and yet it had neither length nor breadth, for these, like time, were things which had yet to come into existence.

The Universe should never have been born from such an unpromising start, but something unknown – something at which modern science can only guess – disturbed this timeless serenity. The disturbance itself was minute, but the chain of events which it started was dramatic. Time started, but it was a close race, because within infinitesimal fractions of a second the entire Universe had erupted into being in the unimaginably ferocious explosion whose violence we can still detect today, the eruption known colloquially as the Big Bang.

'Perkloip,' went Junior's bubblegum for the zillionth time.

A space machine was indeed also a time machine, as Bran had feared, and Tompion had inadvertently set the calibrating dial to infinity – the symbol like an eight on its side. The fablundium, unable to travel an infinite number of years back in time (the substance had only been invented recently), had seized upon the nearest item of matter of approximately its own weight – seventy-five kilograms.

Tompion.

And so, think back to the beginning of the Universe
. . .

A small disturbance . . .
A seventy-five kilogram disturbance, to be precise . . .
Tompion.

12

And as Junior sits thinking, nearby, in another darkened room, Avedon Patella is sleeping the sleep of the profoundly sexually frustrated: she has just failed, despite all the odds in her favour, to make love with Lucius Apricot.

When finally, a couple of hours ago, she allowed herself to be lured into his bedroom she was fully aware of what she was letting herself in for: a charitable act. Cornwall was gone, and it seemed, now that the MT experiment had apparently failed, that the rest of the Earth was doomed, too. So she forced herself to think positively about doing the particle physicist a favour – and, as he stumblingly lowered his trousers, she gazed at him in feigned admiration and remarked, just as she had been taught in those sex-education classes that Trevelyan had organized, 'Wow! Oh gosh! It's really . . . magnificent. It's grrreat! I don't know the word to use. No – no, I *do* know the word. It's – like, well, Lucius, it's just *titanic*!'

Now Lucius, while she sleeps, lies in the darkened bedroom, worrying away at his fingernails.

What will it be?

Lightning?

6

Plan 666 from Outer Space

I am very pleased to note the author's term for extraterrestrial vehicles. He excludes the expression 'flying saucer', which is a deplorable misnomer because they come in so many different shapes and sizes, and does not call them 'unidentified flying objects' (UFOs) because that's a contradiction in terms . . . Mr Morison's term is alien space vehicle (ASV), which means what it says. I should like to see the term adopted by everyone investigating the phenomenon.
– the Earl of Clancarty, introducing Robert Kingsley Morison's *An Experiment with Space*, 1979

1

'Who be there?' Jeb muttered reflexively to the closed door.

Sick, came the eldritch whisper.

Jeb thought: *Oh by buggery, I did be a-seeing that dretful godless film, five times, to think my darling anthrax-spore Rachel might be a-heaving and a-spewing all radioactive green belike . . . Happen I should fetch overall.* But still he said aloud: 'Sick who?'

Sick sick sicks . . .

Scratching his head, Jeb decided this wasn't anything like as funny as the one about the National Farmers' Union and the goat. Impatiently he reached for the door handle, which as his hand approached became a smallish Gila monster and took him firmly by the thumb.

'This be no time for buggering finesse!' shrieked Jeb.

His size-sixteen boot, hardened and tempered with the
blood of a hundred hikers who'd strayed from the public
footpath, impacted the flimsy door. Toothpicks flew
everywhere. The Gila monster metamorphosed into a
scattered shower of frogs, and then nervously reverted to
being a door handle. It occurred to the plucky farmer
that some occult power was at work here: heedless of his
bloody thumb, he wrenched the lid from the cardboard
box and plucked out – an Emergency Quick-Draw
Talisman.

At least, that was what Jeb thought it was. Comprising
as it did the mummified relic of either a rhinoceros or
John Dillinger, adorned with two lusty garlic cloves
strategically a-dangle, it was a totem which Jeb preferred
not to let his eyes dwell on. If Rachel were to see it . . .

'Why, Jeb darling, how charmingly old-fashioned of
you.'

It was she – now reclining quite normally on the
crumpled bed, and yet not quite normally. She radiated a
throbbing, sensual attraction which welled out in slow,
sultry waves to strike him hard in the pit of his stomach;
while as for her pose, it heartbreakingly called to mind
the 'men only' pages of *The Cattle Breeder's Artificial
Insemination Supplement*. Now seemed the ideal time for
Jeb to act naturally and reclaim his woman; but a small
lingering worry tainted the back of his mind. What was
it?

'O Jeb, you truly magnificent rutting he-man, throw
down your burden, throw off your trammelling garments,
and be at one with me for an eternity of timeless ecstasy!'

Moving as in a dream, he was half-way through the
prescribed course of action when the lingering worry
brought a remembered voice to mind. *Happen you'll be
wanting to play ferrets and rabbit-holes afore we get a
wink of sleep, Jeb you old goat?*

'Why pause, why linger and delay? Come now to me, lover fore-ordained since time began, and taste the forbidden fruits of unendurable pleasure indefinitely prolonged!'

He couldn't put his finger on it, but something had surely . . . changed. And now that he'd managed to divert his attention to Rachel's face, wasn't it odd how the light reflected from her eyes with such an eerie, murky, crimson flickering? Particularly as the room was lit by a 40-watt fluorescent tube?

It was too late to retain his braces, but he made a sudden snatch at the exorcism kit, spilling a scatter of icons, amulets, periapts and runes, until he triumphantly brandished a small plastic marble. The transformed Rachel looked suddenly wary: she licked her lips and (briefly and alarmingly) her ears.

Jeb remembered the plastic marble from the instruction booklet. 'A holy economy special from Popular Relics Inc! No longer a rich men's and rich churches' preserve; you now hold your own very authenticated fragment of the True Cross! Yes, using the latest high-tech molecular shear, Popular Relics Inc have sliced a guaranteed True Cross splinter into 10^{18} individually personalized chunks, each plastic-encapsulated for your miraculous convenience. Safe when taken as directed . . .' He couldn't actually see the tiny, precious particle at the centre of the seeming marble, but he had a simple countryman's faith, by flaming buggery he did!

The light in Rachel's eyes flashed – flashed and seared out in a tight, coherent beam of 6563 Ångstrom units wavelength (corresponding exactly to the red C emission line of the solar hydrogen spectrum, as its target distractedly failed to note). The hellish beam struck straight and true for Jeb's heart, only to be somehow refracted by the plastic marble and diverted through the window on a steep, upward-slanting course. With a snarl of totally uncomprehending triumph, Jeb strode forward – and gradually sloughed to a halt in the suddenly treacly and ectoplasmic air. *So this be Yankee pollution,* he thought.

'Looks like a standoff, Pop,' said Rachel. Terror stalked on frosted feet along Jeb's vertebrae, wriggled down the back of his Y-fronts and (after manoeuvres not convenient to describe) took up its chilly abode amid his short and curlies. The voice had been the voice of Nathan. And Jeb had always *hated* being called Pop.

2

'So this is . . . it,' slobbered Captain Sc'smv, braiding its/her eyestalks at the viewscreen in the immemorial Cygnan gesture of distaste. The image of Earth hung there in space like a ripe and rotting fruit, a diseased persimmon, perhaps, or a medlar of great age; maggot-gnawed by earthquakes, poxed with volcanoes and liquid-natural-gas explosions, eaten away by cancerous pollution and great red weeping sores which once were oceans, spotted with the leprosy of misplaced and fractured icecaps, distended by cruelly irresponsible overwriting, stiffening even now into deadly hypothermia thanks to the little predicted 'Bureaucratic Winter' (whereby a single nuclear explosion in Sun Plaza, Tenerife, can by wild chance hurl numbing masses of Inland Revenue Schedule D Tax Assessment forms high into the stratosphere, forming a self-sustaining layer of paperwork and cutting off the Sun's last sickly rays) . . .

'That is it,' guggled Stf'ndnl'dsn in sombre confirmation.

'We came all this way for . . . that,' the Captain reticulated.

'Even so,' the First Mate oozed.

'By the sacred cloaca of Lr'nhb'bd!' the Captain erupted (not a figure of speech, but a Cygnan conversational mode whose meaning is painfully literal: their lowly office of 'ceiling effectuator' corresponds roughly to a combination of the Earthly 'telephone sanitizer' and 'sewage farm operative'). 'After all our trouble! As you are already well aware, despite my need to repeat it for ignorant readers, we have painstakingly studied this backward world's culture. We have learnt their language from radio broadcasts and speak it even when conversing between ourselves in private, for the sake of practice and the plot. We have adopted such names as our psychologists agree the natives will find most reassuringly appropriate to extraterrestrial visitors . . .'

Across the room, handsome young Lieutenant Rt'hrcc'lrk retracted his proprioceptors in convulsive embarrassment. His computer-selected *nom de guerre* incorporated two of the vilest obscenities in the aliens' language; he looked forward to nothing but the end of this mission and the resumption of his true name, Fred.

'We took the trouble to encode and transmit a message distilling the essential elements of all the locally hypothesized alien first-contact communications, which Earth culture could find familiar and therefore soothing . . .'

'WE COME TO ANNIHILATE YOU PAINFULLY AND RAPE YOUR PLANET,' the First Mate quoted wetly and reminiscently: she/he/she had composed the sentence, which in the Cygnan original formed a perfect triolet.

'We have even learnt to pretend we enjoy snacks of live hamsters, to licentiously carry off female primates, and to utter essential phrases such as "Take me to your leader", "*Klaatu barada nikto*", "Resistance is useless" and "EX-TER-MIN-ATE",' peristalsed the Captain. 'To set Earthlings' minds at rest we have with great difficulty constructed lethal Heat Rays, impenetrable force fields, matter/antimatter pods, cute robots, and endless hand-held lasers which, as in Earth's dramatic art, can fire an infinite number of charges without ever hitting an important character.'

'Yes, yes, I know all this,' the First Mate conjugated – not a moment too soon. But the Captain was in full spate, as testified by the gurgle of the bridge's drainage units.

'Only thus can we unobtrusively assess this planet for membership in the Galactic Union. If this sorry, shattered wreckage (which looks more like a regurgitated *mgr'ttht'chr* than anything else) is capable of membership in anything . . .'

But the expression in her/its mucus organs belied the harsh words. The Galactic Union was, after all, a noble ideal. It was all that protected intelligent life-forms from exploitation by the monetarist Cosmic Brotherhood of the Inanimate – a coalition of impersonal, non-living forces, mindlessly bent on expansion like some deadly virus.

Earth's fate therefore hung in the balance. The Galactic Union could not permit the existence of independent, blackleg intelligence! Did General Relativity itself not prescribe that the shape of the Universe was a closed shop? If the human race was found wanting, the Cygnan fleet would be forced to swiftly and mercilessly . . . strike.

Hordes of alien spy-drones were already prowling Earth's atmosphere, adding a statistically significant 0.2% to the mounting wave of UFO sightings which accompanied the run-up to apocalypse. 'We need specimens of the highest local life-form,' the Captain infarcted:

within twenty *sx'tysc'nds* (a Cygnan time-unit approximately equal to one Earth minute), such a specimen had been located and beamed up to the mother ship, and the spy-drone responsible brought back for severe reprogramming. The giraffe was kept by the First Mate as a souvenir.

'There are signs of life in New York,' reported Midshipthing M'cffr. That area was receiving quadruple surveillance: if unable to gain Earth's attention, the Captain planned as a last resort to convey typical and lovable alienness by the traditional means of attacking Manhattan Island.

'ENEMY ATTACK!' grated a harsh voice. 'SPY DRONE 5-271-009 STRUCK BY LASER BEAM OF 6563 N'GS'TRM UNITS WAVELENGTH! STANDARD MIRROR DEFENCE SUCCESSFUL BUT MUST REGARD AREA AS HOSTILE! PROPOSE EITHER [A] SATURATION BOMBING OF HEMISPHERE WITH MK III ULTIMATE WEAPONS, OR [B] TRY SOMEWHERE ELSE. THIS IS YOUR FRIENDLY COMPUTER SIGNING OFF. PS: DOESN'T [A] SOUND MORE FUN?'

'I prefer [B],' secreted the Captain, who at both hearts was a kindly soul. 'Let's focus on that little island known to the natives as "Britain", over there on the other side of the ocean which in local parlance might be termed the "Atlantic" . . .'

It wasn't long before they had located, subdued (with some difficulty) and beamed up a large group of natives – large enough, statistically, to provide a full, reliable picture of Earthling personalities and cultural aims. The group comprised 216 males ('These lower life-forms all look alike to me,' the Captain exuded to the First Mate), 78 females ('Same goes for the other of their paltry two genders,' was the gelatinous reply), and one large reptilian organism which the First Mate tentatively classed as a pet.

The Captain's painfully acquired knowledge of English was soon taxed to its limit by phrases like *'Himmel!'*, *'Dumkopf!'* and *'A-yllough-why kewsel Kernewek?'*

3

'It's our only chance,' said Dr Nevin. 'Earth is doomed. This old planet of ours is on its last legs – like a hot fudge sundae at ground zero of a multiple thermonuclear blast.'

'I still don't like it,' quavered the cringing Mayor of Los Angeles. 'It'll never take off . . .'

'Bullshit!' snapped Dr Purnell. 'When a 200-kiloton nuke goes *blam* right under the ass of the good ship *Libertarian* – comprising this entire reinforced city block – believe me, it's going to *move*.'

'This, as you should be well aware, is the *Orion* concept,' put in Dr Nevin, leaning back and sipping Irish coffee. 'Pogoing into the sky on a column of nuclear fireballs! Being batted once every second towards the stars, by God's own fist! The mere idea ought to give any red-blooded American wet dreams. In fact, the entire Los Angeles SF Society has volunteered as crewpersons . . .'

Purnell touched his Sony Walkman, and the 'Battle Hymn of the Republic' blared tinnily forth. 'Out there in brave new worlds, we can establish a new order that will last for a thousand years.'

'But,' whined the Mayor, 'what about the environment, and flattening Greater LA at take-off, and all the poor folks who can't go along to found space colonies?'

Purnell shrugged. 'The environment's had it – get it through your head, this is the *end of the goddam world!* As for the whiners, they make me sick. Welfare cheaters and wishy-washy liberals: if they had a milligram of the American frontier spirit they'd all have built their own getaway ships. This is going to be the first large-scale, practical test of Social Darwinism.'

'People who opposed Star Wars defence systems have only themselves to blame,' confirmed Nevin. (Being an American, he pronounced it 'defense'.) 'We *needed* those orbital weapons, just in case the inevitable aliens from 61 Cygni turned out to be hostile. As it is, we'll have to play it by ear.'

'ALL-CHANNELS OVERRIDE,' interjected the seeming Sony Walkman, dead on cue. 'COUNTDOWN COMMENCING: THIRTY MINUTES TO THE FIRST DETONATION . . .'

'My God. What *are* your plans for contacting the extraterrestrials?' quavered the Mayor.

Dr Purnell looked proudly up into the lowering sky, and said: 'Nuke 'em till they glow, then shoot 'em in the dark.'

4

Apricot had spent several hours conducting thought experiments about matter transmission. He'd never quite got the hang of thought experiments before: the apparatus had always had the awkward habit of dissolving without warning into a simmering conceptual pool of mulled gin-and-tonic. This was why he'd always found it handier to assemble his epoch-making experiments very slowly and in person, with frequent pauses to lie down or clean the vomit out of the mass spectrometer. At least, that way, the gadgetry was solid enough that you didn't risk anything worse than fatal radiation doses or 200 kilovolt shocks.

(Even this had been strangely comforting. Statistics had conclusively shown that people who habitually worked with raw plutonium and 200kV potentials almost *never* died from kidney failure or other diseases of alcoholism – so, as long as he didn't change his laboratory practice, Apricot clearly didn't have a drink problem.)

Today, trembling with superstitious fear, he'd found it soothing to hide in the clean recesses of his mental laboratory, staying away from the imaginary cupboard numbered with the prime factors 2, 3^2 and 37, and confining himself to the big picture, the major issues, the hoped-for MT breakthrough which could be the most tit –

Big, anyway.

His list went:

[1] An ideal matter transmitter will move objects instantaneously from *here* to *there*. Normally the speed of light, c, is an absolute limiting velocity. Take away this absolute limit, and relativity crumbles. (Apricot had paused at this point, and looked over his shoulder, fearful of seeing the spectre of Einstein poised to hurl titanic lightnings at the blasphemer . . . *don't think about it!*) Quantum mechanics is shored up by relativity. Quantum mechanics accounts for the fact that atomic electron-orbits do not decay and spiral madly into the nucleus, where negative and positive charges would cancel cataclysmically. No relativity equals no quantum mechanics. Bye-bye, atoms. Bye-bye, world. *Conclusion:* try other line of research.

[2] An ideal matter transmitter is regarded as a hole in the fabric of space, a hole through which (bypassing relativity in a way we will reserve for a future paper when we've thought of it) objects can pass from A to B. According to my calculations, such a discontinuity would be stable once first established (in a way we will reserve, etc). Thought experiment: permanent MT

221

portal, can't be turned off, irrevocably connecting my laboratory to [a] a dead point in interstellar space to which the pressure difference would eventually force Earth's entire atmosphere; [b] the centre of a sun or black hole, which . . .*Conclusion:* try other line of research.

[3] An ideal matter transmitter comprises a 'gate' to somewhere else in space. A simple calculation based on the zero-point energy fluctuations of free space should yield a maximum stable size for the MT gateway. Working along these lines, I estimate a diameter of no more than 1.926643 centimetres, which is something of a limitation . . .*Conclusion:* try other line of research.

[4] An ideal matter transmitter is instantaneous. Therefore the 'limiting' velocity of light is locally altered – to infinity. By Einstein's $E = mc^2$, infinite energy will therefore result from any spontaneous nuclear transformation. Thought experiment: natural radioactive decays are taking place all the time. As c approaches infinity, any single such decay will release sufficient energy to wipe out the entire Universe, or in fact any finite or countably infinite number of universes. *Conclusion:* file under 'useful ultimate weapons' and try other line of research.

[5] An ideal matter transmitter will establish a nice, stable, controllable gateway between A and B. But in what frame of reference is the MT gateway stable? Thought experiment: MT gateway is set up. Earth continues to move, shifting along a gigantic vector compounded of Earth's own spin, its orbital motion relative to the Sun, the Sun's motion relative to the galaxy at large, the galaxy's motion relative to, er, something or other. Immediate effect: the gateway appears to zoom off in an unpredictable direction, possibly carving a *fff* large hole through the MT equipment, the experimenters, the laboratory, the Earth . . .*Conclusion:* try other line of research.

[6] A matter transmitter is – *eureka!* This is a truly wonderful solution, but I am at the bottom margin of the paper, which is too small to contain it . . .

'*Eureka!*' cried Apricot aloud, a hideous sound which brought lovely, inquisitive, pert-bosomed Avedon Patella running into the room, ravishingly clad in one of the sheer, filmy night-dresses which unaccountably were the only sleeping wear located by Bran's looting expedition. (They looked particularly unconvincing on Bjørgstrøm.)

'What was that?' she enquired seductively.

'I said, my dear, *Eureka!* The problem is cracked and I have saved us all! The word means *I have found it*, or in your native Cornish, *Dün-ny, glybyn agan mȳn!*'

She started uncontrollably, stopped short in astonishment, and then started again. Such musical phrases were the throbbing key to the infinite, artesian wells of passion which burnt deep within her; she could respect Dr Apricot at last. Throatily she said: '*A-yllough-why kewsel Kernewek?*'(*Do you speak Cornish?*)

Not for nothing was Apricot a world-famous researcher and a quick study. With a confident leer he replied, '*Gwra mellya orth daclow dha honen!*' (*No, but I saw the movie.*)

Avedon sobbed in ecstasy, flung herself down on her perfectly formed knees, and fumbled urgently at Apricot's trouser-zip. Burning in her shapely loins she felt the force of Destiny, and the need to balance the long and inadequately salacious scientific passage of just a few paragraphs ago.

'Gosh,' said Apricot after a brief but eventful pause.

'Perhaps first I should tell you the MT insight which could yet save the entire doomed world?' Apricot gasped.

'This is amazing!' said Apricot.

'Out of the window, which I am facing and to which you have your exquisite back, I can see a small and silvery UFO!' Apricot continued.

There was a sudden red flash, which his trained physicist's senses interpreted as coherent light of 6563 Ångstrom units wavelength. The lurid after-image seemed to show a double beam: one emanating somewhere close by, one bouncing back from the curiously alien object hovering there. The time, he noted mechanically, was

7:06 P.M.; or, as one might jokingly phrase it, 6:66 . . .
Apricot felt a sharp, searing pain.

Distracted from her sensual pastime by a strange
scorched smell, voluptuous Avedon glanced upward. Her
mouth was too full to scream, but her dark, ravishing
eyes widened in stark horror.

5

'GREETINGS, EARTHLINGS! RESISTANCE IS
USELESS! WE COME TO ANNIHILATE YOU PAIN-
FULLY AND RAPE YOUR PLANET. TAKE US TO
YOUR LEADER. WHICH SHALL IT BE, PASSWOR-
THY, WHICH SHALL IT BE? WE'RE GOING OVER
THE TOP, GONNA TRY AND HEAD THEM INJUNS
OFF AT THE PASS. ACTION STATIONS! THERE'S
A HERD OF KILLER RABBITS ON THE WAY
HERE . . : IT'S ALIVE! IT'S ALIVE! AN INTELLEC-
TUAL CARROT! I'M WALKING BACKWARDS
TILL CHRISTMAS TIME, AND THAT IS THE END
OF THE NEWS.'

The broadcast was so powerful that, even though all
radio reception apparatus aboard the *Mary Poppins* had
been converted into X-ray lasers, stills, or emergency
clamps for embarrassingly situated wounds, the very
quartz of the viewports resonated after the fashion of a
crystal receiver. Few human beings have been privileged
to hear a crystal set with an unamplified output of 200
watts, full stereo (there were of course two viewports).

'Kind of interesting,' said Bart Malone listlessly. 'Reading between the lines, it seems to me there's this fleet of
gigantic alien spacecraft in Earth orbit, all armed with
heat rays, ultimate weapons and impenetrable force fields,

delivering an ultimatum from 61 Cygni in terms they've sort of gleaned from English broadcasts.'

'Capitalist lickspittle running dogs,' Dimpla defined, with a cynical thrust of her lusciously bra-less, free-falling bosom. 'Perfectly good Russian broadcasts to learn language from. Full of hard facts on boot production and continuing Afghanistan peace initiative. Aliens clearly have poor taste, politically unsound, not *kulturny*.'

Malone didn't really feel like arguing. Not only did he have a wound which left a much-loved part of him swathed with bandages until it resembled Tutankhamun's cat, but his ultimate, last-ditch ploy had failed. 'I am a poor, hapless and indeed unwilling gay whom no woman has been able to wean from his unnatural longings to the One True Way . . .' In all his wide experience, stretching over five separate continents and including initiation into the Mile High Club during a *ménage a trois* parachute drop, Malone had never known a woman who could resist the challenge. Until now. Evidently Comrade Adrianna Dimpla was made of drop-forged steel, despite all the deliciously jiggling evidence to the contrary.

'Can only hope terminal radiation blast as we impact antimatter will also wipe out Earth's invaders,' pouted Dimpla.

'Yeah, about a tenth of a second before it sterilizes Earth,' Malone grumbled. 'Even then, it might not make too much impression on all those impenetrable forcefields and stuff. I've seen the movies: bullets won't stop them, phasers always fail to operate, your only hope is they all catch cold. Aliens . . . they're always bad news.' Having defined US foreign policy in a nutshell, Malone sucked moodily at the stains on his trousers which were where he'd spilt the very last of the booze. At least, he hoped that's what they were.

'Surely even aliens have other weak spot?' Dimpla

asked, pleased that the conversation had for several sentences stayed off the subject of free-fall sex.

'Sex,' said Malone, shattering her hopes. 'Aliens always wanna carry off Earth's fairest daughters . . . statistically proven. Of course this isn't necessarily a full analysis, like, but apart from germs the only documented alien weakness is they've got the hots for [a] girlies, and [b] mindless insensate violence.'

'Is like your way of courtship?'

'No, Dimpla . . . Hot ziggety! I've got it!'

'If is herpes, keep even greater distance, thanks.'

'*Violence!* See, that fleet up ahead probably has the hardware to smash planets and eat the left-overs for breakfast. They could zap this ship easy as picking your nose!'

'Nice to know,' Dimpla sulked. 'Can pass time making bets on whether invaders' weaponry or comet destroys us first.'

'Strip poker would be more fun – ouch.' Dimpla had pushed the revolver barrel a certain distance into his left nostril.

'So explain great stupid plan?'

'It's like this. See, we take advantage of their natural and incredibly violent offensive/defensive reflexes.'

'Ah, you mean wait till they make mistake of marching on Moscow.'

At this, Malone's tone became offensively superior, though not for long. 'Not quite, gorgeous – *ouch*. OK, look at it this way. Attack them, they'll come back with some kind of planet-busting disintegrator ray, you betcha.'

'No way for us to attack, Yankee fool. No use even if way.'

Malone leered. 'Oh yes, we can attack, Dimpla. *Your revolver!* We'll have to go out of the airlock and start shooting at the invaders' mother ship. Only a tiny provocation, admittedly, but the response is likely to be pretty damn terrific. Sledgehammers and nuts, and we're the nuts.'

'First sensible sentence yet.'

'Listen. We synchronize our watches and time it for when the comet's real close to us – just before impact – so their return fire zaps noble self-sacrificing us *and* the comet, both! Giving Earth at least a chance!'

Dimpla sighed. 'Almost I admire foolish courage. But is useless, bullet which – ' (she blushed divinely, in a shade of naughty pink never, never to be found in the GUM store) 'which injured you went on. See? Space-suits perforated, useful only as makeshift colander, no repair possible.'

So much for decadent Western boasting about tool of steel, by Bog! she thought to herself.

'I figured that out, too.' Malone licked his lips nervously. 'There's gonna have to be a real hero-type sacrifice. Out of the airlock into naked space, and float there shooting as long as I goddam can!'

'Am trained shot, imperialist pig,' said Dimpla, hefting the revolver meaningfully. '*I* make sacrifice, in name of glorious international amity under Supreme Soviet.'

'We need you for the shooting, yeah,' said Malone. 'But you're kinda low-mass, darling. A big lunk like me would retain body-heat longer, be able to shoot longer in the terrible cold of space.'

'Lickspittle sophism is proper dialectical analysis of argument.'

Malone exerted all his failing charisma in one last effort. 'We hafta load the odds any way we can, honey. Like: my mass, your skill. We can share body heat by wrapping ourselves together in one big parcel, with heads and your shooting arm free – and then, out of the airlock!'

Dimpla's eyes narrowed in suspicion. She had never looked more gorgeous or unattainable: and yet there was a chance. He had exaggerated his intimate injury, biding his time until . . .

'Of course,' said Malone, sweating slightly, 'to get the most benefit we'd need to maximize thermal contact between our bodies. That means, naked inside the bedcl – the wrappings. So: you got the courage to chuck out your inhibitions and try to save Earth the best way we can? Ready to go out with a bang?'

I mean that last sentence, baby, he leered inwardly. *If you didn't know about the matter/antimatter radiation flash, you sure won't know it's the vacuum that screws you long before the cold! And maybe Bart Malone before either of 'em . . .*

6

'Looks like trouble,' remarked Al D. Bran, peering from the skyscraper window. 'Wolves! Wolves in the streets of New York! I never knew a wolf pack could swim.'

'Ah,' said Bjørgstrøm, 'this makes excellent sense, climatologically speaking.'

'You mean,' said Abramowitz with many a palpitation of her perfectly, maddeningly shaped ears, 'that wolves, like lemmings, are seasonal? What an amazing insight!'

'Not quite. What I happened to notice, since we climatologists are trained through a long and gruelling education to take an occasional shrewd look at the weather and the sky, is that the Moon is looking bigger. You have to allow something for subjectivism, but I'm persuaded to the conclusion that maybe its orbit is decaying.'

'How,' breathed Abramowitz, 'could you make such a

daring intuitive leap?' She tried to close her eyes before Bjørgstrøm's answering smile, but failed to save her contact lenses.

'Sheer daring intuition, my darling. Eked out just a little by the fact that, being as I am a trained climatologist, I happened to notice the two total eclipses this morning. Yes, the Moon is orbiting faster – therefore closer – therefore it really does look bigger!'

'So Hörbiger's theory, scorned by the fuddy-duddies of orthodox science, was right after all,' put in Zenna Brabham, who with delightful female attention to minor details was painstakingly removing almost invisible pieces of fluff and dust from Bran's clothing. Bran hadn't realized he harboured so much detritus inside his vest. 'Earth's aspiring civilizations are in fact successively smashed by the falling of a sequence of moons!'

'That Moon'll have to hurry,' grunted Bran. 'Anyway, haven't we kind of sidled off the wolf topic?'

'Not at all,' Bjørgstrøm twinkled, detaching various persons' retinas. 'Our parapsychic researches into the "Earthdoom Effect" have made me a great deal more open-minded. From all your scientific experience of bad horror movies, what kind of behaviour would you expect to be intensified by a larger, closer, brighter, fuller Moon? This is a rhetorical question, meaning you will be very stupid if you cannot instantly answer it, my friend.'

'The trouble with having an open mind is that people come along and put things in it,' Bran groaned, and turned to Nadia Finkelstein – a difficult task, since she was lovingly cleaning wax from his left ear in what he hoped was a maternal fashion. 'Nadia honey, we're fresh out of silver bullets: can you be a real caring person and check the spice rack for garlic or wolfbane?'

'But Gwynfor,' said Zenna to Bjørgstrøm, 'can this theory account for the coincidental fact that the few

229

people we see from the windows of this last outpost of scientific rationality have developed strangely long and pointed incisors?'

It was Joyce Abramowitz who replied. 'I don't think the answer to that one lies in climatology, Zenna! It needs a biologist – and I was hot on the track of the Nobel Prize, just as soon as they started giving one for lemming studies. As a snap judgement, I'd say this "Dracula effect" was the result of mass fluoridation: those people's teeth have just got *too* healthy!'

'That suggests a further scientific line of enquiry,' mused Bran. 'How does Charlton Heston escape in *The Omega Man*, when he's holed up in this beleaguered skyscraper surrounded by rabid hordes of albino vampires?'

'He doesn't,' confessed Zenna tearfully. 'They waste him.'

'Well, maybe we can try some other line of research,' Bran chuckled hollowly. He looked out of the window again. 'Amazing the way they can swim while brandishing flaming torches, isn't it?'

7

Oxford, immemorial city of dreaming spires, dreamt on. Cuckoo-echoing, bell-swarmed, lark-charmed, rook-racked, river-rounded, glacier-spared, earthquake-untouched, fallout-devoid (as Gerard Manley Hopkins, who held a lucrative patent on the hyphen, had so beautifully put it), the city still moved serenely down the long stream of eternity, wrapped as ever in its dank, crystalline, donnish reverie, cocooned as ever in long, slow, euphonious sentences replete with rhythmic, poly-syllabic and multiple adjectives, whilst on every side the livid clouds of apocalypse passed Oxford by.

Almost.

A sharp-eyed don, had such a prodigy existed, might have raised a quizzical eyebrow while perambulating the south edge of Christ Church Meadow – might even have constructed a well-bred antithesis, indicative of mild perturbation, as along the turbid currents of the Isis moved by fits and starts a slow log-jam of corpses from the river's western reaches, paying their final respects to learning before the long graduation of London and the sea.

Another clue lay closer to hand.

The Warden of Judas College sensed that there was something obscurely *wrong* about the atmosphere of tonight's dinner at High Table – but he couldn't pin it down.

'Leadbetter, have you been doctoring the food with your infernal concoctions again?'

'No indeed, Warden,' protested the Regius Professor of Aphrodisiacs.

Then what could it be? Perhaps the port even now being drunk. The previous Warden, a physicist who had been over-impressed by discoveries about parity conservation and its failure on the nuclear level, had decreed that henceforth port should be circulated in a repeatedly randomized direction with only a slight bias to the left. The calculations were entrusted to the Benson and Hedges Lecturer in Mathematics (Judas, an impecunious college, relied heavily on sponsorship), who on bad nights tended to keep the decanter in close orbit round himself. At such times it would never wander further than n places from the Lecturer, where n was the square root of the number of Fellows and guests dining:

the Lecturer offered some glib explanation about this resulting from a statistical phenomenon known as the Drunkard's Walk, but the Warden had a dark suspicion that cause and effect had been confused. But the port distribution seemed equitable tonight . . .

Then perhaps the food had disagreed with him. The dessert had been *Bombe Surprise à la Professor Kurti,* the scientist's famous Inverted Baked Alaska. Its core of brandy-laced jam was selectively microwave-heated (taking advantage of the fact, well known to all gourmets, that alcohol absorbs microwave radiation far more effectively than ice, enabling one to produce such high-tech treats as iced mulled wine). The gush of scalding jam from within a seeming block of ice-cream had moved many a don to surprise, alarm, and agonizing pains in the fillings. Habitués of High Table at Judas could always be recognized by their instinctive distrust of ice-cream, and a tendency to check it out with long probes and pyrometers.

No, the Warden admitted to himself, *my sense of wrongness has some other, deeper cause. Yet what false note has been struck in this perfectly ordinary High Table dinner? Is it, perhaps, too . . . quiet?* Being nine-tenths deaf, he dismissed the delusive thought impatiently.

Beyond the raised, illuminated dais of High Table, the long, full benches of Judas College Hall stretched away in silence through scholarly twilight. Not a whisper or clink of cutlery came from the solemnly gowned figures in the body of the hall. What the Warden had subconsciously noted was the barely detectable absence of raucous conversation, loud and merry vomiting, rugby songs, the playful crossfire of time-hardened bread rolls . . . in short, the undergraduates.

Oxford had already fallen. Not so much as a croquet ball or a college tortoise stirred in all the chequered expanse of its dispopulated quadrangles. In every toilet of every college staircase, a sickening sight awaited matutinal scouts and cleaners. The hall's long benches were filled with rows of gowned skeletons, each nodding to each across the crested but untouched plates and silverware, each superglued in its place. Judas High Table was now the final bastion of living academia: partly because prowling lemmings had not as yet negotiated the high step to the dais, and partly thanks to a quirk of college regulations.

The Fellows of Judas would have nothing to do with new-fangled gimmicks: they chafed immoderately about this traditional idiosyncrasy, but such (as the Hovis Professor of Legal History had dryly quipped) were the rules. Water closets were deemed a passing fad, and the Fellows' rooms at Judas remained the chief employment of the last night-soil collector to ply his trade in Oxford. Thus the way was blocked to the ravaging symbiotes. Thus, unwittingly, Judas High Table had so far been spared.

Didn't I read something like this in a book once? mused the Warden.

8

Other tremors of doom continued to reverberate . . .

Ponderously the Earth flipped end-for-end on its axis . . .

Giant psychokinetic and carnivorous insects stalked from the South American jungles, followed by a reserve force of man-eating plants whose killer instincts made them go for the crotch (they had mutated from the Venus Fly-Trap) . . .

All-Knowing Zen and Sufi masters exchanged cryptic,

meaningful observations: 'The sound of no hands clapping.' 'The Tao is silent.' 'I told you so.'

A tiny black hole, accidentally created by the mental twisting of space involved in Dr Lucius Apricot's final and incredibly potent thought experiment, plummeted to the centre of gravity of the Earth itself: it brooded there, beginning the long, slow gobbling process which could eventually suck all Earth's substance into a sphere no bigger than a marble . . .

The first deadly wavefronts of the Sirius supernova explosion neared our Solar System . . .

A feisty new AIDS mutation began to spread, transmitted by mere contact even at second hand (such as through the postal system) . . .

In North America, the legendary Bigfoot tested his first crude thermonuclear device and primitive ICBM/MIRV delivery mechanism . . .

Nobody took much notice, really . . .

Except Death, who is having an identity crisis.

Having at last briefly managed to tune the recalcitrant *aurora borealis* and display candid-camera pictures from a certain New York skyscraper, he is wondering:

Why does he, an impersonal manifestation of total evil and inexorable doom, have the hots for luscious, brilliant mathematician Dr Lise Panther?

9

'I was just wondering what happened to our physics and Cornish-language experts,' pouted Zenna Brabham, with the ravishingly sulky expression which had inflamed a thousand pupils' first infant lusts, and set their uncertain feet on the primrose path to herpes.

'No time for that!' snapped Bran, feeling masterful again. Psychologists always feel masterful when they've thought of an excellent new reason why you shouldn't follow your natural impulses. 'Get the Team together. This is urgent – Junior is registering!'

Looking uncertainly down at the writhing figure of Junior Finkelstein, Zenna asked: 'You mean like a movie screen test? He's registering terror, or delirium, or epilepsy, or something? He may be a cute kid, but he's not a very convincing actor . . .'

A pink, foam-flecked bubble grew from Junior's lips; as they watched in alarm, it popped and three tortured words emerged: '*Loams . . . Evil . . . Catastrophe!*'

'Now isn't that good,' beamed Zenna. 'He never was able to pronounce "catastrophe". Guess he's been keeping up with his studies!'

The door was flung open; Bjørgstrøm strode in. 'Something's happening!' he barked. 'In the Loams' room. Something evil . . . catastrophic!'

'Gee,' said Bran. 'I must just jot this down in the notebook of successful psychic observations which although a hardened sceptic I have begun to keep.' He added a brief memo, just after the entry about Junior's uncanny ability to foam at the mouth and blow bubblegum at the same time, a feat beyond most politicians' talents.

Pert-kneed Joyce Abramowitz, hot-tongued Lise Panther and frisky-cheeked Nadia Finkelstein were already standing in the litter of the Loams' door, peering fearfully at the tableau within. The air of the room was no longer air but a murky, impenetrable jelly, as though space itself had thickened and swelled, inflamed by some feverish battle between spiritual disease and spiritual antibodies: a ghastly, metaphysical boil on the delicate epidermis of space/time as we know it. Through the hellish miasma, shafts of chilly white and hot red radiance flared and

235

coruscated, outlining two shadowy forms embedded in the murk like flies in ointment.

'These are interesting symptoms,' Bran announced cautiously.

'Smells like a mound of century-old lemming droppings mingled with butyl mercaptan,' whispered Abramowitz, wrinkling her delightfully tip-tilted nose.

'Despite my lack of practical experience,' said Bjørgstrøm, 'I think I can positively identify this as the climate of hell itself!'

Not to be outdone, Panther added: 'As a mathematician I may be able to give valuable advice on the construction of pentacles.'

And through some psychoacoustic freak, a soundless voice emanated from the inner pandemonium: *Happen I can't hold out much longer. Only a few buggering shots left in holy-water pistol . . .*

Panther took the initiative and clapped her hands decisively. 'Right! This is clearly a cusp point of the entire mathematical model representing the "Earthdoom Catastrophe" – the point at which the material and spiritual disaster-graphs cross. Kind of like points on a railway, only at the same time kind of different. Decisive action now *might* just reverse the whole pattern of destruction!'

'So long as it doesn't involve more matter transmission . . .' said Nadia Finkelstein wearily.

'Tough luck, Nadia,' winked Panther. 'To the lab, everyone.'

Since he was in a different room, nobody noticed that Junior, exactly as Panther clapped her hands, had emitted a long stream of luminous bubbles which drifted frantically about before bursting with cries of *No! No! No!* Ninety-nine per cent of his mental power was devoted to blocking off the ravages of Antichrist: he hadn't even enough left over for normal consciousness, but with every fibre of his being he still tried to project his hopeless message . . .

The lab work took twenty minutes. Psychic shockwaves reverberated from the mini-Armageddon raging between the possessed Loams: whenever they did, all the knobs and dials in Bran's laboratory jerked convulsively to settings like 0.666, while any tool shaped even vaguely like a cross tended to shatter into impalpable dust. Despite these minor setbacks, the experimental MT apparatus was realigned almost exactly as it had been for Tompion's ill-fated vanishing. Junior, now dribbling and unconscious, was strapped into the 'electric chair'. Only one change was made: the gadget's mass-intake was (according to Panther) redirected by a jury-rigged antenna of concentric pentacles aimed squarely at the Loams' bedroom.

'It'll never work,' snarled Bran, miffed that he'd again lost the initiative. Why wouldn't they let him tackle the whole problem by psychoanalysis?

'*Doom!*' cried Junior, from the stygian depths of his mysterious coma.

'Let me tell you my theory,' soothed Panther, brushing back a sensual strand of hair which had strayed out of her hot-pants. 'We hypothesize that poor darling Professor Tompion was displaced in time by a backlash effect. We can take advantage of this – using the same effect to eliminate the present psychic disaster-node. My mathematical model suggests that this raging spiritual energy can be interpreted as mass (thanks to Einstein's famous joke $E = mc^2$) and shunted harmlessly into eternity. We can flip the balance of doom! This is the time of decision!'

And you're about to make the wrong one, thought Junior hazily; since the words never actually reached his lips, they went unheard save by two far-off Tibetan sages

237

– one of whom leant toward the other and, nodding, summed up the perilous situation in six cryptic words meaningful only to sages. ('The wise man avoids fried foods.')

Wow, Zenna Brabham was thinking, *I can't wait to write to Mom in Ohio and tell her I've been in the same apartment as the Beast 666. Will she be impressed!* Then – not for nothing was she arguably the finest schoolmarm which Western civilization had yet produced – her eyes clouded over and her jaunty mammaries heaved in gorgeous alarm. As in a dream she saw before her a page from Graham Flegg's *Numbers: their History and Meaning,* which she'd recently used while giving the second grade their initial lessons in *gematria.* Could it be that 666 was a false trail – that all this was misguided, even though brilliant Dr Apricot had mathematically proven it to her Smurf mascot only yesterday? Flegg had explained how 'Nero Caesar' could be interpreted as 666; that later writers including John Napier had argued that 666 referred to the Pope, only for an improbably named Jesuit (Father Bongus) to show it actually meant Martin Luther, while later thinkers preferred to pin it on the Kaiser or Adolf Hitler. Then had come the sentence which now rocked the foundations of her world:

However, as it is possible that the original Greek text of *Revelation* reads 'Six hundred and sixteen' and was altered later, many of these efforts may have been somewhat misdirected.

But it was too late to interrupt. The controls were already set, precisely as before. The marijuana cookies had been ritually gobbled, precisely as before. The long red second-hand swept finally towards the twelve, and under her breath Panther began the countdown.

'. . . six *(they don't know my real hope)* . . . five *(that either the MT will take me as it took Mark, and I can go find him) . . .* four *(or some kind of exchange phenomenon will bounce him back to here and now) . . .* three *(even if it means he exchanges places with me – funny, never thought of myself as a heroine) . . .* two *(I don't think even Nadia spotted my faked-up math – but why's Zenna looking at me like that?) . . .* one *(losing Mark made me realize I kind of) . . .* zero *(love . . . him) . . .'*

And she pulled the lever down with all her might.

Almost instantaneously, nothing happened.

There was a brief period of silence, while Junior stirred fitfully, and each person in the lab surreptitiously counted all the others, until the internal phone rang.

'Another damned block of fablundium,' came Bjørgstrøm's bored voice down the line. 'If the economy still existed, and fablundium was actually worth anything, we could open a profitable little shop . . . Any absentees?'

'Not that we've noticed,' said Panther cautiously. *Nor any surprise visitors either . . . damn it.* But now she saw that on the mighty control panel, every dial that had flickered at 666 had fallen back to zero.

In the Loams' room they found Jeb and Rachel Loam in what seemed to be deep and tranquil slumber. Tranquil, that is, save for the trifling fact that Jeb (whose hair had turned dead white with a worrying hint of blue rinse) was hanging trapeze-fashion from the wardrobe door, while Rachel (on whose forehead the numerals 666 could be seen in slowly fading crimson) was arranged on the bed in a pose that made Zenna blush and Bran get very sentimental and reminiscent about a former patient whom all his efforts had never quite cured of nymphomania. The remnants of what might have been a cardboard box had apparently suffered a charge of thermite, while on every wall, appalling runes in laser-incised pokerwork hinted at eldritch and forbidden 'knock knock' jokes with which the impious hand of Man was never meant to meddle.

'All back to normal,' said Bran cheerfully, forcibly reminding the others that fashionable psychiatrists had to take a pretty liberal view of normality. Especially in New York.

Zenna and Nadia were soon serving root beer and chocolate chip cookies in celebration of what might be the turning point of the disaster sequence, while Panther brooded in silent exhaustion and Bjørgstrøm demonstrated his new party trick of converting UHT milk to yoghurt by twitching one corner of his mouth by half a degree.

'A toast,' said Bran optimistically. 'To what may be – the end of it all!' As the glasses were raised . . .

'*You did it wrong!*'

Stumbling through the door came the small, pudgy and tearful figure of Junior Finkelstein, accompanied by a chill of nameless dread and a faint aroma which reminded Zenna that she should really have taken him to the little boys' room before that experiment.

'The end,' Bran repeated feebly. 'Don't worry, son . . . Have a grass and chocolate chip cookie.'

The awesome fact that Junior was not distracted even by chocolate chip cookies crystallized a general feeling that perhaps something might be very, very wrong . . . even apart from the minor point that no one had yet got round to looking for Apricot and Patella.

'Not the end, *the start*!' shrieked Junior, red in the face. '*You just started it all!*'

Only the rose-complexioned Panther, with that swift intuition so common among sensuously beautiful woman mathematicians who are secretly far gone in love, grasped even a hint of his terrible, paradoxical meaning.

10

Look back. Look back through time and space, which over these immense vistas tend to get snarled up with each other anyway. On a clear day you can see forever, so maybe if the interstellar dust and chronic fog should thin a little, you might for one stark moment see clear back to the beginning.

It's crowded at the beginning. A small, seventy-five kilogram disturbance is only the start of it. Thanks to the folly of those who've, as it were, fed foreign coins into the mighty one-armed bandit of Time, Tompion is not long alone at the mathematical point in space/time from which a Universe is to blossom. Something else shares what we might call the same space, if only there were any space yet. In that unimaginable micro-instant before the Big Bang (if only there were any instants before the Big Bang), before he can so much as get his bearings (if only there were any directions in which to move or bearings to get), Tompion feels *something else* coalesce with him, like an immense, affectionate slug crawling into the same confining straitjacket:

Knock, knock . . .
Who's there? wonders Tompion.
You . . .
You and who else?
UNIVERSE! Ha ha ha . . .

And then it is the Big Bang and all very traumatic, and Tompion doesn't remember much more. Nothing, not even matter, not even the tiniest nuts and bolts of the intricate DIY kit which is matter, can survive the Big Bang, but Tompion more or less manages to pull through, being now intermingled with the unspeakable psychic vortex which was the Antichrist (plus Reuben and Nathan as supporting cast, additional dialogue by the Beast 666), and which Lise Panther's genius or folly has projected back with him to the Beginning.

There's nothing like company.

Or, as it were, symbiosis.

The first interesting stuff about Creation is over very quickly: stable nuclei start forming as soon as space is cool enough, in about fourteen seconds. Free neutrons more or less vanish at the three-minute mark, and most of the other important changes have run their course in half an hour or so, when the cosmos becomes a Nuclear Free Zone as spontaneous nuclear processes stop happening.

During the following 700,000 years, while the Universe cools to the point where your actual stable *atoms* can begin to form and stay formed, Tompion/666 has a lot of time to think and very little to think about. He looks different now, as would you if you'd picked up your tan at a time when all of space was at a cosy 100,000,000,000,000 degrees Kelvin. He doesn't remember too much about that first 700,000 years, or even the billions more years which follow, during which protogalaxies, galaxies, stars, planets, atmospheres, life, intelligence and income tax pop up in their inimitable, inevitable way.

He thinks he may have got through it by inventing and telling himself 'knock knock' jokes.

Only floating memory-shards of a former existence remain with him, like those odd keys on a key-ring which open locks no longer fitted to the doors of houses one no longer lives in. After long, forced symbiosis with immortal Evil, both the Tompion mind and the Tompion body are . . . changed. Luckily mirrors will not be invented for a long time yet.

Some dim, unremembered homing instinct brings him to Earth, where the first flush of life in the teeming, shallow seas reminds him rather nostalgically of something. He wades into the water for a closer look, and a dozen terrified proto-amphibians immediately leap out, each straining to be the first to develop good, fast legs (the lungs can wait a bit longer, they unanimously decide).

After sulking for a number of millennia, he looks around him again to discover a steaming swampland populated by huge, terrible lizards. A brontosaurus negligently steps on him. In a fit of pique he snaps his fingers in the general direction of the sky: by and by an Earth-grazing asteroid takes a wrong turn, smashes into Earth's tortured crust in a retaliatory way, brings on a new Ice Age, and kills off all the dinosaurs. *That was kind of fun,* he thinks dimly.

His first encounter with primitive Man leads to a spontaneous mass realization that the recently invented cricket bat can be also used as a weapon to try and beat terrible strangers to death. He tries to zap the enraged mob with a lightning bolt, but hasn't yet perfected his aim, and instead hits a nearby tree. Distracted, the tribe turns aside to speculate on uses for the strange, hot, red flowers licking up from the wood. Retreating for another long sulk, he wonders whether he is making any difference to this world's evolution, and considers peaceful coexistence.

However, the Emperor of Atlantis makes an unforgivable joke about his complexion, with consequences well known to twentieth-century science.

He drifts on through history, going under many names: the Wandering Jew (despite a small voice inside which insists he is not Jewish and has hated bagels since long before they were invented), Melmoth, Vanderdecken (which had to stop when that fool Wagner wrote a musical about him), the Man in the Iron Mask, the Oracle at Delphi, the Elephant Man, John Grant . . . He doesn't much like the name superstitious folk give him, but that's showbiz.

Generally he's reclusive, amusing himself with occasional plagues, earthquakes, fires (something about the number of the year makes him very bad-tempered in 1666), hurricanes, volcanoes and Conservative governments. Once in a while he comes out of the closet for an incognito chat with somebody who's in one sense or another blind: he tells the story of his life to Milton, fills up Nostradamus with a load of rubbish invented (so he believes) on the spot, and inspires rather too much of Poe.

(Milton later wrote:

> . . . Him the Almighty Power
> Hurl'd headlong flaming from the ethereal sky
> With hideous ruin and combustion, down
> To bottomless perdition, there to dwell
> 'Mid adamantine chains and Knock Knock jokes . . .

But afterwards he changed it.)

Then . . . the final quarter of the twentieth century! The period for which, over billions of years, he's been feeling an unknowing nostalgia. Sure enough, in the late '70s a host of strange new feelings begin to course through him. (Does he still have glands? He's never looked.) Something new has come into the world. In fact, Lise Panther has reached puberty.

The torment increases. He is torn by lust without knowing its object. One slender thread of information, though, trickles down the occult grapevine as the clock of the century ticks mercilessly towards 1990.

Somewhere out there is what he's lusted after since the Big Bang, without ever achieving even a little bang.

Somewhere out there, too, is a guy (Professor Mark Tungsten? Mark Tappen? There was a lot of noise on the vine) who is fooling around with the absolute one and only woman . . .

Revenge!

A world which can allow this intolerable situation must . . . pay for it! Must be laid waste, must groan at his feet as his acknowledged kingdom!

Earthdoom!

For the first time, he consciously takes to himself the name given him by superstitious peasantry when, disguised as a wandering friar, he tried to earn a little small change by offering to scythe people's lawns.

After almost twenty billion years, Death still has the hots for Lise Panther.

11

BLAM! The third-floor windows of the skyscraper are blown in by the first aquatic attack wave of maddened vampires and werewolves, eager to wreak untold havoc and carnage amid security men, secretaries, technicians and other characters not required for the denouement . . .

BLAM! Air rushes fatally from the *Mary Poppins* as events on board take a far from foreseen turn . . .

BLAM! In the bridge of the *Libertarian* (formerly the Los Angeles SF Society clubhouse), Captain Pelz winces at the apocalyptic launch blast which flattens LA; he has time to make a note in his official Trip Report book during the brief pause before the unique Orion drive's second *BLAM!*

BLAM! The CHANCRE research establishment detonates in an explosion equivalent to the simultaneous spraying of enough fluorocarbon aerosols to stretch to Pluto: far above, Earth's tattered ozone layer cringes in anticipation . . .

BLAM! Willing at first to parley, the Hitlers lose their collective tempers and let fly with concealed Lugers – at the realization that the unmistakable evidence of their names marks these 'Cygnans' as, in fact, Jewish!

BLAM! With a grossly melodramatic thunderclap of displaced air, Death materializes awesomely on the New York skyscraper's top floor. 'Missed,' he snarls, and begins to look for the fire stairs.

BLAM! Bigfoot ruefully blames his large, clumsy fingers (so awkward at setting tiny adjustment screws) for the fact that his peaceful test nuke has inadvertently hit Washington and precipitated World War III.

BLAM! Using a little known climatological karate trick, Gwynfor Bjørgstrøm bursts in the locked door of Apricot's laboratory and gapes at what he sees.

BLAM! is by no means the sound heard as Comrade Adrianna Dimpla's puny revolver is discharged at the mighty Cygnan mother-ship, either because it isn't in fact discharged or because, of course, in space no one can hear you *BLAM!* . . .

7

D-E-A-T-H Spells 'DEATH'

He was wearing a plaid jacket, porkpie hat, carried a raincoat
and wore a camera around his neck, like an ordinary American
tourist. As with all Watchers, the hat, jacket and raincoat were
soft and reversible, providing six combinations.
 – Frederick Forsyth, *The Fourth Protocol*, 1984

Nothing puzzles me more than time and space; and yet nothing
puzzles me less, as I never think about them.
 – Charles Lamb

1

Officer Hotchkiss gunned his big, black gleaming Honda
90 down New York's Broadway, opening up the throttle
and hitting the engine for all it was worth. The result was
a surge of speed to nearly seven knots – the big machine
never had worked at its best underwater. Come to that,
neither had he. He was experiencing some discomfort,
not just because of the lack of oxygen but because he'd
swallowed several gallons of water and his bladder was
bursting. He was reluctant to stop and find a tramp
somewhere to urinate against (as a small-town policeman
he had *standards*, goddammit: there was no *way* he was
going to piss against a lamppost like an animal), because
that would have involved exposing his generative organ –
briefly and only partially, to be sure, but it's better to be
safe. As he was beginning to realize, in the sad sequence

of events which had overtaken the Earth and all its inhabitants no male member was safe.

To take his mind off the pressure, he did his best to concentrate instead on the possibilities of there being a solution to Earth's problems. 'Never did see a problem that didn't have a solution, somehow,' his old station chief had been fond of saying. 'Most times it ain't too hard to find. Youth problem? – I shoot the bastids. Nigger problem? – shoot the bastids. One-parent-family problem? – same thing.' Then the old man would bow his white-grizzled head and giggle with homespun wisdom.

The young Hotchkiss had listened carefully, even though outwardly he'd pretended to be as casual as all the other cops in the briefing room. And he'd taken the words seriously – even after that sad day when Chiefy had been told by his doctor that he had a heart problem. The trouble was that, as far as he could see, there were very few things around right now to shoot. The shoals of mackerel were just too damned elusive, and the one shark he'd come across – with its curiously overdeveloped teeth – had seemed to be totally unaffected by the six bullets he'd put through it. And now his gun had become waterlogged and wouldn't work any longer. For the first time in his adult life it seemed that he would be unable to rely on Chiefy's wisdom.

If Hotchkiss had been a religious man, he would probably have prayed right then; but he wasn't and so he didn't. Besides, things seemed to be changing around him. The water surface above was showing a rainbow effusion of livid colours, as if somewhere nearby a sky-scraper was lighting up in apocalyptic fashion as the Antichrist fought for survival, every one of the building's windows a different colour in a dazzling (not to mention coruscating) display of supernatural pyrotechnics. More-over, just up ahead he could see a great mass of furry

248

jostling bodies, as if some pioneer had invented the ultimate dog-whistle and had just given it a first experimental blast. But those weren't dogs, as Hotchkiss could now see. At first he had taken them for German Shepherds, but now it was patent that they were . . . ommigod, *wolves*. But not just normal wolves: these ones seemed all to be partly dressed. Ripped garments, cruelly torn as if they had suddenly been expected to conform to a shape for which they had never been designed, adhered to the wolves' eagerly milling bodies. And some of them were carrying ('toting', Hotchkiss's mind corrected) firearms, for all the world as if they were possessed of fully human intelligence.

But intelligence deliberately perverted to foul unholy ends!

Werewolves have had, over the centuries, a pretty unfavourable press: would you like your daughter to marry one, and so forth. But this has been unfair. Werewolves – *normal* werewolves – are very much like you and me: just easy-going, good-natured joes, a little grumpy perhaps on the morning after the night before, but all in all just average peace-loving good guys. And, in a general sense, they're not supernatural in any way: those tales so beloved of the horror-novel writers are just that – tales. Werewolves represent evolution's perfectly natural answer to one of the problems faced in filling every available ecological niche. An organism that is adapted to being human during the daytime – when it can go out and earn itself a decent wage – and vulpine at night – when it can do things a hell of a lot more profitable than worry about why the decent wage it earned during the day just somehow wasn't decent enough – is an obvious evolutionary Good Idea. In fact, this new creature you've invented is a better candidate for filling the ecological niche of Dominant Organism on Planet

Earth (top dog, as it were) than is the species *Homo sapiens*.

Which explained, although Hotchkiss hadn't the scientific training to realize it, the reasons for the scene of unbridled hostility and hatred being played out in part before his awestruck eyes. For centuries now the werewolves had been fully aware of their evolutionary potential: they were to inherit the mantle of Dominant Organism when finally it was shucked off Man's unworthy shoulders. However, being amiable and superhumanly compassionate, wise creatures, they had seen no reason to hurry the process along: they were content with peaceful coexistence for however many millennia were necessary for the change to be effected gradually. But now, but now . . . it seemed that the Earth would be utterly destroyed before they had had a chance to come into their birthright! And who was responsible?

Death had come across a pack of them baying furiously about the issue in a moonlit clearing in Transylvania some weeks back, and his fertile brain had instantly realized that here was an opportunity to exploit their justifiable fury for his own vengeful purposes. He had watched their debate for a few moments secretly, his brain (if brain it was) buzzing energetically; and then, with a few gratuitous flashes of lightning followed by appropriate claps of thunder, he had materialized dramatically in the centre of their gathering.

'You seek a villain in this piece,' he had said, holding up one strangely misformed hand to silence their whining howls of astonishment. 'Well,' he had continued, 'the answer is surely obvious to you – if you will only think about it. Who else could it have been but . . . *Man*! But what you don't know is which particular snivelling collection of craven humans were ultimately responsible for the forthcoming annihilation of Earth and all things terrestrial. I can tell you that.'

He had paused for dramatic effect.

'Meet me in New York City in a month's time and I will even point them out to you!' he had said, and a chorus of eagerly bloodcurdling yowls of assent had filled the night air. Timing his moment to perfection, he had vanished as enigmatically as he had arrived, leaving behind only a retina-scarring image of himself, twice life-sized (as it were), which slowly faded away into the chilly forest blackness.

Hotchkiss, of course, knew none of this: all he knew was that he was within a few feet of a pack of seething werewolves; the one small mercy was that they had yet to master the art of howling underwater. Still, he didn't much like the look of all those gas-bubbles floating upwards towards the water's surface. *I've gotta get outta here*, he thought to himself. *And fast!*

But how?

The only way seemed to be upwards – the big bike could never achieve more than a few knots down here. In fact, he sadly recognized, the big bike had had it. It had served him for many years now, ever since he had been a rookie, and he was sad to see it go. *Well, old partner . . .* he thought to himself sentimentally; but then he thought instead: *What the shit am I getting emotional over a goddam hunk of metal for, when I should be getting the hell out of here?* Automatically, his spinal cord added a reflexive: *And fast!*

The surface of the water was fully fifty feet above him – a problem to which his nervously strained bladder had just added – and it seemed a heck of a long way away. Besides, he couldn't swim. His mind went back to those long hours he had spent as a child splashing around in waterwings and rubber rings, never able to remove such aids and carry himself unsupported in the water. He had had to confine his seashore activities to kicking sand in people's faces. Now he wished that he'd tried a little harder to . . . *My God! That was it! Rubber rings!*

In moments he was off the big bike and frantically pulling open its toolbox. Mere milliseconds after that he was down on his knees, his skilled spanner hard at work on the bike's wheel-hubs. It seemed like light-years but it can only have been quintillions before he had the wheels off the bike, the tyres off the wheels, and the inner tubes out of the tyres. Thank some wise providence that he'd had the foresight to pump some air in them back in Phoenix (or had it been Nashville?) so that now they were still taut and full, not flaccid and empty-seeming like so many other things nervously were these days.

He lost his hat getting one of the inner tubes slung around his body, but he didn't care. The other tube he held protectively against his chest. He proceeded to squeeze it with all his might until the rubber threatened to rupture. Then he put his right hand round to the lowest point of the tube's circumference (still squeezing powerfully with his left) and shot his fortunately razor-sharp index fingernail into the tormented rubber.

In a great stream of angrily foaming bubbles, Officer Hotchkiss shot upwards, up through the water and hundreds of feet into the air. At the very highest point of his trajectory he saw beneath him the roof of a skyscraper, where a hauntingly familiar figure was making its way unknowingly towards the fire stairs. Hotchkiss closed his eyes as his body began inexorably to accelerate back towards the distant Earth.

The impact came a lot sooner than he had expected, and did a lot less damage. He lay there, tangled in wet rubber, for a moment or two before he dared reluctantly to open his eyes. His fall had been broken by what he at first assumed to be a heap of foul-smelling clothing which someone had left lying around, for some inscrutable reason, on the skyscraper's roof. But then the bundle of clothes moved, and a face emerged from it. Hotchkiss's gaze was drawn relentlessly to the eyes in that face. The pupils were thin vertical lines, and fl :ne was flashing from them – in a concentrated silence that was more spine-wrenching than any crackling or hissing could have been.

'Say buddy,' said Hotchkiss, reaching reflexively for his now useless gun, 'haven't I seen you someplace before?'

2

'Brothers,' ejaculated Captain Sc'smv, holding up her/its/some*when*'s knotted alimentary canal in order to gain attention amidst the gallons of excited anticipation being excreted in the great Mother Ship's main conference hall. 'I have called this Emergency General Meeting to discuss the problem of the Earthlings now infesting our vessel.'

'Point of procedure!' osculated Ch'rspr'st immediately. He/me had always been a troublemaker at meetings, reflected the Captain wearily.

'Yes, Ch'rspr'st, he/me/you have the floor.'

'Point of order!' rattled another bucketful of intestinal fluids at the back.

The Captain, again wearily, recognized the splatter: it was J'nkkls. 'Go ahead, J'nkkls.'

'Why should Ch'rspr'st have the floor? Surely we should all have a share of it?' Bile washed to the edges of the conference chamber, where the disposal units strained their last resources.

'We can *all* have a share of it, J'nkkls,' Sc'smv oozed,

'but one after the other. At the moment Ch'rspr'st can have his/my share, and then afterwards you/they can have you/theirs.'

'But that's not fair!' eructated J'nkkls. 'Why should he/me have his/my share of it *first*? Surely we should *all* have first turn of it. Or, at least, surely the subject of who gets first turn should be put to the vote.'

'I'll/it'll vote for it if you/they will vote for me/it,' chipped in the diminutive form of E'nwts'n. As usual, however, no one paid too much attention.

'Further point of procedure,' expectorated Ch'rspr'st . . . but by this time Sc'smv was no longer listening. *It's always the bloody same,* it/she thought. *You try to get something done in a hurry and the whole meeting is constipated by these 'hard-liners' and their ridiculous, trivial points of order. The Great Spong alone knows what they hope to achieve by it. Certainly it/I don't. We'll still be sitting here debating whether or not to go through the minutes of the last meeting after the Earthlings have taken over the ship. And then, of course, it'll all be my fault, and we'll have another meeting to discuss a motion of censure, and then . . . Oh, by the sacred meatus of L'ngfd'r, why the hell did it/I ever let them elect me Captain?*

Its/her thoughts were scattered by the door to the great chamber being thrown open. Brandishing his Luger maniacally, a Hitler rocketed into the room, slithered with his arms flailing for a heart-stopping moment, and then vanished with a despairing wail into a six-foot-deep puddle of amendments to the general constitution. Cygnan relief – that this suddenly appearing menace had as suddenly disappeared – flooded the room.

'However,' flexed Captain Sc'smv firmly, masterfully taking command of the meeting once more, 'we cannot expect fortune to treat us as kindly when the next intruder gets here. Or the one after that. We must somehow cut through all this red tape and get to the point at *schlpp*. It/ I suggest we ignore the points of procedure put up by brothers Ch'rspr'st and J'nkkls and try instead to decide what should be done about the Earthling threat!'

'I have an interpolative amendment to propose on that,' gushed E'nwts'n enthusiastically.

It/I could have been a ceiling effectuator, the Captain mused.

3

'Gosh, Lucius,' simpered Avedon Patella, 'you never told me you wore a toupee.'

'Well,' the world-renowned particle physicist said with a youthful, boyish blush, 'the subject just never seemed to come up. Besides, I wanted you to have a romantic image of me, not to be confronted by the . . .'

'Don't say it,' giggled Avedon. 'Look – all that's left is the label.' She picked up the charred piece of leather with her exquisitely contoured fingers. '"Titanic Hairpiece Corporation," it says here. "Not to be taken orally."'

There was an imperative *rat-a-tat-tat!* at the door.

'Tush,' said Lucius.

'Are you in there?' came Nadia Finkelstein's elegantly configurated (albeit on this occasion perhaps a trifle shrill) tones.

'I might have been, in another couple of minutes,' muttered Apricot.

'Yes!' trilled Avedon, with a 'sorry, dearest, but business comes first' expression appreciatively wandering across the fleshly perfection of her face. 'We'll be with you in a moment. Say – what's the matter? What's happened *this* time? And anyway, shouldn't that have been *"knock, knock"*?'

'Oh, fer chrissakes,' said Nadia Finkelstein, but she rapped her knuckles on the door again, this time producing a satisfactory *knock, knock*.

'Who's there?' cried Avedon Patella, with a mentally sophisticated chuckle.

'Nadia.'

'Nadia who?'

'Nadia Finkelstein, you dumb assholes. Can you open up this door?'

'I thought she was going to say "Nadia Ears Washed Out?",' said Apricot sadly, clambering into his underpants.

'Just a sec,' said Patella. 'We've just got one or two hypotheses to confirm.'

'Confirm, schmonfirm,' said Nadia Finkelstein. 'We need every expert we can get ahold of – and, like, fast. If not faster.'

'Well, blast it, what's the matter?' said Apricot, squeezing with difficulty into his Bod-EE-Line Shape-Improver.

'Whazza matter? Why, *every* goddam thing's the matter,' Nadia Finkelstein blurted. 'We thought everything was going A-OK until Junior warned us that . . . well, that it wasn't; and until Gwynfor Bjørgstrøm saw what the hell was happening in your laboratory upstairs!'

'Another of Junior's dire predictions, no doubt,' said Apricot merrily. 'Why can't he be like all the other psychics and predict something cheerful for a change? What was it this time? – only fourteen shopping days 'til Christmas, or something? Don't tell me – I don't really want to know.'

'He says that we've accidentally initiated the final Armageddon, you dumb lunk,' snapped Nadia furiously.

'Knock, knock,' giggled Avedon felinely.

'Who's there?' responded Apricot dutifully.

'Armageddon.' She was beginning to eye his zip in reassuring fashion again.

'Armageddon who?'

'Armageddon a bit pissed off with the way Junior keeps telling us that the end of the world is nigh. How about some *news* for a change?'

'You can laugh!' Nadia Finkelstein howled furiously through the door.

Oh, no, thought Apricot, *this is the last thing we need: dissent among our own ranks. We've got to be all together on this one.* So, in order to spread oil on boiling waters he said: 'OK, so just what *has* been happening in my lab? Don't say we've started having spontaneous matter transmission?'

'No, nothing as serious as that. It just seems that *something* you've been doing in there has had the effect of beginning to screw up reality. We're not sure as yet exactly how it works – and so far we've seen nothing of the effects – but an off-the-wall ballpark analysis suggests that a beam of concentrated reality-randomizing factors was emitted in a quantitatively indeterminable direction just a few hours ago.'

'Not a – uh, kind of – laser beam?' said Apricot seriously.

'No – Jeez! Why should it have been that? All we can guess is that it was a pair of photons, oppositely polarized.'

Apricot groaned inwardly: the news relentlessly thrust his memory back to the ideas that had been bustling through his mind before Avedon had come surging into the bedroom where he had been conducting his thought experiments.

Every particle physicist worth his salt (and we all know about the definition of the word 'salary') had heard of the

infamous pair of oppositely polarized photons. No one –
by definition – had ever actually captured a pair of them
(as the theory had it, you could know either *where* they
were or *what* they were, but not both at the same time),
but many a time and oft the world's most distinguished
physicists would awaken from their inscrutable dreams in
the wee small hours and mutter about the independently
polarized pair.

Imagine that you take a pair of photons. Photons, shall
we say, can wiggle in one of two directions, vertically and
horizontally. (Of course, those aren't the directions at
all, but we're aiming for simplicity here.) If you take one
photon that's wiggling horizontally and flick it off in one
direction, and another photon that's wiggling vertically
and flick it off in the other direction, you naturally expect
that the two will retain the directions in which they're
wiggling right through until they either decay (into π-
mesons) or reach the Heat Death of the Universe. But it
just don't work out that way – if (and it's a big *if*) you
happen to have the opportunity to stick a polarizing
screen in the way of one of them. Say, for example, you
take the one that was wiggling horizontally and shift it so
that now it's wiggling vertically. Instantaneously, without
any delay due to things like the velocity of light, *the other
particle will be found to be wiggling vertically as well.*
And the same's true the other way around: tamper with
the one that was wiggling vertically so that it starts to
wiggle horizontally, and, as soon as you get over there to
look, you find that the other member of the pair of
independently polarized photons you first started off with
is now doing exactly the same.

Shucks, that's physics for you.

The paradox is a genuinely fundamental one . . . as
Apricot, with his incredibly high-powered academic training, realized only too well. Although the odd photon

whizzing here and there might seem unlikely to effect any general changes on the overall structure of the Universe, such independently polarized pairs *can* – and do. Because . . . well, consider this:

It is obviously impossible for the information to be communicated from one photon to the other that its direction of polarization has been changed; not only would this violate Relativity, because faster-than-light travel would have to be involved, there is also the problem of how the photons would actually *do* their communicating. Miniaturization may have taken great strides, but nobody has yet produced a telephone or walkie-talkie sufficiently small for convenient use by a photon. No, the only possible way for the situation to come about is if, in some essentially incomprehensible fashion, both photons in the pair have somehow *always* been polarized in the 'new' direction. The idea that they were polarized any differently is essentially just a misconception on the part of the experimenter. This is difficult to appreciate – even more so to accept – on the part of normal people, but quantum physicists are accustomed to such stuff.

Now, tall oaks from little photons grow. The change in the direction of a single photon's polarization fundamentally redesigns the very fabric of reality, but it might seem that it does so only on the most trivially minute of scales. Obviously, this is most often the case; but in something with the vastness of the Universe – vastness in both space and time – a minutely small alteration of reality can have colossal consequences by the time a few billion years have passed and the shock-waves of the reality-change have spread out a corresponding few billion light years. (The 'communication' between the photons 'travels' at 'infinite speed', but the shock-waves travel more sedately, at the velocity of light.) You recall the old nursery rhyme in which a kingdom was lost 'and all for the loss of a horse-shoe nail'.

It is rather alarming to realize that the entire pattern of reality is changing the whole time – and that *you* are changing with it. The only consolation is that, for very obvious reasons, you don't know anything about it. According to some fictitious (and theoretically impossible) 'independent observer', it might well be that yesterday you – along with the whole of the rest of the human race – were a purple cabbage with an acne problem, and that your memories of having been a fleshy pink biped all these years are erroneous, but in actual practical fact it doesn't really matter – *because everyone else agrees with the way you remember things*. Stuff the 'independent observer' who thinks we all used to be purple cabbages: he/she's a loonie.

This is all very well in the general way, but *close to the point of emission* of a pair of independently polarized photons one can't be quite so blasé about things. The reality-changes may be pretty small-scale individually, but there are a heck of a lot of them, all happening very rapidly, and their effects tend to accumulate. Quite how drastic the net result of this could be, no one is yet sure: so far as Apricot knew from his studies in the technical journals, no experimenter had yet plucked up the courage to risk generating a photon pair – and indeed the very possibility was legally forbidden in most of the Western nations. It could well be highly dangerous to start littering the place up with alternate universes (because, obviously, each 'new' version of reality, no matter how insignificantly different from its predecessor, creates an alternate universe) – and no one wanted to find out the hard way!

Apricot's brain thudded as he pondered for a second time the implications and hazards of all this. It was perfectly possible, he knew only too well, that that mysterious lightning-flash had in actuality hit a much more sensitive part of him than his toupee (come to think of it, like Avedon, *he* hadn't realized that he wore a toupee, either), but that a subsequent reality-alteration had wiped out that indubitably painful event from the Universe's collective memory. Except, of course, that in some unfathomable alternate universe, Somewhere Else, there would at this very moment be a Professor Lucius Apricot howling with pain, clutching his injured anatomy, and wishing that he weren't doing so at arm's-length.

The idea didn't bear thinking about, so he thought about something else instead. Whatever reality-changes were going on, the *apparent* effect of the independently-polarized-photons scenario was that a message was flashed instantaneously between the two. Might it be that he had been approaching the whole subject of MT from precisely the wrong direction? He had been tackling the problem in a rather outdated way – decide what you want to do and then see if you can do it – whereas the modern approach could possibly be more fruitful: decide on the *effect* that you want to bring about, and then see if you can create the circumstances whereby that *effect* is created! If he could conjure up a device that would alter reality in such a way that the Earth 'had always been' in a different part of the Cosmos altogether, then that was every bit as good as having brought about the same effect by use of instantaneous matter transmission. A purist might say that the two effects were in fact identical, being indistinguishable, but that purist would be wrong, because the two would *not* be indistinguishable at all: in the case of an MT having been used, everybody would remember what had happened, whereas in the alternate-reality scenario everyone would be completely oblivious to the fact that anything had happened at all. In fact, Apricot reflected ruefully, this was one serious drawback of the new approach he was considering: no one would know that *he* was the saviour of the world. No flocks of nubile lovelies would be pounding on his door and in his bed, night and day. He would have to get his Nobel Prize for something else. He might still have Avedon to nurture him, but it was possible that Avedon – in the new reality – might be a purple cabbage with an acne problem. All in all, he thought that Avedon in her current, histrionically curvaceous form was probably a heck of a lot more fun.

That's enough thinking, he thought. *It's time for a bit of action.*

As he ran for the door, though, he did permit a final thought to scurry with the subtle scampering of a fairy's feet across the veneer of his conscious mind. *In fact, I've rather come to the conclusion that matter transmission by any other means is completely impossible!*

He was not to know that, only a few miles above his head, he was being proved wrong.

4

'My friends in the bowels of the Lord!' bellowed the Reverend Rick Hamfist into the microphone. The huge astrodome of Dayton, Ohio, was packed out with over 150,000 swaying figures who moved their bodies rhythmically in time to the words that boomed at them through the sound system. Only a few weeks ago the Reverend had been a minority cult figure, his adherents numbered in the tens, at best. But recently, since all these signs that Armageddon was upon the world, his following had swollen, and swollen. With any luck, he mused to himself while waiting the necessary five minutes for the echoes to die away, he now had more disciples than that bastard

the Reverend Hunk Brady, whose oleaginous counten-
ance and insincere pseudo-charm had, in the old days,
filled the television screen every week and reminded *him*,
Hamfist, that he was something of an also-ran in the
revivalist stakes. It had been the same back at drama
college, where he and Brady had attended Practical
Evangelism together: somehow, whatever they were
doing, Brady would pip him to the post. Anyone else
might have been happy always to take the second prize,
but not Rick Hamfist – no sirree! Especially since there
were only two students in the class.

But now, he gloated, things had changed. *Wish you
could see me now, Brady, you garbage-eater!* he thought
viciously, and cuddled himself gleefully. *Oops, the echoes
have nearly disappeared.*

'The evil that we see is the evil that we do!' he roared,
and the marks swayed their approval.

*What really puts the shine on the ointment is that all
these cretins keep me rolling in the good old greenstuff,* he
thought, lighting a cigarette. (The best part of these really
big rallies was that no one was close enough to see what
the fuck you were doing in between sentences. He'd
once, just for the hell of it, laid a couple of student
nurses during a sermon on the nature of hypocrisy, and
no one had noticed – except, possibly, the student nurses.)
*I don't even have to invest in getting appeals printed: they
just seem to expect that they're supposed to bankrupt
themselves by sending all their capital to me. The Lord
looks after those who look after themselves, as I've always
said, so who am I not to rip off a few million credulous
bumheads who think I'll show them the way to get into
God's good books? Say, there's an idea. I could make a
few extra megabucks if I . . . it's about time someone
published another testament. The other two are beginning
to get really goddam dated!*

'When sin is among us we should sing Hallelujah!' he thundered, and then returned to his thoughts. *I can see it now: come publication day I should actually start being invited to appear on legit TV for a goddam change. Johnny Carson will be letting me tell a few theological jokes. Jeez. And I bet all the girls will be impressed . . . though it's hard to see how I could fit in more of them (interesting turn of phrase, that) than I already do. Lemme see now, whaddami gonna call this masterwork? It's a pity 'The New Testament' has already been used . . . I guess I could go for the upfront, hard-sell approach: 'The All-New IMPROVED Testament'. Say, I like the sound of that!*

'So I say unto he who is without sin: "Repent"!' he shouted into the microphone, but his mind was on this fantastic new money-spinning idea of his. *Although the real bullet in the pastry is that that bastard Hunk Brady has never published a goddam whole goddam testament! He's gonna eat his booze-rotting heart out over this one when he sees me stuck there in the numero uno position on the goddam* New York Times *bestseller list! It won't be him being the one who gets all the classy groupies on the ol' revivalist circuit any more! Yeah – it's gonna be Also-ran Brady for a goddam change . . .*

Just then the sky lit up in great washes and waterfalls of brilliant colours, creating millions of random patterns of coruscating flashes and sparks. But only for a moment. Then order was created out of chaos, and the Reverend Rick Hamfist – and his 150,000 dumbfounded Dayton, Ohio, followers as well – saw a miles-high, full-colour hologram of the Reverend Hunk Brady, his silvery locks of wisdom flirting with the stratosphere, breaking into a horizon-stretching unctuous smile.

'Repent, for the world is at hand!' boomed this apparition, and as it did so the Reverend Rick Hamfist's heart sank leadenly and without trace . . .

'Is better not naked,' said Comrade Adrianna Dimpla, frowning in concentration. 'The aim is – yes? – to maximize our bodies' retention of vital heat – no? – in the cold immensities of the interplanetary medium. I always get cold when naked in bed – get goose-pimples and . . . other effects. We wear clothing, yes?'

'No, baby,' said Malone, suddenly sweating profusely: he'd thought he'd got the whole thing unbuttoned up. 'No way, ya commie temptress! Because there'll be, like, *two* of us we'll stay warmer for longer if our bodies are clamped close together. Preferably rubbing against each other so that we get an infinitesimally increased heat-contribution from friction.'

'Your idea, Comrade Malone, sounds a trifle capitalist and lickspittle to me. Were it not for the fact that you have self-confessed your idiosyncratic homosexuality to me, I would suspect that your interests were more in the frictional abrasion than in the saving of dear Mother Earth. Besides, there disadvantage is in such manoeuvrings. Consider: you may become sexually aroused. This means, if I have medical terminology right from having read issue of *Knave* for mischief once during cultural-exchange trip in Harrogate, England, that your penis becomes engorged with blood. That is saying, the veins and arteries in it dilate, as also the teensy little capillaries close to the dermis. Think, my friend, of the heat-loss from your body as a result of that dilation! Perhaps only a very minuscule heat-loss . . .'

'A goddam *enormous* heat-loss!' exclaimed Malone before he could stop himself.

'As you say. You doubtless better medico-mathematician than I am, though I educated in such disciplines in Moscow Academy of Arts under Rudolf Nureyev. A titanic heat-loss. So you die a few seconds earlier than perhaps should, which means I get less of the body-warmth from you, which means I too die a few seconds too early, which may make big difference if I fire that vital one shot too few. Perhaps difference between Earth dying and Earth rising triumphant from ashes.'

'Ah,' said Malone, brain racing – but racing *what*? 'There's another way of looking at this. One of the main problems on the kinda heat-loss and fluid-loss front is gonna be our mucous membranes – regions like the eye and . . . well, like the interior of the, uh, female genitalia. Now, you can either do a bit of closing off with a few safety-pins I c'n probably jury-rig from the air-recycler . . .'

Dimpla winced.

'. . . or you can cover that mucous membrane goddam *up* with something.'

'But I not know how to do this.'

'And, at the same time, you can help solve the problem of the mucous membrane in my, er, um, you know, like, Big Boy.' Malone had never really thought about the fact that there might be a mucous membrane tucked away beneath his jealously guarded foreskin: the whole idea vaguely revolted him. Still, all's fair in love and war.

'But how you suggest we do this?'

'Well, if, uh, we're both as naked as Mom's apple-pie and I, despite myself, become inadvertently aroused, we could use the two . . . ah . . . mucous membranes to, like, shield each other from space's infernal coldness. I could, to put it bluntly, insert you.'

'"Insert" me?' said Dimpla, her rampant breasts heaving with mystification. 'Insert me into what? I not understand.'

'Like, I could . . . say, have you never actually *done* sex before?'

'Oh, yes, sex. Is fun. I have sex with champion studs of Communist Party in various eugenic experiments. They real ace-100% performers! They men hung like rhinoceros yet knowing every subtle secret of the erotic arts. They know how to give girl real good time – yes? – not vaguely frustrating experience girl gets by fooling around with *little* boys with clumsy manners. But what this got to do with anything we discussing?'

'Ulp! Nothing at all. You know, I think you may be right that we'd be better off dressed. Keep warmer that way. Be really kinda shitty if ya had to go out giggling.'

'I have heard it say that Western capitalistic string vests are good at keeping out cold. What you say we . . .?' But Dimpla never finished the sentence, for behind her, through the viewport, there was a sudden dazzling display of uniquely conjured light.

The reasons are complex.

If you were an independently polarized photon, where's the last place in the Universe you would choose to head?

Right. Towards the heart of an antimatter comet.

But if you were an independently polarized photon and you had no choice in the matter you might indeed find yourself heading straight towards the heart of such a comet, dragged down by the implacable force of coincidence, so to speak. And if that happened, why, hell, you'd find yourself involved in a matter-antimatter annihilation situation.

With a difference.

You see, your 'partner' would be forced independently to encounter another antimatter comet – *but one which was oppositely polarized!* So, as the radiation flash from your own annihilation rocketed towards the Earth, the equal and opposite (but *differently polarized*) radiation flash from the *other* interaction would likewise be rocketing towards the Earth. And the net result would be that the two would cancel each other out by the process of interference – just in the same way that ripples on the surface of a pond can cancel out when you've dropped two stones into it. Furthermore, by the very nature of the situation – its perfect symmetry – the cancellation would *have* to be perfect!

This was cheering for the inhabitants of Planet Earth (as also for the Cygnan fleet, which was close enough to be considered as part of the same entity).

It wasn't too bad for the pair of photons, both of which emerged – mentally scarred but intact – from the experience.

But it was far less cheering for the occupants of the *Mary Poppins*, who were exclusively close to one of the annihilations.

They were vaporized.

Apart, that is, from Malone's incipient erection: he would have been proud of it. Tougher than pure diamond, it remained in orbit around the Sun – a tiny *(Not so goddam tiny!!)* planetoid in the solar family – until, millennia later, a race much wiser than Man might stumble across it. It and a smaller replica inexplicably created on the Moon.

But that was in a different story.

So it goes.

6

Only a few miles above Lucius Apricot's unknowing head, Captain Sc'smv was flushing. Very noisily. And into a vidcom unit that connected it/she directly with 61 Cygni C, where the Great Spong him/it/herself was communicating.

'The brothers are debating whether or not a debate should be started,' flushed Captain Sc'smv, 'but I've slithered away to seek emergency clearance to override the democratic procedure and see if there's something that can be done about [a] the Terran infestation problem and [b] the Terra problem in general.' Its/her intimately excreted fluids were gathered automatically by the vidcom's sensor units and squirted instantaneously through space to splatter lustily into the Great Spong's anticipatory 'face'.

An aide of the Great Spong courteously answered. 'While it is unthinkable to anticipate the result of their vote,' excreted he/them/they (the game of 'Twenty Questions' had never caught on on 61 Cygni C, for obvious reasons), 'it might perhaps be worth considering the wisdom of your proposal.' Once again, the exuded words were captured by the vidcom unit and hurtled across interstellar space to be shot out of the receiver at high velocity into the welcoming mucus of Captain Sc'smv's proprioceptors. 'Spell it out to us, litre by litre.'

'I have the feeling that, despite all – ugh! – appearances to the contrary, the Earthlings may be potentially friendly to our cause,' urinated the Captain, 'but I conjugate that this can only be tested by an expedition, *phllpd* by myself, down onto the Earth itself, as soon as we have successfully scoured from our vessel the last vestiges of the infesting aliens. In the ordinary way, this expedition might have gone down onto the lawn of the revoltingly coloured house which the natives call "white" in the city which, for all I/she know, they call "Washington", but happily that seems to have been eliminated in a thermonuclear emission.'

'I/they/them do just *love* those thermonuclear emissions. They're the best of all,' emitted/admitted the aide. 'But please continue.' The words hit the Captain forcefully in the 'solar plexus'.

'So,' micturated Sc'smv, 'I/she think that the best plan would be to go down to what now seems the last bastion of Terran resistance against the unfortunate events that are befalling this miserable little planet.'

'Well,' spat the aide, 'do so – now!'

'But,' the Captain osmoted, 'what of the views of the Great Spong?'

'Ask not the views of the Great Spong,' warned the aide. 'He/it/sheself is ignominiously constipated.'

'But I need to know,' copulated the Captain.

'Well, don't say I didn't . . .' produced the aide.

But it was too late.

Squirted across the light years at hypersonic speed, the adamantine bullet hit the Captain squarely between the proprioceptors and slammed it/her against the bulkhead.

'Well,' bled the Captain internally, 'at least now I've/she's got some orders.'

7

The suspect was no pin-up, Officer Hotchkiss reflected. True, you couldn't always tell whether people were guilty or not just by looking at them but, over the long years of working the streets of the city he had learned to love in all its womanly ways, he had developed an intuitive understanding of the outer manifestations of the criminal persona. It was an understanding a man could never share with another – not even with his closest buddies in the locker-room, where secrets were as a matter of course allowed to hang out. Yet, it was also an understanding that all of the guys back in the precinct shared . . . each in their own individual ways. Curious, that – the way that something can be at one and the same moment totally intimate and personal and individual and private and specific and express and intimate and personal and individual and private and specific and – well, I guess, express as well, while it's also completely shared and communal and general and universal and nonspecific and public and shared and impersonal. It was not a thought that had ever passed through Officer Hotchkiss's mind before, and it was doing so rather slowly now, but it seemed to him that somehow the insight struck right at the very heart of the relationship between a police officer – *any* police officer, from the humblest rookie right up to the commissioner himself – and his fellow police officers, not to mention that analogous relationship which they all shared – individually as well as generally and nonspecifically – with the city which they all loved as if she were a woman.

Not a *perfect* woman, it's true, but a . . .

'Will you kindly get your fat form off me,' groaned

Death. He'd been under pressure quite a few times down the long billennia, but never before had he been under pressure like this.

'Don't address a police officer with disrespect,' snapped Hotchkiss automatically, wrenching his thoughts back to the present from the arcane depths of philosophical floundering which they had been plumbing.

'I'm sorry, Officer,' grunted Death with difficulty. 'But I think you've broken a few bones.'

'No,' said Hotchkiss, feeling himself warily, 'I don't think I have. What's your name? And you might as well tell me your address, too, while you're about it, buddy boy. Don't dodge the issue or I'll make sure you get – oh, shit, this gun's not working. How does the idea of getting *squashed* to death while evading arrest grab ya?'

'We've been through this conversation, or one very like it, before,' sighed Death, his voice like the soughing of a winter's wind through a deserted pine forest. 'Please, please, just let me up!'

The thought began to lurch through Hotchkiss's brain that perhaps he could do the greatest service to his fellow-humanity (a rather remote concept to him) and, more significantly, to himself by very simply *not* climbing off this bizarre character whom he now recalled only too well having encountered previously. At the time, it had struck him that the fellow was suspicious – could be a shoplifter or a pickpocket, the way he looked, and was probably a nancy with that funny walk of his. Now, finding him here on top of a New York skyscraper, his suspicions were hardly allayed. 'Yeah,' he said, 'I remember what you said last time, that your name was "Death". Well, buster, I didn't believe you then so there's no way I'm gonna believe you now. You sure you're not that English fugitive guy they never caught? Whassname, Lord Looker, sumpin like that?'

'If I said I were Lord Lucan would it make you get ⟨⟨ me?' gritted Death with difficulty.

'I don't know as it would,' said Officer Hotchkiss. 'Sheeit! What's *that*?'

That was a silverly gleaming spacecraft, slowly and deliberately vaporizing large areas of deserted downtown New York as it settled towards the ground. It was an awe-inspiring sight. The ship was perhaps 6–7 kilometres (3.73–4.35 miles) across, and shaped like an enormous teacup, although, rather than a single handle, it had two handle-like tori placed symmetrically, one on either side. Flying in attendance around it during its majestic descent were countless tiny robot drones, buzzing and darting for all the world like an inadvertently disturbed hornets' nest. The air was filled with the overwhelming, awesome thunder of a billion supernovae as the craft activated its retrothrusters and ponderously came to rest. Even after it had stopped moving, the memories of that titanic sound still filled the ears.

Traffic violation? thought Hotchkiss optimistically.

Aboard the vessel, Captain Sc'smv was beginning for the first time in a long while to feel reasonably complacent about the way the expedition was going. There had been problems, not least the fact that debate was still raging in the conference chamber as to whether a motion could be seconded before it had been properly proposed through the chair (it appeared that the likely decision would be that the matter would be referred upward to the next meeting of the Spiral Arm Ancillary Organizational Sub-Committee, but there were still plenty of speeches to come before this could be taken for granted) so that the Captain was having to run everything itself/herself, assisted only by its/her loyal First Mate, Stf'ndnl'dsn. However, most of these problems had now been solved. A rather puzzling attempt by the Terrans to reverse the

rmal order of things – by sending part of Los Angeles
up to meet the visitors, rather than the other way around
– had been easily enough tackled by placing a force-field
bubble all around the city, inside which the good craft
Libertarian was even now battering itself to pieces like a
demented fly at a sunny window. The Hitlers, too, had
presented something of a dilemma, but then Stf'ndnl'dsn
had come up with the bright idea of broadcasting, through
all the ship's systems, the constantly repeated message
'CAN YOU TRUST THE PERSON NEXT TO YOU?
HE LOOKS A BIT SEMITIC TO ME/ME/ME', until
the Hitlers had all been either drowned or digested by
the corrosive fluids that sprayed from the loudspeakers.
There was still the minor difficulty of the vast reptile
which had come aboard with the Hitlers, but it seemed
not to be significantly hostile, and Sc'smv was, in fact,
becoming rather fond of it; even now it was squatting
contentedly in a corner of the control chamber munching
and sucking some Hitler-corpses it had come across in
the corridors.

So Sc'smv had good reason for contentment – pro-
visionally, at least.

As the last shudderings left the great behemoth and it
settled down onto what had once been 17th to 29th
Streets and 1st to 8th Avenues, Sc'smv moved into action.
It/she knew from long months of studying the speculative
CETI scenarios produced in terrestrial movies that the
craft should now sit silently where it was for a few
hours – its inscrutability acting as a trigger to yet more
widespread panic – but that didn't mean that it/she could
afford to waste any time. It might have been easier if the
rest of the crew had been available to help . . . on second
thoughts, it might not.

Firstly, it/she had to transmogrify itself into pseudo-
human form. In itself, this was not too difficult – the

Cygnans had mastered complete control of their perso▨ physiologies millennia earlier – but, in the case of Eart▨ there was an additional problem. Sc'smv did not regar▨ itself/herself as in any way a traditionalist – no, its/her opponents in the election for the position of Captain had accused it/her, by contrast, of being all too bohemian – but nevertheless it/she found even the *thought* of adopting that repulsive, fleshly, bipedal configuration indescribably repulsive.

Still, it had to be done, or the contact could hardly hope to be successful. Pausing only to ingest a much needed dose of tranquillizing ethanol (the Cygnan equivalent of alcohol) from a nearby wall-dispenser, it/she headed off towards its/her private (although scrupulously shared) stateroom, where it/she could undergo the transformation without being observed.

This was not a matter of shyness, but of kindness.

The Captain found the prospect of adopting human form personally repugnant. But there was no reason why simple Stf'ndnl'dsn should be subjected to having to watch the procedure.

There were limits to her/his/her loyalty.

8

Far, far away, on a distant hillside somewhere in a lost land, the number of sages seated around the reluctantly crackling camp-fire had increased as Zen masters from all corners of the globe had been drawn inexorably to contribute their reflections to the vast pool of spiritual *tao* energy that was accumulating. Several hundred of them dotted the snow-filled landscape where the winds soughed like a dying man's final resentful breath and the

..ce howled like a lonesome werewolf. They sat there, ..cased in their rank, foul-smelling garments of festering ..nimal skins, and they did so without a sound . . . save only their strangled grunts as they practised holding their breath for minutes on end. They knew now that the future of Earth was assured, thanks in large part to their efforts. What they did not know was what that future would hold.

They stiffened yet further in the omnipresent blizzard as they were joined by the migratory spirit of Junior Finkelstein.

There is one comes among us from the distant land of America, sighed a thought, or was it only a trick of the wind?

It is I, whispered Junior's mind, and they all nodded, content. The circle was complete and unbroken, the *tao* from here on led through broad and pleasant countryside.

Why have you come? came their collective thought.

To convey great occidental wisdom to you.

Tell us your wisdom, oh young one.

Knock, knock.

Who's there?

Still Junior.

Oh, God. Still Junior who?

Still Junior meditation, you guys?

The eldritch scream of laughter from the soul of Junior Finkelstein as it departed from the Himalayas never to return was almost drowned by the gust of relief from several hundred minds.

I prefer the one about one hand clapping, they thought unanimously.

9

It had taken the lemmings that were infesting Ambledyke Farm a long time to work out how to open the cylinders of Tabun and Sarin, but at last they had done it. The project had been assisted by the superhuman intelligence which they now could tap, thanks to the consciousness lurking in the world's sewers: the difficulty had been that the individual lemmings tended unpredictably to adhere to any and all surfaces. Nevertheless, they had finally succeeded.

And what a success! As soon as the eyes of the lemmings had relayed details of the contents back to their controlling consciousness, a great cry of exultation had gone up from billions of furry throats. Here were complicated molecules a-plenty for the collective organism to experiment with, extending and enhancing its powers.

Moving swiftly and efficiently, the eager worker-lemmings manoeuvred the cylinders to the flush toilet housed in the traditional-style wood-look polythene shed at the far end of the farmyard. They tilted the cylinders up and then finally controlled the taps so that great gushes of the toxic chemicals shot directly down into the Devonian sewerage system, from where they were spread at top speed to those of the rest of what had once been Britain. Even . . . even to the dream-enshrouded spires of cob-webbed Oxford, where silence now filled the time-honoured quadrangles even out as far as Botley, whose own archaic splendour was now a scene of cloudless stillness. But wait. One sound could yet be heard.

Had a solitary and temporarily sober undergraduate been walking through the quad of Judas College he

...have heard through the lead-framed stained-glass ...ows the hum of desultory conversation among the ... few steadfast representatives of long-forgotten aca-...mic glory. And had that undergraduate paused in ...everie for a while to listen, his ears would have been rewarded by the mellifluous tones of that establishment's Dr Scholl's Reader in Anatomy confessing to his companions at High Table that, after these last few days of their endless formal dinner, the urges of brute biology were at last making themselves felt even within his august corporeal framework.

'If you will forgive me,' the undergraduate might have heard that personage enunciate, 'I must leave you for some moments to attend to a small matter.' The euphemism, tastefully deployed, passed unnoticed for, as the don discovered upon raising his eyes over the edge of the now-drained port decanter, his erstwhile companions had long since, one by one, departed from the table upon a similar errand. Moreover, none had honoured that ages-ancient hall with a return.

Bastards have all pissed off, thought the Dr Scholl's Reader in Anatomy, delighted at last to be able to escape to the sanctuary of his own unheard thoughts, where he could express himself with a crispness and concision deemed over-worldly elsewhere within the Judas College confines. *Guess I can go and point the old J.T. at the porcelain without all the usual prefatory protocol*, his thoughts continued, revelling in their exquisite *naughtiness* – a naughtiness enhanced rather than petrified by the rarity of the occasions upon which he permitted his intellectual processes to function thus.

There was, therefore, a glimmer of complacency reflected in the smile which ornamented his physiognomy as he pushed his chair precisely back from the table and trod his measured steps to the edge of the dais, down its

278

hallowed step (immortalized by the late George, Lord Byron, in a verse scrawled as part-payment to a tavern-owner not long before he had been sent down, as 'the singing stair that outshone fair Helen's lips'), and over to the time-darkened oaken door of the hall. As he stood there, he glanced back for what, although he knew it not, was the last time, and some figment of consciousness within the chambers of his vaulted mind seemed to be bidding it farewell.

Our undergraduate would not, as a matter of normal course, have followed the Reader to his rooms; but had he done so his eyes might have been exposed to a sight that defied all adjectival circumscription.

Empowered by the straying radicals made available to it by the admixture of the potent chemicals but recently discovered by its agents within the purlieus of the agrarian holdings owned by one Master Jeb Loam in the western reaches of these blessed islands, the integrated consciousness had succeeded in transmitting its agents through wood and steel, through plaster and concrete – through all the materials that normally shield frail humans from the fetidly odoriferous passages where their waste products congregate – such that no longer was there any part of the land that was safe. Having elected upon the target of its choice, the group mind needed only to plot out with infernal cartography the route through the underground sewers to the point of closest contact between its own subterranean realm and the point above the dull clay where it wished to strike, and then send its hirsute messengers scrabbling through the obstacles of wood and concrete, subtly softened by the actions of the virulent compounds which it now exploited. They could go anywhere on land or sea. To wit: into the earth-closet of the Dr Scholl's Reader in Anatomy at Judas College, Oxford.

The results need hardly be described.

10

'Nadia,' said Zenna Brabham, 'now that Al's esca . . . had to go to the lavatory for a few minutes, I think it's time that you and I had a talk.' The finest junior-school teacher in the Western hemisphere – well, certainly in what was left of the Western hemisphere – pouted one of the finest bosoms in the Western hemisphere shyly while looking coyly out of the sides of her curvaceous honey-blonde eyes at the statuesque, thrillingly sensual figure of the world's top space scientist.

'A talk? What about?'

'About . . . well, about *things*. About you and me and Al. The situation between the three of us is – how can I put it? – inherently unstable. Sooner or later Al's going to have to make up his mind between the two of us, like in the Judgement of Paris, and that's going to be hard on the one who's rejected. You, in short.'

Nadia Finkelstein's pristine brow wrinkled. She wondered which trial in Paris Zenna was talking about. Must have been the arraignment of some of the Nazis after the war, or something. She couldn't see the exact relevance of the reference. 'I don't see why you're so confident that Al is going to select *you* to be his soul-mate,' she said. 'I get the very strong feeling that he regards you as nothing more than a nuisance, with the way you're constantly fawning over him, never allowing the poor man a moment's peace and quiet to spend getting to know *me* a little better in private.'

'You say *I* fawn over him!' Zenna Brabham exploded, her breasts heaving with barely suppressed indignation. 'What about you? Only yesterday, at breakfast-time, I saw you feeding him his cornflakes, one by one, on the tip of your tongue. The poor dear looked harassed — that's the only word to describe it.'

'Well, you were spreading the marmalade on his toast with your left breast at the time!' countered the NASA boss.

'I just couldn't find a knife anyplace,' muttered the youthful schoolmarm, easing her memorable buttocks into the soft, grateful caress of one of Bran's office chairs. 'Besides, he liked it.'

'Liked it! That's a good one! He looked as if he were going to be sick!'

'That was because of what you were doing with the cornflakes!' Zenna snapped, throwing her silky hair in a great cloud over her shoulder with an impetuous, wild glower. 'He was running his fingers gently up and down the soft, downy hair of my spine the whole time!'

'No he wasn't, you stupid cat!' cried Nadia Finkelstein, aware that, as so many men had remarked in the past, she always looked maddeningly beautiful when roused to anger. 'That was Junior doing that.'

'*Junior?* But surely Junior's far too . . .' And then, with heartwrenching sorrow, the truth began to dawn on the charming young educationist. Over the years of her teaching experience, she had thrilled the hearts (and other regions) of scores upon scores of eight-year-old prepubescent boys, but hardly once had a full-grown man exhibited anything towards her other than perfect, polite correctness. Was it possible that she would never be able to find adult love? For, now that the first shock of Nadia Finkelstein's words was beginning to wear off, she realized that there was a certain amount of truth in what the rocketry buff had said. Al *did* seem to look around him for the nearest available exit every time she came into the room; and she had more than once seen a glaze come over his eyes as she had launched gaily into some coltish reminiscence which she had assumed would enrapture the heart of any male. But . . . but, well, his attitude towards Nadia Finkelstein seemed to be not dissimilar – as, in fact, the space boss herself was now likewise beginning to recognize.

For a few moments more they stood there in silence, facing each other like a pair of Victorian erotic bookends, each woman thinking her own restless thoughts. Then Zenna Brabham stuck out her sensitive hand, which was gripped daintily by Nadia Finkelstein's deliriously elegant one.

'May the best gal win!' they said simultaneously.

They giggled together, their laughter mixing like the water rushing over a cataract in some divine ophthalmologist's surgery.

The mood was shattered by the door being thrown open.

'Have you seen what's going on out there?' blustered Bjørgstrøm forcefully as he slammed the door back against the wall. 'It's the moment we've all been dreading – the arrival of the aliens!'

'Gosh, we've got too many clothes on,' said Zenna, and Nadia nodded her agreement.

Bjørgstrøm looked baffled, a reaction which destroyed three alien drones which had been spying on the scene through the window. It was hard to see how either of the women could wear any less without beginning actually to flay themselves.

'We've got to be scantily clad for when the aliens arrive,' explained Nadia to him gently, 'so that while they're trying forcibly to abduct us you guys can be saving the world with your atomic blasters and all.'

Bjørgstrøm wondered how he could explain to her that he, Bjørgstrøm, didn't actually *possess* an atomic blaster, and that he was pretty sure that none of the other males of the party did either; but he was saved from potential embarrassment by the swift arrival in the room of the remaining members of the Think Tank – with the exception of Junior Finkelstein and the Loams.

'Right,' said Bran, immediately and instinctively taking command, 'time for a quick update on the situation. We all know by now that the extraterrestrials have arrived here in New York, but we have no idea as to whether their intentions are hostile or not. To judge by the messages decoded by Dr Panther and our late, departed friend and dear colleague, Professor Tompion, we have good reason to suspect that they are far from friendly – in short, that they plan to exterminate the human species. But we could just be jumping to conclusions.'

Lise Panther nodded miserably. The consolation was that soon she would be joining Mark in the hereafter – wherever that was. For some inexplicable reason she found herself becoming almost sexually excited by the thought of her own imminent encounter with death.

'If we assume that they are indeed unfriendly,' Bran continued, 'then that means that we really need to put the accelerators on the matter-transmission programme. Dr Apricot?'

'Progress is really rather exciting,' said the world-famous particle physicist excitedly, warming to his theme and to an encouraging squeeze from an adoring Avedon Patella. 'I've now worked through most of the theoretical considerations, and I can see few difficulties remaining. By this evening, at the latest, I should be ready to brief a team of engineers as to exactly what I need by way of hardware. After that, it shouldn't be long at all before we have a fully functioning device that will replicate – to all practical intents and purposes – the effects of an MT and safely transport this entire planet to some distant realm of the cosmos. Fine-tuning facilities can easily be installed such that the alien spacefleet is simply left behind.'

There was a burst of applause.

'That's great, Dr Apricot,' said Bran enthusiastically. 'So just how long do you think it will actually take for the engineers to do their stuff?'

'Well,' said Apricot, 'assuming that we have no difficulties in appropriating the various raw and processed materials that we require, then, as I say, it shouldn't take long at all. Perhaps two decades – maybe even less.'

There was a total silence in the room. Apricot began to wonder if, perhaps . . . 'That's no time at all for a project of this size,' he said hesitantly.

'Look, Apricot, you stupid ivory-tower asshead!' It was Joyce Abramowitz who was speaking, her frustrated fury overriding her accustomed jaunty pertness. 'Those goddam aliens are liable to blast humanity to smithereens *tonight*, and you're talking about twenty goddam years. Our chances of escaping through your matter transmitter aren't worth a flying fuck at a rolling doughnut!'

'Well, I wouldn't say that,' muttered Apricot. 'Not in mixed company, anyway.'

'What in hell are we going to *do*?' wailed Bjørgstrøm miserably, his bumptious confidence for once shattered. A crack splintered its way across Bran's onyx-topped desk.

For some while Lise Panther had been silent, sitting in the corner, her face growing steadily more ashen and perspiration appearing like nectar on her forehead. Now she began to speak . . . slowly, and with apparent difficulty. 'There's a voice,' she said, 'speaking *inside my head!* It's . . . it seems like it's Junior's voice. It says that he's wanting me to take him up onto the roof, where . . . where I Must Meet My Destiny!' Her eyes had rolled up in their sockets now, so that the whites ranged around the room like gibbous moons. 'It says that I . . . must . . . go . . . n-o-o-o-o-w-w-w . . .'

She rose on unsteady legs, and tottered towards the door. None of her friends and colleagues gathered there dared to approach her: they all just watched her as she left, stunned into immobility by their sense that something greater than all of them was at work. After she had left there was a further silence.

It was smashed into its component pieces by the booming, ear-rupturing tones of a thunderous voice that filled the entire skies of New York with bels upon myriad bels. **'Repent ye, for the Lord will fill your hearts as the waters cover the sea!'** it said, shattering the city's few remaining unshattered windows – Bjørgstrøm looked unashamedly envious.

Bran was first to the window, peering with bulging eyes at the mind-numbing sight that greeted him. Some miles beyond where the alien spaceship squatted enigmatically there towered the vast holographic figure of a paunchy, cleanly dressed middle-aged man with a nervous artificial halo around its head. It was grinning blindly down upon the wreckage of New York with an oiliness that was indescribable and yet terrifying. **'There is more joy in Heaven over a single sinner than over the eye of a needle!'** thundered the Reverend Hunk Brady, standing safely in his nuclear-fallout shelter somewhere in the wilds of Massachusetts. That this was only a holographic representation and not really a visitation from God Himself became apparent only to his startled audience when a high-level cloud solemnly passed apparently in through one of the evangelist's ears and out through the other.

'Jeesk,' said Nadia Finkelstein, 'as if we didn't have enough problems on our plate without somebody coming along and trying to save us!'

Inside the alien Mother Ship, Captain Sc'smv had just given vent to similar emotions, and four of the drainage units overheated and expired. 'Parsecs and parsecs we cover!' it/she erupted. 'It/I spend *skri* after *skri* battering my brains' (it/she meant this quite literally) 'trying to contrive a suitable First Contact scenario that will appeal to the Earthlings' subconscious, and then *this* happens! *By the Great Spong, I've been UPSTAGED!*' Hectolitres of raw fury swashed down every one of the ship's corridors, penetrating even into the great conference chamber, where the assembled delegates looked up in astonishment as they were swept willy-nilly along by the tidal wave of wrath. Thus it was that two lengthy and valuable contributions to the debate, by the ship's astrologers Ptr'ckm'r and C'hrsb'yc, were rudely ignored and lost forever – awesomely changing the fate of the plot itself.

'This planet is unfit for recruitment by the Galactic Union,' Captain Sc'smv frothed. 'Prepare to depart!' Its/her torrents of indignation washed vitriolically (again, literally) to all parts of the ship. 'And get that blasted Terran reptile out of all of my sights!' ordered the crazed Captain, picking up the miserable Stf'ndnl'dsn by the anterior sphincter and throwing her/him/her bodily at the cowering monster. 'It/I want all things Terran evacuated from this ship within the next five *sysbys* – and then we blast off!'

Stf'ndnl'dsn obeyed – with some difficulty. The reptile might be slow-thinking, but from the moment of the start of the Captain's tirade, some minutes before, comparatively fast-moving panic reactions had been twitching their way up to its double brains. It wrapped its forelimbs defensively around the Cygnan communications terminal and held on for dear life as the First Mate struggled with it. The two were roughly equally matched for size and weight, and the fight could have gone on indefinitely had

not Captain Sc'smv thrown itself/herself into the fray
Finally, between them, the two aliens succeeded in forcing
the primeval monster out through one of the airlocks, still
dragging the majority of the interstellar communications
console with it.

With a loud splash, monster and machine fell into the
dark waters of the Hudson.

11

Will it come to this, thought Death, *that even I will die?*
Every fresh breath that he took was a torment to him
now as Officer Hotchkiss's weight, bolstered by a lifetime
of eating MacDonald's hamburgers in parked police
cruisers, thrust him inexorably into the unyielding tar-
topped roof.

'Damnation is the name of DEATH!' thundered
the Reverend Hunk Brady's holographic image, the sound
filling the sky from horizon to horizon.

Can't even get my bloody name right, thought Death,
and he began to give up hope. *Failure! My vengeance will
fail! The world will cease to feel the terror of my righteous
wrath!* He sobbed inwardly. *Will anyone even notice that
I'm gone?*

'Soon as I landed on you I knew you were up to no
good,' grunted Hotchkiss, totally unimpressed by anything that was going on around him. Except – well, there
was a good chance he'd be able to book the big holy
roller for something connected with the noise regulations;
the occupants of the now-departing alien spaceship, if
only he could catch it (*damn it, but I miss my big
bike already!*), could undoubtedly be thrown in the cells
overnight for dropping litter into the river; and if this

eird-looking customer didn't peg out first he could sure
as hell have him in for a little questioning at the wrong
end of a night-stick. Looked like Officer Hotchkiss might
well get himself a citation for today's work – yes, sirree!

'What are you doing?' said a voice from behind him,
and he looked over his shoulder to see, standing at the
top of the fire stairs, a pulsatingly dressed if somewhat
tear-bedraggled brunette accompanied by a small boy
with a weird light in his eyes.

'Makin' an arrest, ma'am,' said Hotchkiss. 'Probably
best if you and the youngster get outta here in case
there's gunplay. Wouldn't want to disturb a hair on your
pretty little head.'

'Get off him,' said the child, firmly.

Hotchkiss boggled. This little half-assed runt . . . but
to his amazement he found himself obeying. He climbed
off Death's crumpled form and carefully walked backwards to lean against a nearby air-conditioning tower.

For a moment nobody moved, and then Lise Panther
stepped forward instinctively to help up the fallen figure.
Death moved with difficulty, assisting her only a little as
she pulled him to his feet. His gaze ranged around the
shattered horizon before finally coming to rest on her
face.

'You!' he said.

'You?' she responded, puzzled. 'Do you know me from
somewhere?'

'Lise – oh, Lise, I thought I'd never see you again!'

'I'm sorry, I don't know what you're talking about.'

Death looked at Junior, and his eyes narrowed – a
process easier to describe than watch. 'And you, you've
been my enemy since all this' (he gestured with one arm
at the wreckage of the world) 'all this began. I ought to
hate you – but strangely enough I don't. If it hadn't been

288

for you I wouldn't be here now, reunited with my darling Lise!'

Junior stared at him impassively, popping a bubble of gum.

Death looked at him apprehensively for a moment, then turned back to the well cushioned mathematician. 'Lise,' he said. 'Isn't it fantastic to be together again? It's been the best part of twenty billion years, but you seem hardly to have grown a day older!'

'I'm afraid I don't know you, sir,' she said, edging away from him, her face a caricature of distaste.

'Is this bum causing you trouble, lady?' growled Hotchkiss in a deep voice.

Death's attention was momentarily distracted by a rumpus from a few storeys beneath: Dr Al D. Bran had thrown his head out of the window of his office and was bellowing at the vast alien spacecraft, as it rose slowly from the ground on pillars of turgid flame, 'Take me with you, for God's love! Take me with you!' He was drawn back inexorably by two pairs of perfectly formed and very determined arms.

It was this distraction that changed the future of the Earth, for Officer Hotchkiss, impatient at the way that potential arrest after potential arrest seemed to be slipping out of his grasp, took his opportunity to step forward and strike the suspect firmly in the throat. Death doubled up in agony, blood starting from his eyes, his hands clenched around his neck.

'E-e-e-e-u-u-u-r-r-r-g-g-h-h-h-h!' he gasped.

'Pesterin' innocent womenfolk, you bastid!' snarled Hotchkiss in a synthetic fury. And he struck him again.

This time the force of the blow – to the kidneys, if Death had had any kidneys – rocketed the frail figure sideways, off-balance. A few lurching steps . . . and then Death was teetering on the edge of the roof, flailing his arms wildly in an attempt to preserve his balance. This he succeeded in doing for quite a long time, because naturally enough it took a fair while for all the events of his life to be replayed before his inner eyes. But finally the struggle was lost, and he plummeted helplessly into thin air.

As he fell he thought only for a moment of using his superhuman powers to save himself . . . but then that look of distaste on his beloved Lise's face came back to him, and his age-old spirit at last abandoned all hope. *I wonder what kind of a place the Universe is going to be without me*, he mused.

It was his last thought before oblivion mercifully enshrouded him.

12

'This scene had to be enacted,' said Junior Finkelstein softly to Lise Panther, who was weeping quietly, from the reaction, into his thin, youthful shoulder. A shattered skin of bubble-gum had impacted over her ear so that she could not make out his words, but the sense of them somehow communicated itself to her.

'There's regulations against neckin' in a public place,' said Officer Hotchkiss with an expectant twinkle in his eye.

Perhaps all hope was not yet lost.

8

The End of the Beginning of the End
(Part One)

The world then to an end shall come
In Eighteen Hundred and Eighty-One.
> *Life and Prophecies of Ursula Sontheil* (Mother Shipton).

The world then at an end we'll view
In Eighteen Hundred and Eighty-Two.
> *Ibid*, reinterpreted 1 January 1882.

The world then to an end shall come
In Nineteen Hundred and Ninety-One.
> *Ibid*, reinterpreted 1 January 1883.

The world in fact will self-abort
In Nineteen Hundred and Ninety-Nought.
> *Ibid*, reinterpreted by Junior Finkelstein, 1990.

The Universe will go to pot
In that same year; or maybe not.
> *Ibid*.

1

Dick Ingrams, erstwhile lavatory attendant, had been screaming for what seemed like days. Screaming and running. Running and screaming. Shrieking his pitiful message of terror at the grey uncomprehending sky. Stumbling and cursing and once again screaming as again raw horror exploded in the no man's land of what in kinder days had been his mind. Screaming and running wondering why novelists' syntax got so unconvincingly jerky when they wanted to inject a bit of spurious excitement. Running. Screaming. Remembering a bloody, emptied pair of trousers and writhing in guilt at his own past indulgence of sucking oranges dry, just like . . . *No! No!* No hope in sight, not a human face, not an unwrecked building amid the lemming-torn ice-plains of southwest England, not a properly constructed sentence with a verb . . . Screaming. Running. Falling over.

He did not know how long he'd lain there in the soft blanket of snow. Long enough, clearly, for fever and hallucinations to have set in. For, before him, a steep curve of the hilly ground trembled and slowly yawned open. From the cleft hillside there issued a soft, mystic light which transformed the desolation to a scene of glowing enchantment. Somewhere a gong was struck, a solemn knelling whose reverberations went on and on, echoed by the deep and brazen voice which followed:

'The hour is come. The hour is come. The hour is come.'

Bloody hell, thought Ingrams. *Their Pershings were bad enough, I didn't know we had Minuteman silos as well.*

Out from the throbbing cave of light moved the armoured and crowned figure of a man. The deep voice spoke again: 'It is time. Now that all England lies in peril, it is time. Through the centuries my hundred knights and I have slept: now we ride forth against the final foe. I, Arthur, once and future King of England, have spoken.'

He raised his visor and looked around – saw the shattered land, the jagged, stained horizon, the smoke and the ice, the moribund figure that lay twitching at his feet . . .

'Oh,' he majestically said.

292

'I think you left it a bit late,' said Dick Ingrams bitter

'This is what comes of relying on a ruddy sundi₁
over fifteen sodding centuries,' complained King Arthur.
'Personally, I blame Merlin. Er, well, you seem a *worthy
knight*. Would you care to come in for a cup of tea and
maybe a millennial slumber? You look as though you
need it.'

A minute later, the last surviving inhabitant of England
had vanished from the face of the land. Wandering
lemmings were moved to a dim wonderment by the
awesomely final sound of ancient bolts being drawn and
door-chains re-attached.

2

After feistily disposing of a flock of plot inconveniences
such as left-over secretaries and security men, the attack
on the skyscraper had petered out at the appearance of a
new threat in its rear. A literally monstrous threat.
Werewolves (and vampires) were still swimming ineptly
about the New York streets, trying to avoid the former
denizen of Loch Ness, both of whose brains had decided
vampires (and werewolves) were tasty and nice.

Now Dr Lucius Apricot and Joyce Abramowitz kept a
nervous eye on the carnage from their improvised raft, as
they struggled to haul a certain object from the Hudson
River with their improvised block-and-tackle, powered
by an improvised Gwynfor Bjørgstrøm.

'An alien artifact! It could be the matter transmitter
with which we could yet flip the entire Earth into a more
upmarket region of the Universe,' Apricot had enthused
with the strange prescience typical of awkward expository
moments in novels like this.

We don't need to do that any more,' Patella had _ked sensuously.

'But alien super-technology could yet solve the lemming problem, purge my guilt, and save ravaged England,' Abramowitz had delightfully, poutingly cried.

Now, dented and dripping but still holding the promise of cosmic knowledge undreamed of by the hidebound fuddy-duddies of the entrenched and conservative scientific establishment (not that there were actually any of them left), the Cygnan interstellar communications console was raised from the depths in all its malodorous majesty.

'That's interesting, there's a kind of container clipped to the side,' Apricot noted, and incautiously prised the lid off the strange alien cylinder to which he referred. '_Argh!_'

Within the cylinder there pulsated a veined, jellylike fluid resembling a mixture of borscht, thousand-island sauce and untreated effluent. All three of them reeled and gagged at its appalling stench.

'Pooh,' said Abramowitz, voluptuously quoting from the works of A. A. Milne.

'Get rid of it,' grated Bjørgstrøm.

'Yes, I think we can safely discard _this_,' Apricot choked, suiting the action to the word, and watching the Hudson's immemorial waters close over several litres of detailed Cygnan instruction manual.

3

Champagne corks popped on the skyscraper's 113th floor. The time of disaster was clearly over, and a great weight of oppression had lifted from the tortured, miasmic Earth.

'All over,' crooned Abramowitz to Bjørgstrøm. 'We tiny band of survivors have made it through all the horrors of earthdoom . . . and now, since that mysterious out-of-control nuclear-pulse ship has for reasons of plot tidiness sterilized the rest of the USA with its fallout, it's our duty to repopulate the world!'

The ravaged climatologist replied: 'Of course. Do please accept this fifty-carat engagement ring which this morning I looted just for you. And *here* is my engagement gift to you, Joyce, my lovely anticyclone.'

'A . . . a chastity belt? Gwynfor, I don't think that's very nice.'

'No, dear. *I* wear it, not you – for your sake. An iron mask.'

Her last inhibitions blown away, she flung herself deliriously upon him. Bjørgstrøm looked fondly at the sparkle on her ring finger, which forthwith disintegrated into a cloud of industrial-grade sanding diamond.

'I wonder which of them the children will take after,' pouted Nadia Finkelstein with a slight shudder. 'And, speaking of children . . .'

In a flash, Al D. Bran had rushed to check the push-bar on the fire escape door. Nadia idly noted that he'd taken to wearing spiked running shoes at all hours of the day and night. *I guess these psychiatrists have a word for shoe fixations,* she thought. *Pedophilia, something like that?* Aloud she said: 'Dear Joyce has been telling me about genetics, everyone. It seems that two excessively brilliant, highly-strung geniuses should never marry – the result could be a complete over-the-top freak. I know this is going to be a big disappointment to you, Al . . . but it looks like my duty to the future human race is to go for, like, a man of the people.'

'Wow,' said Harcourt, that deeply populist technician and spear-carrier whom everyone had as usual forgotten.

'Not you, oaf,' snapped Nadia. She smiled shyly, nipples popping romantically erect, as her hand slipped into Officer Hotchkiss's.

'Gee,' said that pillar of the law. 'I guess maybe under the circumstances I won't run you in for propositioning a guy in a public place.' It was his simple, rough way of saying *Darling, my darling, I am thine, thine, thine, until the very warranty of eternity has expired!*

'So that leaves you a clear field, Zenna,' Nadia concluded with sensuous magnanimity. 'Just think what a magnificent genetic inheritance could come from a Nobel prize-winning psychiatrist and the finest schoolmarm in this room – in the Western hemisphere – the world – it comes to the same thing, after all.'

(Bran muttered something about checking the mailbox, and seemed ready to sprint down 112 flights of stairs, even though the US Postal Service had collapsed several years ago, and the mailbox was underwater anyway.)

'No, no, no,' said the perky-nippled schoolteacher stoutly. 'I've been thinking hard, and at last I know where my true destiny lies. I've confronted my inner self. My true attraction, I now realize is for . . . younger men.'

'My darling! I'll always look up to you in your maturity,' said Harcourt.

'Not you.' A tear trickled erotically down the perfect curve of Zenna's cheek. 'Junior, Junior, the time is not

yet . . . but I want you to know . . . in just a few year
. . . I'll be waiting for you.'

'Mmm,' said Junior, blowing a stolid bubble. His gigantic psychic talents had mapped out enough of the future to know that the remaining world supplies of bubble-gum would last him only so much longer. When they were exhausted, it would be as well to have another pleasure-source in reserve. Logic dictated it. 'This has been willed where what is willed must be,' he clairvoyantly belched.

With a thrust of gorgeously rounded, silken knees, Avedon Patella looked up from where she was tenderly holding a fourth bottle of champagne to Apricot's lips (he had had a slight relapse on realizing the disaster was truly over). 'We feminists don't usually do well in disaster novels – we either get wiped out by male chauvinist authors or stuck with some ghastly romantic happy ending. I've worked out my own compromise . . .'

Harcourt stared at her with dumb adoration tempered by dumb lust.

'Not you . . . Lucius is the man for me, a man who unlike most is not dominated by fantasies of rape, a man who is gloriously incapable of the ultimate physical expression of male dominance. Living with Lucius and filling his glass, I can love – in Cornish – without that oppressive *physical* element contaminating all our joy!'

'Hic,' agreed Dr Apricot. Or disagreed. It was hard to tell.

'Ah, Rachel, my little marsh-tigget, 'tis sweet as the cry o' mating water-voles to hear such stuff,' said Jeb Loam, sitting with an arm twined romantically round Rachel and his free hand thrust lovingly between her adorable thighs.

'Ah, give over, Jeb, you do be like hippopotamus on heat,' twinkled his wife, tickling him privily. Though otherwise recovered from their brush with Absolute Evil,

...e Loams had found themselves curiously gifted with erotic knowledge far beyond the basic position (gleaned from the *Pig-Breeder's Companion)* which had resulted in Nathan, Reuben and the baby they had finally – as a sort of *in memoriam* gesture – christened Mark. As a consequence of these new insights, they'd spent most of the last few days in their room, loudly recuperating.

'Like do be calling to like, seed to egg and sire to dam and sheep to booted farmer,' quoted Jeb profoundly. "Tis as my old mommet told me, "when swallows be leaving, girls be conceiving". Eh, and maybe Dr Bran and Dr Panther do be making eyes at each other, seeing as how there bean't a buggering lot of choice left?'

Bran and Lise Panther both choked suddenly over their champagne (provoking Apricot into a dim horizontal resentment – he'd spent several hours that morning synthesizing the bubbly in a converted X-ray diffraction apparatus, and was unjustly proud of the result). It was Bran who recovered his breath first:

'No, folks, I have to tell you I finally completed my own analysis this morning. Seemed to me kind of significant, the curious anti-erotic syndrome I experienced when Zenna or Nadia were, er,' (he coughed) 'close to me. Well, you'll be glad to hear I figured out just what I was suppressing! After calculating a suitable erotic object, I smoke-signalled an invitation across the wreckage of the continent, and any minute now . . .'

Knock. Knock.

'Come right on in,' called Bran hastily, before anyone could make the fatal mistake of saying *Who's there?* And with eyes that were twin stars, he took the hand of the newcomer – the Reverend Hunk Brady.

'Who looketh on wine when it is red is as a worm that dieth not!' boomed Brady conversationally, accepting a glass of (pinkish) champagne from the eager Bran.

'Looks like it's you and me,' whispered Harcourt to Lise Panther, who all this time had remained silent and ravishingly aloof.

'Not you. I realize now that I could never love any other man but Professor Tompion. With him gone . . . I can be nobody's.' A frozen, irresistible beauty, she betrayed no emotion bar that indicated by the heap of empty bottles at her feet.

Mutely accepting his destiny, Harcourt obscurely wandered over to the window and unobtrusively threw himself out. *As such a minor and unimportant character,* he thought as he passed the 97th floor, *I suppose I should be grateful . . .* (he continued as the 23rd floor whizzed by) *. . . that I made it as far as the last chapter . . .*

Far above, the happily coincidental pop of a champagne cork masked any trace of unpleasant splatting noise which might have ruined the party atmosphere. Joyce was gaily tightening the straps of Bjørgstrøm's new iron mask. Nadia regaled Hotchkiss with risqué little anecdotes about Hohmann transfer orbits. The Loams were engaged in trying to achieve the 'Lithuanian Typewriter' position without anyone noticing. Apricot struggled to explain to Avedon, using only minute twitches of the left eyebrow, which was all that seemed functional, that he needed to visit the little boys' room. Zenna was telling Junior the raw facts of life, such as when it was socially acceptable for grown men to clear nasal blockages with a dexterous finger. Bran, master psychologist, had already persuaded Rev. Brady to demonstrate the early Christian kiss of brotherhood. And Lise Panther stared unseeingly into space, clinging to her one last hope.

I don't know Mark is dead . . . do I?

Unnoticed, one other intellect brooded in that cheerful post-holocaust room.

When the Antichrist had been hurled back to the

Beginning, along with the soul-stuff of Nathan and Reuben, the third, unnamed Loam child was left a soulless hulk whose 'thought' was a mere collection of reflexive responses – not unlike a mainstream literary critic. A tiny blob of psychic vacuum that craved and yearned . . .

Nature abhors a vacuum.

I thought the bloody thing was finally over, brooded Death, alias Professor Mark Tompion, alias Mark Loam, whose spirit had failed to escape into the freedom of eternity but had instead been sucked into this ill-fitting container with a metaphysical *pop* curiously like the noise of a champagne cork played in reverse on a spiritual tape recorder of dubious quality.

All might be for the best in this best of all possible worlds, mused the infant. *In a little while I'll be able to talk, and then I can persuade exquisitely voluptuous Lise Panther to . . . wait for me.*

Just the same, there was a slightly worried look on the unformed, deceptively cherubic face. He realized instinctively that for a long time before any fun stuff like puberty, he'd have to put up with the ghastly, foreordained horror of being dreadfully bullied by Junior Finkelstein.

You bet, conveyed Junior with a menacing pop of bubble-gum.

4

'And now,' moaned Dr Apricot through the obscuring fog of his hangover, 'we finish the cleanup of Earth.' By sheer intuition and reckless guesswork he'd fathomed all the workings of the Cygnan communicator/matter transmitter – or almost all – and had explained his conclusions in a lengthy technical lecture which fortunately took place offstage but probably accounted for jaunty-buttocked Avedon Patella's air of having suffered a recent prefrontal lobotomy. The rest had been a sleekly disciplined team effort:

'Joyce . . . you've tuned the controls to the physiology of the rabid lemmings which still infest Europe. Gwynfor . . . you've corrected for the effect of those little lines on the weather maps. Lise and Nadia . . . you've programmed in the precise mathematical coordinates of intergalactic space. Al . . . you've given me an aspirin (very important that). Junior . . . you've warned me of doom, as usual. Hotchkiss . . . you've very decently waived the penalties for operating illicit matter transmitters within city limits. Zenna . . . you've helped with elementary stuff like the three-times table which we rarified theoretical physicists are apt to forget. Jeb and Rachel . . . you've sustained me with your simple, earthy wisdom (and I hope you can teach some of the positions to Avedon). God, what a *team* we make!' With shaking hands Apricot drained one of the all too few Bloody Marys left to this depleted world.

'And now, when Rev. Brady has given his blessing – '

'Cast generations of vipers before swine!' elucidated Brady.

' – I press the button!' said Apricot.

PZZZZOCK
BLINNNNGG
FTOOOOEY

With a mighty wrenching of the very fabric of time and space, the Cygnan MT unit was perverted to a function for which it had never been designed. The lemming hordes, worst of the terrors which afflicted the world,

301

were instantaneously transmitted into the depths of inter-galactic space. Caught up in a vortex of plot convenience, the superglue, Bigfeet, mutant cockroaches, glaciers, black holes, nuclear fallout, plague virus, fluorocarbon molecules, falling Moon and traffic wardens were swept after them. Earth was cleansed.

A long way away in the Himalayas, the massed mystics and sages joined Junior Finkelstein in thinking, *Oh, no . . .*

Apricot's genius had mastered all but one of the Cygnan device's settings. Had anyone on Earth been able to interpret the patch of oozing purulence over the relevant dial, they would have read: VOLUME CONTROL. Drawing on energies outside the Universe as we know it, the communicator was resistlessly able to *amplify* the mass of the surging, guggling Cygnan conversation-stuff, so that the tiniest trickle of received signal could emerge as a comfortably gooey torrent.

In the last struggle to eject *an Niseag* from the ship, the volume control had been set (as it had never been set before) to full amplification . . . and twisted even further, beyond that point. Need one say more?

Amplified by technology, lemmings the size of galactic superclusters seethed and burgeoned in what used to be protected wilderness areas of empty space. The mass of the universe was dramatically swollen. Far, far away, a conveniently placed alien astronomer peered through its telescope and had time to cry, 'At last I have solved the problem of the Universe's missing mass, as required by our theories of cosmology! And it's not the shape you thought it'd be . . .' Then gravity came into play, and Isaac Newton was revenged on the apple at last. Sucked inward by the monstrous added gravitational pull of the lemming clusters, the expanding universe shuddered, did a brief impersonation of a quivering blancmange, and began to contract.

As any physicist knows – at least, any physicist who learnt his/her stuff from books like the present one – this means that the Arrow of Time itself goes into reverse. Entropy begins to back-pedal. Events stop happening, and start unhappening.

. . . *on hO*, think (or unthink) the mystics. Apricot, talking backwards, backs away from the Cygnan device. Soon last night's party is replaying, with champagne emerging from people's mouths into glasses, levitating into the bottles and being neatly corked away. Harcourt rises from obscurity through 113 storeys and throws himself in at the window. The Cygnan ship reverses its course and heads back for Earth, narrowly missing the newly recreated antimatter comet and *Mary Poppins* module which are hurtling away . . .

!niaga toN, is the thought which passes through all minds: but it is too late, or too early. Tompion contemplates his next chance to meet Lise Panther, umpteen billion years in the future/past. Will he still fancy her then? Or will he go mad telling himself *kconK kconK* jokes? Thus, inexorably, time unravels and unwinds, back and back to the first and awful Word which was spoken in the Beginning, and which goes:

!MOODHTRAE

TNARG NHOJ DNA DROFGNAL DIVAD

The Great Spong was soon to have a very unpleasant experience . . .

2,

23, 24, 25